CROSS
MY HEART

Also by Megan Collins

Thicker Than Water
The Family Plot
Behind the Red Door
The Winter Sister

CROSS
MY HEART

Megan Collins

ATRIA BOOKS

New York   Amsterdam/Antwerp   London   Toronto   Sydney   New Delhi

ATRIA
BOOKS

An Imprint of Simon & Schuster, LLC
1230 Avenue of the Americas
New York, NY 10020

First Atria Books hardcover edition January 2025

ATRIA BOOKS and colophon are trademarks of Simon & Schuster, LLC

For information about special discounts for bulk purchases, please contact Simon & Schuster Special Sales at 1-866-506-1949 or business@simonandschuster.com.

The Simon & Schuster Speakers Bureau can bring authors to your live event. For more information or to book an event, contact the Simon & Schuster Speakers Bureau at 1-866-248-3049 or visit our website at www.simonspeakers.com.

Interior design by Davina Mock-Maniscalco

Manufactured in the United States of America

3   5   7   9   10   8   6   4

Library of Congress Cataloging-in-Publication Data

Names: Collins, Megan, 1984- author.
Title: Cross my heart / Megan Collins.
Description: First Atria Books hardcover edition. | New York : Atria Books, 2025.
Identifiers: LCCN 2024019301 (print) | LCCN 2024019302 (ebook) | ISBN 9781668048078 (hardcover) | ISBN 9781668048085 (paperback) | ISBN 9781668048092 (ebook)
Subjects: LCGFT: Thrillers (Fiction) | Novels.
Classification: LCC PS3603.O454463 C76 2025 (print) | LCC PS3603.O454463 (ebook) | DDC 813/.6--dc23/eng/20240429
LC record available at https://lccn.loc.gov/2024019301
LC ebook record available at https://lccn.loc.gov/2024019302

ISBN 978-1-6680-4807-8
ISBN 978-1-6680-4809-2 (ebook)

For anyone who relates to "The Prophecy" by Taylor Swift,
and for every woman who's ever been called crazy by someone she loves.

AUTHOR'S NOTE

There are two pets in this book—a dog and a cat—who never come to any harm.

I can't, however, promise the same for the humans.

PART ONE

YOU BELONG WITH ME

From: DonorConnect Communications
To: Morgan Thorne
Date: May 3, 2025

You have received the following message from your loved one's organ recipient. As a reminder, DonorConnect encourages both organ recipients and donor families to refrain from sharing identifying information (including name, address, and personal email) until a time when both parties have consented to giving and accepting those details.

Hi.

I've decided there's no way to begin this message that isn't either (1) creepy or (2) awkward, so I'm just going to dive right into the Creepy/Awkward Pool and hope I don't drown.

One year ago today, your wife saved my life. And it breaks my heart that, in order for me to live, she first had to die.

Actually, I shouldn't say that. I know it's just an expression—breaks my heart—but it feels a little reckless for me to use it. Because, this time, I plan to be careful with my heart. With your wife's, I mean. I plan on keeping it whole.

I don't remember a lot about the day of the transplant. For that whole week, I'd been in and out of consciousness. But I remember the light in the operating room, just before they put me under, so sharp and bright it felt like a slap of sunlight. I remember realizing, then, that it had been months since I'd felt the actual sun on my face, because even before the hospital, before my symptoms, I'd been in such a dark place. From November 16 to that day, May 3, I'd barely stepped outside.

Sorry if that's too bleak or too much. I just want you to know your wife gave me even more than her heart. She gave me light again. Gave me the reminder that, despite all the darkness I'd indulged, there was still, somehow, sun.

But while I'm potentially oversharing: I wonder sometimes what *else* she's given me. In the past year, I've read a lot about heart transplants, and there's one article I keep coming back to. A woman in Canada claims she feels love differently with her new heart. The love is colder, she says. More clinical. To be honest, I'm not sure what that means. How can love be cold? To me, love is so blazing it hurts. But the article did make me wonder if there's residue inside my new heart of all the love your wife once felt.

I say that in the hopes it'll be some comfort—the love she had for you didn't necessarily die with her.

We're not supposed to use names right now, but I thought you might like to know a little about the person your wife saved: I'm a thirty-year-old woman living in a Boston suburb. I work as the manager of my parents' bridal salon. I don't have a partner, pet, or children, but one of the best parts of my day is when I walk my parents' dog. I always say I'm doing it to help my dad, who's recovering from a hip replacement (this has been my family's Year of Upgraded Body Parts), but really, I do it for me. I do it to spend time with that soft, sweet Australian shepherd whose love is unconditional, who's never known anything of heartbreak (except, of course, when I deny him a fifth treat in as many minutes—then he's the most deprived dog who's ever lived; cue that Sarah McLachlan song). I do it for the exercise, too, so I can put my hand on my chest and feel my new heart beating. So I can remember that each of those beats is another chance to live the life that, for six excruciating months before my transplant, I was sure I'd never have.

And while I can't thank your wife for everything she's given me, I've decided to start using DonorConnect so I can at least thank *you*—

the person with whom she trusted her heart. The person who kept it safe.

From: DonorConnect Communications
To: Rosie Lachlan
Date: May 5, 2025

You have received the following message from your donor's loved one. As a reminder, DonorConnect encourages both organ recipients and donor families to refrain from sharing identifying information (including name, address, and personal email) until a time when both parties have consented to giving and accepting those details.

Well, hello there.

First of all: don't worry; I medaled in the Awkward Olympics. Second: before you even reached out to me, I was already thinking of you. (How's *that* for awkward?)

As I'm sure you can imagine, the anniversary of my wife's death is a difficult day. But as I neared it, the date looming in front of me like a noose, I decided I'd spend it thinking of all the people—those unknown, unnamed people—who received organs from her, who carry pieces of her into the future, who keep her, in some small way, alive.

Mostly, though, I thought about you. I don't imagine my wife's essential qualities were stored in her kidneys or pancreas. It's the heart we always talk about. And yes, it's just an organ, as indifferent to love as a lung or liver; it's only a metaphor—that our emotions, our very selves, are contained in our core—but if any bit of my wife truly survived, I like to believe that whatever remains of her can be found in you.

Normally, that's not something I'd actually say to someone—most would find it weird or creepy (see? I'm right there with you, splashing around in the Creepy/Awkward Pool)—but I appreciate that you seem to see it the same way. And I'm grateful you reached out to me. Grateful for these small details you've told me about yourself. In return, here are some details about me: I'm a thirty-eight-year-old man who, like you, lives in a Boston suburb. I'm a writer (if you can't tell from that paragraph above where I explained in obnoxious poetics what a heart is and isn't. But hey, are you a writer, too, by any chance? I love "slap of sunlight." I might just have to steal that.). Finally, I have an orange tabby named Sickle. Short for Creamsicle. Creams might have been a better nickname (my wife fought for that, believing that pluralizing any noun makes it an adorable pet name—go ahead and try it: Marbles. Sweaters. Even, somehow, Bandages)—but his claws have always been unnaturally sharp, even for a cat. Hence: Sickle.

What's your parents' dog's name? And—a better question: Will you be petitioning for them to change it to something that's a plural noun, now that you know the Foolproof Trick to Naming Pets?

Speaking of your parents, tell me more about managing their bridal salon. I'm not close with my family, so the idea of actually working with them is enough to give me hives. Hopefully, in your case, it's a rashless experience. Also, have you ever been attacked by a bridezilla?

On a more serious note, I'm sorry to hear you weren't having the best time before you got sick. This dark place you say you were in—do you want to tell me about it?

CHAPTER ONE

At first, I mistake the blood for sequins. Bright red sequins sewn onto a white gown.

Then I spot the blood on my thumb, seeping from a cut near my cuticle. I've been scraping at it, I guess, tugging a scrap of skin as I studied Morgan Thorne's latest Instagram post.

He had Chinese takeout for dinner. Dipped his dumplings in ketchup. Does anyone else do this? he asked in the caption. And the answer is me. I do. I've gotten strange looks for it all my life.

As I lingered on that post, I stopped seeing it for a moment. Instead, I saw us together, me leaning across a table to extend a dumpling toward Morgan, who took a bite, moaned with pleasure, before licking his lips, tongue wet with grease. Then it was my turn. He teased me first, inching the dumpling closer only to pull it away when my mouth tried to clamp around it. His smile was wild. Wolfish. He stared at me like I was the meal.

But then the red. It bloomed in my peripheral vision. I looked at the sequins—no, not sequins—and my eyes snapped wide.

Now I realize I must have touched the gown, stroked the lacy fabric as my mind lured me into fantasy. The dress is a Maggie Sottero fit and flare we received last week. My parents—my bosses—will not be pleased.

I tuck my phone into the pocket of my black dress and suck the blood from my thumb. Then I fold the gown over my arm to haul it down to Fittings.

"One of my brides had a nosebleed," I tell our seamstress, Jane.

Jane tsks at the gown, even grabs the fabric, squinting at it through her glasses.

"She felt *so* bad," I add. "My bride." I look at my shoes, sorry to give Jane this extra work to do; I know her son is visiting from New York.

"It's fine, Rosie." As Jane pulls the dress off my arm, her gaze catches on my thumb. Fresh blood pools in the nail bed.

"I'll take care of it," she adds. With one hand, she slips me a Band-Aid from the top drawer of her desk. Then she winks—and I flinch.

Brad was a winker.

I take a breath, attempt a smile. It baffles me, still, how something so tiny, literally the blink of an eye, can yank me back to him. Or—not him, I guess. The dark pit of it all. The days in bed. The tangled spirals of grief and shame. The pain in my heart that started as a metaphor, before it worsened into a symptom. Then, always, the smell of the hospital: citrus and urine. The hope, even then, that he'd hear what happened and return to me.

Back upstairs, I march through the front room of the store—all sleek gray hardwoods, subtle blush walls, ivory couches and armchairs—to lock the door. Without the chirp and chatter of brides, the salon is the kind of quiet I can feel in my head, a pleasant pressure after a packed day of appointments. The second it turned eight tonight, I let Marilee and the other consultants go, tiny thanks for all their hard work, so there's not even the sound of their heels clicking across the floor as they sweep and straighten, tidy and tally.

Thumb freshly bandaged, I flick through a rack of gowns, ensuring the bodices all face to the left. I pivot to a mannequin, reaching to readjust a silky strap, when there's a knock behind me—one so frantic I clutch my chest.

A woman stands outside, pressing a garment bag against the door, Just Say Yes's rose gold logo embossed on the fabric. Her lips open and close, fogging the glass with muffled words.

We're closed, I mouth, but that just makes her knock even harder.

Her eyes, red and puffy, shine beneath the light outside. Her cheeks are streaked with mascara. Her shoulder-length white-blond hair is nested and knotted against one side of her head, as if she's been burrowing into pillows. *Please*, her lips say—and I recognize something in her. Despair. Desperation.

I hurry toward the door to let her in.

"Are you okay?" I ask as she steps inside. She hunches to the left, weighed down by her garment bag. "Here, let me—" I take it from her, hang it from a nearby rack.

"Thank you," she says, almost breathless. "I'm sorry to just—I need to return my dress."

"Is there a problem with it?" I unzip the bag a few inches, and the woman winces like I've squeezed lemon on a cut.

I peer inside to find a Stella York ball gown, and right away, I understand her panic. It's a gorgeous piece, but one I never would have pulled for her. The voluminous skirt would swamp her small frame, and the bustier top would shorten her torso. She'd do much better in a fit and flare. Actually: she'd look amazing in the Maggie Sottero I bled on.

"No, the dress is—my dream," the woman says.

Ah. This happens a lot. A bride comes in with a specific vision, a style they've admired on tall, hanger-thin models, and despite the consultant's efforts to steer them toward more flattering dresses, they can't let go of the fantasy, end up ordering a gown they fell in love with online before they ever saw it in real life.

"It's just—" The woman swipes at her errant makeup but only smudges it more. Her cheeks blush with kohl, giving her a gray, decomposing look. "I don't need it anymore." She attempts to smooth her hair before dropping her hand to her side. "My fiancé broke up with me. The wedding's off."

It's so fast: the dizzy whirl of memories. My reflection in a full-length mirror. The door behind me opening. Brad's freshly shined shoes entering the room.

"And now I'm stuck with— This dress, it's—"

My vision prickles at the edges. I blink the darkness back.

"Every time I see it in my closet, it's like—"

"Like seeing a ghost," I say.

The woman's face opens—eyes widening, lips parting—like my response unlocked something inside her. "Exactly," she whispers, fresh tears tumbling onto her cheeks.

Steady as I can, I walk to an end table, pluck a tissue from the box we keep there for parents who cry at appointments. "Here," I say, handing it to her. Then I pick up her garment bag, carry it to reception, and drape it over the counter. The woman follows, dabbing at her eyes.

"Sorry," she says. "I know I'm a mess. I've *been* a mess for days. This week has been—" She shakes her head, no words for the horror of watching her future dissolve. "But you're right. This dress is a ghost. Thank you for putting it that way."

I shrug off her gratitude. "I just . . . know what it's like, owning an unused gown."

She freezes, tissue still held to her face. "You've gone through it too."

The dress that haunts my closet is a Casablanca A-line with a beaded lace bodice, cap sleeves, and sweetheart neckline. The satin skirt is both dramatic and simple—no appliqués or other embellishments, just a stunning chapel train. The second I saw it, shimmering on its hanger, I knew it was The One. Same as I knew Brad was.

I click the keyboard to wake the computer, force my voice to be strong. "What's your name, so I can look it up in our system?"

"Edith Cole," she answers, and as I type it in, I feel her studying me. She leans forward to whisper: "How did you get through it?"

She cringes at her own question, taking a step back. "Sorry. I hope that's not too intrusive, it's just . . . As you can probably tell"—she gestures toward her face, then to her T-shirt and sweatpants, too—"I'm still in the Cry All Day phase. I'd love to know what other phases are available to me." She chuckles wetly, a bubble of snot escaping her nose. "Oh, gross, sorry." She blows into her tissue.

"Well, there's the *Gilmore Girls* phase," I say, thinking of my non-Brad breakups. "Doesn't matter how many times you've seen it; the *Gilmore Girls* binge is an important part of the process."

"I've actually never seen it."

"What! Oh my god, you *must*. Half the characters are kind of insufferable, but that doesn't matter. It's actually part of the fun."

Edith nods. "Love to hate an insufferable character."

"Exactly." I click my nails on the counter. "Then there's the Horror Movie phase. The bloodier, the better."

She scrunches her nose. "Those tend to give me nightmares."

"Heist movies then. The point is: nothing romantic."

"Got it. What else?"

"The Danish for Dinner phase. I recommend two at once: one raspberry, one cheese. It's got all the major food groups: fruit, protein, dairy, joy. Sweet Bean next door"—I gesture toward the café that shares the L-shaped plaza we're in—"has the best Danishes."

Morgan Thorne loves them, too.

Last Sunday, he posted a photo from Sweet Bean: his laptop on one of their tables, an open notebook beside a Danish and cappuccino. One does not simply go to Sweet Bean and not get a Danish, he'd captioned it, and I wished I'd been working that day so I could skip next door, brush by his table, then accidentally—

"I'll definitely get some," Edith says. "This is great; I should be taking notes."

"Oh, and don't forget the New Hair phase."

"Ah, yes. A classic."

"For good reason. Breakups always make you feel like you have no control, you know? Well—they do for me, anyway. I've always been the one getting dumped. So changing your hair is this tiny thing you can do to feel some control again. It's like training yourself to become a new person."

Edith stuffs her tissue into her pocket. "Is that why yours is pink? Because your wedding got canceled?"

I finger the ends of my hair, the waves I added to it this morning still holding after eight consultations. "Uh, no. I did this . . . a while after that."

Seven months after.

Four weeks out of the hospital.

My best friend, Nina, drove me to the salon, helped me pick out the perfect shade. And as the stylist swept the dye into my hair, I watched my old self disappear in the mirror. No longer the woman who'd crumbled so completely after Brad that not even my breakup phases could piece me together again.

New heart, new hair, new me, I said to Nina as we stared at my reflection. But when she hugged me after, her chest pressed to mine, I felt Brad's absence in every inch of my incision.

"Oh," Edith says. "Well, it's a great color."

"Thanks. It's very cotton candy, I know." This has been my refrain, the last eleven months, whenever someone mentions my hair—safer to pretend I'm in on the joke in case they think I look crazy. In truth, I love its gentle pink, a shade inspired by the spray dye Nina used last Halloween, when she dressed as cotton candy herself. All that night, I kept holding her hair up to mine, enamored of the color, despite how it clashed with my *evermore*-era Taylor costume.

"Nothing wrong with cotton candy," Edith says. "And that means something coming from me—when I was like ten, I puked all over this boy I liked after eating too much of it on a field trip. Totally traumatizing." She grimaces at the memory. "But is it weird if I admit the puke was a pretty color?"

I laugh. "My childhood puke food was Twizzlers. Right after a friend's birthday party. The back of my mom's car looked like a bloodbath."

As Edith smiles, her eyes brighten, despite the shadows of smudged mascara.

"Anyway," I say, "I'm so sorry this happened to you. The dress, your wedding." I look at her order on the monitor. "Do you want me to apply the refund to the card we have on file?"

"Wait. You're actually letting me return it?"

"Of course."

"Oh, wow, okay. I came here thinking this was a long shot, but"—her eyes dim as they drop to the garment bag—"I had to try."

We do have a no-return policy. If my mom were working today, she would advise Edith to sell the dress online. But I'm taking advantage of a different policy, one specific to me as the manager: every four months, I can comp one bride a dress. Maybe it's less a policy than it is my mother's way of managing *me*; I used to beg her to let me comp gowns all the time—for brides with money trouble, or terminal illnesses, or recent losses of loved ones. *Can't we do this one small thing?*

Rosie, your heart is so soft, she'd always tell me, in a way that sounded like a warning, and I'd picture my heart as a giant wad of gum, malleable enough for someone to chew.

But after my transplant, my mother never said those words again, too spooked by how soft my heart had actually become. Instead, she gave me my new policy—an effort to make me happy, I think—with one stipulation: the dress must be under fifteen hundred dollars.

Edith's cost thirteen fifty. I click the button to initiate the return.

"Refunds are rare," I admit, dragging the garment bag off the counter and hanging it from a rack behind me. "But we allow them in certain cases."

I just didn't intend to use my second comp of the year so soon.

"Wow," Edith says. "Thank you so much." She shakes her head through a tearful smile. "I'm so grateful."

"It's no problem."

Edith wipes at her cheeks. "How many Danishes do you think I can get with thirteen hundred dollars?"

As I laugh, Edith picks at her sleeve, shifts on her feet.

"What is it?" I prompt, sensing she has more to say.

"Nothing, I was just—" She fidgets with the canvas tote slung over her shoulder. "Would you want to hang out sometime, maybe? My friends have been great this week, but none of them have actually been through this, and it'd be nice to talk to someone who's . . . made it to the other side? Plus"—she shrugs—"you seem fun."

It's not butterflies I feel in my stomach, not that half-sick flutter I get when I look at Morgan's photos or reread his message, but it's still something winged and wonderful.

"I'd love that," I say.

I've kept my circle small as I've healed—mostly just Nina, my parents, my sister and brother-in-law—but it's been a year since the hospital. I'm already opening myself up to love again; why not friendship, too?

"Yeah?" Edith says, surprised and almost giddy, as if she'd been expecting me to say no. "Awesome! Can I give you my number?" She stops to laugh at herself. "God, I sound like I'm dating again already."

I laugh with her. "It's good practice! And yeah, let me get my phone."

I slide a key off its magnet under the counter and unlock the drawer where I store my purse. I plop the bag onto the counter and rummage through it, taking out items—lip balm, compact, wallet, book—as I dig for my phone.

"Sorry," I say. "I have way too much stuff in here."

"Oh, I'm exactly the same," Edith says, indicating her bulky tote. "I treat mine like it's half purse, half garbage can."

My chuckle stops short when I reach the bottom of my bag and remember my phone is still in my pocket.

"Oh. Duh," I say, pulling it out. I look at Edith, waiting for her to recite her number, but her gaze is stuck on the mess I've made of the counter.

"You like Morgan Thorne?" she asks, reaching for the paperback I tossed from my bag. It's *Someone at the Door*, the thriller that launched Morgan's career six years ago, spent eighteen months on bestseller lists, earned a splashy film adaptation. I read it when it first came out, but I plucked it off my overstuffed bookshelf this morning, intent on revisiting it on my break. Still buzzing from Morgan's message, I was hungry for more of his words. More of his stories. More of him.

"Um, yeah." I finger the book's cover. "I like him a lot."

It was Nina who first suspected our connection. She was there, working in the ER, when Daphne Thorne was brought in. There to hear the hurried discussion about her organs—the ticking clock of transplantation. There, days later in my hospital room, to say, *I know this is a hard-core HIPAA violation, but . . . I think your heart came from that author's wife.*

Now I know she was correct. As I sat on my bed last night, reading Morgan's response on DonorConnect, I grew almost dizzy from all the details he confirmed. A writer in a Boston suburb. Thirty-eight years old (in March, he posted a photo of him and his best friend digging into a cheesecake on the floor—Celebrating my thirty-eighth birthday by re-creating that one Friends scene that's always made me salivate). And then, the clincher: Sickle. A cat I've adored since I first started studying Morgan's Instagram. Initially, I'd done a deep dive on his profile because I'd been curious about Daphne, who had no social media of her own, and whose elegant but spare obit offered scant details: loved poetry; taught English at Emerson. But the more I searched Morgan's socials for specifics about his wife, the more I realized that, even if Daphne wasn't the person who saved my life, Morgan was someone I was meant to know.

I, too, have salivated over that *Friends* episode; a few years ago, it even inspired my statewide Quest for the Perfect Cheesecake. I listen to the same music Morgan uses in his Instagram Stories, rewatch the same movies he references in captions. And once, he wrote that Taylor Swift is the Sylvia Plath of our time, a sentence that had me swooning.

We have so much in common—connections that shimmer between us like starlight in constellations. So as soon as I read Morgan's message, I felt so potently what I could only hope for before: fate is nudging us together.

"Do you like him, too?" I ask Edith.

"Oh, of course. I work at the Burnham Library, so liking Morgan Thorne is basically a condition of my employment."

I laugh, even though it's probably not hyperbole. The library has a dedicated nook for Morgan's three novels, adorned with a placard referring to him as "our hometown hero."

"Isn't it so sad about his wife?" Edith says—and my smile slips. "One of my co-workers was really close with her, and she's still shaken up about it."

Deep in my core, there's a punch of guilt, a reminder that my being alive is at the cost of other people's grief.

"Yeah, it's—awful," I force out.

Edith nods, her mouth a straight, sober line. "I guess it puts my problems into perspective, right? Like, at least my fiancé only dumped me. At least he didn't crack his head open and die."

My eyes widen as she continues.

"Actually, he might deserve something like that." She laughs, weakly, before gasping. "Oh god, that's dark." Her gaze dips from mine, self-conscious again, as she nudges her chin at the phone still clutched in my hand. "You *sure* you want my number?"

I assure her I do. I know better than most the way dark thoughts intrude, the way a broken heart can break your brain a little, too.

Once Edith's number is in my contacts and I've texted her mine, she scrambles through a series of thank-yous and apologies before rushing out of the store. I return to my phone, reflexively open Instagram, and revisit Morgan's post about his Chinese takeout. Then I switch to my Notes app, add another bullet point to the document titled "MORGAN THORNE." Eats his dumplings with ketchup, I type, right beneath my most recent entry: Thinks the best pet names are plural nouns.

Back on Instagram, I read his caption again. Does anyone else do this? Normally, I don't look at the comments—they only remind me there are others who might feel a connection with him too—but this time, I scan the responses, as if to prove I'm the only one who shares this particular quirk.

A few people have written variations of lol gross. Others are less opposed: I don't hate the idea, or We stan a trendsetter.

But it's a comment from four minutes ago that freezes my thumb mid-scroll.

The only food you should be eating is the kind they serve in prison.

I frown at the words, then open the replies to find I'm not alone in my confusion. Someone's responded with three question marks, to which the original poster—their handle a chaotic string of numbers and letters—has answered: His wife's death wasn't an accident.

My head rears back.

The comment has nine likes but only one response: WTF why would you say that??

I dart back to the accusation, staring at it until it blurs. Finally, I refresh the post, hoping for clarity, for others to have piled on in defense of Morgan. But as I scroll, I can't find it anymore. I check again—and again and again—but no matter how many times I re-fresh, it still isn't there.

The comment is gone.

I shake my head, shake it off—just a sick joke, deleted as soon as the poster was scolded.

I swipe back to the picture and focus on Morgan's face, partially obscured by the dumpling he's holding. I zoom in, admire the pool-water blue of his eyes, the tortoiseshell frames of his glasses. I study the stubble along his cheeks, imagining the feel of it—a texture be-tween velvet and Velcro—and notice a bit of ketchup in one corner of his lips. It's small and round, like an errant drop of blood.

For a moment, I stop seeing the picture, see only the two of us together.

Morgan's smile is red at the edge, and I lean in close, thumbing the color away.

From: DonorConnect Communications
To: Morgan Thorne
Date: May 6, 2025

You have received the following message from your loved one's organ recipient. As a reminder, DonorConnect encourages both organ recipients and donor families to refrain from sharing identifying information (including name, address, and personal email) until a time when both parties have consented to giving and accepting those details.

Hi again.

First, I want to thank you for your reply. I'm sure my message brought up a lot of complicated emotions for you. It did for me, too. So I'm grateful you're engaging with it at all. I'm sure that some people would have found it crazy.

Second, I want to answer your questions. No, I'm not a writer, but I'm flattered you asked. I did take some creative writing classes for my English major in college, but it's not something I've kept up with. I'm impressed *you're* a writer, though! Is that as glamorous as it sounds? I'm just now realizing I imagine all writers to be dressed in cashmere robes, surrounded by mahogany bookshelves, while they feast on fancy cheese. How close am I? And more important: How's the cheese?

For the most part, I do enjoy managing the bridal shop. I haven't had too many bridezillas, but I've had *plenty* of mother-of-the-bridezillas. I like that I get to work with people when they're at their happiest, and I like feeling I've had some small impact on the most important day of their lives. I also love the origin story of the shop. It was my mother's dream to open it, ever since she became obsessed with bridal magazines as a teen, and my dad actually proposed to her in an empty storeroom, a space where he'd just signed the lease, so he could "start making all her dreams come true." I'll admit, though, it's a lot to live up to, finding a love like that.

My parents' dog's name is Bumper, but I'm definitely going to start calling him Bumps, because you're right—plural nouns do make the best pet names. I've been brainstorming some other good ones: Beans. Buttons. Bundles. (Wait, why do those all start with the same letter? I'm suddenly nervous I only know nouns that begin with B. Oh, except "noun" is a noun. Okay, I'm cured.) (By the way, where can I sign up for that Awkward Olympics you mentioned?)

As for the dark place I was in before I got sick, it's a long story best summed up by three words: I got dumped. Although "dumped" makes it sound so casual when it was anything but. My breakup was literally a formal affair. As in, I was wearing my wedding dress when it happened. Turns out, I had *not* found a love like my parents'.

I'll leave it at that for now. To be honest, it's hard for me to think about that time. I truly believed we would be together forever. So when that belief was shattered, the rest of me shattered, too.

I know, though, that what I went through is nothing like what you've experienced. The person I loved didn't die. He's still out there somewhere, doing his daily sudoku and five-mile runs. So I know that my "dark place" is trivial in comparison to your grief.

Do you want to tell me about your wife? I admit I'm more than a little curious about her—particularly what she loved. I have this weird theory she really liked potatoes. I used to hate them in any form (boiled, mashed, or stuck in a stew, if you catch my *Lord of the Rings* reference), but ever since my transplant, I crave them all the time.

And I'm curious, too, what you loved about her, what made you certain she was The One.

From: DonorConnect Communications
To: Rosie Lachlan
Date: May 7, 2025

You have received the following message from your donor's loved one. As a reminder, DonorConnect encourages both organ recipients and donor families to refrain from sharing identifying information (including name, address, and personal email) until a time when both parties have consented to giving and accepting those details.

Hey, you.

Let me start by answering your most important question: Yes, I caught your *Lord of the Rings* reference, and it made me very happy. So much of your message did, actually. Not many people can make me laugh out loud with their writing, but every time I reread the paragraph where you panicked about only knowing nouns that start with B, I can't help but chuckle.

As for my writing life, I'm afraid it's a lot less glamorous than you've imagined. While I do consume a fair amount of cheese, it's usually presliced cheddar that I cram between crackers in lieu of making a sandwich. I also don't have any mahogany shelves. At least, I don't think I do. I actually have no idea what kind of wood my office shelves are made of, but they came from Ikea, so there's only a fifty-fifty chance they're even made from wood at all. And I don't believe I own any cashmere, let alone an entire robe of it. Sometimes, though, I wear my least-stained college sweatshirt when I write—does that count as glamorous?

On a more serious note, I'm sorry to hear about your broken engagement, and I don't think your experience sounds trivial at all. Unlike the Awkward Olympics, pain isn't a competition. And even though your ex didn't die, it *is* a kind of death, isn't it? The death of the future you thought was guaranteed. That's brutal, and it warrants every ounce of grief you felt, for however long you felt it. And for the record, I took a poll, and one hundred percent of people surveyed agree that anyone who does sudoku and runs five miles a day is the worst. I've read only two letters from you, but I already know he didn't deserve you.

And sure, I'm happy to tell you about my wife—especially because your theory is right: she *did* love potatoes. In our five years of marriage (seven together), I saw her eat an impressive, if not alarming, amount of Russets and Yukon Golds. She also loved thunderstorms and lunar eclipses and reality competition shows. She loved peeling stickers off books. Collected photos of vintage bicycles. Her favorite scent was vanilla. Her favorite musician was Van Morrison. Her hobbies included crocheting (which she was adorably bad at; ask me how many "hats" Sickle owns), baking banana bread (and *only* banana bread), and writing poetry on the weekends.

As for what I loved about her. She'd experienced something terrible in her childhood—and she was so open about it with me, shared the whole story on our second date. "I want us to get to know each other," she said, "and you can't know me without that story."

I felt so honored by her trust in me, and I was in awe of what she'd gone through, the fact that she'd grown up in spite of it, made a life for herself full of passion and laughter when others might simply have withered. After that second date, I saw her differently. Before, she'd seemed almost innocent to me; she had this way of scrunching up her nose when she smiled that was so enticingly wholesome—I used to crack jokes just to see her do it. And I thought I was drawn to that, the idea of someone untouched by darkness. But when she told me what had happened to her, I knew better. What I'm really drawn to is someone who's seen darkness—breathed it, even—and survived.

As she finished the story, I felt something vibrate inside me, the same kind of buzz I get when I'm particularly inspired. *Here is a woman*, I thought, *who could endure anything.*

I bet you know a lot about that—enduring things. You're only thirty, but you've already lived through so much. Illness. Hospitalizations. A broken engagement. And yet here you are, now: making me smile with your messages.

I'd love to know more about you. What makes you laugh? What makes you cry? I've found you can learn a lot about someone in the answers to those questions. And if you're up to talking about it, I can't help but be curious about the part of you that's connected us in the first place. To put it bluntly: What happened to your heart? What made you need my wife's?

CHAPTER TWO

Nina isn't picking up her phone. This is the second time I've called her on my way home, and the answerless drone is a trigger, shooting me back to the days after Brad: those nail marks I stabbed into one palm as I clutched the phone in my other, the broken glass at my feet, the blood on the floor.

I shake the echoes from my head—this is nothing like that, this is *good news*—and leave Nina an excited shriek of a voicemail: "Neens. Call me back. Morgan responded again."

When I received Morgan's initial response earlier in the week, I read it to Nina over the phone, dissecting every sentence. So ever since his new message landed in my inbox on my lunch break, I've been eager to share it with her again. Maybe I misremembered her schedule and she's at the hospital, hustling from patient to patient. Or maybe she's out with Alex for date night.

I smother a flash of jealousy as I turn into my driveway. Nina and Alex have been married three years; Alex is basically a brother to me now. But there are times—selfish, childish times—when I want to come unquestionably first in my best friend's life. Like tonight, when the man I'm into has messaged me again.

You're not "into" him, I hear Nina scolding me. *If anything, you're into his Instagram.*

And his writing. And his sense of humor. His kindness and self-deprecation.

I climb the stairs to my apartment, then unlock the door as I reread Morgan's words on my phone. My eyes skip to the parts I love best.

Hey, you . . . I already know he didn't deserve you . . . I'd love to know more about you . . .

In my bedroom, I set my phone beside the books and prescription bottles on my nightstand, then swivel toward the mirror. I force myself to laugh, checking to see if, like Morgan's wife, my nose scrunches when I do, but instead, I'm confronted with a face I'm still getting used to, moon-round and puffy from high doses of prednisone. There's a twinge in my chest, like I've already disappointed him. He asked me to tell him more about myself, but after the details he shared about Daphne, I'm afraid I'll come up short. I don't have endearing, hyper-specific hobbies like collecting photos of bicycles and baking only one kind of bread. I don't crochet. I don't make anything, really. My only focus lately has been Morgan and the continued work—meds, checkups, tests—of staying alive.

I start to change out of my work clothes, but my bracelet snags on the zipper of my boatneck dress, as if reminding me that even my jewelry—a MedicAlert ID—is part of my survival plan. When I wriggle free, I catch my reflection again, see the scar on my chest that's the wrong kind of pink. Not cotton candy. Not a match for my hair. A color like raw meat. What happened to your heart? Morgan asked. But there's a better question, one I ask myself all the time: What *will* happen to it?

I slide into yoga pants, pull on a T-shirt. Then I open my closet, close my eyes, and grope for my sneakers. When my hand brushes a too-familiar garment bag, I flinch like I've been cut.

The night is cool when I step back outside. Zipping up my jacket, I jog down the exterior stairs and walk thirty feet to the house I grew up in. Since my transplant I've lived above my parents' garage, a one-bedroom space they used to rent out, then ushered me into after the hospital. Before that, I lived fifteen miles away, close enough to commute to Just Say Yes, far enough that I didn't feel like I'd rebounded straight from college back to my hometown.

This living arrangement was supposed to be temporary, just the first couple months of recovery, my parents cooking for me, refilling my prescriptions, driving me to weekly follow-ups for blood tests and biopsies. But by the time I was well enough to return to my own apartment, just the thought of that place—where I'd loved Brad, mapped out our future, then grieved it as if both of us had died—resurrected symptoms the transplant should have cured: deep fatigue, shortness of breath, pressure in my chest. So Nina packed up my haunted apartment for me, and for some reason, despite her offer to get rid of it, I insisted she bring me my ghost. Insisted she hang it in my new closet, as if I might wear it again.

Inside my parents' house, the TV is on, a laugh track wafting from the living room. Bumper bounds over to me, tail and tongue wagging, and I crouch down to greet him. "Hey, Bumps," I say into his fur.

"Hey, Rosie girl," Dad says from his recliner, eyes fastened to a *Frasier* rerun. Bumper's nails click on the floor behind me, his tail thumping against an end table, eager for his walk.

"Rosie, did you authorize a refund the other day?" Mom asks in lieu of a greeting. She sits on the end of the couch closest to Dad, his chair positioned so they can still hold hands.

I scratch the top of Bumper's head. "It's one of my comps."

"Already? Rosie, it's only May."

"But it was a return. So we can resell it."

"At a lower price point," Mom tuts. Her disappointment is futile, though. She gave me this policy knowing full well I'd use it. "Was there something wrong with the gown?"

"Um. No." I think of Edith, her face splotched with tears, and make a mental note to get in touch with her soon, make sure she's doing okay. "The bride's fiancé canceled the wedding."

My parents slide a look at each other, their brows denting with the same worried crease.

I pretend not to notice, heading to the hutch where we store Bumper's leash. My eyes catch on the two picture frames perched on its shelf, and I brace myself against a familiar pang. The frame on the left displays my parents at twenty-three, Mom beaming up at Dad, the sleeves of her wedding gown puffing around her arms. To the right of that photo is one of my older sister, twenty-five at the time, dressed in a strapless Lazaro, while my brother-in-law kisses her cheek.

For a while, there was another picture on this shelf, one I'd planted there myself, a placeholder for my wedding portrait with Brad, where I'd be smiling out from the glass just like my mother and sister—young, in love. Loved in return. But in the placeholder, as I gazed up at Brad like a flower stretching toward sun, his eyes were pointed off camera, and now there's only an empty space where that frame once was, lined with a film of dust.

"I can start walking him again, you know," Dad says as I clip on Bumper's leash. "I've finished my PT. The doctors encourage me to move around. So if you're not feeling up to it, or too tired after being on your feet all day, just say the word."

His tone is casual, but I know there's concern in the offer. My transplant was traumatic for them, too.

I dip down to kiss the top of his head, then squeeze Mom's shoulder. "I'm good," I assure them, and I glance back at the pair of frames on the hutch—seeing, for an instant, only Brad inside them.

I blink and force a different image: Morgan Thorne, his hand on my chest, warming the heart that guided him to me.

"I've never been better," I add.

Nina calls as Bumper and I reach the end of the sidewalk and step onto pavement.

"Sorry," Nina starts, "Alex took me thrifting and I left my phone in the car."

"Did you find anything good?"

"Yeah! A suitcase of wigs!"

"That's . . . creepy."

"No, it's awesome. They're good quality, and there's one I can use for my Jem costume this year. I'm making Alex be one of my Holograms."

Nina is evangelical about Halloween, so I'm not surprised she's already piecing her and Alex's looks together, five months in advance. She's crafty, too—she'll sew whatever she can't find already premade. I think of Sickle with the hats Daphne crocheted for him, think how, if Morgan ever meets Nina, he'll love her creativity.

"But anyway," she adds, "Morgan wrote back again?"

"*Yes*. Here, I've screenshotted it for you."

I pause to send the message, and Bumper sniffs at a leaf. As Nina reads, I tug him along. Our route has grown progressively woodsier, and if given the chance, Bumps would investigate every pebble and pine needle skirting the street.

"Hmm," Nina says when she finishes. "That's kind of fucked-up."

I stop short. "What is?"

"That the thing he loved about his wife was that she had some kind of childhood trauma."

I continue on, shaking my head as if Nina could see it. "That's not what he said. He loved that she was able to *endure* the trauma. He said he's drawn to people who've lived through darkness and survived it."

Am I someone like that? In every relationship I've ever been in, darkness has been the thing I fear most—the way it settles in with time, keeps a couple from seeing each other the way they once had, when everything between them was dizzyingly bright. For me, that darkness has always been inevitable. It's just how things go: sparks become fires, and fires burn out.

But then there was Brad. Then there was darkness like none I'd ever known—so deep it wasn't only him I couldn't see anymore; it was myself, too.

"It just seems weird to me," Nina says. "And now I'm curious what her childhood trauma was."

"I think her sister died? Daphne's obituary said she was predeceased by her sister, but I couldn't find anything else about it. I wish there was a subtle way to be, like, 'Hey, about that terrible experience your wife had . . . Could you elaborate on that? Preferably in a five-paragraph essay with footnotes and citations?'"

Nina doesn't laugh at my joke.

"I'm kidding," I say. "I'm not going to mention it."

"But you *are* planning to respond to him?"

"Yeah, as soon as I get back from Bumper's walk."

By habit, Bumper slows as we pass a house I love to admire—a yellow colonial with a half circle of stained glass above a green door. Not too long ago, that house was for sale, and I wish I'd been ready then, wish I'd had a partner to move there with me. I glance at the hand holding Bumper's leash, see the glint of my MedicAlert bracelet—which, with no other options, lists my mother as my emergency contact.

"Rosie," Nina says, before gusting out a sigh. "What is your plan here? I thought all you wanted to do was confirm that Daphne was your heart donor."

"I mean, yeah, that's how it started, but—"

"Okay. And now you've done that. So why keep messaging him?"

"Because we're having a good conversation. I want to see where it goes."

Bumper pulls to the right as we approach the entrance to another street, but I hold his leash tight, steering us straight. Dad always takes him that way, but I prefer a different route.

"Where it goes?" Nina echoes, her tone a little scolding. "I know you have this . . . crush on him—but, Rosie, you can't, like, *date* Morgan Thorne."

A car rumbles up the road, and I click on my headlamp so they know to stay clear of me and Bumper. After they pass, I keep it on. The woods around us are thickening, the trees with their new leaves blocking out the moon.

"You have his wife's heart," Nina continues through my silence. "You can't have her life, too."

I'm not surprised by her reaction. I can't expect her to understand. Not when she met her soul mate three weeks after graduating from college. Before that, she was always the dumper, kindly quitting her relationships with a reassuring hug. She's never had to fight for love, never felt it as a luxury. And because it came easy to Nina, the kind of love people promise at altars, she can't comprehend my chronic anxiety that I'll never make it to an altar at all. And because of that, I haven't told her my most urgent truth—that I feel each beat of my heart like the tick of a clock.

I've done the research, spoken to my doctors: heart transplants last, on average, about fifteen years. And that's if something else doesn't attack the body first; immunosuppressants keep me from rejecting my new heart, but they're nearly as likely to welcome infections and cancers as they are to keep me alive. Then there's the vasculopathy, an artery disease that eventually clobbers all transplant patients, that will come for me no matter how diligent I am in taking my cyclosporine every twelve hours. That means, someday, I'll be back in that hospital bed, and I might not be so lucky the second time, might not live long enough to accept someone else's heart. With Daphne Thorne's, everything aligned: our proximity, our matching blood types, her organs becoming available while I was a Status 1 candidate. It was a miracle, really, and another isn't guaranteed.

I think of that empty space on my parents' hutch, and how I'm dying to fill it with a frame of my own, while I can still enjoy the life, the love, my wedding portrait would hold.

"You agree with me, right?" Nina says. "I mean, transplant aside— you don't actually know this guy. He could literally be a murderer."

I nearly trip over a stick that Bumper's picked up and abandoned. "Why, did you see that Instagram comment?"

"What Instagram comment?"

His wife's death wasn't an accident.

I've thought about it a lot since the other night. The sheer cruelty of taunting Morgan on his own page, almost a year to the day he found his wife unconscious on the bathroom floor, blood blooming from her skull. For an instant, I see myself there, beside him at the moment of discovery, holding his hand, holding him back, so he doesn't slip in all that blood, doesn't leave his footprints there.

I tell Nina about the comment, there and gone with its bot-like handle. I tell her I've combed his recent posts for other trolls and, thankfully, none have turned up.

"First of all," Nina says when I finish, "I don't follow Morgan on Instagram—so no, I didn't see that. I just meant: he's a complete stranger, so he could just as easily be a nice, normal guy as he could be a serial killer."

"Really? Just as easily?"

Nina ignores my teasing. "DonorConnect is not a dating app. This can't actually *go* anywhere. You see that, right?"

No. I don't. Because my heart is a ticking clock—and it's led me straight to Morgan.

"He's expecting me to respond," I say, trying a different tack. "He asked me questions. And don't I owe him answers? I'm only alive because his wife is dead. Doesn't he deserve to know about the person who . . . who has her . . ."

My sentence slows to a stop in sync with my steps. Bumper pauses, too, nosing at familiar ground. To our right, the trees have opened up, revealing an acre of grass—a wide, dark carpet unfurling toward a house where floor-to-ceiling windows glow from inside.

I turn off my headlamp.

"No," Nina says. "You don't owe him anything."

Inside the house, Morgan sits on his couch, watching something on his laptop. As he reaches for his wineglass on the coffee table, he doesn't break his gaze. He sips as he stares.

I see his screen in my mind. My most recent message pulled up. I see him hover over my words with his cursor, an almost-touch. Then he refreshes his inbox. *Click. Click. Click.*

I see me sliding onto the couch beside him. See us clinking our drinks. See Sickle purr in our laps, belly-up, velvet-soft, his namesake claws retracted.

"Rosie?"

Morgan sips. He stares. He sits behind his window, like a picture in a frame.

"Rosie? Are you still there?"

"Yeah," I answer, but even I can hear how distant I sound. My thoughts—my future memories, maybe—are still inside that house, the blueprint of which I already know so well, its Zillow listing bookmarked on my browser. "Sorry, what were you saying?"

Bumper lifts a leg to pee, and in my ear, Nina sighs.

"Just—forget all this, okay? Don't write back to him. Don't fixate on his Instagram. Just leave it alone. Leave him alone."

"You're making it sound like I'm stalking him," I say—and then I wince, aware of where I'm standing.

But Morgan's house is less than a mile from my parents', and Bumper needed his walk.

"I'm not crazy," I add. Then, away from the phone: "Come on, Bumps." As he trots beside me down the street, Morgan's house disappears behind us, the trees closing ranks again.

"No, not stalking," Nina says. "And *not* crazy. But we both know you tend to"—she pauses, and I sense her choosing her words—"go a step too far."

"That doesn't sound a lot better."

"You know what I mean. You're . . . enthusiastic."

"Ugh, fine," I say—because I can't deny that. When I love someone, I simmer with it, my excitement bubbling higher and higher until I boil over with devotion. In high school, I left a letter in Noah's locker every day, turning the bottom into an overflowing recycle bin. In college, I celebrated Jared's run as Brick in *Cat on a Hot Tin Roof* by plastering his dorm room with pictures I'd taken of him during the show—something his roommate complained was "creepy." Every man I ever dated eventually accused me of going overboard with my displays of affection. And they're probably right. But on my four-month anniversary with Brad, when I baked him four of his favorite desserts, he said, *Oh wow*, biting into the crème brûlée before kissing me with sugared lips. *You know I'm going to expect this forever now, right?*

The memory clamps around my heart, quickening my breath, and I'm glad when Nina continues.

"So promise me you'll leave it alone, this thing with Morgan?"

I know why she's insisting. It's my own fault. *I want to see where it goes*, I told her, but she already knows where it—a crush, a relationship—has taken me before. She remembers me crumpled on concrete, remembers the blood on my hands. If I keep arguing, she'll speak of that night—my very worst—in specifics. No dancing around it, no dressing it up as *a step too far* or *enthusiastic*.

So I tell her okay. I continue on into the night, Bumper by my side, and I do what she asks. "I promise."

From: DonorConnect Communications
To: Morgan Thorne
Date: May 8, 2025

Hi again.

I've decided to answer two of your questions as lists. Writers like lists, right? Or is that just another fact I made up, like the cashmere robes and mahogany shelves? I genuinely would love to know about your writing life. Is there a particular kind of music you like to work to? Is there only one kind of pen or notebook you'll use? Where do you find inspiration?

Anyway. The lists!

What Makes Me Laugh:

- Blooper reels (I *love* seeing the person behind the actor)
- Baby chicks wearing cupcake liners as skirts (I have printouts of this in my office at the salon)
- That old episode of Family Fortunes where a guy keeps giving the answer "turkey" (google if needed)

What Makes Me Cry:

- Elderly people eating alone at restaurants
- Dogs reuniting with their owners after a long time apart

- Calling the pharmacy, getting their automated system, and saying "Speak to a pharmacist" at increasing levels of desperation until you decide no medication is worth the torture of a robot mishearing you twelve times in a row

Honorable mention in the Cry Category goes to your kindness about my Dark Place™/breakup, especially the part about feeling my grief for as long as I need to. I really did tear up when I read that—I'm so used to people just expecting me to be over it. And I get where they're coming from. It's been eighteen months since my ex approached me in his black suit, said, "I can't, this is too much," but sometimes I swear I'm still there, hairpins stabbing my scalp, dress clinging to sudden sweat.

Thanks so much for the details you shared about your wife. She sounds like someone I would have loved to know. I'm sorry she experienced something traumatic as a child, but it's inspiring that she was, as you said, strong enough to survive it. When I read about that in your message, I couldn't help but put my hand over my heart, more grateful than ever to carry a part of her inside me.

A lot of what happened to my heart is still a mystery to me. What I know is this: I had already spent a few weeks in bed after the breakup when the first symptoms appeared. My chest felt full, like your stomach after eating too much. One time, I even thought I heard something gurgle, deep behind my breastbone, like the bubbling of a watercooler. I'd walk from my bed to the shower and have trouble catching my breath. And though these sensations were weird, they didn't concern me much. They sort of made sense: my heart had recently been shattered—of course my chest felt different. I'd barely been moving, let alone exercising—I was just out of shape. And the nausea that made meals feel like punishments? Well, who can eat when they're impossibly sad?

But it wasn't long before I passed out—three times in two days. Then I vomited blood. Then I was driven to the ER, where the doctor ordered a chest X-ray. And when he saw the results, there was an urgency in

his voice I'd never heard from a medical professional: "I've made an
appointment for you, tomorrow morning, with a cardiologist. This really
can't wait."

More tests with the cardiologist, where—despite the ER doctor's
alarm—I still felt almost embarrassed, wanting to explain to the
nurses, "No, it's nothing, just an epically bad breakup. I'm sorry for
wasting your time." But then, much sooner than I expected, I received
a diagnosis: cardiomyopathy. The word meant nothing to me at the
time, but when the doctor explained it, I learned a disorienting truth.
While I thought my heart had shattered inside me, it had actually
become so enlarged it was failing.

In the weeks that followed, the *why* of my disease became much less
important than the *what next*. My doctor believed a virus had caused
it, but other than shrugging out that hypothesis, he remained focused
on keeping me alive. On prepping me for a transplant. On waiting,
alongside the bedside phantoms of my family and friends, for my
turn on the list. In the meantime, I deteriorated so rapidly, fatigue
solidifying like concrete in my bones, that it became impossible
to imagine ever leaving that hospital again. But then—the rush of
doctors and nurses. The lights in the operating room. Your wife's
healthy heart.

It's a strange, symbiotic relationship she and I have—I keep part of
her alive, just as part of her keeps *me* alive—but what I've told you
here is only half its origin story, and I can't help but wonder about the
rest. So . . . this might be asking too much—and please don't answer
if it crosses a line—but would you be willing to share what happened
to her?

———————

From: DonorConnect Communications
To: Rosie Lachlan
Date: May 14, 2025

You have received the following message from your donor's loved one. As a reminder, DonorConnect encourages both organ recipients and donor families to refrain from sharing identifying information (including name, address, and personal email) until a time when both parties have consented to giving and accepting those details.

Hey, you.

Sorry it's taken me so long to respond. I was on deadline, and my tunnel vision became so severe I apparently missed a dentist appointment, a coffee date with my friend, and a FedEx delivery requiring a signature. I'm slowly catching up again—the dentist, date, and delivery have all been rescheduled—and now I can finally focus on you.

First off, I don't know if *all* writers like lists, but I definitely do. Lists are sexy. *Especially* when bullet points are involved. So, to answer your questions about my writing life:

- I've never been able to listen to music while I write. I actually require complete silence. Sometimes I hear Sickle using a scratching post from three rooms away and it's all I can do not to yell, "Excuse me, sir, I didn't ask for your weird percussion solo!"
- The only pen I'll write with is a Lamy Safari fountain pen. It's elegant and smooth and basically indestructible. (My wife once tested that claim by throwing mine in the garbage disposal, and though it gained some scratches, it was otherwise fine.) As for notebooks: I'm a Moleskine man.
- A lot of my work explores the darker side of humanity—the impulses we shouldn't follow, the secrets we'd kill to keep—so I tend to consume a lot of pretty twisted stories. But inspiration

is, at times, difficult to identify. Some days, I have no idea where the words I write originate. They simply rush onto the page, as if running from something inside me. And in those moments, there's nothing—absolutely nothing—that could keep me from getting them out.

I have to admit, though: *you've* been inspiring me lately. I said it before, but I love the way you express yourself, the details you choose that anchor me to the experience: "hairpins stabbing my scalp," "the bedside phantoms of my family and friends," "fatigue solidifying like concrete in my bones." You say you're not a writer other than some classes you took in college, but honestly, your prose has impressed me, and if you ever want to tell me more about your Dark Place™ (very smart to trademark it, by the way), I'm here to listen. I know we're still almost strangers, but I firmly believe in writing the worst things down, in writing them *out*—like bacteria from a cut. Because words are how we heal our wounds. So please know that these messages are a safe place for heartbreak.

In that vein, I want to thank you for sharing so much about your heart. I can only imagine how terrifying it was—having your chest sawed open, a vital part of you ripped out; the uncertainty of whether your body would accept the foreign organ or if you'd end up even sicker than you started. I admire, too, your resilience, the fact that you've survived a year since then. Since we began messaging each other, I've done a little research on posttransplant life, curious about your experience. I was surprised to learn how easy it is for a good heart to go bad—especially those first twelve months. I was even more surprised that the meds you must be taking are saving your life while risking it further. That my wife's heart might not be the last one you need. To carry that knowledge, day after day, requires a tremendous amount of strength. And here you are, introducing me to hilarious game show videos, caring enough about others to cry when someone dines alone. To be honest, if I lived with the fears I assume you do, I don't know if I'd have any room in me for humor, if I'd be able to see anyone's pain beyond my own.

All that is to say: I think you're remarkable.

In closing, I want to answer your last question, which didn't cross a line at all; I completely understand why you'd ask. My wife died in a tragic accident at home. She fell and hit her head. Even a year later, it's hard for me to comprehend. I'd seen her trip dozens of times— she was pretty clumsy, actually—and I'd even seen her hit her head before: on cabinets she didn't know were open, on stop signs she walked right into while looking at her phone, on her car door when she stumbled in our driveway. She'd had bumps and bruises, and one time she had a concussion, but still, I never imagined she'd die that way. In fact, if she'd made her own list of what made her laugh, her first bullet point would have been videos of people falling—grooms fainting at weddings; businessmen tossing their briefcases in the air as they slip on ice; college students having to crawl across a particularly slick spot on campus, their backpacks like turtle shells. So sometimes, when I think about finding her there, on our bathroom floor—alive, still, but just barely—I have this intrusive thought: if she hadn't actually died from it, she'd have laughed so hard at what happened to her that night.

CHAPTER THREE

There's a forty-year-old bride in the shop. She pivots in front of the mirror, considering the dress: backless, deep V, illusion neckline. Decades ago, when my parents first opened Just Say Yes, this woman might have stood out on the floor. She might have raised a brow or two for wanting to see something sleeveless and sparkly instead of understated and demure. Now, nobody blinks an eye. Her girlfriends coo from the couch, champagne glasses in hand, and Marilee grabs a cathedral veil that complements the lace on the gown.

Once, these older brides were a comfort to me. As my twenties ticked by. As each of my relationships ended. As man after man included in their breakup speech some iteration of "You're just . . . too much, Rosie." Older brides gave me hope that, even though my parents and sister and best friend all found their soul mates young, true love doesn't have an expiration date.

Now women like that prompt a stab of panic in my chest.

My phone vibrates beneath the reception counter, and I drag my attention from the bride to read a text from Edith.

I'm okay, thanks for asking. I actually might venture a little outside my house/work comfort zone today and pick up some takeout. With my own two hands. From an actual restaurant. Or do you think that's a betrayal of my frozen dinners from Trader Joe's?

I smile as I type a response.

Def do takeout.
Joe will understand.

I've checked in on Edith a few times since meeting her last week, and we've tossed around dates to get together, but she hasn't committed to anything yet. I've been worried that, despite her initial invitation to hang out, she's been too ground down by grief to actually leave her house. But picking up takeout is a good first step. And it's a positive sign she's answering my texts at all. If it were me— No, when it *was* me, my eyes were too blurred by tears to even read my friends' words.

I swipe out of Edith's text and open DonorConnect to reread Morgan's message, which arrived last night, after nearly a week of silence, with a tone that felt a little flirtatious.

I can finally focus on you . . . Lists are sexy . . . I think you're remarkable . . .

All week, I'd felt nauseated from Morgan's lack of response, nervous that, even to an almost-stranger, I'd once again become "too much." I'd labored over my third message, same as I'd labored over the first two, and as the days passed, I was sure it had turned him off, the way I crafted and polished each sentence, the way I'd studied his style as a model for my own. But his opening paragraph (not to mention his compliments) put me at ease. He'd been slow to reply only because he was on deadline. Because he's Morgan Thorne. Still,

I promised myself last night that I would take his cue and wait a few days to respond. Tyler, my boyfriend before Brad, once complained that I was "always available" to him, and I guess that was a bad thing.

It doesn't mean I can't keep memorizing Morgan in the meantime, though. I open the list in my Notes app and add a couple bullet points.

- Needs complete silence to write
- Uses Moleskine notebooks and Lamy Safari fountain pens

"This is it," Marilee's bride says, eyes glittering with tears. "My dream dress." She twists to admire her bare back in the mirror. "It's definitely the one."

Her friends leap off the couch to hug her, and Marilee takes a step back. In a minute, she'll interrupt the bride for measurements, but for now, she allows the women to swarm their friend, to gush about a dress that none of them—not for a single second—can imagine as a ghost.

Her gown has buttons down the train. Mine had buttons, too, all the way up its lacy back. They'd been my favorite detail, but they made it impossible to fasten the dress on my own. So when Brad stepped into the room that day, his tie already unknotted, he didn't see me as he should have, as I'd planned; he saw me with the gown gaping open—unfinished, unflattering—and that only added to the agony of it all.

My stomach churns with the memory, or maybe just with hunger. I haven't eaten since breakfast. It's five thirty now, still a few hours from closing, and I've got a returning customer with her second consultation at six. If she's anything like she was at her appointment a few weeks ago—analyzing the placement of every bead, requesting estimates on every possible customization—I'm going to need some fuel.

I call out to Marilee, still on the sidelines of her bride's celebration: "Want anything from Sweet Bean?" She shakes her head, distracted, then steps into the group of women.

"Let's make this official!" she says.

Outside, it's raining, the sky all steel, so I slide into my jacket and flip up my hood before making the forty-foot trek to the café. When I step inside, I'm greeted by Sweet Bean's cinnamon scent, their leafy plants, the strings of fairy lights. I get in line behind a couple holding hands and crane to see the late-afternoon offerings. With five Danishes left in the case, my stomach gives a loud, anticipatory rumble. I turtle deeper into my hood, blushing as I scan the people around me—and that's when everything stops. My awareness of the other customers. Sweet Bean's folksy music. Even the rain outside.

He's here.

Tortoiseshell frames. Dark scruff. Eyes like the bottom of a pool.

This is the closest I've ever been to him. I can actually see the gray in his beard—just a few tinsel strands—and the hair on his arms, the loose button on his shirt.

I watch from under my hood as he sips a cappuccino, sitting across from a woman. No—not just a woman. His best friend, Blair. I shouldn't recognize the back of her head so easily, shouldn't instantly know that shiny dark hair as hers, but I've studied every photo on Morgan's grid, and she's been a fixture in them for a long time, even before his marriage to Daphne eight years ago.

He laughs at something Blair says, and my lips part, the sound so rich I can almost taste it.

"Hey, Rosie, ready to order?"

I turn to see a gap between me and the counter, the couple in front of me vanished. With a glance back at Morgan, I step toward my favorite barista, then recite my usual—two Danishes, one cheese, one raspberry—adding, at the last second, an apricot one for Marilee.

"Switching things up a bit—nice," the barista says. "Is that for here or to go?"

"Um . . ." I'd planned to take it with me to Just Say Yes, scarf it down in my office before my six o'clock shows up. "The apricot is to go. But the rest are for here."

When she hands me my bag and my plate, I take them to the only empty table—diagonally across from Morgan. If he were to look my way, we'd be facing each other. But he's focused on Blair. I nibble at my Danish, about to shrug out of my jacket, when I realize it's best to keep it on, my eyes slightly hidden by its hood.

Only now does my pulse begin to pound. I know it's just an effect of my transplant, my denervated heart. I know adrenaline rushes no longer happen in real time for me. Instead, I'm on a perpetual delay, my body needing a few extra minutes to react to things like this Morgan sighting. Still, it's as if whatever remains of Daphne can sense her husband nearby.

"I had no idea there was so much involved," Blair says, and it's easy to eavesdrop. Most of the customers are staring at laptops, earbuds in. I take out my phone, scroll through some news app without really seeing it, trying to look as occupied as everyone else.

"Every day's another urgent project and I'm going insane trying to keep track of it all. There's the florist. The caterers. The band. I kind of thought that all just . . . came with a venue. I never considered all the research involved. I swear, if I have to read another review of, like, linen providers, I'm going to call the whole thing off."

"Is a linen provider a thing?" Morgan asks, and his voice is as foreign to me as it is familiar. In the past year, I've listened to some of his podcast interviews, but hearing him now in person is like seeing a painting in real life after loving it first on a screen.

"I don't know," Blair says. "But napkins, tablecloths—they've got to come from somewhere, right? And apparently it's too much to ask the owners of the rusty—I'm sorry, *rustic*—barn to include that."

"See, this is how I know Vanessa is *it* for you. You've only been together for like eight minutes, but—"

"Excuse me. Eight months."

"But you're willing to forgo AC, not to mention complimentary linens—which I'm just now learning you care about—so she can have the cottagecore wedding of her dreams."

"Wow. I was not aware you knew the word *cottagecore*."

"I've used it with you before."

"When?"

"In one of my emails."

Blair slumps back in her chair, playing exhausted. "When are you going to learn? I do not memorize your emails."

"You should. They're very well written. Basically deserve a Pulitzer."

I take another bite of Danish to smother my smile, but Blair is not amused.

"They're like ten pages long!" she says. "It's like you're drafting an entire novel to me. Don't you get enough of that all day?"

"It's not like drafting at all. With drafting, there's an outline, a plan, a story you're building with an end already in mind. My emails to you are . . . a way to record and shape the events of my days. Clarify my thoughts."

"I'm not your diary, Morgan."

"Aren't you? You know all my secrets."

I look up in time to see something pass between them. A current of silent communication. A brief hesitation where their eyes stay locked.

"Whatever," Blair says. "All I'm saying is: I don't need setting details and dialogue tags for every half-interesting interaction you have."

"Wow. I was not aware you knew the term *dialogue tag*."

He grins to show he's teasing, and I marvel at how they volley with each other. Marvel, in particular, at Blair, who isn't afraid to give Morgan shit, be dismissive of his interests. Maybe it helps that they're friends instead of lovers, but I've never been like that with men. For Tyler, I feigned a love of football so I could still see him on Sundays. For Gabe before him, I taught myself video games until my fingers were dented from the controllers. For Jared in college, I studied Shakespeare, bought tickets to plays so I'd have an in with his theater-major friends. And for Brad, I slept in a faded Arcade Fire T-shirt—*Oh this? I've had it forever*—that I'd bought at Goodwill one week after our first kiss.

"Anyway, what about the dress?" Morgan asks. "I think there's a bridal shop next door. We could go after this if you want."

I almost choke on my pastry. Morgan at Just Say Yes? We don't take walk-ins—appointments book weeks in advance—but there are always exceptions.

I see the scene: welcoming Morgan and Blair into the salon, shaking their hands in introduction. First, me and Blair—professional, perfunctory. Then me and Morgan—our touch lingering. Electricity zinging through our skin. Gazes paused on each other.

"You'd actually want to go dress shopping with me?" Blair asks.

"Isn't that part of my man of honor duties?"

"I don't know. I've never had a man of honor before. But either way, I'm good. I have an appointment in Boston with my mom."

My shoulders sag, my fantasy dissolving—even though it felt as real as a memory.

"Wait. Seriously?" Morgan says. "Do you really think that's the best idea?"

"It's fine. She's been . . . better lately. Both my parents have. The dress appointment was *her* idea, believe it or not."

"Oh, I believe it. Come on, Blair. They always do this. They make you jump through hoops for scraps of attention, and then, just when you're finally about to call it quits—like that whole thing at Christmas—they reel you back in so they can start the cycle all over again. The dress appointment is bait."

Blair takes a slow, measured sip from her drink. "Are you done?"

"You said it yourself: they use love as a weapon."

I draw my gaze back to my Danish, guilty about listening in on something so personal.

"I should go with you to that appointment," Morgan says.

Blair punches out a laugh. "Oh, sure, *that* would make it better. You know my mom just loves when you're around."

"Well, unfortunately for Janet, I'm always going to be around, because I'm always going to be the number one man in your life." He gives Blair an exaggerated wink.

"Please," she says, monotone, "if you don't stop flirting with me, I'll melt right here."

My phone vibrates in my hand, delivering a text from Nina.

> Proof of life please.

This is a frequent request of hers. A holdover from my tissue-clutching, fetal-position weeks, when I met Nina's check-ins with silence. It's a reminder, too, that while I've survived a year with someone else's heart, Nina knows I'll never be out of the woods.

I send her a picture of my Danish before returning to Morgan. He's laughing appreciatively at Blair, and then, as he leans back in his chair, his eyes shift—clicking onto mine.

There's a jolt of connection, like the tug on my heart during bi-opsies. A smile lazes on his face as he gazes at me. I hold my breath.

Then I break our stare.

My cheeks heat up; I feel him studying me still. I try to seem unfazed, thumbs skating across my phone.

> OH MY GOD NEENS OH MY GOD.

> What???

> I'm at Sweet Bean and Morgan is HERE. One table over. We just made eye contact.

I slide another glance toward Morgan—ready, now, to return his smile—but his focus is back on Blair. Part of me is relieved. I wasn't prepared for the intensity of his attention. The blue of his eyes that's deep enough to drown in.

An ellipsis pops up as Nina types. Then it disappears. Flashes and dies again. Finally, her text comes through.

> How did you know he'd be there?

I frown at the screen. She thinks I followed him. Stalked his Instagram Stories to zero in on his location, orchestrate a meet-cute.

> I didn't! It's a complete coincidence.

As I wait for her to respond, I tune back into Morgan. "Seriously, though," he's saying, "wedding planning is stressful; it can make even the coolest, most capable people"—he pauses to point at Blair—"a little crazy. So just: lean on me more. I'm not here simply to write the greatest man of honor speech of all time. I genuinely want to help. Do you want me to learn guitar so I can be your wedding singer? Learn calligraphy to write the invitations? Choreograph your first dance? Whatever it is, I'm your man."

Blair laughs. "You think I'd trust *you* with my first dance? Do you even remember yours with Daphne?" My back straightens, a piece of Danish crumbling between my fingers. "The two of you swayed like a couple of eighth graders with zero chemistry."

I bite my lip, looking at Morgan, who dips his gaze toward his mug.

"You know as well as I do that chemistry was never our problem," he says, flicking his eyes back to Blair. I see her body tense, and so does mine, because there's something so pointed in his stare. Heavy with implication.

"And anyway, first dances are awkward," he adds. "All those eyes on you."

I wait for Blair to apologize. Wait for her to see in the slump of Morgan's shoulders that it was a step too far, dragging Daphne into the conversation. But her response—"Oh, right, because you *hate* when you're the center of attention"—makes Morgan break into a devilish grin.

My phone vibrates again, drawing me back to Nina.

> Good. And you didn't respond to his message, right??

My thumb hovers above the screen. I don't want to lie to her. But I also don't want to argue over a decision I've already made—one that felt, even as I defied Nina's advice, more inevitable than illicit.

> Right. But maaaaaybe this means I'm supposed to keep talking to him.

> UGH. You're making me want to go all Veronica Mars and find out he really IS a murderer or something, just so you'll get ideas like THAT out of your head.

> He is NOT a murderer! He seems like a good guy. End of story.

> Orrrrr that's just your Rosie-colored glasses talking.

My Rosie-colored glasses. Nina's been using that phrase for years. And she's right; I tend to see things a little tinted. A little brighter and better than they are. But sitting one table from Morgan, I can't help but notice his hands. They're cupped around his mug with a loose, almost tender grip. How could hands like that hurt anyone?

I'm staring at my phone, pondering how to respond to Nina, when a text arrives from Marilee.

> Hey, your bride is here.

I almost groan out loud.

I glance between Morgan and the message, then back to Morgan again.

"I know," Blair is saying—a response to something I missed. She's gathering her trash. "But Vanessa's in Oregon until the end of the month, helping with her mom's recovery, and I'm trying to get it done before she gets back because I'd rather be the one to make that decision."

"You'd rather have the control, you mean."

"Always," Blair says, standing, and she's taller than I expected. On Instagram, when she's tucked beneath Morgan's arm, the two of them laughing together, she seems a lot smaller. But maybe that speaks to Morgan's height more than hers. I won't know until he stands, too.

"You coming?" Blair asks, snatching up her jacket and umbrella.

"Nah." He pulls a laptop from the bag at his feet. "I've got some emails to write."

For a second, I wonder if one of those emails will be to me—until I remember I haven't even responded to his latest. Part of me itches to type a reply right now, if only to watch his reaction as he reads it. But I'm determined to do things right with Morgan. Learn from my mistakes with other men. Appear less available than I actually am.

Blair snorts. "You and your emails," she says, then bends to kiss his cheek before heading for the door.

With her gone, Morgan has a clearer view of me, but his eyes remain on his screen. Still, I feel the space go taut between us, like a rubber band pulled tight.

I type out a response to Marilee about my bride.

> Can you take her?

Because I could stay here, in Morgan's line of sight. I could wait a minute, then pick up my plate, my bag with Marilee's Danish, and accidentally bump into his table. I could apologize. Tuck my hair behind my ear. Ask if I jostled his cappuccino, if I splashed his laptop. When he says no, I could grab him napkins anyway. Our fingers might touch as he takes them. His eyes might zip to my face. He might recognize something in me—an old but enduring pain that fits snugly against his own. Because sometimes that's all it takes: being in the right place, at the right time, with the right person.

> Why? Are you okay?

I write back to Marilee quickly—Totally fine, just caught up with something—because I know she's worried it's my heart, that I'm stuck in the Sweet Bean bathroom, wheezing against the wall. It's not a baseless fear. I'm weaker than I was before the transplant. Which is exactly why meeting Morgan through DonorConnect—or by chance, in a café—is so perfect. I don't have the stamina for bars or parties or other places where relationships might spark.

Still, I'll need to be careful. I should pocket my MedicAlert bracelet. It IDs me as having a heart transplant, and I'm not about to announce to Morgan, *Hey, I'm who you've been talking to on Donor-Connect.* Because that would be too much. Too soon. I'd seem like such a stalker. And I can still use those messages to my advantage. I can ask more questions about his wife—learn what it takes to be a woman Morgan loves. I can gather evidence in writing that he *is* a good man, then show it to Nina when I come clean about us growing closer.

And once Morgan and I have a strong enough bond in person, I can come clean with him, too, tell him I'm the woman he's already fallen for online.

But for now, I watch Morgan type. His eyes are stitched to his screen, his brow creased in concentration, and I wonder if he gets that focused when he writes to me. *Hey, you*—a greeting both gentle and intimate, like a thumb stroking a cheek.

Another vibration on the table. Another message from Marilee.

> The bride's insisting she work with you. She says you're familiar with her "preferences."

I pinch the bridge of my nose. The customer in question is picky and demanding, but she doesn't have a budget, which means one sale from her could equal five, even ten combined. When she booked her return appointment, she told me she wanted to see *what you'd pull for a Kardashian. Then we'll customize from there.* I can't risk her taking her business elsewhere.

Across from me, Morgan's fingers dance across his keyboard, nimble and knowing. His hands are so close to me—mere feet away—I can almost feel them on my skin.

Still, Marilee nudges.

> What should I tell her, Rosie?
> Are you coming back?

From: Morgan Thorne <morganthorne@morganthorne.com>
To: Blair Hawkins <blairhawkins@gmail.com>
Date: May 15, 2025
Subject: Dear Diary

Okay, B. Here it comes. Your greatest joy. Another email from me.

I know you're rolling your eyes. You're saying to yourself, "Is he serious? I *just* saw him!" But a lot has happened since you left Sweet Bean today.

I met someone.

Collided with her, actually.

I ordered a second cappuccino (I know, I know, but I don't sleep anyway, so what's the difference?) and when they called my name, I went to the counter, took the mug, spun around—and smacked right into something pink. A woman, it turned out.

The pink was her hair. Not Gwen Stefani pink, which I know is where your '90s-child brain immediately went (with more than a little judgment). No, the color was much more muted than that. Like a cherry blossom.

Of course, I apologized profusely—I'd spilled cappuccino all over her shoes—but she barely seemed to notice. Instead, she stared at me with that slightly starstruck look I see a lot at my book events: seventy percent awe, thirty percent fear.

"You look a little familiar," I said, giving her an opening, space to admit what I suspected: that she was a fan, that she'd maybe even attended one of those events. "Have we met before?"

The woman shook her head. Smiled a little shyly. "No, but I, uh . . . I know who you are."

I tried to put her at ease: "Well, that's not fair. Because I have no idea who you are. What's your name?"

She opened her mouth, then hesitated, as if in telling me the most basic information about herself, she'd be divulging a secret.

"Rosie," she finally said.

The name suited her. All that petal-pink hair.

"Rosie," I repeated back, and right away, her cheeks colored to match her hair, making me a little starstruck too. I love a woman who blushes.

"I'm so sorry for crashing into you," I said. "Here, let me get you some napkins, and—could I buy you a coffee to go with your—" I gestured to her take-out bag, which she was gripping like a purse I'd tried to mug.

"Uh. Danish," she said.

I smiled. "I love their Danishes." I handed her a stack of napkins from the dispenser on the counter. "And one sec, I'll get you that coffee."

"Thank you," she said, before blurting out, "Oh, wait. I don't drink coffee. The caffeine makes . . ." She trailed off, glancing at her shoes, and only then, for the first time, did she seem to register the mess I'd made of them.

"Herbal tea?" I offered.

"Sure. Thanks."

I placed the order, then watched her struggle to clean her shoes, swiping at them while half crouched, the fold of her take-out bag tucked awkwardly beneath her arm.

"Here, sit with me while we wait," I said. She seemed surprised by the invitation—and I liked that. Right away, I could tell she wasn't *that* kind of starstruck, the kind that praises me in Instagram reviews, then curses me out in DMs because I didn't thank them quickly enough. It was clear Rosie didn't believe she was owed my time—even though I'd disrupted hers.

I showed her to my table, pulled out the chair you'd recently vacated, and she sat to wipe at her shoes in earnest. When she was done, she balled up the napkins and tossed them into her take-out bag.

"Weren't you going to eat that?" I asked of the Danish she'd mentioned was inside.

Her eyes went blank for a moment, then widened. "Oh god, why did I do that? I wasn't even thinking." She moved to pluck out the napkins, then seemed to think better of it, her mouth puckering in disgust.

"You were . . . creating a new flavor," I said. "Cappuccino Danish."

"Shoe Danish," she said, and when she smiled, her cheek dimpled in a way that made it look delicate, like the tiniest touch could dent it. And I knew immediately: I wanted to see that dimple again. I wanted to create it.

The barista called me up, Rosie's herbal tea now on the counter, and since there wasn't anyone in line, I went back to the register and ordered her another pastry.

"They were out of Danishes—shoe and otherwise," I said when I returned to the table, setting the plate and mug in front of her. "But their raspberry pie twists are the next best thing."

"Oh." She blinked at the treat. "You didn't have to do that. But thank you, that's so nice."

"It's the least I can do. And—sorry, I forgot to tell them it was to go."

I hadn't forgotten.

"But feel free to eat it right here," I added. "Looks like all the other tables are full. Unless—are you in a hurry?"

I watched her think about it. And I could tell she did have somewhere else to be. Which made it even better when she shook her head and told me she was free.

She opened up after that, laughing easily at my stupid jokes. She even moaned a little when she bit into the pie twist—then blushed, adorably. "Sorry," she said, "I think I just sexualized this pie crust." I told her not to worry, that I've already proposed marriage to half the menu items at Sweet Bean, and I loved that she played along: "Oh, when's the wedding?"

"Haven't been able to set a date," I said. "You know pastries. Always so flaky."

Again: a stupid joke. You never would have laughed at it, not in a million years. But Rosie did.

Then I asked her what she did for a living—genuinely curious how this woman with the pink hair and dimpled cheeks spends her days—and I was surprised she got a little cagey. That, of course, only made me more curious. "Is it illegal?" I asked. "Do you sell, like, bootleg DVDs?"

She laughed again, and I swear, B, the sound was intoxicating. Like a contact high. "Does anyone sell bootleg DVDs these days? No, I just . . . I'd rather not talk about my job, if that's okay." I cocked my head, letting my silence coax her into saying more. "It's been an exhausting day, and it would honestly bore you to hear about it."

I wondered, then, if she didn't want me to know where she worked, where I could find her each day, and I appreciated her caution. You can never be too careful.

"And anyway," she added, "it's nothing as glamorous as what you do."

It was the first reference she made to my writing, besides her initial acknowledgment that she recognized me.

"Is that what you're doing here?" she asked with a gesture to my laptop. "Writing?"

"Oh—no. I can't write in places like this. I was just emailing my editor about my next book."

She lit up at that. A kid on Christmas. "What's it about?"

"Well, technically it hasn't been announced yet, so I'm not supposed to talk about it. But it's a multi-POV, multi-timeline story centered around some fucked-up family secrets. More in the vein of my second book."

"*Chaos for the Fly*," she said. "That's my favorite of yours."

I leaned back in my chair, unable to hide my smile. "Really? Wow. I think you're the first person to ever say that."

(Besides you, of course.)

I explained that, though it sold relatively well, *Chaos* hadn't had the same critical success as my other books, that one reviewer found it "cloyingly clever," while a prominent blogger said it might be "too highbrow for your average thriller reader."

"That's so insulting to readers!" Rosie said. "And insulting to you. How dare you be clever."

I grinned so wide I probably looked deranged, my mouth a Venus flytrap.

We talked more about books after that—what she's reading, what I'm reading, which film adaptations completely slaughtered the source material. She asked how I felt about my own film adaptation, and I told her the truth, that I'd never even watched *Someone at the Door*, that I closed my eyes during all two hours and three minutes of the cushy, velvet-seat premiere. I told her I was grateful to the filmmakers, the actors, the studio for all the extra attention the adaptation brought to the book, but in a weird way, it felt like sanctioned plagiarism, like strangers were stealing my characters—their stories and backstories, the words I'd labored to write for them—and presenting them as their own.

Rosie nodded. "That makes sense. Like the film is just an impersonation of the book."

I swear, Blair, I wanted to kiss her.

Before tonight, I'd been thinking it was best to let my love life die with Daphne. I've always known it's a risky thing, letting women get too close to me. You're the only one, Blair, who knows the real me and somehow hasn't suffered for loving me.

Still, I didn't leave the café. I couldn't. I allowed the evening to keep spinning on. We moved from books and writing to music, TV shows—nothing incredibly important, but the things that give texture to a person—and we had so much in common there. Our textures, it turns out, are the same. She agreed that *Friends*, though often problematic in a current-day context, remains one of the most memorably funny shows. I told her, "People only shit on it because they think that makes them intellectual, when really it just makes them boring." (Yes, I stole your argument.) And she referenced the paste-pants scene, the English trifle Thanksgiving episode, David Schwimmer's perpetual pitch-perfect delivery as reasons why we shouldn't trust those people. It was all such simple, easy conversation, our laughter ping-ponging between us. And all the while, I basked in the warm glow of Rosie's attention, giving her the entirety of mine in return.

When a barista approached our table, told us they were closing, I was shocked to see that the café had emptied out, that we were the only two left, that we'd been smiling and staring at each other for—I had no idea how long. So when Rosie and I gathered our things, stepped outside, stood beneath a sky that had suddenly cleared, I did what I knew I shouldn't.

"I'd love to see you again," I said.

But I think she sensed something in me. The darkness like a storm beneath my skin. Because she hesitated, glanced at her feet, a bit of her earlier caution seeping back into her face.

"Okay," she said. "Sure." And then her eyes sparkled—just a little, just a wink of light between her lashes—but enough to let me know her caution was, at least in part, an act.

She was worried she'd seem too eager, I think. So I went first. Showed her how impatient I actually am.

"When?" I asked. "How?"

And she stepped away from me, walking backward—slowly, tauntingly—out from under Sweet Bean's lights, into the inky night.

Then, these six words before she turned around: "I know where to find you."

It was a strange thing for her to say.

But god, Blair, I swear. It was so sexy, too.

CHAPTER FOUR

I wake the next morning to a hot, fizzy feeling in my stomach, like I've swallowed a sparkler. I reach for my phone and, for a second, there's a part of me that thinks I'll see a text from Morgan—even though he doesn't have my number. Still, when I got home last night, filled with a giddiness that bordered on intoxication, I had to stop myself from immediately messaging him through DonorConnect, had to remind myself I'm trying to be a different kind of Rosie. One with *restraint*. One who's less available to men, and therefore more alluring.

Instead, I funneled my energy into the list in my phone, adding each new detail I'd acquired about Morgan at Sweet Bean, sifting through every single minute of the memory for another treasure. Another gesture. Another specific thing he'd said. That way, I could keep that day forever. Make him a little more mine.

Now, I sink back into the image of us: smiling, gazes locked, time growing slippery as his words drift over me like music, as I fidget with a napkin, itching to reach for his hand.

I open Morgan's Instagram. No new posts, but that's okay. I'll revisit the selfie in his yard where, in the background, a deer grazes, Morgan's eyes wide with wonder. Or the selfie at his desk, his face tired but satisfied, a document of blurry words on the laptop behind him. There's a gap of a few weeks, right after his wife died, when he did not post, aside from a tribute to Daphne. But scrolling backward through time, I resurrect her: Daphne in overalls, paint roller in hand; Daphne with a stack of books; Daphne sipping wine.

His photos of her were always in black and white. And there aren't many. Over their seven years together, there's little more than a dozen. Even their wedding photos are colorless, making Daphne's long, glossy hair appear pure black in contrast to her white dress.

It's a flattering look. It makes me wonder if I should ditch the pink, dye my hair dark, alter my style to one I know Morgan likes. I even twist to see myself in the mirror, hold the sleeve of my black sweatshirt against my cheek to test out the color. It's . . . not terrible. Then again: I don't love the dark like I do the pink, which is pretty and romantic enough to soften the strange new landscape of my face. And more important, pink is the color I had during my first real-life encounter with Morgan, which feels like reason enough to keep it for a while.

I scroll deeper, faster, on his Instagram until the years erase Daphne—because there's something so private, almost forbidden about his pictures of her. The scarcity of them, their shadowy grays. As if Morgan wanted Daphne all to himself. As if everything about her was secret and sacred, even the color of her eyes.

Or maybe I'm projecting. Maybe her photos only seem illicit because, in some ways, I feel like I'm betraying her. Daphne saved my life, and in return, I lie here hoping for messages from her husband, all the while knowing—up close and personal—the color of *his* eyes.

I scroll past the feeling, find Morgan in 2016, a year before he started dating her. Here he is, sharing a beer with Blair, whose hair is blunt and blond, her face free of any makeup, so different from the mature, thick-lashed woman I saw last night. For a second, I stop seeing the older photo, imagine instead one with Morgan and Blair and me, his best friend having become one of mine, her dark hair mingling with my pink as we press our faces close for the camera. There's a hint of mischief in Morgan's smile, and afterward, he teases us both: *I think you guys love each other more than you love me.*

The thought of his voice has me instantly craving more. I open YouTube, search for interviews with Morgan, ready to rewatch ones I know by heart. I filter the results by date—then jerk upright when I find a new video, uploaded last week.

It's a virtual bookstore event, a conversation between Morgan and another author, Sally Andrews. As his voice rumbles out of my phone, I melt back against my pillows, but when Sally speaks, I scroll through the comments, interest already waning.

@SarahCain 3 days ago
This book sounds amazing!! Can't wait to read.

@oliviawright9 3 days ago
Love these two!

@9ts612ithdibijcpi 2 days ago
Anyone else think Morgan Thorne straight-up murdered his wife?

I almost drop the phone. I gawk at the comment, then the poster's handle—a set of random numbers and letters that looks strikingly similar to the one from Instagram last week—before scrambling to read the replies.

@samanthamains 1 day ago
THANK YOU for saying this, my friends all think I'm crazy!!

@ReginaTate 1 day ago
Wait, WHY do you guys think he murdered her???

@samanthamains 1 day ago
He didn't even have an alibi. He was HOME when it
happened. Also, the victims in his books are ALWAYS women.

@jessesomers 12 hours ago
Omg I've been WAITING for someone to say this. It would
not surprise me if he killed her. There's SO much misogyny
in his books. He clearly thinks women are dumb as shit. His
protagonists are always diving headfirst into danger even
when a million red flags are waving.

@MichelleCloud 10 hours ago
I meannnnnn this is straight from the acknowledgments page
in Chaos for the Fly: "I'm grateful to Detective Connor Dolson
for fielding my myriad of after-hours questions about police
procedure; thank you for helping me make a murder look like
an accident. On the page, of course."

@jessesomers 10 hours ago
omgomgomgomgomgomg

My head swims. I rub my right temple, then review it all again.
It's just gossip, of course. Speculation from people who have listened
to too many true crime podcasts. They're twisting Morgan's words,
trying to create a more lurid story, and it's left a slushy feeling in my
stomach. Morgan doesn't deserve this.

I exit YouTube, pull up Morgan's house on Zillow instead. It always
comforts me, studying the pictures from before he bought it in 2019.
I love to admire the wainscoting, the recessed lights, the built-in
bench seat in the kitchen, and I wonder how the 2,300-square-foot
space might have transformed since then. I know he's already filled
and decorated it with the last woman he loved, but now, I'm picturing

how we'd make it ours. The photos we'd hang in the living room, black-and-white portraits of us. The space he'd make on shelves so my books could sit beside his. The reading chair we'd pick out together. The blanket I could learn to crochet.

I pull up the picture of his kitchen, focus on the French doors that open to a backyard patio. At the time the photo was taken, the glass wasn't covered by shades or blinds—just big, blank panes that blurred the line between inside and out. Maybe Morgan and Daphne changed that. Or maybe they liked the clean, curtainless look. Either way, I'd need drapery of some kind; otherwise, just about anyone could walk the stone path to the back and see right inside.

As I'm zooming in on the doors, thumb and finger bracketing one of their handles, my phone rings. I glance at the time—8:03—before answering: "Is this a wake-up call?"

After exhausting nights at the hospital, Nina likes to talk on the drive home.

"You know it. Better than coffee. But also: we never finished our conversation."

I sit up, fluffing my pillows against the headboard. "Which one?"

"You know which one."

I stall with a beat of silence.

"Sweet Bean," Nina presses. "Morgan Thorne. What happened with that?"

"Nothing," I say, even as Morgan's laugh reverberates inside me, rhythmic as a heartbeat.

"Uh-huh." Her response is flat with doubt. "So, you didn't, like, deliberately crash into him? Spill a drink on his stuff just so you could talk to him?"

I shift beneath my blankets. It's scary how well she knows my mind. I'm glad, at least, I can answer her honestly: "I did not spill a drink on his stuff."

In her pause, I hear a gust of static—wind or a sigh. "That is not the full denial I was hoping for."

"I went back to work," I tell her, keeping my voice sincere. "I have no idea what happened with Morgan after that. I promise."

Again, she hesitates, but finally relents. "Okay. Good. It's just— You've been so fixated on him, and it was starting to feel a little like last time, so I—"

"This is nothing like that," I say, sharp and sure.

"Okay, fine, I'm sorry. But listen: I asked around the hospital, talked to one of the nurses who actually interacted with Morgan after Daphne was brought in, and she said—"

"Wait, what? Why were you 'asking around'?"

"Because I was worried you were still full steam ahead on this guy! Especially once you went radio silent yesterday. So I wanted some info on him."

I squeeze the bridge of my nose. This is so Nina that I'm surprised I didn't see it coming. She may think I "go a step too far" when it comes to love, but she goes a step too far with friendships, inserting herself into situations that don't require her help. A few years ago, after Tyler broke up with me, she snuck into my phone and erased his number so I couldn't reach out to him. Later, I learned she texted him herself, too. Told him if he ever contacted me again, she'd *Tonya Harding his kneecaps.*

"Either way," she continues, "my co-worker said there was something weird about Morgan that night. Like, he was acting really strange."

"Well, yeah. He'd just found his wife half dead in the bathroom."

"No, like—he had his laptop with him, in the waiting room, which is weird enough. Who brings their laptop in an ambulance? But he was typing like crazy. The nurse saw a document open on his screen, and . . . she thinks he was *writing*. While waiting to hear if his wife had *died*."

"That doesn't—" I curl my toes, fighting a sudden, unwarranted chill. "I'm sure he was scared out of his mind, and writing is just how he copes."

"I knew you'd say that. But I've seen tons of people at the ER who are scared out of their minds, and you know what they do? They cry. Or pace. Or call family, friends. They don't drop off their bleeding wife and then *write their novel*."

I open my mouth to protest, but Nina barrels ahead.

"So I don't trust this guy. But fine, if that doesn't sway you, I'll find something that does. Because I *know* you're still tempted to talk to him. I know you're, like, imagining your future together. But, Rosie, you can't pursue someone you've been obsessing over. We've seen how this ends: it isn't healthy for you."

I fidget with the hem of my sheets. I don't want to keep things from Nina. Don't want to see and speak to Morgan only in secret. He could be in my life for a while—forever, if I'm lucky—which means he'll be in Nina's, too. And I don't want her on permanent alert when the four of us are together: me and Morgan, Nina and Alex. I don't want cookouts and game nights to be sullied by Nina's suspicions. Not only of Morgan, but of me, too. Of what I might be missing. What I might have convinced myself to overlook.

Nina thinks my track record sucks. When one of my exes, Gabe, got so drunk at a Fourth of July party that he lit a Roman candle and, cackling, aimed it at my face, its exploding shell grazing my ear, Nina applauded me for having "enough sense" to leave him at the party. But she couldn't believe that when he called the next day, admitting he'd been an idiot, I rationalized it—he'd been wasted, joking; he hadn't actually intended to hurt me.

Then there was Tyler. When I woke one morning to a sharp, persistent pain in my side—a kidney infection, I'd later learn—I called him for a ride to the doctor. His refusal hissed through the phone: *I've got my own shit to deal with, Rosie.* His "shit," as it turned out, was putting new rims on his tires, but when he finally texted, hours later, to check on me, Nina got annoyed at me for responding.

God, Rosie, she said once, *the things you let men do to you*. But it's just because I want—no, need—what Nina already has. Without it, my future terrifies me: back in another hospital room, alone this time, my parents too old to care for me, if they're even still around; my best friend and sister too busy with families of their own. And it's not only that. Ever since Nina's wedding day, there's been something asymmetrical about our friendship. For our whole lives, from kindergarten on, it had been the two of us, loving each other first and best. But when she married Alex, she updated her emergency contact forms, checked with him whenever I suggested a night out, in case they already had plans. And as much as Nina and Alex have tried to make me never feel like a third wheel, it's always there in my mind, that my presence is a kickstand, keeping them from riding as fast and far as they want.

That's why I want her to love who I love. I want that sense of symmetry back. Four instead of three. So when it comes to the person I choose as my partner, I need my best friend to be on board.

"For the hundredth time," I tell Nina now, "you don't have to worry and you don't have to dig up dirt on Morgan. I'm *not* obsessing over him."

As soon as we end our call, my fingers act on reflex, pulling up his Instagram again. I return to the photos of Daphne, hold the phone closer to my face, as if I'll hear her whispering secrets through the screen: *This is how you keep him*. But the pictures are as muted and monochromatic as ever, like shots from a silent film. I note the clothing she favors—silky V-necks that would never work on me, exposing too much of my scar—and the way she does her makeup: cat-eye liner I've struggled to perfect in the past.

I close the app, a little defeated, and the time on my phone alerts me that I have to take my meds. I pad to the kitchen, pull the orange juice from the fridge, my eyes catching on a wedding invitation I've stuck to the door, the RSVP card still blank. It's from my college roommate, and beneath the line where I'd specify my plus-one, there's a typed request from the bride and groom: "Significant others only, please." I turn my back to it, smothering a fresh sting, and drop a syringeful of cyclosporine into a glass of juice. Then I swallow the mixture as fast as I can, cringing at the bitter, sulfurous taste that, for now, keeps me alive.

Leaning against the counter, I brace myself for the side effects—nausea, shaking, a dull throb in my head—and distract myself with recent texts, picturing some future good-morning message from Morgan, something that would soothe my heart as it ticks the time away. But then I see Edith's name, and I'm soothed in a different way. Unlike Nina, she's actually sympathetic toward Morgan, not suspicious. *Isn't it so sad about his wife?* she asked when we met—just before mentioning that someone she knows was close with Daphne.

I open our text thread and type a new message.

> Hey! Didn't you say you have a co-worker who was friends with Daphne Thorne?

She responds a minute later.

> Yeah! Why?

> This is so dumb, but I've seen a bunch of people speculating online that Morgan like KILLED his wife haha. (Not laughing because murder is funny, laughing because the comments are ridiculous) But it did make me wonder what your co-worker thought of him, assuming she knew him through Daphne.

I'm expecting an immediate, emphatic answer: *Omg that's insane, my co-worker LOVES him.* Instead, Edith responds with three surprised-face emojis before typing again.

> Wowwwww I have not seen that. I think my co-worker said she doesn't like him though.

> Wait, really? Why not?

> I'm not sure. Something about bad vibes? It was a while ago.

Well, that's not much of a reason. But this vague answer presents a good opportunity.

> Do you think you could connect me with her? So I could ask her myself?

> Why, are you like . . . investigating him? lol

I hesitate only a second before crafting a lie with just enough truth.

> A friend of mine has actually started talking to him after meeting him online. They've only seen each other once so far, so it's definitely early, but if he's got bad vibes . . . I don't know. Makes me want to find out more haha.

I watch as Edith's ellipsis appears. Oh, she says after a while, an answer so curt that I worry my request seems crazy. It's not that I even care about Morgan's supposedly "bad vibes." Nina thinks yogurt has bad vibes; the phrase is so overused it's meaningless. But I am curious what someone close to Daphne could tell me. Not just her impressions of Morgan, but insight about his wife, too. Details beyond her makeup and clothing that I can use to keep him interested.

Edith's ellipsis blinks on and off again, and it's another few minutes before her answer comes through.

> Can you make it to the library at 9?
> I'm not working today but Piper is.
> She says she's happy to chat.

———————

I show up with a Danish.

I stopped at Sweet Bean on my way to the library, hoping that Morgan would be there again, that I'd be forced by fate to pick up where we left off yesterday. As I stood in line, scanning each table, I saw the scene so clearly: Morgan with another cappuccino, his eyes hooking on to mine, his mouth curling at the corners—a smile set to snare me.

Now, as I climb the steps to the library, I find a woman sitting on the top stair, huddled beside shopping bags. From the dirt on her cheek and the hole in her sleeve, it's obvious she isn't just resting here before heading home. Obvious, in fact, that she has no home at all.

I pause beside her, glancing at my Sweet Bean bag. I brought it as a thank-you to Edith's co-worker—Piper, apparently—but now I hand it to the woman instead.

"Oh. Th-thank you," she says. She peers into the bag, then inhales deeply, her eyes rolling back in pleasure. "Oh my."

"They taste even better than they smell," I tell her.

When I open the door and step inside, I inhale deeply myself, savoring the scent of books, feeling a buzz I only get in libraries and bookstores. I've always wanted a library of my own, a room in my house reserved for all the books that currently sit in stacks around my apartment. I wonder if Morgan has one. Wonder how soon it'll be before I see for myself.

Piper's waiting for me by the door, taller than she seemed in the picture Edith sent, but I recognize her honey-colored curls.

"Hi . . . Piper?" I reach out my hand. "I'm Rosie. Thanks for meeting with me."

Her grip is limp with distraction. "Yeah, hi," she says, eyes combing through my hair. I touch the tip of one pink wave, ready to preempt any comments about the color—*I know, it's like cotton candy*—but Piper mutters something else: "Okay, now I get it."

"Sorry? Get what?"

She glances over my shoulder to the steps outside. "Did I just see you feed Margaret?"

"Oh—that woman?" I look back through the glass in the doors, find her licking raspberry filling off her fingers. "Yeah— Sorry, I thought she was unhoused. Did I get that wrong?"

I blush at the thought that I might have offended Margaret—or just looked insane, handing a random stranger an even more random Danish.

"No, she is," Piper says. "Just . . . people usually pretend she isn't there." Piper tilts her head, as if considering me anew, but her eyes are still tangled in my hair. "Edith *did* say you're a good person. Come on, we can talk in one of the meeting rooms downstairs."

When we reach the bottom floor, Piper leads me down a corridor before turning into a windowless room. She flicks on the overhead light, revealing worn gray carpet, a watermarked table, a handful of mismatched chairs.

"My shift starts at nine thirty. I came early to help a patron apply for jobs, so I've only got a little time to chat." Piper slides into a seat, gesturing for me to join her. "But as soon as I got Edith's text, I was like—" She cuts herself off as I sit across from her. Her eyes rove my face as if registering it for the first time. "Wait. Are you Rosie *Lachlan*?"

I stiffen in surprise. "Yeah?"

"God, sorry. The hair kind of threw me so I didn't notice upstairs. I'm Piper Bell." She waits for recognition, and I wince with none to offer. "I was a couple years below you at school."

"Oh!" I scrutinize her face. There might be something familiar about her, but I struggle to place her in my memories of Burnham High. "I'm so sorry, I don't—"

"It's okay." She waves off my embarrassment. "I'm freakishly good at names and faces. But how have you been? I'm friends with Nina Burke on Facebook and I remember her having a big post about you a while ago. Something . . . happened to you last year, right?"

My mind leaps to Brad—a tear-smudged phone, twelve unanswered calls, then thirteen, fourteen, the car keys in my hand, blood on his driveway; *You're crazy, Rosie, you're fucking crazy!*—before I realize Piper couldn't know any of that.

"I had a heart transplant," I say.

"Right, that's it! Wow." Her eyes drop to my chest, as if looking for the place they sawed me open. "Was it— Did you have, like—"

I cut her off, used to this question. "I had cardiomyopathy."

She nods, curiosity lingering in her gaze, so I rattle off a condensed version of the story: at first, doctors thought my disease had been caused by a virus they found in my system, but the autopsy later showed I'd actually had a congenital heart defect, the virus only worsening a problem that was already there. What I don't mention is how, when my symptoms first appeared in the weeks after Brad, my parents wrote it off as anxiety. Depression. The physical toll of my shredded mental health. *You're making yourself sick*, Mom said. And I believed it. Because what is *crazy* if not a sickness?

"Basically," I sum up, "I was born with a broken heart. I just didn't know it until I was twenty-nine."

"Wow, that's so intense." Piper reaches across the table, flattens her hand close to mine. "I'm so sorry."

"Thanks."

My eyes drop to her ring finger—a reflex I've recently acquired. I check everyone's these days, searching for solidarity. Hers is naked, and I wonder if she loses any sleep about that, if she dreams of gowns that haunt like ghosts.

Probably not. Because no matter how many single people I meet, I'm always alone with my specific fear, my pulse that feels like a timer. It's a burden I'll only be able to share if I find someone to love me. And even then, if I do manage to get married, that fear will only double, felt not just by me, but my husband, too. Intrusive as an asterisk in our vows. *Till death do us part.* *

**Which might be pretty soon.*

It would be a terrible thing to put someone through. And of course I think of Morgan—how I'd be sentencing him to an unspeakable fate: losing a second wife, who has the same damn heart as his first.

But then I think of what we could have in the meantime: sun-soaked mornings with Sickle, Sweet Bean weekends, reruns of *Friends*. And even better than all that, what I've craved in every relationship, what seems so easy but is actually extravagant: the simple pleasure of sharing space—a bed, a couch, a home—blanketed by silence that doesn't feel like an absence or a gap, but a presence and fullness all its own. With Morgan, I could read on one end of the couch while he writes on the other, and every so often, I'd glance over the top of my book to watch him work, wondering at how he conjures the words that spread chills across skin.

"Anyway," Piper says, shattering the image. "Sorry to be so nosy—you didn't come here to talk about that. Edith said you were asking about Morgan Thorne?"

As she says his name, her voice hardens. Her cheeks sink inward, like she's sucking on something sour.

"Yeah," I say. "It's not a big deal or anything, but my . . . friend started—well, they've been talking, and Edith said you got, like, bad vibes from him? So I just—"

Piper swats at the air, cutting me off. "Trust me." She punctuates the sentence by pressing her finger onto the table. I watch her knuckle turn white, as if she's holding the wood in place. "You need to get your friend away from Morgan," she says. "Before it's too late."

CHAPTER FIVE

Piper's expression is so intense I lean away from her, back pressed to the chair.

"Too late?" I repeat, throat tightening. I laugh to loosen it. "What do you mean?"

But she doesn't answer that. Instead, she says, "I met Daphne here. At the library."

She gestures to the walls, beige and blank, and her gaze softens as she studies them, as if her memory of that day is projected over my head.

"We were hosting an open mic night—something we'd done dozens of times. But this was the first time Daphne came. And right away, I was starstruck."

"Because she was Morgan's wife?"

Piper's eyes snap onto me. "Hell no. I didn't care about Morgan Thorne. I know that's basically blasphemous for someone in this town, but I've always been skeptical of anything that's massively popular. If it appeals to *that* many people, it can't have much substance."

I bristle at that, reminded of Brad. His taste skewed so indie that, in solidarity, I actually stopped listening to Taylor Swift, whose music he dismissed as "sparkly breakup songs."

"Honestly, I knew so little about Morgan Thorne," Piper continues, "that until I met Daphne, I assumed he was a woman."

When I only frown in response, Piper sighs, as if annoyed she has to explain: "His protagonists are always women. And his name is Morgan—which can be a woman's name—so I just figured Morgan Thorne had to be a woman. Otherwise, he was appropriating women's voices and stories. Which: now I know, that's exactly what he did."

"Wait." The desire to defend him nearly lifts me out of my chair. "He can't help what his name is."

Distaste flicks across Piper's face—now I've disappointed her.

"He knows what he's doing. Women made his genre what it is. Gillian Flynn with *Gone Girl*, Paula Hawkins with *The Girl on the Train*. So when readers see someone named Morgan writing thrillers about women, they're going to assume the author is a woman. Daphne even said that when *Someone at the Door* first came out, he didn't have his photo on his book or website, and his bio didn't use any pronouns. It's a disgusting sales grab."

She sticks her finger in her mouth, pretending to gag, and it's so childish that it suddenly clicks for me who she was at Burnham High. I saw her do that same gesture my senior year, when she and some other girls mocked a freshman named Winnie, who often dressed like she'd just left a Renaissance Faire and, that day, had brownie stuck in her braces. As Winnie blinked back tears, I touched her arm and improvised: *I've been looking everywhere for you! Your dad's still getting us backstage at Gaga tonight, right?* Most of the girls' jaws dropped open, but Piper rolled her eyes, clearly unimpressed.

Now it makes sense, her aversion to Morgan. In the last minute, she's accused him of manipulation, appropriation, and writing books that lack any substance—but it seems she's always been prejudiced against popular artists.

"All that is to say," Piper adds, "I wasn't starstruck about Daphne because of who her husband was. I was starstruck because of *her*. She was a writer, too, you know."

I blink, taken aback. "No, actually, I didn't know that. I just know she was a professor. At Emerson?" I try to seem foggy on the details, like I didn't study every sentence of her obituary, which made no mention of a writing career.

"Yes, but she was also a poet. An amazing one. When I read her debut collection, I highlighted so many lines that some pages were completely yellow. She had another book, too, which won an award."

"Wow. I had no idea." I'm careful to sound more impressed than surprised, but the truth is: I'm caught off guard by the information. This never came up when I searched her name. Even in Morgan's second message, when he shared that his wife liked "writing poetry on the weekends," he tacked it onto the end of a list of Daphne's hobbies. As if she filled a notebook or two with quaint, cursive musings—not penned entire collections.

This is good information, though. It's making me glad I worked so hard to polish my messages to Morgan—he clearly likes women who have a way with words. I should write more often, buy a few Moleskine journals. Maybe he and I could have writing dates together, sneak smiles above our notebooks as I weave him into my stories.

"She published under her maiden name, Whittaker," Piper says—which explains, I guess, why I never saw her work online. "But I'm not surprised you had no idea. Poets aren't exactly known outside the poetry community, even if they've published a lot. Unless they're, like, Instagram or TikTok famous."

She does it again, the fake gag, and I try to keep the irritation off my face. After catching her taunting Winnie back in high school, I spent weeks coaching Winnie to ignore mean girls like Piper.

"But when Daphne came to open mic, she blew everyone away," Piper says. "There was this pause after she read. Just . . . stunned silence before everyone erupted. They were applauding so loud our director heard it from two floors away. And Daphne looked shell-shocked. Like she wasn't used to so much noise. Like she couldn't believe she'd inspired it.

"I went up to her, afterward, told her how much I loved her work, and she was so humble about it. She kept saying, 'I wasn't sure I should even come,' which I thought meant—well, because she's Daphne Whittaker. Leagues above the average open mic performer. But then I got the sense that what she really meant was: she didn't think she had anything to offer in coming. Didn't realize her work would be so well-received. And of course, *now* I know why she felt that way. It was because of Morgan."

She coughs up his name like phlegm. Then she scrapes her nail across a gouge in the table, inspecting the imperfection, her brows sinking deep.

"Daphne and I became friends after that. We'd meet up for coffee, go for walks. We became very close very fast—which was a dream to me, having an actual relationship with a writer I loved. But on Daphne's end, it seemed like there was something . . . urgent to our friendship. Like she knew we *had* to get close quickly. Because otherwise, we wouldn't have time to get close at all."

Her fingernail, still scratching, stutters against the table. "Turns out, that entire time we'd been getting to know each other—about two weeks—Morgan had been away on some book tour. And when he came back, everything changed. It was harder to see her. Harder to make plans. Harder just to get a response to my texts."

There's a dull, haunted edge to Piper's voice, as if Daphne's availability, or lack thereof, was a symptom of something horrible.

"Isn't that just married life?" I suggest, thinking of Nina and Alex. I talk to my best friend almost daily, but I haven't actually seen her since the end of April. "You have certain routines with your partner, and the rest of your social life sort of . . . molds around it?"

"Sure. That's what I thought too. At first. But when we did meet up again, she was . . . different. On edge. Her eyes were always darting around, like she needed to be hyperaware of her surroundings. And she kept getting calls from Morgan, checking to see where she was, when she'd be home. Like he was keeping tabs."

Piper says this last part with so much weight I have to replay the words in my head, just in case I missed something. But it doesn't sound sinister to me, Morgan checking in with Daphne; it sounds sweet. Some of my exes went entire days without initiating contact. I'd try to hold out, wait for them to want me first, but in the end, I always caved, nudging them about making plans. With Brad, it was different—for a while, at least. Until my dress became a ghost. Until he made me feel like a ghost myself: unseen, unheard, but still a pestering presence. I'm actually envious of Daphne; even when she was married to Morgan, he continued to pursue her.

Maybe that's the secret to something that lasts: if you love someone, you never give up the chase.

"I asked Daphne if everything was okay at home," Piper continues, "and she snapped right out of it. Like she realized she'd revealed too much. And she said it was nothing like that, it was just: the anniversary was coming up and—"

Piper stops, her mouth tightening, as if realizing she, too, revealed too much.

"Her and Morgan's anniversary?" I ask.

Piper shakes her head, silent a few more moments, her eyes fastened to the table. "The anniversary of her sister's murder."

I pull in a breath so jagged I nearly choke on it. "Oh god, that's awful."

"Yeah. It happened when Daphne was only twelve."

In an instant, tears coat my vision. I clench my teeth against the sting. I'd guessed her sister's death, alluded to in Daphne's obituary, was the childhood trauma Morgan mentioned, but I imagined something like cancer or a car accident as the cause. Never even thought of murder. It's so tragic I can almost feel it in my chest, the weight of Daphne's pain like a brick where my heart should be.

"What—" I start, unsure how to ask the question. "Who killed her?"

Piper scrapes harder at the table, her gaze fixed to her finger.

"They don't know. It's a horrible story. Daphne's parents were out of town for the night, and they'd left her older sister in charge. Daphne thought she heard footsteps on the porch, so she got up to look, told her sister, 'There's someone at the door,' and that was the last thing she ever said to her—because one second later, the glass in the door was smashed. A hand reached in for the lock. And Daphne ran out the back and just kept going. Through the woods. Into other neighborhoods. She said she thought her sister was behind her, but when she finally stopped to pound on someone's door for help, she realized she was alone." Piper swallows. "Her sister never made it out of the house."

I sink inward, rubbing my ribs. I feel Daphne's horror, sudden and searing, like a cramp in my side.

"She was shot," Piper says. "But the police think it was meant to be a simple robbery. The house was dark—they'd been watching a movie—so the intruder probably hadn't expected anyone to be home."

Intruder. It's a word that conjures danger, violation, and still, it isn't nearly sharp enough. I can't help but imagine it—the safety of their night together, Daphne and her sister cocooned on the couch, TV screen glowing before them. And then: the muted thump of shoes outside. Daphne cleaving the curtains to glimpse a person on the porch. A stranger at the door.

My spine snaps straight, a piece of the story slotting into place. "Wait. The last thing she said to her sister was 'There's someone at the door'?"

It's almost identical to the title of Morgan's debut. *Someone at the Door*. The first word has been carved away, but the rest of Daphne's sentence remains intact. And not just intact: preserved. On book covers. On title pages. In the opening credits of a film.

"Yes." Piper grips me with her gaze. "That's why I told you that story. So you'd see what he did to her, that son of a bitch, naming his novel that."

"It . . . must be a coincidence," I say. Because Morgan's book isn't about an intruder. It's about a woman who knocks on a couple's door, introduces herself as their new neighbor over cookies and conversation, then vanishes, leaving behind a note addressed to the wife: *Your husband isn't who you think he is.*

"It's not," Piper says, resolute.

But it has to be. Otherwise, it would be too cruel. Every time Daphne heard that title, it would sound to her like glass breaking, like a door banging open.

"She asked him about it once," Piper continues, "and he said it hadn't even crossed his mind—those being her last words to her sister. He said it was just a phrase he liked because it felt ominous when attached to a thriller. Yeah fucking right! That sentence has haunted *me* ever since Daphne told me about it. But Morgan, her *husband*, conveniently forgot it?"

I bite my lip, absorbing her argument. She's right that the sentence, the significance of it, should be burned into Morgan's memory. But what would he gain from doing that to Daphne?

Piper taps her phone to check the time. "He was always careless with her feelings. Like, she went to so many of his book events, but he never went to of her readings. She played it off like it didn't bother her, like oh, he's just not that into this stuff, he only reads a few poets and I'm no Pound or Sexton, haha! But of course it hurt." Piper shakes her head, exhaling through a tight, cold smile. "I swear, I never even saw Morgan and Daphne together, but I got such bad vibes from him."

I tense at that—*bad vibes*—the phrase Edith referenced in her text. When I read it, I assumed Piper had some awkward interactions with him, glimpsed things that didn't sit quite right. But no: it's all speculation, just Piper filling in the gaps about an an author—a person—she'd already made assumptions about as soon as she learned he was a man.

"So . . . you never even met Morgan?" I ask.

"Never. I went to Daphne's funeral, of course." The corners of Piper's eyes pinch. "But I never got a chance to talk to him. People were fawning all over him, offering the poor widower a shoulder to cry on—as if he hadn't killed her in the first place."

"Whoa— What?" I pitch forward, hands on the table.

"He doesn't have an alibi. He told police he was writing in his office with music on, so he didn't hear Daphne fall or cry out—which is the flimsiest thing I've ever heard."

I straighten, her words grazing a memory. But I shake my head, brush the half-formed thought away. "You seriously think he murdered her?"

Piper crosses her arms, smug in her silence, and I think of the comments on YouTube, on Instagram, the random string of numbers and letters.

They could have come from Piper.

"But," I start, "even if everything you've said is true—"

"It *is* true."

"Even if Morgan wasn't . . . supportive of Daphne's writing, or was . . . inconsiderate when titling his novel, that doesn't mean he—"

"You're using the wrong words," Piper cuts in. "Morgan wasn't *unsupportive* or *inconsiderate*. He belittled Daphne's work. Used her trauma as *plot*. Because I've read his books since she died, and it's not just *Someone at the Door*. Daphne's past is *all* over Morgan's work. Would you want your friend—the one seeing Morgan—to be treated the way Daphne was?"

I open my mouth, but when my answer isn't immediate, she forges ahead. "And you didn't see her, those last couple weeks before she

died. She was really . . . scared. Completely freaked out about something. She just wouldn't tell me what it was." Piper leans on one elbow
as she rubs her right temple. "She kept dismissing her own mind: 'I
don't know, I might be imagining things.' After she died, I went to the
police with my concerns, but they didn't give a shit, especially since
she hadn't told me *what* she might be imagining. But I knew it had to
do with Morgan. Every dark emotion she had in those months always
had to do with him."

"But—" I hesitate, wanting to be sensitive. Tears swim in Piper's
eyes, the wound of losing her friend cut open again by our conversation. I keep my voice soft, my question slow. "Did she actually *say*
that her . . . dark emotions were about him?"

"She couldn't! Daphne's default was to protect Morgan. Defend
him. Because that's what people like him do. They trick you into thinking you need them. Because if you're as worthless as they make you
feel but they *still* demand you stay, then—they must be amazing, right?
They *have* to be, if they're willing to slum it with someone like you."

I pull back a little. *Someone like you.* I know Piper's speaking
in general, that *you* doesn't actually mean me, Rosie Lachlan. But
there's something about the way she says it—or maybe just what she
says—that vibrates beneath my skin, striking an uncomfortable chord.

"So," Piper adds, "I'm sure of it. Daphne was scared of him at the
end. He'd done something that freaked her out. And before I could
find out what it was"—she stops, gaze drilling into mine as if desperate
to fill me with her belief—"she was murdered."

———————

The text comes as I'm walking Bumper, my headlamp slicing through
the dark.

How'd it go with Piper?

I stare at Edith's question, then drop my hand to my side. I'm so exhausted I don't even bother tugging Bumper when he slows, when he noses the ground so long it's like he's sniffing for someone buried beneath the soil.

I take stock of our surroundings. We've already passed my favorite house, the yellow one with the stained-glass window above the door, but I drifted by it without even noticing. The library tired me out more than I expected, and afterward, work was relentless. One bride had a breakdown because her future mother-in-law, who was paying for her dress, demanded veto power over the woman's choice; another decided, at her second fitting, that the silhouette she'd picked was completely wrong and nearly ripped off the gown. I snuck breaks between appointments, slumped in a chair, hand over my heart, which seemed to race at random. Delayed adrenaline from my indignation at Piper's fiery, fervent claims.

I glance at the text again, Edith's question waiting for an answer I'm not sure how to articulate.

Piper tried to paint Morgan as cold and controlling—maybe even cruel: dismissing his wife's writing; restricting her time with friends; threading her trauma into his books. But one thing that portrait lacked was proof. By Piper's own admission, Daphne never said a bad word about her husband. And Piper never even interacted with him.

But I have.

And I sensed nothing sinister in his presence. Nothing worrying in his words.

It does still strike me as strange that I had no idea Daphne was a writer. Even Morgan's Wikipedia page makes no mention of the poet Daphne Whittaker, lacking a section for Personal Life altogether. Maybe if I'd looked deeper, I would have found the information somewhere, but with few hits for Daphne Thorne on Google and social media, it wasn't long before I pivoted my focus from her to Morgan.

I'm going to remedy that, though. As soon as I got home from work tonight, I put in an order at Burnham Bookshop for both Daphne Whittaker collections. It'll be a few days before they come in, but I'm hoping they'll give me further insight into who she was—and maybe, if she wrote about Morgan, what made her marriage tick.

Still, it's that possibility, the two of them writing about each other, that nudges me to another thought. Even her obituary, which I assume Morgan wrote, only mentioned that Daphne "loved poetry," and when I read that line, I figured it meant she loved *reading* poetry, didn't once consider she wrote it, too.

Piper would say that was deliberate. That he was minimizing his wife's legacy. But I shake my head, pulling Bumper along, because it's hard to trust any of Piper's opinions—including that Morgan was unsupportive of Daphne—when, in her mind, Morgan's as guilty of that as he is of murder.

I'm sure it helps Piper to have someone to blame. Otherwise, her friend's death was too senseless, too random, a fall that never would have happened if Daphne's foot was only inches from whatever tripped her up. There must be a strange kind of comfort in what Piper sees as Morgan's "flimsy" alibi.

Admittedly, though, I'm confused about it myself. If he told police he didn't hear Daphne fall because he was working in his office with music on, then why did he tell *me* he needs "complete silence" to write? He even mentioned he can hear Sickle's scratching—from three rooms away—while he works, and compared to a scream or thud, a scratch is just a whisper. So if it's true he can't write to music, wouldn't he have heard the crash of her body, or at least a yelp of pain?

Then again, maybe he can't listen to music *anymore*. I bet it's a trauma response, a fear he developed *after* Daphne's accident; I bet there's a throb in his gut, blows of guilt and anguish when he thinks of how he didn't—couldn't—hear her. Of course he needs silence now to write. It's like me, unable to listen to Florence & the Machine because I'd been spinning to "Cosmic Love" only minutes before Brad spoke the words that blackened my world.

I return to my phone, where Edith waits for a verdict on my chat with Piper.

> It went well! Thanks again for setting it up. The "bad vibes" Piper got aren't really based on anything substantial.

Of course, I can't mention that, from my limited experience with Morgan, everything Piper said about him actually seems pretty far-fetched. With me, he's been kind, thoughtful, funny, each of us laughing so easily at the other's jokes. He's been vulnerable and curious, too: I'd love to know more about you, he said on DonorConnect—and in that same message, he spoke so tenderly about his wife that, when I first read it, it was hard not to fall a little in love with her myself. I adore that she crocheted hats for Sickle, that she loved baking only one specific kind of bread. It makes me wonder—if given the chance—what Morgan might tell someone about me. What details of mine he'd highlight. What he'd find in me worth loving.

After Brad, I didn't believe I was good enough for anyone. I thought I'd sickened myself from the inside out, that even my skin was permanently tarnished, that no one could look at me, ever again, and find something shining. But when I close my eyes, I still see Morgan's words on my screen: I think you're remarkable.

It's not that I'm an authority on Morgan. I haven't known him long enough to be sure of who he is. But that only seems like a reason to try to know him better. To see how close I can get.

As if sensing my thoughts, Bumper stops again, and this time, it's at a stretch of grass he's beginning to know well. I click off my head-lamp, look across the lawn to the house glowing golden in the dark.

Inside, Morgan's watching TV, and from the massive screen mounted above his fireplace, I recognize an episode of *Friends*.

There's something so comforting in this view—so simple and ordinary and familiar—and I allow myself to indulge in it, watching with Morgan as Ross, Rachel, and Chandler struggle to carry a couch to Ross's apartment. And though I can't hear the words from here, I see David Schwimmer hit his line, "PIVOT," delivering it with such drama and precision that, even outside, I can't help but smile. In his living room, Morgan tilts his head back, and I hear his laughter—in my memory, anyway, because I finally know what it sounds like: a rumble deep in his throat, like a distant roll of thunder.

My phone chimes—a reply from Edith—pulling me from the scene.

> Oh, good. Sorry if I worried you for no reason then! Do you think your friend will keep seeing Morgan?

Bumper tugs on his leash, impatient to continue our walk. I look up from my phone—and register that I've strayed from the curb. Without noticing, I've walked halfway up Morgan's driveway, as if the heart in my chest is still pulled to his, two magnets never meant to separate.

I remain in place as I type my response to Edith.

> Yeah. She definitely will.

From: Morgan Thorne <morganthorne@morganthorne.com>
To: Blair Hawkins <blairhawkins@gmail.com>
Date: May 17, 2025
Subject: Pink flags

Well, B, Rosie was right. She did know where to find me.

When I brought in the mail this afternoon, there was a handwritten note at the bottom of the stack. I almost missed it. Almost threw it right out with the insurance offers and take-out menus. The note was on the back of a faded receipt, like it had been in a pocket for a long time, like the message itself was impromptu.

If you still want to see me, I'll be at Burnham Grove Park 6 p.m. tomorrow (May 17). —Rosie

I hear you screaming at your screen: "Red flag, Morgan! Red fucking flag!" But I think you're wrong about that. If anything, it's a *pink* flag (yes, that's a pun about Rosie's hair), and you know how I feel about playing things safe. "Safe" becomes uncomfortable. It itches like a sweater with a too-tight collar.

And anyway. Red has always been my favorite color.

I arrived at the park at 6:10—late enough to make her wonder if I'd stood her up, to flood her with relief, and gratitude, when I didn't. I found her easily, her pink hair a beacon among the monotony of grass and stone. She was bent forward on a bench, spilling a bit of her water bottle onto a leaf at her feet, not yet aware of my presence. The water pooled inside the leaf, which was curled up at the edges, like a cupped palm.

"What are you doing?" I asked, and she jumped at my voice.

"Um. Oh god." She covered her face with her hand, laughing at herself. "I was—" She shook her head. "Making a birdbath."

I laughed too. "A birdbath? In that leaf?"

"Yeah, or—a bird . . . bowl? There was a sparrow here, a minute ago, hopping around. And then it stopped, and I swear it was watching me drink my water, tilting its head like a dog begging for food. So I joked at it, 'You thirsty, bird?' And it didn't answer—obviously—but then I got worried it *was* thirsty, and I saw this leaf, and—"

"And you made a birdbath."

"Right. Well. I tried. Size-wise, it might be more of a bugbath."

I slid onto the bench. Slid Rosie a smile. "Bugs need water, too."

She scrunched up her nose. "Do they? Do bugs drink water? I mean, they must, right? Don't all living things need water? But I can't picture a bug actually *drinking*. Do bugs have tongues? Oh my god, do they have *lips*?" Her eyes widened at the thought before she slumped back against the bench. "Sorry—I just got really freaked out about bug anatomy for a second."

"Happens to me all the time."

Rosie giggled, her gaze dipping toward her bottle. "So. You got my note."

"You left me a note? I thought I just had really good Rosie Radar."

She smiled, tucking her hair behind her ear—and I loved that, her touches of shyness. Loved that she was two women at once: one who was bold enough to drop a note in my mailbox, instructing me when and where to meet her, and one who blushed beneath my gaze.

In the past few days, I've been preoccupied with ideas for my next book. I think it'll be about a woman who had a heart transplant. She connects with the husband of her heart donor and then . . . something terrible happens. (I haven't gotten very far. I'm still waiting for the protagonist to take shape.) But as I sat there watching Rosie today, I couldn't help but sketch a different character in my head: A woman with pink hair. A woman whose smiles vacillate between sheepish and coy. A woman whose caution is undercut by intense vulnerability, like a squirrel crossing a street, pausing middash to avoid danger—only making it easier for a car to crush her.

"I appreciate the old-school approach," I said. "Felt like finding a note in my locker from a secret admirer." Then I paused for three seconds, counting them in my head, so she'd worry, just for a moment, that I saw the edge of a red flag. "How'd you know where I lived?"

Her reply was quick enough to sound rehearsed. "Everyone in Burnham knows where Morgan Thorne lives. The bookstore practically prints your address on receipts."

"Ah, yes, Burnham Bookshop. The owner there is very . . . enthusiastic. I guess it makes sense that, after promoting my books so much, she'd move on to promoting my address."

"It's great customer service," Rosie agreed.

She looked off at the trees rimming the park, and we fell into a silence that felt like static—something and nothing at the same time, a soothing white noise.

I was the one to break it.

"There's a heart over there," I said, pointing to a gap between two branches, the blank space through which some blue sky bloomed. "Do you see it?"

She squinted into the distance, and I took the opportunity to slide closer to her so she could look down the length of my arm, follow my finger to the heart-shaped break in the trees.

"A blue heart," I clarified. "That patch of sky outlined by the branches."

"Oh, yeah!" she said, excited for a second, before she frowned. "It's broken, though." Now it was her turn to point. "See that one little twig on that branch? It looks like a crack, running from the bottom of the heart." She traced it in the air with her finger.

"You're right," I said. "Kind of like a fault line."

She shrugged, slow to lower her hand. "I guess every heart has one."

I liked that exchange. In part, I'm sharing it with you, B, so I'll have a record of it later, when I'm writing that pink-haired character. A woman who's observant, who makes metaphors of nature in casual conversation. A woman with fault lines of her own.

"Do you have a broken heart?" I asked.

The turn of her head was sharp. "Me?"

"No, the ants in the bugbath." I tapped her knee—a playful imitation of a slap. "I'm just wondering if you saw something of yourself over there." I gestured to it again, that blue gap in the trees.

I watched her force a smile. It was sweet but stiff. Her cheek didn't dimple. "No, I'm fine," she lied.

Maybe the pink-haired character is running from something—someone—in her past. Maybe the pink is a mask. Maybe somebody loved her before, when she was blond or brunette. Then maybe that love turned ugly—more fists than kisses—so she changed her look, her life, squirreled away in a generic suburb. A place where no one confuses love with cruelty. A place where it's safe to loiter at the house of a man she really doesn't know.

"You sure?" I asked, bumping her shoulder with mine.

That close to her, I could almost smell it, her pain like perfume.

She twisted off the cap on her water bottle, stalled by sipping, and as she swallowed, I admired her neck, her throat, pale and exposed. She recapped the bottle and seemed to think very carefully about what to say next. In that pause, I sensed her wound more clearly. Darkness welled from it like red-black blood.

"It's nothing a little Taylor Swift won't cure," she said, slipping me a guarded but expectant glance.

I had to keep myself from grinning.

"Love Taylor," I said. "She's basically the Sylvia Plath of our generation."

This time, Rosie's smile was sincere, though not as surprised as I'd expected. Her dimple winked at me. "You think so?"

"Oh, definitely. Are you familiar with Sylvia's work?"

"Not as much as I should be," she admitted.

"Well. She and Taylor are really similar in how they memorialize heartbreak—at times, writing these beautiful, breathtaking lines, while still being scathing, too, completely skewering the men they believe have wronged them. Well, not 'men' in Sylvia's case. Mostly just Ted Hughes."

"Wait, who's Ted Hughes again?"

"Her husband. He was a poet, too, more famous than her at the time. They met at a launch party for *St. Botolph's Review*, and they kissed that same night, this really wild, explosive kiss—'kissed me quite insane' is how Sylvia put it in 'Mad Girl's Love Song.' Then she bit him on the cheek."

"Yikes," Rosie said.

I shrugged. "Passion can be like that."

She laughed. "Violent and painful?"

"Exactly," I said, but when something flickered in her expression—
a quick crease between her brows—I laughed too. "Anyway, both
Sylvia and Taylor have had tumultuous relationships with men, but
they got their best work from it. Taylor's *Red* album, which she's called
her one true breakup album, is phenomenal. Sylvia's *Ariel*, written after
separating from Hughes, is the gold standard of poetry."

I made sure to stop while Rosie was eager for more. Her body tilted
toward mine, so subtle I doubt she even noticed.

"Sorry," I said. "I tend to nerd out sometimes."

"Do *not* apologize for nerding out over Taylor Swift."

"Apology rescinded. Do you want to listen to her?"

"What, like, right now?"

I pulled my phone from one pocket, my earbuds from another. I
passed one of the buds to Rosie, and it was so sweet, the way she
gaped at it a moment, like it was a diamond ring.

"Right now," I said.

We listened for a long time. Long enough for the sky to shift from blue
to pink as the sun dissolved behind the trees.

"Look," I said, pausing the music. "The sunset's your biggest fan."

The sound of her laughter was infinitely better than Taylor's voice.
"What?"

"It's imitating your hair." I pointed to that heart between the trees, now a patch of pink. "Sincerest form of flattery and all that." I reached out to touch her hair, pausing before I actually made contact, seeking consent with my eyes. She nodded, just a little, and my fingers twisted through the strands. "But to be honest," I added, "it looks better on you."

It was so heavy-handed. I'm sure you're cringing, B. But Rosie blushed until her skin matched the sky.

So I kissed her. No pause. No questioning gaze. I pressed my lips to hers, which were soft and warm and already parted.

She responded by pulling me closer, her hand on the back of my head, her fingers twisting through *my* hair now, and I'm surprised I didn't think of Daphne. I thought for sure I'd feel her clawing at me if I kissed someone else; I thought her ghost would grow teeth. But in that moment, on that park bench, beneath that pastel sky, it was like Rosie shut down that part of my brain—the part that never stops remembering my wife on our bathroom floor, her mouth open but unmoving, her cries for help long since silenced.

When we pulled away, Rosie was slow to open her eyes. I mirrored her smile—hesitant and hopeful.

"So," I said, "while I genuinely enjoyed the note in the mailbox and plan to hang it on my fridge—"

"Oh god, please don't."

"—I think it would be easier if I just gave you my number." I leaned forward, so close I could kiss her again. "For next time."

Seconds passed, Rosie sitting frozen—wanting, I knew, to seem unsure. I waited her out, let her pretend to waver. Then she dug through her bag before finally excavating her phone. As I recited my number, she plugged it in, and I told her to text me so I'd have hers, too. In a moment, my phone dinged with two emojis: an ant and a tub.

"Nice bugbath," I said, adding her number to my contacts. "Wait, what's your last name?" I showed her the empty field.

Again, she froze—committed to her performance. Careful, mysterious Rosie.

"That's third-date info," she joked, "so if you really want to know, I guess we'll have to see each other again."

I only half heard her. In my head, I was working on the pink-haired character, brainstorming the darkness that haunts her. The thing that's made her leash up her heart—an old dog that refuses to learn a new trick.

"I should warn you," I said, pocketing my phone. "I'm not a big texter. I don't like how casual it is. So expect a call instead."

"Oh, so—will the call be formal, then?" she teased. "What's the dress code exactly? Cocktail attire? Ball gown?"

"Black tie optional." I let my lips curl up. Then I stared into her eyes, touched her cheek. "Because I'm hoping this won't be casual."

From: DonorConnect Communications
To: Morgan Thorne
Date: May 18, 2025

You have received the following message from your loved one's organ recipient. As a reminder, DonorConnect encourages both organ recipients and donor families to refrain from sharing identifying information (including name, address, and personal email) until a time when both parties have consented to giving and accepting those details.

Hi again.

You encouraged me to write the worst things down. Actually, I'm obsessed with how you put it: "words are how we heal our wounds." That's so beautiful. So true. And you can't know how much I appreciate the invitation to tell you more about my Dark Place™. I'm usually hesitant to talk about this with people. Some don't get it—my sister, for example, who visited me while I was at my worst and asked me if it really hurt "this bad" (she genuinely wouldn't know; she's never had her heart broken). Then there's the people who wish I'd move on already, drown my darkness with light.

But the thing is: my darkness *started* with light.

My ex and I met on a dating app, which shouldn't feel fated or romantic, but somehow, with us, it did. I was seconds from deleting the app altogether when I received his message: "Quick question. I'm new here, so what do I say in my profile when it asks what I'm 'looking for'? Because I've been looking for the 'strangest delicious pizza' for about six years now. But I have a feeling that's not what that question means."

It might have been a line. An opening he used with everyone. But I did not delete the app.

We wanted to meet up right away, but he was in London for work, so for the next month, we texted throughout each day and FaceTimed for hours on the weekend. When he finally came home, he drove straight from the airport to my apartment. He brought me British candy, took me out for pizza at this restaurant inside an old train car where we ordered their Jif's Jubilee (peanut butter, bacon, and provolone), which he ultimately ranked second in his Strangest Delicious Pizza Spreadsheet—a system he took very seriously, with ratings for odd ingredient pairings, crust, creativity, and overall taste. It was our first date, but for all the talking we'd already done, the stories we'd already shared, it felt like our fiftieth. And just before we said goodbye, he held his lips an inch from mine. "I've been dreaming of this," he said, and then our mouths met, and I felt the kiss in every part of me—my chest blazing, limbs sizzling, blood fizzing like champagne.

For months after that, we saw each other every day. He often had gifts for me: a set of pastel Sharpies he'd seen me admiring at Target; a pint glass he'd gone back and bought from the train car restaurant; a cake stand after we binged one season of *Great British Bake Off*. He showered me with adjectives—I was amazing, wonderful, awesome, special, incredible—and he always sounded awestruck, like he couldn't believe I'd chosen *him*.

We carried on like that. I woke each morning smiling into my pillow. And then, one day, in an otherwise ordinary moment on the couch, he asked me to be with him forever.

And I said yes to that, yes to forever. Yes to the end of breakups and boyfriends. Yes to the future, which was no longer blank as an empty frame.

But in the weeks that followed, something changed. We should have been staggeringly happy, drunk on joy, dizzy with the commitment we'd made, but instead of growing closer, I felt some barrier between us—invisible as air, solid as a wall. When we sat together on the couch, some part of us still touched—arms, legs, hands—but I could barely feel him there. He still called me amazing, incredible, etc., but the words were dispassionate, like he was reciting information he'd been forced to memorize. He started working more, talking to me less, even when we were in the same room. Same bed. And I couldn't understand it. I still don't.

So when he wouldn't let me hold his hand, I held on to forever, to *yes*, instead. I kept planning our future. I bought the damn dress. I imagined that when he saw me in it, gliding down the aisle, he'd snap back to himself. Back to us.

You already know that didn't happen.

Still, two weeks after he broke it off, he texted me: "I miss your face. Come over?" And I did. I drove so fast, positive he'd undo it all, positive I'd stop spending my days in a lonely bed. When he opened the door, there was no preamble, not even hello—just his hands on my face, his mouth on mine. Ravenous, gluttonous kisses. I broke for breath and asked if we should talk.

He didn't want to talk.

When I fell asleep in his arms, the first real sleep I'd had in days, it felt so much like the beginning, skin touching, legs tangled, that my heart instantly healed. It would all be okay. We could start again. My wedding dress, now forced to the back of my closet, would wait for us.

"Last night was fun," he told me, hand on my car door as he saw me off in the morning. "We should do this again."

"When?" I asked.

"I'll text you."

It was enough for me. In the wake of his silence, the simple promise of a text felt as significant as a vow. I actually went to work that day—the first time since it happened. I smiled through appointments, glancing at my phone whenever I could. I returned the next day, too. And the next. But on day four, when I still hadn't heard from him, I called out.

Called him. Called again when he didn't answer. I texted, too: "Hey, are my calls going through? Haven't heard from you, so I'm just a little worried." Still: silence. Silence, again.

On the seventh day, I couldn't take it anymore. Something must have happened. He must have been hurt. Otherwise, why would he say those things? *I miss your face. We should do it again. I'll text you.* Not to mention, that night in his bed, *You're amazing.*

You don't say those things and then say nothing.

So I drove back to him. I knocked on his door, expecting more silence—because he'd been in an accident and the hospital didn't know to call me; or he was back to working late, his phone tucked in a drawer; or his boss had sent him to London again and with the time change—

But then I heard footsteps. The door opened. And he was there, TV remote in hand.

It was the remote that broke me. He'd been free, been fine—just hadn't been in touch. I collapsed in front of his door. Spat out questions and half-finished sentences: "Where have you been? Didn't you get my calls? I thought we were— I figured you meant—"

He stared at me as I cried and told me I was crazy, showing up like that, "calling a million times."

He told me it had been a mistake: him missing my face, that night in his bed.

He told me, "Stop calling, stop texting, it's over for good. Forever."

I shook my head no to that. *No* to forever. *No* to for good. When he closed the door, I was still saying no. When he turned up the TV, no, no, no. When his lights went out: no. When he yelled out the window, "This is crazy, you're crazy, go home!": my head jerked back and forth.

No to a future that's nothing but fog.

No to loneliness like lightning, striking me again and again.

That's what I've been grieving, all these months. The loss of him, yes, but maybe even more: the loss of partnership. The loss of tables for two and a permanent plus-one.

It's only lately that I've been thinking I might not have lost it forever; there might, in fact, be hope for *forever* again—or at least *my* forever, however long that is.

I'm sorry if this has been too much. You wrote that our messages are a safe place for heartbreak, but I'm sorry if I took that offer a little too far.

I probably *do* sound crazy. The whole story of him, of us, likely does. You're probably thinking, *Why did she hold on so hard to someone who was intent on letting her go?*

All I can say is: the beginning was so blindingly beautiful, it kept me from seeing the end.

But in exchange for my oversharing: please know that *your* heartbreak is safe here, too. I'm grateful for everything you've told me about your wife. It's obvious, just from the little you shared, how much you loved her, so I'm sure your marriage never suffered the kinds of storms I described above—and I'm sure, too, that made it even harder to lose her. But if you want to talk about your wife beyond just her hobbies and interests, please feel free. Admittedly, as someone still recovering from an epic romantic failure, it would be nice to hear about a happy marriage.

From: DonorConnect Communications
To: Rosie Lachlan
Date: May 20, 2025

You have received the following message from your donor's loved one. As a reminder, DonorConnect encourages both organ recipients and donor families to refrain from sharing identifying information (including name, address, and personal email) until a time when both parties have consented to giving and accepting those details.

Hey, you.

Do you know that, twice now, in two separate messages, you've made essentially the same apology? *Sorry if that's too much.*

I wonder what it is that makes you worry about being too much. I wonder if it's *him*, your unnamed ex that I now want to put in my next book just so I can make him suffer.

Perhaps you're haunted by all the calls you made, all the texts you sent, by the night you fell apart at his door. If that's the case, I want you to know I understand your actions. He promised you something—first, forever; then, the most casual thing on earth: a text—and he didn't follow through.

Your trust was a gift that he refused to handle with care. I see your openness, your willingness to be vulnerable, and I think you're wonderful for that. I'm honored you trusted *me* with this story, with the specifics of your Dark Place™, and I promise you, your trust has not been misplaced.

I also want you to know: I don't think you're crazy. You were in love. And if I've learned anything from my own experience, it's that love turns you inside out. It changes you—on a deep, cellular level—until even your skin feels different, your voice sounds foreign, until you do and say things you never thought you could. Some days, love makes you look in the mirror and admire your own reflection; others, it makes you a monster in the glass.

Not to mention, I've *seen* crazy, and what you described is not it.

Actually, I shouldn't use "crazy" there. There's a long tradition of men calling women "crazy"—which your ex-fiancé was all too happy to continue—and it's a lazy label, one that's reductive of women's true experience. I'm just not sure what word to use in its place. Unwell? Unstable? Unhinged? Those don't feel right either. The prefix "un-" implies a lack. Something missing. But what my wife exhibited was not an absence. Her behavior made her into something more. Something louder and bigger than herself. Something that, at times, unnerved me to witness. To live with. To close my eyes and sleep beside.

Let me back up a little. You were so forthcoming about the darkness of your past; in return, I'd like to show you mine.

I met my wife before I was published. We were instructors at the same local college, both of us teaching freshman comp, and we'd often commiserate in the copy room, trading the worst student writing we'd read that week. That probably sounds cruel, but that's what the torture of teaching composition does: it whittles you down to your worst impulses.

Admittedly, I liked the smidge of meanness in her. It made her human. Because otherwise, she was so undeniably *good*. Case in point: on our first date, headed to dinner together, she made me stop for roadkill. It was a fox some driver had left for dead, its fur torn open by tires. Still, she stooped over the animal, checking for movement, for breath, before finally accepting she was too late to save it. In the passenger seat, as we drove away, she dabbed at tears in her eyes.

She was like that with her students, too. She wanted to rescue them all. Even the ones whose writing we groaned at. Maybe especially those. The limp-necked, dead-eyed ones who drooled through class. She believed she could reach them through writing—theirs or someone

else's. She believed once they found the right author, the right
passage, the right line, it would unlock something inside them, unbury
the hidden treasure of their own words. She taught freshman comp like
she was training those students to survive.

I never took it that seriously, and honestly, it exhausted me, trying
to get those students to care. I found it difficult, too, to teach
something that came so naturally to me. Which is why, as soon as I
was published, I quit teaching, while my wife took a tenure-track job
at a more prestigious school, where she'd teach one section of Intro
to Creative Writing (she was a poet) in addition to composition and
literature courses. Now I wonder if she should have followed me out, if
teaching was not a calling for her, but a curse; over the years, she gave
so much of her mind to her students, to work, that it's no wonder it
ultimately fractured.

But first: the early years of our marriage. I see them in sepia, like
vintage photographs, all brassy light, an almost unnatural glow—each
moment pretty and preserved. I'm aware that's overly romantic, but
that's because the beginning always is. "Blindingly beautiful," you
called it, and I couldn't agree more. My wife and I were blind to the
truth in each other.

It was my writing that started to unravel her. She'd come to
my readings, my book talks, and if someone in the audience
complimented my work, she'd squirm in her seat. Sometimes, if the
comments were particularly gushing, she'd sigh. I wondered if she
was jealous of the attention I'd received. As a poet she'd likely never
see herself become a household name. Not because her work lacked
quality, but because the best-known poets are usually dead.

Now I don't think it was jealousy she felt. I think it was fear. I think
the more successful I became, the more scared she was I'd see her
as insignificant, superfluous to my life. We'd begun, together, as
teachers, all but begging our students to listen, to care, to simply show
up—but now I had a built-in audience. Of course, that didn't change
how I felt about her. But the fear—that I'd tire of her, leave her, unlove

her—grew like a tumor, the kind that presses against the brain, alters the personality.

She began lashing out. At first, it was only words. She'd disparage my work, call it derivative, as good as plagiarized. She always apologized after. She'd had a bad day, hadn't meant what she said. She asked for forgiveness, and because I loved her, I gave it every time.

Still, the tumor grew.

When I hesitated to share new plot ideas with her—afraid I'd jinx them, make them jump ship before they'd officially set sail—she accused me of "keeping secrets." Shouted, "You can't put me through this again!"

Put her through what? I was so confused. So concerned. I encouraged her to see a doctor, but the suggestion just agitated her more. "I already know what's wrong with me: you make me sick." She'd spit out those words, then leave to read for an hour, or crochet, or bake some bread—before returning to me with apologies, the scent of banana on her fingers as she gripped my hands in hers.

It wasn't always bad. In between her storms, there was light again. Laughter. But for every soft, sepia moment between us, there was one so dark I could barely see her.

My wife was not well, the last year or so of her life. She was paranoid, delusional, dangerously dissatisfied. Most days, she returned from work—where she'd spoken kindly to her students, inspired their writing, then shrugged off the credit they tried to offer her—and she looked so . . . content. Like she'd served her life's purpose. Then she'd look at me, and her face would instantly change. Distrust. Distress. That enduring, tumorous fear.

Then it got even worse. I went away for a couple weeks to promote my latest book, and when I returned, she told me she'd met someone. My heart crashed into my stomach, cratering me, and she must have seen

that on my face. "Not a man," she clarified. A new friend. She seemed
so much happier, almost giddy, and I was thankful to the friend. I even
asked my wife to set up a time when the three of us could get together.
That set her off: "You can't let me have even one thing, can you? She's
mine. Don't go near her." Those comments, defensive as venom, made
me worry. Made me wonder. Why didn't she want me to meet this
woman?

After that, whenever her moods spiked, I suspected she'd just seen
or spoken to the friend—but maybe that was my own fear, my own
paranoia at work; maybe, even now, I'm just looking for answers. All
I know is, after my wife met that woman, her outbursts left marks.
Gouges in the walls where she threw my books past my head during
an argument. There was one night in particular, close to the end,
when she burst into my office. "Look at me!" she snarled, slapping
my laptop shut. "Don't you write another fucking word until you
LOOK. AT. ME." But I already was. My eyes were so wide they hurt
as I looked at the woman I'd married. Looked *for* the woman I'd
married.

Now, my biggest regret is I didn't force her to get help. It wasn't long
after that night that she had her accident, that I lost every version of
her, even the ones that were strangers to me.

I know this isn't what you expected. You asked about our happy
marriage and I gave you the real one instead. Still, I'd go through all
of it again—her storms, her scowls, her misplaced accusations—to live
just one more sepia moment with her. I loved her, even when it felt
like she no longer loved me. Even when I started to believe that, had I
been an animal she saw on the side of the road, had it been *my* body
broken by some car—she would have driven on by.

It seems there's a lot in our pasts, yours and mine, that haunts us. So
I'm wondering if you'd ever want to talk about it in person. I think we
live close to each other. That restaurant you mentioned, the one in an
old train car? That's Pizza Depot, right? I've been there; I've actually
had the Jif's Jubilee. Pizza Depot is only one town away from me.

I know DonorConnect is meant to be anonymous, but I've just told them they have my permission to give you my information, assuming you ask for it first. I've really enjoyed our messages so far. It's been cathartic for me, telling the truth about my wife, both the beautiful and the bad, and even though I didn't live your exact situation, the grief you described resonates with me—you're an amazing writer; your pain pierced through the page. I have a feeling, though, there's so much more we could tell each other, so much more we could share, if we were face-to-face.

Think it over. I understand if you feel hesitant, and there's no need to decide right away. But in the meantime, I want you to know one thing: you are *not* too much.

CHAPTER SIX

Proof of life, please.

Nina's text forces me to pause my music. I've been reading in bed, listening to Taylor Swift, thinking of Morgan. Now I sit up, slide Plath's *Ariel* off my lap, and smile for Nina's picture. It takes more effort than I'd like; my meds have made me especially nauseated today, and I've taken the morning off to rest. It disturbs the brides, I've found, when I grin with gritted teeth.

Wait. Why is your dress like that?

At Nina's response, I jerk my head to the closet—I forgot it was open behind me in the shot. And right in front: my wedding dress, free of its garment bag for the first time in eighteen months.

Just had a craving to see it

I pulled it out a couple hours ago, after Morgan's latest message arrived on DonorConnect. My fingers shook on the bag's zipper, but

I wanted to honor the hope I felt inside me, to look at the dress with fresh, unswollen eyes and see if it still haunted me. Because maybe it's not some specter of the past. Maybe it's a premonition for the future. Even though I bought it for a wedding to someone who decided I was *too much*, that doesn't mean I can't ever use it.

If the dress really is a ghost, then maybe that just means it has unfinished business.

> Are you sure that's a good idea?

I set my phone aside, leaving Nina's text unanswered. I can't explain it to her—not without revealing how things have progressed with Morgan. With *me*.

When I ran my fingers down the dress this morning, the satin did not scrape me. The buttons didn't feel like blades. I was surprised how much I still loved it, even if there was a painful edge to that love, a jagged breath caught in my throat. But that's true of all love, isn't it? There's always some part of it that hurts.

Morgan's message certainly made that case. Toward the end with Daphne, he felt like roadkill she would have driven past without care or compassion.

I had nearly identical thoughts after Brad. When he ignored my texts, my calls, when I stood on his doorstep and registered disgust in his eyes where there'd once been only desire, I was sure if he ever saw me stranded in a ditch somewhere, he would not stop to help. He'd pass that crazy woman on the street, without so much as a glance in the rearview.

But Morgan said, *I don't think you're crazy*—and that's unclenched something long held tight inside me. He read the details of one of my ugliest nights, and he didn't even flinch.

Still, I didn't exactly tell him the whole story.

Didn't mention my blood at Brad's door.

I'd cut myself, earlier that night. I'd been fiddling with a glass in the kitchen, my phone pressed to my face, the ringing tone from Brad's throbbing in my ear, when my hand slipped, shooting the glass to the floor. Except it wasn't just any glass. It was the one Brad bought me after our first date, the logo for Pizza Depot now jigsaw pieces on the tile. And in my rush to salvage them, I sliced open my palm, the blood soaking through tissues already soaked with tears.

I drove to Brad's house that way, bleeding, because I'd just lost this part of us, this stupid but significant pint glass, and I couldn't waste another second wondering what else I was losing, why he stayed silent after proposing we *do this again*. When he answered the door, he gaped at my blood: the puddle in my palm, the drops at my feet. He saw my keys smeared with red, saw my car door open, heard the engine still running, like I'd catapulted from my seat to his steps. And even after he told me to leave, I stayed there, crouched and crying, bleeding on concrete.

So I couldn't blame him, could I, for calling me crazy? For deeming me too much?

I was worried Morgan would deem me that, too, after reading my latest message. In all our prior interactions, I've held back, answering questions with only a few sentences each, but all that caution was a cork in me, adding new pressure to old pain—until two nights ago on DonorConnect, when I took advantage of the anonymity and finally let the story spill out. Afterward, I buried my face in my hands at how detailed I'd been, sharing even my first kiss with Brad. "That was way too much," I hissed.

Not according to Morgan. And his response has reminded me there are other first kisses that will matter even more. I see mine with Morgan, his palms cupping my face, his lips as soft as moths, and heat rushes through me—until I remember he wants to see me in person. Not knowing, of course, that he already has.

I can't risk him thinking I'm a stalker or that I figured out who he was and forced our proximity at Sweet Bean. It's a steep slope from *remarkable* to *crazy*, but I know so well that it's slippery, too—and I couldn't bear for Morgan to take back assurances he's already made. *I don't think you're crazy. You are* not *too much.*

I unfollow him on Instagram, remove myself from his eighty-two thousand fans. Just to be safe. Then I switch my account to private so that, even if he somehow stumbled upon it, all he'd see was the sunset in my profile picture.

Still, the stalker fear is not my only hesitation in revealing myself as the woman Morgan's been messaging. As much as I've clung to his words all morning, I can't ignore his haunting descriptions of Daphne's behavior—and wonder what caused it.

Piper was right that there was something strained about Daphne and Morgan's marriage. But that seems to be all she and Morgan agree on. In his message, Morgan paints himself as a baffled victim of Daphne's moods. Not just verbal assaults, but acts of violence, too— books thrown, walls gouged—the latter only starting after Daphne met Piper. But in Piper's version, Morgan controlled Daphne, tormented her, stirred up all that darkness inside her.

If only I could read Daphne's version, in her own words, see how she wrote about the people in her life, get insight into why she lashed out at Morgan. Maybe I could use her poetry as a road map, memorize all the warning signs and danger zones so I can keep my own relationship with Morgan from veering off course.

According to her bio on *Poets & Writers*, Daphne's poetry is marked by its "sharp, confessional nature." I'm still waiting for her books to arrive, but the poems I've found online lean more political than per-sonal, with titles like "The Day After the School Shooting, I Teach My Students *Lolita*" and "The Canceled Comedian Reenters the Club." In a half-hearted effort, I open my laptop and type "Daphne Whittaker poetry" into Google, skimming for poems I might have missed. It's not until the fourth page of results that I find a reason to stop.

Podcasts Archive – Writer Couples: Thorne and Whittaker

I jolt up straight. Click on the page. Gulp down the description: As part of *Open Vein*'s quarterly series, a bestselling thriller author and an award-winning poet join host Andrew Salazar to talk about their "interwriter relationship."

It's dated fifteen months ago.

I press Play and pull the laptop closer. A split screen appears with the host on one side, Morgan and Daphne on the other. At first, it's disorienting, seeing her alive, watching as she absently scratches her sternum, fingers so close to the heart that now beats in my chest. She looks different from her pictures on Morgan's Instagram, where she's silent and still, where the black-and-white filter drains her of the flush in her cheeks. In the video, she runs a hand over her long dark hair, settling in for the interview, while the host introduces his guests. I focus on her fresh, unfractured face, and I can't help but think: *She has no idea what's coming.*

I recognize the room they're in, Morgan and Daphne. I know it by the burnt orange of the couch, the same color that blazes through Morgan's living room windows at night.

Morgan grins for the camera. Daphne sits with her shoulders back, hands clasped in her lap. From the bland, white-walled studio where he's recording, Andrew Salazar thanks them for taking part in *Open Vein*'s series on writer couples—"I'm fascinated by these relationships, always wondering if it's more collaboration or competition"—but I lose track of his words, focusing on body language instead. I search for signs of tension, something sharp in their smiles to signal that, just that morning maybe, Daphne shouted at Morgan, hurled words and objects across a room. But Morgan only reaches over to rub Daphne's knee, a gentle gesture that looks as automatic to him as breathing.

"Before we get to your relationship as writers," Andrew says, "I want to talk to you, Morgan, about the start of your career. With your debut novel, you became this kind of overnight success, and I wonder if—"

"Oh, believe me." Morgan waves a hand in protest. "It wasn't overnight. I have three shelved thrillers that publishers simply weren't interested in. It wasn't until I wrote a fourth novel that I actually got anywhere."

"Okay, see, as a writer myself, that makes me feel a lot better," Andrew says. "It's always been hard for me to believe your debut was actually your first novel. It's so masterful. Of course, we're talking about *Someone at the Door*," he adds for the benefit of the listener, "which had me from the very first sentence. If not just the title! I love how it's this ordinary phrase that's also instantly unsettling. It lets readers know, right from the start, that they're in for a treat."

Daphne stiffens. The polite smile she's worn dissolves. It's so stark, the change in her demeanor, that it's hard not to see it how Piper would: by praising the title, Andrew's struck a nerve.

"Daphne," he continues, and her smile reappears. I hit Pause and focus on that, how one side of her mouth curls up higher than the other. I try to move my lips the same way, mimic the smile I bet Morgan loved, but it's an uncomfortable fit on me, more grimace than grin.

I give up, pressing Play on Andrew again: "I'm assuming you got one of the earliest looks at Morgan's debut, so what did you think when you read it? Did you know right away that publishers would scramble to scoop it up? That it would go to auction with"—he glances at his notes—"nine different publishers?"

"Oh, well, I mean—" Daphne brushes at her pant leg before reclasping her hands. "I don't think anyone can ever anticipate a nine-publisher auction." Andrew chuckles appreciatively. "But actually, I didn't get the chance to read the novel until the galleys arrived. I kept asking Morgan if I could see it, but he was protective of it. Sometimes I wondered if it had the nuclear codes in it." She bumps his knee with hers, a playful jab.

"It's true," Morgan says. "I couldn't bear for Daphne to read it before an editor got their hands on it. I wanted her to experience its best possible version. Because I guess"—his smile turns sheepish again—"I was still trying to impress her. We were engaged then, not yet married, and I didn't want to hand her something atrocious and give her a reason to back out."

"I highly doubt you could write anything atrocious," Andrew gushes. "But I love that—it's like you wanted your book to be on its best behavior with her. That's sweet, actually."

Daphne tilts her head at his response. "Well, at the time"—she laughs a little—"it seriously felt like classified information. He wouldn't even tell me what the book was called. I didn't learn it until the deal was officially announced."

"Wow, really?" Andrew voices my own surprise. Given the story Piper shared, it's a troubling image: Daphne eager to celebrate her husband's success, refreshing her browser until the announcement went live, only to finally see the title he'd kept a secret—and feel the smack of her own past.

"Yeah, I'm a little superstitious," Morgan explains. "And I'd experienced so much rejection before that book went on submission that it was daunting to put myself out there again. I know it's illogical, but it felt like, 'Okay, if I don't even speak the book's name out loud, then it can't hurt me.'"

"Sure," Andrew says. "Like Bloody Mary."

"Exactly. Maybe that should be the title of my next one."

The men laugh, but Daphne doesn't. She stares into the distance, past the camera.

"So have you dropped the secrecy around your work now that it's too late for Daphne to back out of marrying you?"

"Oh yeah, she's stuck with me now; these rings are welded to our bones," Morgan jokes, holding up his hand, where a platinum band catches the light. He tilts toward Daphne—"Can you weld metal to bone? What even *is* welding?"—before turning back to the camera. "My point is: even when we're dead and buried, our skeletons will be wearing these rings."

I straighten. Goose bumps stipple my skin.

"Spoken like a true thriller author!" Andrew says. "Seriously, what a sentence."

What a sentence, indeed: dark, but strangely romantic, too. An ache pulses inside me, stronger than my nausea—because I've never had that, someone who actually means *forever*. Someone who wants me to belong to him even when I'm nothing but bones.

I pause the video, move the cursor to trace Morgan's face. Seeing him in person is great, of course—but I love this, too: studying his features without the worry that I'm staring too much. As he smiles at the camera, stuck in this single frame, it feels like he's staring right back.

When I hit Play again, Daphne leans forward, as if reminding me she's there. "But Morgan's still very secretive about his writing. I never see it until the advance copies come in, when it's basically too late to make any changes. He even—"

"Yeah, like I said"—Morgan shrugs—"I'm superstitious. An idea, a story, it's so fragile. I never believe it'll actually survive until those galleys arrive and it finally looks like a book."

"Makes sense," Andrew says, but Daphne shifts on the couch, frowning.

Was this the root of her issues with Morgan? He said it stemmed from her fear that he'd outgrow his love for her in the face of success. But maybe it was the fear of being blindsided again, like she was by *Someone at the Door*. Still, would that really warrant the behavior Morgan described? Shouting at him. Throwing books past his head. I look at their walls, scanning for gouges, but the paint is as smooth as Morgan's face while he waits for another question.

"Daphne, how about you?" Andrew asks. "Do you like to keep your work under wraps until it's published, or do you have Morgan critique it during the process?"

"Oh, I told her from the very beginning not to trust me with that," Morgan says. "I'm clueless when it comes to poetry."

Daphne shakes her head. "He always says this. And yet, every single time we're in the produce section at the grocery store, he busts out some random William Carlos Williams line."

"Well, it's not random," Morgan says, "when you consider how much fruit appears in Williams's work."

"I know, but—"

"But no, she's right—I read the greats. Williams. Keats. Hughes. Plath by extension. But I have no idea how to do what they did: distill a specific feeling down to a few stanzas. I always need a few hundred *pages* just to come close to what I'm trying to say. So no, I don't usually see Daphne's work until it's already out in the world. I'd have nothing to offer her."

"That's so interesting," Andrew says, "because as I prepared for this interview, I noticed a lot of similar images in both of your work. Morgan, your debut has the motif of the titular door, which comes to represent how breachable our sense of security is, and, Daphne, your poems include a lot of doorknobs, dead bolts, thresholds. Then there's the intersecting themes in your second books: the oppressive weight of guilt and blame, alienation from family. I guess I always assumed those similarities sprang from being involved in each other's work, but—maybe not?"

"Well, it's funny," Daphne starts, "because I always—"

"Yeah, it's weird, isn't it?" Morgan says. "We've noticed that before but can't really explain it. I guess it's like . . ." He returns his hand to Daphne's knee, squeezing it as he searches for the right words: "We spend so much time together that our minds have started to behave in the same ways."

"The same violent ways," Andrew emphasizes. "Of course, there are the murders and abductions in your books, Morgan, but, Daphne—even though your writing is beautiful, there's a lot of violence in your word choice. 'Branches *knife* the sky.' 'The silence *suffocates*.' Is that a conscious choice for you?"

Daphne cocks her head, considering the question. "I don't know if *conscious* is the right word. But it's definitely a natural choice. I find that beauty and brutality often go hand in hand. To the point where—" She bites her lip before clearing her throat. "You know, I actually worry sometimes that—" She knots her fingers tighter in her lap. "I worry that everything beautiful, even love, eventually ends in bloodshed."

Morgan jerks his head to look at her, and she pivots hers to appraise him, too. Their eyes remain locked together while Andrew fumbles for a response.

"Wow, that's . . . heartbreaking, of course. But powerful. It sounds like the start of another poem."

Daphne returns her gaze to the camera, her smile gracious and demure.

"Maybe I'll write it," she says.

Then she flinches, mouth popping open like something's surprised her. Andrew doesn't seem to notice; he's peering at his notes. Morgan doesn't react, either, but when Daphne looks at her husband again, her eyes are narrowed.

I must have missed something.

Tugging the laptop closer, I replay the last several seconds.

". . . worry that everything beautiful, even love, eventually ends in bloodshed."

I tune out Andrew's response, watch Daphne and Morgan share a look, watch Daphne turn and smile and—

There. Movement in Morgan's hand, the one resting on her knee. But it's not relaxed anymore. It's clenched around her kneecap—until a second later, when it's back in his own lap.

It happens so fast. I go back to be sure. But the image repeats: his fingers stiffen, digging into her leg like a claw, and as soon as Daphne jolts, Morgan lets go.

My phone chimes, startling me. I pause the video, and in the instant before I check the notification, I'm sure it's Morgan. He's sensing, somehow, that I'm scrutinizing this moment. And when I look at the screen, I do see his name there—but it's in a text from Edith.

> Hey, so . . . I've been curious about those comments you said you saw about Morgan Thorne, so I've gone down a rabbit hole (is Rabbit Hole a breakup phase? Anything's better than crying, right? lol) and I just found this.

I open the screenshots she's attached. The first is a thread on Reddit. Someone's asked for a book recommendation—"something that will freak me the fuck out"—and in the initial batch of replies, Morgan's *Chaos for the Fly* is mentioned. The second screenshot appears, snapped from farther down the thread, where there's a pile-on of theories and accusations that are quickly becoming familiar. One user writes, I mean yeah that book was good but . . . I'm pretty sure the author killed his wife?? Another giddily agrees: Right?!?! She "fell" at home while he was "writing." Sure, Jan.

My eyes almost glaze over. It's the same baseless claims I've seen on Instagram and YouTube. People love to pick the bones of a tragedy, ravenous for something rancid.

But the next comment snatches my attention again: THIS!!!! Supposedly they found no evidence of foul play, BUT my cousin is a cop in Morgan Thorne's town and he said there was something weird about the scene. Like the wife supposedly slipped in the bathroom, only there wasn't anything for her to slip ON. No bathmat, no puddle, nothing. And she wasn't straight out of the shower or anything, she was fully clothed. Evidence or not, I'm willing to bet he pushed her.

I close the screenshot, but the comment lingers like an echo. Something weird about the scene. It reminds me of a detail Nina mentioned—the ER nurse's perspective of the night Daphne died: *There was something weird about Morgan.*

I return to my laptop, where his flat, placid expression contradicts Daphne's narrowed gaze, and for a few seconds, I'm filled with a sensation like arrhythmia—something out of sync.

Edith texts me another picture, this time a selfie. She's wearing a gray sweatshirt, its hood pulled so tight around her head that only her eyes and nose peek through.

> The hood is in lieu of a tinfoil hat.
> Am I crazy or is that "nothing to slip
> on" detail kind of creepy?

Sure, it's a little creepy, but it's nowhere close to conclusive—if it's even true at all. It's not like we're hearing it from the cop himself; it's secondhand, filtered through a supposed cousin, on Reddit of all places. And more important, I tell Edith in my reply—

> If the cops really thought the scene was
> suspicious, they would have arrested him. Or
> there'd at least be, like, . . . articles saying he
> was a suspect. And I've never seen anything
> like that.

> No, me either. Because believe me
> I LOOKED lol. Just trying to see if I
> need to burn my Morgan Thorne books.
> But okay, I'll take off my faux tinfoil hat.

> I mean, the FTH (faux tinfoil hat)
> looks GREAT on you.

You know, I didn't want to brag, but I thought so too. SO much better than a wedding veil.

Edith adds two emojis—one laughing, one sobbing—and I send her a heart in return, promising to take her to dinner soon. I scroll back to her selfie, where her eyes are puffy from crying, and I remember it viscerally: the splotches on my own skin, the swollen eyelids, the scrape of tissues. It's brutal, what she's going through. And I never want to return to it, that feeling like my heart's been clawed apart.

I look at Morgan, frozen on my screen as Daphne squints at him, the hand that gripped her knee now withdrawn. It's true what I said to Edith: "nothing to slip on" is nothing like evidence. And neither is this strange moment between Morgan and Daphne.

When I resume the video, Andrew asks Daphne, "Are you working on another collection at the moment?"

The question appears to relax her. "Always," she says, a smile sliding onto her face. "And actually, the poems I've been writing lately all circle the theme of—"

"Don't say!" Morgan grins, tossing up a hand like a stop sign. "At this point it's probably bad luck for me to hear your ideas before they're published."

Andrew laughs. "There's that superstition again. Okay, let's talk about writing routines instead. Do you ever write in the same space together? A shared office, perhaps?"

"Well, as a full-time writer, I keep a different schedule than Daphne, who's a teacher," Morgan says—and Daphne's eyes narrow again, her mouth shrinking to a thread-thin line. As Morgan goes on to describe his specific routine, Daphne never breaks her gaze from the camera, but in her lap her hands clamp so tightly together that her knuckles shine white.

From: Morgan Thorne <morganthorne@morganthorne.com>
To: Blair Hawkins <blairhawkins@gmail.com>
Date: May 20, 2025
Subject: Re: you were right

Sorry I didn't pick up when you called this afternoon. I was fleshing out ideas for the next book, the one about the woman with the heart transplant. I think there's something there. Something with all sorts of twisted potential. I'm just not sure yet if the woman is the villain or the victim.

Glad to hear you found a dress, but I'm sorry your mom was her usual toxic self. She did it on purpose, you know, arriving that late. She doesn't really believe you gave her the wrong time. She just wanted you to think she forgot—and she wanted it to hurt. You're her favorite toy, and the game she loves best is pretending she's not playing with you at all. You don't deserve that, Blair. And she definitely doesn't deserve you.

Also—I didn't open the pictures you sent. I want to wait until the big reveal to see the dress. I know you'll look amazing, though.

And yes, I *have* seen Rosie again, thank you for asking/feigning interest. It was earlier tonight, actually. I'd been missing her the last few days in a way that felt like hunger—a persistent, gnawing *lack*—and maybe a few weeks ago I would have told myself that was for the best, that I should only *want* instead of *have*. But I don't know if that's the answer anymore, punishing myself over Daphne. Because what does that even accomplish? It doesn't change what happened that night. So maybe the way forward is to keep seeing Rosie as much as I can—to prove I can care about a woman without things ending in bloodshed.

I called her around lunchtime, hopeful she'd be on break at work, and she sounded strange when she answered, almost muffled, like she was actually lying in bed or keeping the phone, keeping *me*, at a distance.

"Are you free tonight?" I asked. "If so, you have two options. Meet me for dinner, wherever you want, or come over here and I'll cook for you."

She hesitated—which I didn't expect. This is the same woman who stood outside my house without me knowing, who slipped an invitation in with my mail. But she is also the woman who still hasn't told me her job, her last name. She's not an open book like Daphne was. And maybe that's a good thing.

"If it helps sway you at all," I told Rosie, "I have a cat who would *love* to meet you. And he has a collection of crocheted hats."

She arrived at six, her hair curled, her cheeks already blushing to match the color. She'd brought pastries. Two Danishes, two raspberry pie twists—a nod, of course, to the night we met—but she seemed almost embarrassed to be holding the Sweet Bean bag. Or nervous, maybe. She was slow to step inside the house. But when she did, she swept her eyes around the foyer, peered into the living room, curious and reverent, like she'd entered a museum.

"I've just put my famous lasagna in the oven," I told her (yes, B, your recipe), "but I think I might die if I don't eat one of these Danishes first."

"Ah, right. Death by Not-Danish. I hear that's a problem these days."

I nodded, solemn. "I just read an article about it. Doctors are now saying that Not-Danish might have been responsible for more than three hundred thousand deaths in the last year alone—they just didn't know to test for it."

"I'm so glad science finally caught up!"

And that was it, the familiar crackle of our conversation, her hesitation slipping off her like a jacket.

Still, we ate our Danishes on opposite sides of the kitchen counter. As Rosie chewed, she studied the room, looking at the French doors, the magnets on the refrigerator, the knives in the butcher block, the calendar I never took down from last year, the pages still stuck on May.

"Is that . . ." she started to ask, pointing to that one photo on the fridge you hung there a few months ago. She squinted at it, as if trying to zoom in without getting closer herself, and I knew who she thought it was.

"It's my best friend, Blair," I told her. "Well, and me, obviously. But the woman is Blair. She thinks it's hilarious—my eyes half closed, mouth half open. I was in the middle of saying something when she took it. She put it on the fridge as a joke, but it's a good picture of her, so I left it up."

Then I told her all about you. Everything from our time in college together to your current project of sneaking weird, kitschy mugs into my house whenever you come over.

"Do you want a tour of the house?" I finally asked. "We can try to find that cat I promised."

I knew where Sickle was—up in my office, last I'd checked—but I steered her to the living room first. Her eyes stalled on the couch, like she wanted to ditch the tour altogether, fall onto the deep orange cushions, our bodies already tangled, but I led her to the dining room instead, as if the thought hadn't even crossed my mind.

Then: the library. She actually gasped when I opened the door. "This is . . . a literal library."

"Were you expecting a figurative one?"

"Kind of, yeah! Most people put up two bookshelves and call it a library, but this— Is that a real card catalog?"

"Got it at a tag sale. It's from the seventies. Still has the original index cards in it and everything."

Her mouth gaped. She spun around to face the three rows of shelves in the middle of the room. "Morgan, you have *aisles* in here."

"It's not as impressive when you consider how many of these books I haven't even read yet. Like that entire shelf by the window."

"I'm pretty sure that just makes this *more* of a literal library." She glided into one of the rows, grazing the spines with a finger. She glanced back at me but didn't pose the question until her eyes were pointed away: "Are they all yours, or were some of them your wife's?"

We hadn't talked about her yet. I assumed Rosie knew I was a widower, like many fans of mine who live in the area, but this was the first time she'd brought her up. And it occurred to me then that when she'd been scanning the rooms, her eyes veering from mine, she'd been looking for traces of Daphne.

"I got rid of all her books," I said. "Donated them to a real library. It's what she would have wanted."

Rosie pivoted toward me. "I noticed you don't have any pictures of her around. Not down here, anyway." She swept her arm to indicate the entire bottom floor. "Is it just . . . too painful?" As I considered how to answer, she was quick to add: "I'd definitely understand that, if it is."

I decided to go with that. Nod without words. Swallow hard. Let her think I missed Daphne so much that seeing her face was like stubbing out a cigarette right on my heart. You're the only one I've ever trusted with the truth, B—that the photos morphed after that night. Blame settled into Daphne's posture; accusations slid into every smile. It was your idea, wasn't it, to take them down? You knew that if I didn't, I'd never have a moment of peace.

Rosie returned my nod with one of her own, then swiveled back to the books.

"You've alphabetized them!" she said after a moment. "Wait—maybe not. You have *F* and *K* next to each other."

I stepped closer to see the books in question: *Everything Is Illuminated* and *The History of Love*. "Oh, that's because they're married. Or, they were, anyway. Jonathan Safran Foer and Nicole Krauss. They're divorced now. But I came to Krauss by way of Foer, so."

Rosie's gaze was gentle on the side of my face. "You shelve couples together?"

"Yeah, look." I ran my finger down the shelf until I reached the *H*s. Tugged out the corners of *The Hawk in the Rain* and *Ariel*. "Ted Hughes and Sylvia Plath. Just like we talked about the other night. They were separated when Sylvia died—he'd had an affair—but it's impossible not to think of her in relation to him. He edited her *Collected Poems*. He even edited *Ariel*, her masterpiece. The manuscript was just sitting on her desk, the day she died, and he picked up where she left off. Worked on it until it was the best version it could possibly be."

"So he . . . changed the poems?" Rosie asked. "Rewrote them without her permission?" She stared at the shelf. "I didn't know that."

"No, no. He tweaked the contents of the manuscript. Removed some of the weaker poems. Added in some stronger ones she hadn't included."

Rosie's brow sunk. "But would she really have wanted him messing with her manuscript like that?"

"Well, without him, those poems might never have seen the light of day." I cleared my throat, pushing out a prickle of irritation.

"Your wife was a writer, though, right? Do you think she'd be okay with you doing something like that with her work?"

That surprised me a little. You have to scratch beneath the surface to know that Daphne Thorne was also Daphne Whittaker. The only time I remember talking about her work publicly is during some interview we did for a podcast no one's heard of—which Daphne pitched to the host herself and booked without my knowledge. Did I ever tell you about that? It made me a little sad for her, actually. She was so excited about it, her first podcast, but apparently, she'd needed to attach my name just to get it.

"I think she'd understand," I said. "Hughes was only using his influence to help Sylvia expand hers. He cemented her legacy."

Rosie's gaze tightened at that. There was something about my answer she didn't like. When her eyes drifted past me toward the door, I sensed the moment getting away from me. Sensed *her* getting away.

"But enough about poets," I said, touching her palm, holding it in mine. She glanced at our hands, then my smile, and something softened on her face. "Have I told you I'm really glad you're here?"

She tucked her hair behind her ear. "You are?"

I stepped closer. Put my fingers on her hip, watched the blush bloom in her cheeks. "Definitely. And not just because you saved me from Death by Not-Danish."

She exhaled a laugh.

"I haven't stopped thinking about you," I said, "not since the park," and it was so satisfying, B, seeing her wariness melt into wonder. I think that's part of the allure. I know I can have her, but I have to work at it first. Be better than I am.

"I've . . . been thinking about you, too," she admitted.

"Well, Rosie, I'm honored—to cross the same mind that thought of 'bugbath.'"

Her grip tightened on my hand, and even though the space was filling with the scent of garlic, the lasagna almost ready, I closed the gap between us. Kissed her in the room where Daphne used to write.

Her face was soft between my palms, but as we deepened the kiss, I felt the shift of her jawbone, reminding me that beneath that soft skin was a skull so easily crushed.

I pulled back, just a sliver, my breath still tangled with hers. "Can I show you the second floor?"

Her nod came slow. But she bit her lip and smiled.

We held hands as we wound back through the house, our shy glances undermined by the speed of our steps. Upstairs, I made no pretenses. I led her into my bedroom, then spun around, my mouth instantly finding hers. As we kissed, I nudged her back, back, back a little more, until her spine was flat against the wall.

I tugged at the hem of her shirt. Slipped my fingers under. Felt her abs quiver and contract. Her breath came faster. My hand climbed higher. Slid beneath the lace of her bra.

I teased the bottom of her breast with one slow fingertip. I traced the curve of it, my touch so tender it was hardly touch at all. But even that was too much for her. She shivered and pulled me closer, her kiss more urgent.

I grabbed her hands, locked our fingers together, held them against the wall, above her head. She moaned at that, back arching, which only tightened my grip, my muscles clenching, my desire for her a cramping, constricting thing.

"Ow!"

She wrenched her hands from mine. "You squeezed so hard," she explained, rubbing her knuckles in tight, circular strokes.

"Oh, shit. Sorry." I gave a sheepish, head-shaking laugh. "I guess I got carried away. I just—really want you."

I waited for her to soften again, same as she had before, but she kept massaging her hand, her thumb stretching her skin taut over the bones.

So I became the soft thing. Softened my touch. My kisses. Skimmed her neck with my lips, tasting the skin that was just beginning to salt.

Even so, I felt her distraction in the stiff way she held herself. Pulling back, I found her eyes still open. She was staring over my shoulder—straight into the bathroom.

"Rosie?"

I couldn't tell exactly what she was looking at. I only knew what was visible through the doorway: the tile, shining white as moonlight, and the sharp edge of the vanity, a perfect right angle.

"Rosie?" I tried again.

"S-sorry," she finally said, but the word came out in a stutter. "I think I should go."

"Wait. What? No, Rosie— If this was too fast, I—"

"It wasn't," she assured me. But she stepped away from me, her eyes still clinging to the bathroom. "This— It's me. I probably shouldn't have come here in the first place. I haven't been feeling well. I should— I should be in bed."

And just like that, she was walking to the door, marching down the stairs, heading back to the kitchen, the foyer. I followed behind her, bewildered, off-kilter. *She's going to do something crazy*—a knee-jerk thought. I almost grabbed her and yanked her back to me. But she wasn't Daphne; she didn't seem *angry*, just—

Nervous. Apprehensive.

And that's when it clicked: her hesitation when she first arrived, her eyes scanning for ghosts—

For clues.

Twice she invoked her. *Your wife. Your wife.* And just now, she'd stared into the bathroom like, even a year later, there was still a woman on the floor.

Maybe she's read things. Those comments you always find on my posts and tell me to delete. That one that popped up this morning— maybe I wasn't quick enough. Maybe she saw it. Maybe she thinks she knows.

How brave of her, then, to still come over tonight.

How sick, even.

Or, from another perspective: how sweet.

I watched her go, Blair. Listened to her say she was sorry, she'd be in touch. And now the lasagna is charred on the counter, and Rosie is gone—spiraling, maybe, with dark thoughts about me—and I can't let her do that. I shouldn't have let her leave.

Voicemail

Morgan Thorne
mobile
May 21, 2025 at 9:37 a.m.

Transcription

"Hi Rosie it's Morgan I wanted to make sure you're okay I'm not really sure what happened last night but uh I'd love to talk to you about it so um please call me back when you get a chance . . ."

Morgan Thorne
mobile
May 21, 2025 at 8:43 p.m.

Transcription

"Rosie it's Morgan again listen I hate the thought that I might have hurt you or I don't know scared you in any way I'd love the chance to talk about it because I think you might have the wrong impression about some things so um give me a call okay when you get this thanks bye . . ."

Morgan Thorne
mobile
May 22, 2025 at 10:58 p.m.

Transcription

"Rosie hi sorry to keep clogging your phone with all these messages I know it's late and I'm sorry if I've done anything to

make you uncomfortable but it's been a couple days now and
I'm worried about you so um please let me know you're okay
before I go uh combing the streets for you hah but seriously
you can call me back or even just show up I just really need to
talk to you . . ."

From: DonorConnect Communications
To: Rosie Lachlan
Date: May 23, 2025

You have received the following message from your donor's loved one. As a reminder, DonorConnect encourages both organ recipients and donor families to refrain from sharing identifying information (including name, address, and personal email) until a time when both parties have consented to giving and accepting those details.

Hey, you.

This might be unnecessary, but I've been sort of stuck in my head the last couple days—not in the productive, writerly way—and it's causing me to second-guess some things. I know we don't have a regular schedule with these messages, but it's been a bit since you've written, so I can't help but rethink what I last wrote to you.

I meant it, what I said. That I'd love the chance to meet up. These messages have been great (I honestly feel like I know you already), but I'm not sure you can truly understand someone without interacting in real life. A person's gestures, their vocal patterns, the sound of their laughter—that's important texture, and I'm interested in learning yours.

With that said, I don't want to do anything you're not ready for. I don't want to push for too much too soon or accelerate this relationship any faster than you'd like. It's unusual enough, this connection between us, the heart I loved now living on in you, and I'd hate to turn *unusual* into *uncomfortable*. So I want to apologize if I came on a little too strong (now who's worried about being too much?) and say that I hope to hear from you soon—electronically or otherwise.

CHAPTER SEVEN

I rub my scar through my shirt. Trace the seam of skin where they sealed up Daphne's heart. Behind my closed eyes, images strobe: Morgan's hands, his touch like a whisper; Morgan's hands, clenching into bone; a bathroom with his and hers sinks; a bathroom with nothing to slip on, except for blood.

I've called out of work again, and if anyone's reaching out about dress orders or appointments, I won't be able to help them. I've turned off my phone—easier, that way, to ignore the messages I've left unanswered. For weeks, I've wanted nothing more than for Morgan's name to pop up on my screen, but right now, the sight of it makes me uneasy.

My mother's managing the store in my absence. She left a few hours ago, just after she stood above my bed, taking my temperature, counting my pulse. Both numbers were normal, but worry welled in her eyes until I assured her that my heart felt fine, that I didn't need Dad to "come up and sit with me," that it was just my meds again, wreaking havoc on my system.

I don't like to lie to her. But the truth is too confusing: *No, Mom, it's not the cyclosporine unsettling my stomach. It's a famous author and the books on my bed.*

Daphne's books. *Anatomy of Night* and *The Quiet House.*

I picked them up after work yesterday, having received a voicemail that my order had arrived at Burnham Bookshop—and not a moment too soon. The *Open Vein* episode had made me so eager to read them that, hours after watching the podcast, I resorted to the next closest thing: reader reviews. I sprawled on my bed—Morgan so fresh in my memory, I could feel the stunning squeeze of his hand—and lost myself to comments that were mostly complimentary.

Haunting imagery.

This is poetry that grabs you by the throat.

Not enough people are obsessed with Daphne Whittaker.

But there was one review that stood out from the rest: *Daphne Whittaker was my writing professor, but I've only just now read her work. For a long time, I couldn't stop thinking about how troubled she seemed, right before she died. She was distracted in class, looked like she hadn't been sleeping. Now I see through her gut-wrenching poems how much trauma she had in her past. How much darkness she had at home. It's a wonder, really, she ever slept at all.*

When I read those words, my eyes felt stiff and gritty, as if I were the sleepless one. It rang too close to something Piper said to me in the library, something I'd dismissed as paranoia: *You didn't see her, those last couple weeks before she died. She was really . . . scared.*

Of what, though? What kept her up at night? Or perhaps more accurately: Who?

Those questions were still whirring through me last night, especially as the owner at Burnham Bookshop rang up Daphne's collections for me. I stared at their covers, wondering what truths they'd reveal, what "darkness at home" they'd bring to light.

"Oh, wait," the owner said, pausing as she bagged my books. "I think we still have a couple of—" She crouched behind the counter, then reemerged with a postcard. "You'll want one of these. It's Daphne Whittaker's final poem."

I snapped to attention, the sentence tingling along my spine. "Oh. Wow—"

"Well, I guess I don't know that for sure. But when she gave it to me for the postcards, she said it was 'one of her latest.' We made these to promote the reading she was scheduled to do here, last May. But then of course she died and, well, that was all she wrote." The woman winced at her own words. "Absolutely no pun intended."

It haunted me on the drive home: the idea that Daphne's "latest" work had become her last; the fact that she assumed she'd keep creating, that "latest" would be an ever-changing thing. That's why, back in my apartment, I left the postcard in the shopping bag, choosing instead to begin with her earlier collection, published—I did some quick math—two years into her marriage to Morgan. Still, I read only the first stanza of the first poem in *Anatomy of Night* before I needed to set the book aside. The title was "Aubade"—a word I had to google: a poem written at the arrival of dawn—and at the fourth line, my breath caught.

> The light cuts into me, still serrated
> with darkness, and I have to write it down—
> the way the sun seeps like someone else's blood—
> because words are how I dress my wounds.

Hair prickled on my neck. I was certain I'd seen that line before—or something close to it. I combed through DonorConnect to be sure, and yes: there, in Morgan's third message. Words are how we heal our wounds. I'd even parroted it back to him in my response, praising him for writing it. Except he hadn't. He'd changed the pronouns, swapped out *dress* for *heal*, but otherwise, it was Daphne's. And a lesser version at that, because Morgan's missed the wordplay, missed the point entirely: the double meaning of *dress*—both a way to treat her wounds and a way to cover them up, make them presentable to the public.

I closed the book, crawled into bed, tried to sleep away the strange feeling inside me. But my thoughts throbbed like a heartbeat, snippets of Morgan and Daphne together pulsing behind my eyelids. It had been two days since I'd watched their *Open Vein* interview, but the truth of what I'd seen kept brightening, clarifying, like a photo in a darkroom left to develop. Several times, Morgan had interrupted Daphne, slicing through her sentences. And what was it he said about her poetry? He claimed to read "the greats" while also saying he'd have nothing to offer in critiquing Daphne's work. The line had seemed self-deprecating at the time, like Morgan simply didn't know enough to be of any help. But maybe there was a hint of criticism, too, the reminder that Daphne wasn't one of "the greats" herself and the implication that she never would be. So maybe Piper was right; maybe Morgan had belittled Daphne's work.

Then maybe he stole her words anyway. Passed them off to me as his own.

When I woke this morning, it was to another message from Morgan. An apology this time, an attempt to nudge me from my silence. I haven't been able to answer him. Not the past few hours, nor the past few days. It's become too complicated, keeping track of who I am to him. He has no idea the woman on DonorConnect knows so much—the grit of his voice, the grip of his gaze, the strength of his hands. He can't fathom that I've been stuck in bed, pinned between wanting him and wondering what he's capable of, this man who, in just a few weeks, I've let so close to me.

Now I open *Anatomy of Night* again, turn past the page that stopped me before, and immerse myself in Daphne's voice, the words of the woman who knew Morgan best.

Most of the poems circle her sister's death. There are so many references to blood that the whole book feels spattered with it. It's there in the poem about the roads in her neighborhood, the night she ran from her house in bare feet: *There must have been something sharp on those streets to account for the blood on my heels.* It's there, too, when she writes about the home her sister died in, imagining there was no bullet, no man with a gun, but that the house simply swallowed her instead. *For anyone else, that would be its own kind of nightmare,* she acknowledges, *but it's the dream I cling to, to keep from smelling your blood.*

In a poem called "Roadkill," the blood appears as *drops like too-shiny rubies on the grille of his car.* But this one isn't about her sister. *A date derailed,* Daphne writes, *and him in the driver's seat, still buckled in.* She describes a fox on the road, *all wound and fur, the glimpse of a rib cage. Beneath his tires: the tip of a tail.* She crouches over the animal, half of her knowing it's dead, the other half hoping, hoping— *Back in the car,* she continues, *his hands were steady on the wheel.*

I jerk my eyes from the page. This is the second time I've heard this story—the roadkill on Morgan's first date with Daphne. In his messages, he shared it as an example of how Daphne was "so undeniably *good*," crying for an animal she hadn't even known. Except, in Morgan's version, it wasn't him who'd struck the fox; it was "some driver."

Why lie? Accidents happen all the time.

Then again, I've done this, too, with Morgan—slanted my own stories so they find me in a better light. So maybe it's flattering, in a way? He wants me to see him as his best self, even if it's fictional.

I finish the poem, returning to the line where I left off.

> Back in the car, his hands were steady on the wheel.
> It's only now, years later, I wish I'd seen it as a warning.

I pull back from the page. A warning about what, exactly? That Morgan didn't care enough about the animal to get out of the car and try to help it? Or—the thought slithers in—that he could hurt something and his hands wouldn't so much as shake?

I whip to the next page, searching for more about Morgan. There's another poem about Daphne's sister before the final one called "Second Date." *He didn't flinch*, it begins, *when I told him about you*. Other men had, she says, the story of her sister's murder causing them to shrink away from her, clamp their hands around coffee mugs, force sips after their sorrys. They ended up treating her like a stranger, even when she waited months to tell them, even after one had said he loved her. But Morgan was different. Daphne doesn't use his name, of course, but I remember this, too, from his messages, that she told him the story on their second date, that that was when he realized what he was most drawn to in a woman was the darkness she'd survived.

Daphne describes Morgan as leaning forward instead of back, his hands reaching instead of retreating. She writes how his eyes creased with concern, the folds of skin reminding her of pages in a book, a place to keep her story safe. It's a love poem, I realize, a sharp departure from "Roadkill," where she wondered if his composure hinted at cruelty. Here, he's supportive. Solid. Drinking in her trauma and never once grimacing at the taste.

He's been like that with me, too. Adamant that I'm not too much. That my history isn't either. He's not like Brad, whose lip curled as I cried on his front steps. Who, in our final days, would not even let me slip my hand into his as we crossed an icy parking lot. *You'll get cold*, he said, tucking my hand into my own coat pocket, disguising his rejection as care.

I glance at my phone, think of the messages still waiting for me there, proof that Morgan has seen so much of me already—and only wants me closer.

Dog-earing the poem, I smile at the man I recognize in Daphne's words, then read its final stanza.

> I told him your eyes were open—
> shutterless lenses, stuck on the ceiling.

When someone finally closed them,
their gloves were specked with red.
I even mentioned the blood beneath your nails,
how they think you might have reached
for the bullet inside you, tried to tweeze it out
with your fingers. And even then,
even then,
his face didn't flinch. He paid our bill
and kissed your name off my lips.

With the first collection finished, I snatch up Daphne's second, published two years later. Right away, there's a shift in tone, startling as a clap of thunder. The opening lines are an accusation: *Smiling swindler, blue-eyed betrayer, you tore my voice from my throat.*

Fury leaps from the page. She describes herself as *thrashing against the theft*, and that image reminds me of the woman Morgan portrayed in his messages. Daphne's wild moods, the books she threw across rooms. Morgan said he didn't understand the source of her behavior—but in the poem, she confronts him.

What you call inspiration
feels like invasion.
I lay my case at your feet,
body so broken without a voice
that I'm already kneeling,
already bent to beg.
But you sit at your desk
like it's a judge's chambers,
and you offer no mercy.
You tell me my case was flawed
from the start: "There's no copyright
on trauma."

I squint at that ending, taken aback. It's such a cold response. Maybe even cruel. Instinctively, I rub my chest, as if trying to soothe the heart that once endured it.

My college professor once said of poetry, *There's the truth, which is what literally happened. And then there's the Truth—what emotionally happened. So much of poetry exists in that capital T.* So it's possible Morgan didn't actually say it—that cold, cruel thing—but at the very least, Daphne's showing me how she felt. She's hinting at him stealing her story, her words, even if only to title a story of his own.

Diving deeper into the book, I find that, for a while, the poems avoid any mention of Morgan, returning instead to Daphne's childhood. But where *Anatomy of Night* dissected her sister's death, *The Quiet House* tackles the aftermath, the years in which Daphne found herself—suddenly—an only child. There are images of loneliness and alienation: *In my room, I hum half a harmony, while downstairs, my parents play the wordless scrape of forks against plates.* Images of guilt: *I'll bury my toes in soil, bolt my feet to the floor. I'll never—Do you hear me? I will never—run anywhere again.* She describes the distance that widened between her and her parents: *I want to say the silence spread through the house like carbon monoxide, a toxin in every breath. But I think the silence saved us.* Because when they did speak, grief mangled her parents' words into blame. They asked why she ran so far that night, instead of just next door. Why she didn't scream for the nearest neighbor, didn't pick up a phone. They asked question after question—poker-sharp, iron-hot—until they burned her to the bone.

My scar stings, a phantom sizzle of Daphne's pain. But I'm struck, too, by the familiarity in the words—or maybe my mind's just looking for patterns. Connections between Daphne's life and Morgan's stories. Still, I can't help but think of *Chaos for the Fly*, Morgan's best book, in my opinion. In that one, the protagonist's sister died in an accident when they were teens, but when new evidence comes to light that points to murder instead, the woman's parents become convinced that one daughter killed the other. Locking the protagonist in her sister's old bedroom, they devise increasingly twisted ways to push her toward a confession.

My stomach swirls at the similarities. The woman's isolation. The parents' pointed fingers. The murder of her sister as a kid. It's possible the plot was not inspired—*what you call inspiration feels like invasion*—by Daphne's past, but how could it not trigger her?

I read on in Daphne's book, those themes of seclusion and blame bleeding through every page. It's not until the final lines of the final poem that I find another reference to Morgan, after Daphne recounts driving herself to college, her parents not even home to see her off.

> And years later, I find someone to love
> the parts of me you couldn't. The parts
> as dark as too-deep water. The pitch-black
> ocean of my memories, and even
> the monsters beneath.
>
> *I'll never let you go*, he swears.
> A siren's call I gladly crash against.

I pause on those last few lines, and I understand the pull of that promise. I fell hard for *forever*, used it to forgive almost anything. I ignored the change in Brad's voice, his awe sawed down into something abrasive. I dismissed the barbs in his words: *Can't I just sleep alone for one goddamn night?* I still toured the venue, still bought the dress, still would have stood at that altar, smiling. But unlike Daphne, I didn't have the family trauma—all that loss and loneliness and rejection—to drill a need for permanence deep in the core of me. All I had were the wedding portraits on my parents' hutch, and the empty space where mine was meant to go. The Instagram posts from college friends, every month a new engagement. The brides at work who all had someone to go home to. So I get why Daphne clung to Morgan, even when she saw his work as "theft," as a violation. It comes down to a simple truth: it's easier, sometimes, to be miserable in love than it is to be alone.

The books finished, I reach for the postcard still inside the bag from Burnham Bookshop. I've saved it for the end, this poem the owner said was one of Daphne's last. On one side are event details—Daphne's reading was going to be held at the community center, hosted by the bookstore. On the other is the poem, printed in spindly handwriting, and shorter than most of her work at only a single stanza.

> You've robbed me again and again.
> Siphoned my love. My likeness.
> You won't stop until there's nothing left.
> Until my body is drained of blood,
> my clothes decomposed,
> my skin peeled from bones.
> And on my finger, the one token
> you didn't take, my wedding ring—
> taunting me from inside the grave.

A shiver ripples through me.

I gape at the card until it blurs. Then I blink it back to focus and narrow in on the title: "Pre-Mortem."

Before Death.

Too many thoughts compete in my head. I try to tally the poem's references—Morgan poaching her past, stealing her "likeness" for his stories; Morgan on the podcast: *even when we're dead and buried, our skeletons will be wearing these rings.* But above it all, I hear Piper: *You didn't see her, those last couple weeks before she died. She was really . . . scared.*

Was this her fear? That she'd end up "drained of blood"? The image comes back to me: the master bathroom, all that bone-white tile glistening red. The shine as thick as shellac.

But she couldn't have known, despite the poem's title, despite any fear Piper gleaned from her, that she was only weeks from death.

Unless her fear was that Morgan would hurt her. More than just emotionally.

I think of the podcast video, his hand on her knee, how he gripped her so hard she jolted—but his face didn't flinch.

I shake my head, an ache building in my temples. It could easily be a metaphor; when she wrote of her buried, rotting body, she could have meant it not as truth, but Truth—that Morgan had stolen so much of her story she felt stripped of her identity.

Still, it's disturbing, how several of the poems she wrote about him lean more sinister than sweet. At the very least, it's shown me there are sides of him he's been careful to conceal from me. Or sides I've simply missed—me and my "Rosie-colored glasses."

Then again, if Brad were a writer, he wouldn't paint me pretty either.

I turn on my phone to access DonorConnect. As I reread Morgan's messages—as carefully as I did Daphne's poems, looking for phrases that might open to additional interpretations—I see them again, the little lies he told: about "some driver" who killed the fox on his first date with Daphne, about the line of hers he passed off as his own, about his complete confusion over her outbursts.

Then there's something else that unnerves me—a sentence I've returned to even before today: I've never been able to listen to music while I write. In trying to square the discrepancy between his need for "complete silence" and his alibi to police that his music was cranked too loud to hear Daphne's fall, I guessed it was a trauma response, that he needed silence to write only *after* she died. But now I see I'd forgotten an important word in that sentence: *never*. So total and absolute. Encompassing of all times.

Which means Morgan's alibi might be another lie.

Even still, his messages are packed with reminders of why it's so easy to fall for him: his sense of humor; his warmth and vulnerability; his generous—even Rosie-colored—view of me. You've been inspiring me lately . . . I think you're remarkable . . . These are balms that, for so long, I haven't believed I deserved. And after showing him more of myself than I ever dared reveal to a man this early, he gave me only reassurances in response: You are not too much . . . I promise you, your trust has not been misplaced . . .

Don't I owe him—or even myself—the chance to prove that's true? I close my eyes, see his hand near my heart, his fingers almost grazing my scar, and it's not apprehension I feel; it's affection, for a man who'd touched so tenderly the places others scraped raw.

And if he's hidden things from me, if he's tilted the truth— Well. Come on. Haven't I done that, too?

I scroll through my phone, reviewing the rest of Morgan's messages. I've been ignoring him the last couple days, left him thinking he moved too fast. But maybe we haven't moved fast enough. Maybe we've both been so cautious we forgot to be honest.

There's still time. My heart's still ticking, for now, but my future won't wait forever.

As I rip back my blankets, Daphne's books and "Pre-Mortem" poem tumble to the floor, as if reminding me that, without her, I'd have no future at all. I stare at her words on the postcard—you won't stop until there's nothing left—and I know I owe her this too. If there's even the slimmest possibility it was Morgan she was afraid of those weeks before she died, I need to know that. For her and for me. I won't be the blinking, blindsided lamb in white, sacrificed at an altar again.

I step over the books on my way to the shower. Because it's time I ask him everything. No circling the subject. No skirting around Daphne's name. It's time I reveal to Morgan the woman he's been messaging—and find out the man he really is.

From: Morgan Thorne <morganthorne@morganthorne.com>
To: Blair Hawkins <blairhawkins@gmail.com>
Date: May 23, 2025
Subject: Rosie

I was right, Blair. You said I was overthinking it, but you should have seen her just now. She was [Describe the look on her face. Flashing between fear and hope?].

She didn't tell me she was coming. I was chopping vegetables for dinner. Listening to an old John Mayer album. So it was jarring as hell when Rosie was suddenly THERE. I barely had time for surprise or even relief because right away there was something skittish about her. Skittish but [A word that starts with S. Skittish but sssssss. Single-minded?].

Like she'd come with an agenda. But was scared of it.

Normally I love that about her, the way she's all rush and reservation. But there was something wild in her eyes I needed to tame.

I said, "I'm so glad you're here." Took her hand. Reeled her in [or maybe: "Tugged her closer"?]. "When you didn't return my calls, I started to think—"

She opened her mouth to speak, so I covered her lips with mine. I raked her hair from her cheeks. Knotted my fingers in the strands.

She pulled away. "I have to tell you something." Hair tuck. Slight blush. "I haven't been completely honest."

It sounded like bad writing. Like a cliché TV drama [sharper analogy?]. And it made me want to shake her. Pink-haired women shouldn't speak such colorless words.

"I'd like for us to be honest with each other," she added.

I couldn't look at her, Blair. Looked instead at the counter, the cutting board, the flesh and guts of a tomato. I gestured for her to continue, to tell me her truths, but I hated to do it. The wonder of Rosie is IN the wondering. The blank spaces she leaves. The pages I can fill.

But when she started talking, it wasn't to make a confession of her own. It was, it seemed, to coax one from me.

Daphne's name flew out of her mouth. Every sentence a question. She knew so much more about her, about us, than I'd even guessed.

The more she spoke, the more I saw her unravel. I noticed the roots of her hair, a different color than pink. Of course I always knew that, had even brainstormed reasons for the dye job, but to actually see it . . .

I couldn't bear it.

One woman becoming another. Or—no. Daphne never became another woman. She simply [Something about darkness. How delicious it is. Until it devours you.].

So when Rosie—never so much as pausing for me to answer—moved away from Daphne and back to herself, this THING she had to tell me, this THING she'd been hiding, I couldn't bear to hear it.

Her words buzzed in my ears like wasps.

And between us, a tomato, split open on the cutting board, my knife still piercing its skin. My hand reaching for

Draft saved

CHAPTER EIGHT

Morgan's front door is open. A gap just wide enough for someone to slip through.

I stare at the space, the glimpse of his entryway. The narrow table for keys and mail. Music pounds from the house, an old John Mayer song, all drums and guitar and growl.

"Hello?" I call.

My hands shake with what I have to do. A bead of sweat slides down my temple.

I step back onto the lawn, scan the floor-to-ceiling windows, but the sun is still setting, its waning light smeared on the glass, so it isn't dark enough yet for the house's interior to be revealed.

Still, for a moment, I see not only Morgan inside, but Daphne, too. They're swaying to a slow beat with their bodies pressed close, Daphne's hand in Morgan's—until he squeezes so hard she buckles, her lips in the shape of a gasp. She tries to free herself, but he won't let her go; there's something hot and hungry in his eyes. Love, maybe. Or possession. Sometimes they look the same.

I blink the image away. See only smudges of sunset on the pane.

The street behind me is quiet, empty. No passing cars. No people with dogs who might stop on the curb.

I approach the door again, knock on its frame with an unsteady fist. The sound gets lost beneath the music's drums, which thump inside me, mimicking a heartbeat.

"Hello?" I repeat, tossing another glance at the road. "Morgan?"

I'm about to ring the bell when something darts past my feet. I jump back, processing too late what I'm seeing—an orange streak, a blur of fur: Sickle!—and fail to catch him before he disappears into the shrubs lining the walkway.

I dive after him, arms sweeping through thickets of leaves, eyes raking every hollow, panicking that he might have already sprinted farther away.

When I finally find him—tucked within the final shrub I check, crouched low under the branches, almost flat against the grass—my breath spills into the air, coasting on a laugh.

"Hey, bud." I reach for him, but he contracts deeper into the bush, wary of my touch. "I don't think you're supposed to be out here. Should we head inside? Go find your dad?"

He blinks at me and I try again, contorting myself into uncomfortable angles until my hands clamp around him. He squirms and swats, but I manage to pull him out, and when I cradle him against my chest, murmur into his neck, he wriggles a few more moments before relaxing into me, settling down.

"It's okay," I assure him, stroking his fur, dipping my forehead down to his. "I'm a friend." He isn't purring yet, but he nuzzles against me, whiskers tickling my skin.

It's not until I'm back at the door that I notice scratches on my arms—from the shrubs or Sickle, I'm not sure—and two spots of red. At first, I think I'm bleeding, the scratches deeper than they seem, but Sickle's front paws, normally white, are splotched with it, too.

"You poor thing! Did you cut yourself out here?"

I hurry across the threshold and nudge the door shut with my hip, careful to prevent another escape. "Hello?" I call. "Sorry—Morgan? It's— Your cat got out and I think he hurt himself."

Music crowds the entryway, my voice too small to compete. Sickle grows impatient, shifting in my arms before leaping out and landing on the floor.

"Oh— Sickle, no—" If there's something sharp in his paw, he might embed it deeper by walking on it. But as I bend to grab him again, he's already off, dashing into the living room and out of my eyeline.

I follow the faint tracks he's left, whispers of red along the hardwood. Scanning the kitchen, where an electric guitar whines from speakers, I find a laptop on the island, a colander of vegetables, a cutting board streaked with the pulp of a tomato. But no Morgan. No Sickle. And without a cat to keep contained, without a wound to tend to, I have no reason to be here yet.

I turn to go, heel already pivoting, but it's then that Sickle meows, a sound I barely hear beneath the music, a sound I might be imagining, looking for reasons to stay. Still, I step closer to the counter, slow enough not to scare him off, and when I reach the lane of hardwood between the island and oven, his name is perched on my tongue: "Sic—" But it crumbles between my teeth.

Because it isn't Sickle on the floor.

It's Morgan.

Flat on his back. Eyes on the ceiling. Staring but not seeing. Covered with something so dark and rich and red, I might think it was fabric—velvet—if not for the knife in his chest.

PART TWO

LOVE STORY

CHAPTER NINE

My heart gallops. It's been over an hour since police arrived, but the part of me that's Daphne is thrashing as if I've only just stumbled across Morgan's body.

His *body*.

A sob shakes out of me. It breaks my still-stunned silence, draws the attention of an officer, the one standing on Morgan's walkway, tasked with watching me.

His colleagues have been filing in and out, some in uniform, others in plain clothes. There's an ambulance in the driveway, police cruisers flashing blue and red against the dark, the rhythm in sync with the speed of my heart.

"Sorry about that, Ms. Lachlan."

The detective reappears, having stepped inside at someone's request to "take a look at this." Now he towers above me—because I can't stand up; I'm stuck on Morgan's front steps, leaning against a column, unsure how to lift my head to meet the detective's eyes.

He's asking me questions again. Each one crouches in my ears, stalled on its way to my brain. My gaze sinks from his khaki-covered knees to his scuffed-up shoes to my hands in my lap—which is when

I register that I'm still clutching my phone, that I haven't set it down since I stood in the kitchen, dialing 911 for the first time in my life.

Then there are the splotches on my arm, dried from red to rust, their source now blisteringly clear beneath the porch light. Sickle didn't cut himself during his escape into the yard; he'd walked through Morgan's—

"Did the cat get out?" I ask. As I finally look up at him, the detective's face comes into focus. Brown eyes. Heavy brows. Neatly trimmed beard. Hair swooped back on top of his head. There's something vaguely familiar about him, like he could be a sharpened, leaner version of someone from my high school. I struggle to recall the name he gave me when he first arrived: Detective Jackson Dean. It doesn't ring a bell.

"The cat?" he asks.

"The door's been open, everyone going in and out. There's an orange cat. Sickle. He's an indoor cat. He shouldn't get out, he—"

I stop speaking, my throat solidifying to stone. What's going to happen to him? I picture him in a crowded shelter, stuffed into a hard cage, confused where all the softness has gone: stroking hands, crocheted hats. It's almost enough to make me rush back into the house, find him myself, and claim him.

"The cat's fine," Jackson says—and I'm not sure why I do that, think of him as Jackson instead of Detective Dean, like maybe I *did* know him at some point in my life and my mind is too shell-shocked to place him. "Please, Ms. Lachlan. I know this is difficult, but I need you to answer some questions so we can determine what happened tonight. Can you tell me why you were here?"

My gaze falls to my arm again, the rust I could flake off with my nail if I dared. I'm not sure what to tell this man. The truth is too complicated, and it feels like there are too many truths at once.

I keep it simple: "We'd been talking recently. He wanted to meet up."

He writes something in a notebook I only now notice he's holding.

He's left-handed, like Morgan was; I remember photos of him from Instagram, signing books at an event.

"So he'd invited you over?" Jackson asks.

I stare at a crack in the concrete, my heartbeat becoming erratic. Less a gallop than a limp. "It was sort of . . . an open invitation. But I didn't tell him ahead of time I was coming."

There's a pause, and I don't know if Jackson's watching me or writing down my answer. I can't look away from the crack—the same length of my scar, the same line with a curve so subtle it's almost straight. For a second, I wonder if there's something of Daphne down there, too, buried beneath the walkway.

"I see," he says. "And what did you do when you arrived?"

"I was going to ring the bell, but the door was ajar. I knocked, called out to him, but then his cat darted out, and I went after him."

"Him as in . . . ?" He leaves a blank for me to fill.

"The cat. Sickle. I caught him, under those shrubs, and I thought he was bleeding, so I went to bring him inside, clean him up—"

"And so you entered the house?"

"I had to get the cat inside." How do I explain my certainty that Morgan would have been fine with it? He adores Sickle. Poses with him on Instagram in matching sunglasses. If Bumper fled my parents' house, they wouldn't care if it was an escaped convict who brought him back, so long as someone did. "I thought he was hurt. But he jumped out of my arms, and when I tried to follow him, he—he was there. On the kitchen floor."

"He as in . . . ?"

"Morgan. With the knife and—and all the . . ." I shut my eyes, try not to see that cloak of blood. My throat is no longer a stone; it's a straw that's close to closing.

"So between the time you arrived and when you say you found his body, you never spoke to Mr. Thorne?"

I shake my head. "How could I have?"

"Did you move his body in any way?"

"No. I didn't touch him."

"When you first arrived this evening, did you notice anyone else in the area? Anyone at all. A car on the street. Someone walking by. Even if just a neighbor."

"No. I didn't see anyone."

The street had been empty. I remember that. As if conspiring to keep me and Morgan alone.

"What about those scratches?" Jackson asks, wagging his pen at my arm. "They look fresh."

"They're from Sickle. Or the shrubs. I'm not sure which."

"But you didn't have them when you first arrived?"

"No."

He hums an acknowledgment before scribbling on his pad. "Would you be willing to—"

"Detective."

Jackson's head snaps up at the voice in the doorway behind me. I glance toward it, find an officer with gloves on her hands, plastic coverings on her feet. She doesn't say anything else, but by the time I turn back to Jackson, he's rushing past me up the steps.

"Excuse me another moment, Ms. Lachlan," he says on the way.

The officer on the walkway—the watching one—slides back into view. I ignore him, slump against the column again, that crack on the concrete blurring before me. My heart has slowed and steadied to the point where I don't feel it anymore, and when I blink the crack into focus, it looks less like my scar—less like a sealing place—and more like the break that it is. The dark, empty gap between two colorless slabs.

Minutes later, when Jackson returns, I brace myself for another set of questions. I have no answers left to give him. That's why I came here tonight, for answers, for the truth, mine and Morgan's both, but now I'll never know: if there hadn't been a knife, and blood, and pool-blue eyes hazed to almost gray, would tonight have been the end or a new beginning for us?

I look up at Jackson, about to ask if we can finish this later, still too in shock to be useful, but his expression is sterner than before. Everything I thought I recognized about him disappears in a tight mask of suspicion.

"Ms. Lachlan," he says. "I'd like to continue this interview down at the station."

———————

The room is too well lit.

It's nothing like the gray, single-bulbed spaces on police procedurals. Here, the walls are blindingly white, and the recessed lights above me remind me of the operating room, that "slap of sunlight" I told Morgan about the first time I spoke to him. The phrase he praised me for, warning me he might have to steal it.

It feels like hours before Jackson walks in bearing two Styrofoam cups. He sets down the water I requested in lieu of coffee, then takes a sip of his steaming drink. When he sits across from me, he has a folder tucked under his arm and a groove between his brows that looks deep enough to slot a coin into.

"Ms. Lachlan." He slaps the folder onto the table.

"Rosie's fine," I tell him.

"Rosie. Right." He clicks the top of a pen, glances at his watch. "For the sake of the recording, this is Detective Jackson Dean interviewing Rosie Lachlan at 10:06 p.m. on May 23, 2025."

That's when I notice the camera in the corner of the room, perched just below the ceiling. It stares at me with a beady red eye.

"As a reminder," Jackson says, "you're free to go at any time." Then he opens his folder, frowns at the papers inside. "Just to be clear, you say you didn't speak to Mr. Thorne when you went inside his house tonight."

"I couldn't. He was— He already—"

There were bubbles of blood at the corner of his mouth. If I hadn't seen the rest of him, I could have believed it was juice from the tomato he'd been slicing.

"Yeah, here's the problem with that," Jackson says. "Mr. Thorne's laptop was on the kitchen island—"

I nod. A laptop. A cutting board. Two of the last images I collected before the blood.

"—open to an email draft that appeared to be in progress. In it, he described a confrontational encounter at his home this evening with a woman named Rosie."

I squint at the detective.

"A Rosie," Jackson continues, "who he described as having pink hair."

My eyes narrow even more, while Jackson's shift from my face to the cotton candy strands sticking to my forehead. Something thuds in my stomach, like a shoe in a dryer.

"That's—" I shake my head, a slow pivot from side to side. "No. We've been speaking through DonorConnect. But he wouldn't know my name. Or what I look like."

"DonorConnect?" He says it flatly. Not really a question. If he's been looking through Morgan's laptop, then surely he's seen our thread. "What's that?"

"It's a service that connects organ recipients with their donors—or their donors' loved ones, in my case. I was put in touch with Morgan because he's the husband of my donor."

Beneath Jackson's neutral expression, I see a ripple of something. Confusion, curiosity. Maybe anticipation.

"I had a heart transplant, a little over a year ago," I explain. I show him my MedicAlert bracelet, and Jackson leans forward to read its engraving. "Morgan's wife, Daphne, was my donor. He and I have been talking, like I said. But he doesn't know who I am. The service is anonymous."

"And yet," Jackson says, clasping his hands together, almost like he's praying, "you know who he is."

"I figured it out. He told me he was an author in a Boston suburb. He told me about his cat, Sickle, who I'd already seen on his Instagram."

"So you followed him on social media? Before this . . . exchange on DonorConnect?"

"Yeah. I like his books."

"Hmm," Jackson muses. He unlinks his hands to sip from his coffee. Then he picks up his pen, taps it against the folder. "Ms. Lachlan—"

"Rosie."

"Rosie. Why were you at Mr. Thorne's house tonight?"

I don't like this—the recycling of questions, when I have far too many of my own. They're stacked like bricks in my brain, walling up the horrors I've seen tonight, the gush of loss that wants to drown me.

I don't know if my questions should be answered. If I should let those bricks come tumbling down.

"I told you, he asked to see me in person. He left his information with DonorConnect and said I could use it to meet with him. You can contact the service to verify."

I sense it's best not to unravel too much of the truth: how well I already knew Morgan's address, his house, every route and road that could take me to him.

Jackson nods, writing something in the margin of his paper. "Switching gears for a moment: you say you discovered Mr. Thorne's body shortly after entering the house. But you didn't touch it or move it in any way."

"That's right."

"But see, my team has recovered hairs on the body. One was in his hand, actually. It's hard to say for sure at the moment, but the hairs appear to be the same color as yours." He swirls circles into the air with his pen, the tip pointed toward me. "Pink."

"I— His hand? No. I didn't get within five feet of him. I couldn't, I was too— It was— The hairs have to be someone else's." I stretch some strands away from my face. "You can take a sample of mine, check the DNA or whatever. It won't be a match."

For some reason, I expect him to tell me that won't be necessary, that these questions crowding around me are standard procedure, not something specific to a suspect. Instead, he smiles, his mouth pressed tight.

"We'll do that, thank you. Now, you also say you've spoken to him through this messaging service, DonorConnect. But what about your in-person conversations?"

A sigh slides out of me, impatience at not being heard. There's an ache, too, building in my rib cage, uncomfortably reminiscent of my days before the hospital.

"I didn't talk to him at his house tonight," I tell him again. "I couldn't. Morgan was—"

"Already deceased. Yes, you said. But the thing is"—Jackson flips through the pages in his folder, stabbing certain phrases with his pen—"Mr. Thorne has been emailing a friend for several weeks now about interactions he's had with a woman named Rosie. Not on Donor-Connect, but in person. And a couple of those interactions have been pretty . . . intimate in nature."

My lips part but no sound slips out. The information swims through my head, but I can't latch on to it; it floats away from me, just out of reach.

There's been some kind of mix-up. A glitch between my mind and reality. It's as if the papers in front of Jackson are a transcript of my thoughts. As if he's reading the scenes that play out in my imagination—kisses and conversations with Morgan, cuddles on the couch with him and Sickle—and mistaking the fantasy for truth.

"Wait," I say, still struggling to stitch it all together, everything Jackson's said since he entered the room. "Morgan wrote about seeing a woman named Rosie? Wi-with pink hair?"

"He describes a few dates in quite a bit of detail," Jackson confirms.

"Dates? I don't—" I drop my gaze to Jackson's papers, but my vision is clouding, the words a blur of ink. "I've never been on a date with Morgan."

My breath becomes shallow. I take only sips of air.

Jackson pitches forward, pinning his eyes to mine. Between us, his coffee releases wisps of fog. "So you're saying this person he wrote about is not you. That he was married to your heart donor, you have messaged him through the anonymous service, but you have not dated him."

"Yes." My voice is more like a wheeze. I clear my throat and try again: "That's exactly what I'm telling you."

"So you never had a conversation with Mr. Thorne at"—Jackson peels his gaze from me to riffle through his papers—"Sweet Bean Café?"

The room tilts. My ribs feel like the bones of a corset cinched too tight. There's both too much and too little to explain: I saw Morgan at Sweet Bean, locked eyes with him there, thought of creating a collision, sparking a conversation. But I didn't. I returned to work after Marilee's texts, met with the bride who refused to be helped by anyone else.

I keep my answer simple: "No."

"You didn't go to his house for dinner on Tuesday night? And before that, you didn't meet with him at Burnham Grove Park?"

The park? I haven't even driven by it in over eighteen months. I took Brad there one time—just for a few minutes, guiding him through my childhood stomping grounds—and that was enough to turn it haunted.

I shake my head. The too-bright walls whirl around me.

"So you're saying he did all that with another woman. A woman who, like you, is named Rosie, and who, like you, has pink hair. That would be a pretty big coincidence, wouldn't it? Especially since you *were* in contact with Mr. Thorne."

"Anonymously. I was in contact with him on DonorConnect."

I flop back in my chair, stare up at the ceiling where the lights burn my eyes, and for a second, I'm back in the hospital, the room growing staticky with the anesthesia some doctor has just injected. Soon, they'll saw me open, break my ribs, reach inside me for my sick, sick heart.

I pull in a breath. Force myself to sit up straight. Because it's more than a year later, and my heart—pumped full of meds but healthy for now—came from a woman whose husband just died. A husband whose heart I'd hoped would also be mine.

"I don't understand what's going on," I tell Jackson. "But whoever this Rosie woman is that Morgan wrote about in those emails—that wasn't me." I lean forward, make sure he sees the truth in my eyes as I say it out loud: "I've never so much as spoken to Morgan Thorne in person. And before today, I'd never once stepped foot inside his house."

CHAPTER TEN

They don't arrest me—but they don't believe me, either. That's clear in Jackson's eyes, the watchful squint as another officer presses my fingertips to pads of ink. I consented to this, encouraged it even, supplying my prints as proof of my innocence, because I know they won't find them on the knife or anywhere in Morgan's home. A woman in latex gloves plucks hairs from my head, and I focus on the sting in my scalp instead of that knife.

They swab my scratches, too. Snap photos of them. I know what they're looking for—evidence of a struggle with Morgan. When they're done, Jackson says he'll take me back to my car, still parked on Morgan's street right where I left it, hours ago now, but I decline the offer. I don't want to share space with a stranger who thinks he already knows me, what I'm capable of.

I call Nina instead, giving her the scantest details. *I found a dead body. I was asked to come in for questioning.* She doesn't have a shift tonight, so I'm surprised when it takes her a while to arrive. I'd imagined her speeding through the streets, her urgency like a siren shrieking from her car. She isn't even out of breath when she opens the door to the station—I'd imagined that, too, how the panic would pinch her lungs until she saw I was okay. Instead, as she approaches me, her face is furrowed with dread, her eyes zipping to my wrists, as if expecting to find me in handcuffs.

"Rosie," she whispers, "what the hell is going on?"

I rush toward her, collapse into her arms. As she rests her chin on my head, it all floods up in me, the images I've tried to hold back: Morgan's eyes like dull marbles behind his glasses, his body as lifeless as a chalk outline. There's something about seeing Nina for the first time in a month, coupled with the blood I can't rinse from my memory, that has me buckling against her. Tears gush, sloppy and slippery, but as Nina corrals me toward the door, she says, "Not here, not here," which, even in my distress, registers as odd. She's a natural caregiver, someone who bends over backward to stanch people's wounds—physical or otherwise—but right now, she's more concerned with exiting the station quietly than comforting me.

She steers me through the parking lot, then deposits me into her car, where the air freshener greets me with a familiar smell: cinnamon and vanilla, like stepping into a bakery. It's a scent that's accompanied us on late-night snack runs, post-movie debriefs, times when Nina took the long way back to my apartment to give us a few extra minutes together before she dropped me off, and now it hugs me as I lean toward my knees, heaving with sobs.

Nina sinks into the driver's seat, shuts the door with a click that feels too controlled. "Rosie," she says—her voice controlled, too. "What the hell happened?"

I swipe my hand across my nose. Swallow another sob. "You're not gonna like it."

"Uh, yeah, I generally don't like dead bodies."

"No, I mean—" I have to tell her everything now, all the times I've lied to her the last couple weeks, denied I was still talking to Morgan. But as I look at her, cast in the glow of a lamppost just outside the car, I process what I didn't when she first arrived: "You changed your hair."

It's darker—more like coffee beans than the caramel shade she's been favoring the last few years. It lacks her usual highlights, too, making her look, just for an instant, like a Nina imposter.

She passes her hand over her hair, as if self-conscious. "Yeah, I'm trying a new style—guess we haven't seen each other in a while." She shrugs, almost sadly, but then shakes her head, the movement sharp. "*What* is going on? Whose dead body was it?"

"Morgan's."

She blinks at me, struggling to process the name. Then her eyes bulge, staring through the orangey dark, before becoming as blank as Morgan's were.

"Is this a joke?" she asks, but the question is hollow. She knows I'd never joke about this.

"No, he was murdered. There was a knife. In his chest."

When her face unfreezes, she cycles through a series of expressions—disbelief, shock, fear—like an actor unsure how to play a scene. Finally, her features settle on confusion.

"I don't understand. You said you *found* a dead body, so . . . so you just stumbled across him? Dead like that? *Where?*"

"At his house," I say—and before I can clock another emotion on her face, I confess it all: that I continued to message Morgan on DonorConnect, even though Nina told me I shouldn't; that we'd made each other laugh—no small thing after all the darkness we'd endured; that he said our messages were a "safe place for heartbreak," so I shared so much of mine; that for the first time in over a year, all that heartbreak—literal and figurative—had been softened by hope.

"But then I—got confused," I add, and I tell her about Daphne. The tension between her and Morgan on the podcast. The poetry I read just today, the details from her past that Morgan took for his own. I mention the poem on the postcard, too, the one Daphne wrote like a premonition of her own death, pointing her finger straight at Morgan.

"That's why I went there tonight. He told me in our messages he wanted to meet in person, and I was going there to be honest with him, tell him I'd known from the start he was Morgan Thorne. And I was going to find out who he really was. Because . . . because poems aren't facts. And the podcast thing— I could have been misinterpreting that, and I really—"

"Rosie, what the fuck?" Nina cuts in. Her mouth hangs open like it's too stuffed with words to properly shut.

"What?" I ask. "Which part?"

"All the parts!" She grips her hair so hard she could yank out a handful, and the gesture is deeply familiar. In the weeks after Brad, when Nina used her spare key to enter my apartment because I wouldn't answer her calls, she sat on the side of my bed, clutching her head the same way she does now. There have been other times, too: when she listened to me cry about Tyler or Gabe or Jared, answering my descriptions of their hurtful behavior with speeches about how I'm so much better than them, better *without* them, only to watch me answer their texts right in front of her, the second they appeared on my phone.

"You found all this evidence," Nina says, speaking toward her steering wheel, fingers still embedded in her hair, "that, at the very *least*, Morgan treated his wife like shit—and instead of cutting off communication, you tried to *see* him?"

"I don't know that it was evidence. All of it could have been explained away, maybe. And that's the whole point. I needed to talk to him about it. I needed to hear his side."

"His *side*? What if his *side* was that he did do something to his wife? What if, knowing you were suspicious of him, he decided to hurt you, too? God, Rosie, how could you take that risk?"

I shake my head. She won't understand how fated it all felt, even though she was the one, kneeling on the floor beside me, watching me sob in my wedding dress, who evoked fate in the first place: *Everything happens for a reason.* A common mantra for a breakup, and one I initially scoffed at. Her voice had shaken when she said it—with shock, maybe, at how brutally I'd been dumped, the terrible timing of it all—and that quiver only lessened my confidence in the statement. Still, I'd wanted so badly for Morgan and me to prove her right, prove that all our suffering had really been stepping stones straight to each other. Because if Daphne hadn't died, if my heart hadn't failed—or if only one of those things had happened; or both, but at different times—our paths would never have crossed. How could I not think, then, that we were meant to meet this way? Meant to help each other brighten the darkness that dwelled in us both. Daphne's death. Brad. The hospital. Even now, hours after finding Morgan's body, hours after his blood stung my nose like a chemical, I still think it would have been so lovely, so dazzlingly poetic, if he and I could have forged a future together, become the silver lining of everything we'd lost.

"The risk seemed . . . worth the reward," I say—which is something I know quite a bit about. A year ago, I could have died on the operating table. Could have rejected Daphne's heart. I still could, at any moment. But does that mean I should have refused her heart altogether? That would be absurd—not pursuing something that could heal me, just because it might hurt me, too.

And what was the alternative with Morgan? Ignore his messages? Never find out if our chemistry online fizzed the same in person? I don't ask any of this, though, because Nina will literally rip her hair out. She'll tell me yes, that's exactly what I should have done. I should have walked away. Started over. Waited for someone else to come along.

But starting over—even after just a short time—is terrifying. People say that phrase, *start over*, like a new start is even guaranteed. Like there's always someone out there who's definitely going to love you. But what if you're stuck at the end of the last finish line? What if your time runs out, and in the end, you're stuck with only yourself?

"That is *not* a good answer," Nina mutters. "This is so fucked-up and you don't even—" She spins in her seat to lance me with her gaze. "I know we joke about your Rosie-colored glasses, but this time,

they could have literally gotten you killed. If not by Morgan, then—"
She slaps a hand over her mouth, drops it a second later. "What if
whoever murdered him was still there when you showed up? Or even
now—what if they think you saw something, some detail that could
give them away, and they think they have to get rid of you?"

"Tha-that's not going to happen," I stammer. "Nobody's getting
rid of me." But the possibility slices into me. I'm still wrapping my
head around the fact that there even *was* a killer; it didn't occur to
me that whoever stabbed Morgan could have still been inside the
house, watching me discover him. The blood was definitely fresh; in
my memory, I see it in motion, welling around the blade.

"You don't know that," Nina scolds. "You're totally vulnerable, you
were there, you were at the scene, you . . ."

My thoughts drown her out, as if I've slipped underwater. Because
the image of Morgan in the kitchen has surfaced some questions.
Who hated him so much they could plunge a knife into his chest?
The scene was so gruesome, so jarringly red, and only a year ago, one
floor above where Morgan died, his wife bled, too. It's either a tragic
coincidence, or— I touch my temple against a wince of pain. Are
the deaths connected somehow? Is it possible someone did murder
Daphne and has actually been targeting them both?

Something like relief bubbles up through the nausea in my stomach. Because if that's true, then Morgan definitely didn't kill his wife.
Which would also mean I doubted him for nothing. My relief mixes
with regret before both feelings go flat. It doesn't matter if Morgan's
innocent, if I questioned his character. I can't have him either way.

"Wait." The sharpness of Nina's voice jolts me back to her, just
as her eyes fling toward the station. "*Please* tell me you had a lawyer
with you while they were questioning you."

I bite my lip, a wordless response. Nina's head crashes into her
hands.

"Rosie! Oh my god."

"I didn't think of it! I didn't think I was, like, a suspect until suddenly the detective was talking about how there were pink hairs in Morgan's hand at the scene, and—"

"You touched the body?" Nina snaps her head back up, eyes blaring her alarm.

"No, the hairs aren't mine. The detective said Morgan's been emailing his friend about another woman he's been seeing. In person. Who also has pink hair. And—her name's Rosie, too, somehow?"

"*What?* Slow down. You're not making sense."

I knead my forehead with my fingers. "That's because *it* doesn't make sense. I've never even spoken to Morgan in person, only through DonorConnect, so obviously that other woman isn't me. And the police will know that as soon as they test the hair I gave them." I gesture back toward the station, and Nina's eyes, still huge, follow the arc of my hand.

"You . . . submitted your hairs for testing," she says. "Without a lawyer present. Or without even consulting one first."

"The hairs aren't going to match! And anyway, where would I have just . . . *produced* a lawyer? I don't have one to begin with."

"What about—"

I stop her before she can say the man's name, which I can't hear without thinking of Brad.

"I think he's retired," I say. "He only did that as a favor to my dad because they were college roommates."

"You still could have called him for a recommendation! Or called *me* and I would have found you someone!"

"Neens, I'm telling you: none of that crossed my mind because by the time I realized they were suspicious of me, I'd *also* just learned about the woman Morgan's been dating. My head was spinning, okay?"

There was something in that moment—that epiphany that some other Rosie, some other pink-haired woman, had been living the life I'd wanted with Morgan—that felt like Brad dumping me in my dress. The emotional sideswipe of it. The mental scrambling. A cramp in my gut that nearly doubled me over. In a single instant, it rewired my sense of reality. With Brad, I thought we'd been living one story together, only to discover I'd been reading it wrong the entire time. And with Morgan, I believed we were creating something distinct, intimate—that our messages were the start of a romance—only to learn he was already dating someone else.

"A woman . . . named Rosie," Nina says, "with pink hair. Who you say is not you."

"I think I'd know if I'd been dating him, Neens. And if Morgan emailed his friend all about this other Rosie, then he must have written something about her that can help the police identify who she is."

"And they just let you go," Nina says, "on your word that it wasn't you."

"I surrendered my phone," I say, and Nina blinks at me as if I'm speaking a foreign language. "Voluntarily! I want them to search it. If Morgan and this other Rosie were dating, then they'll see that whoever he's been texting or calling isn't me."

"They could have gotten that info from your phone records! You didn't need to—"

"But this shows them I have nothing to hide."

"What about those hairs in Morgan's hand? You're *sure* they aren't yours? Because even the slightest contact can leave DNA."

"Nina, no—I have never once, in my entire life, touched Morgan Thorne. Alive or dead."

Dead. The word slips out easily, but part of me still doesn't believe it. Even with the detective's questions still ringing in my ears. Even with Morgan's blood still blazing on the backs of my eyelids. My body is living a truth my mind hasn't caught up to yet.

I'm not the only one in disbelief. Nina's gaze is foggy with it, aimed at my face but lost in the space between us. I know, though, that it isn't Morgan's death she doubts. It's me.

I say it out loud, the thing she won't: "You don't believe me."

She hesitates—only a moment, maybe, but it feels like a minute. "It's just a shock. You were messaging Morgan for weeks, then you showed up at his house without him knowing, and now he's *dead*, and you're a suspect, and— You have to admit: there are some . . . parallels. To last time."

"It's not the same at all," I snap.

Nina slumps against her seat, cheek pressed to the headrest, looking more exhausted than she does after a sixteen-hour shift at the hospital.

"No, I know," she says. "But this is crazy."

She must see it on my face—the flicker of hurt. The searing brand of that word, *crazy*.

She's quick to amend it: "Not you. The situation. You need to call a lawyer, okay? First thing in the morning."

"I will," I promise—though with my phone in police custody, I'll need someone else's to do it. The thought of asking my parents, explaining what I need and why, makes my stomach shrivel. If Nina's this worried, this appalled by the actions I took that got me here in the first place, I can only imagine how they'll react—my mother, who has never understood that love doesn't simply *arrive*, that sometimes it must be pursued, and that even as the pursuer, you are almost never the predator, almost always the prey; my father, who had to swallow his shame to call his lawyer friend for me, whose hands shook on my shoulders as we sat around the dining room table, reviewing my options.

"I'm late in taking my meds—can you drop me off at my car?" I ask. "I'm parked on Clark Street."

Morgan's street, I don't need to say.

We ride without speaking—a first for us—and after a few minutes, Nina flicks on the radio, as if worried I can hear her thoughts in the silence. Mine keep catapulting back to Morgan. Not just the blood and the knife, but his kindness, his acceptance of me, that beamed from the screen whenever I read his messages. His willingness to meet my darkness with his own. In the past few hours, it's been easy to forget the rumors, the online comments, easy to let Daphne's poetry feel like fiction. And now I realize, with a flare of pain in my chest: I'm going to miss him.

"Right there," I say when Nina nears my car, and she pulls up behind it.

"There isn't a house here." She hunches to peer at the trees I parked alongside.

"It's over there." I nudge my chin up the street, where vans and cop cars line the curb. I don't explain why I parked so far from Morgan's property that you can't even see the house from this angle. Truthfully, I'm not really sure. Maybe I'm too used to there being something secretive about our interactions. Maybe I'm accustomed to skulking around.

I unbuckle my seat belt. "Thanks for picking me up."

"Of course. I'd do anything for you," she says, but there's no emotion in the response. No undercurrent of care, like I usually hear. Instead, Nina sounds distracted, eager to get rid of me, and it makes me feel so alone it's as if she's already driven away.

Still, she squeezes my hand before she lets me go, and when I step out and close the door, I smile at her through the window, my lips pressed tight to keep from crying.

I force a few deep breaths as I get behind the wheel of my car. I turn on the ignition, glancing at Nina in my rearview. I expect her to wait for me to drive off first, but she's already doing a K-turn, heading back the way we came.

Hitting the gas, I steer in the opposite direction. As I pass Morgan's house, I ignore the police cruisers, the mobile light like a second moon illuminating his yard, the yellow tape stretched across the columns flanking his front steps—and with all those images smudged and swirled in my peripheral vision, I can almost believe that I'm leaving them behind.

CHAPTER ELEVEN

Over the next day and a half, I watch fourteen episodes of *Gilmore Girls*. I get Danishes delivered for dinner. I study tutorials for dyeing your own hair—not just to distance myself from the woman who left strands of herself at the scene but to distance myself from me, too.

By the middle of the second day, I've decided to keep my hair as is—no energy for gloves and towels, for scrutinizing instructions on a box—but I convince myself that going back to work will help. I need normal, need routine, need the familiar rhythm of Just Say Yes to keep me afloat. I slip on a boatneck dress, step into wedges, even swipe on mascara and lip gloss. I show up with coffees and pastries for all the consultants, conscious of the extra work I've dumped on them during my absence. But I last only three hours and seventeen minutes before I'm mumbling excuses to Marilee and rushing out the door.

All those dresses. All those beaming brides. All the white, white, white—a perfect, too-clean canvas for the blood still pulsing through my mind.

Back home in bed, I keep Instagram open on my laptop, missing the ease of my phone. For the past two days, I've been refreshing Blair's page, waiting for a post about Morgan. It makes no sense—I saw the body; I've scanned the news stories: bestselling author; homicide; one year since another tragedy in that home—but it won't feel like fact, won't feel permanent, until I hear it from someone close to him. Until I know I'm not alone in my shock.

Finally, almost forty-eight hours after I discovered his body, it comes. A carousel of photos. A caption that guts me. I'm so confused right now, I have no answers, but I know one thing: I loved him so much. I swipe through the pictures, watching the two of them grow into adulthood together: posing at parties in college (Blair with a platinum pixie cut, Morgan clean-shaven); arms slung around each other at bars in their twenties (both sporting a shaggy, shapeless hairstyle); smiling at weddings in their early thirties (Blair with a blond bob, Morgan in gold-wire glasses). Finally, they became the pair I've seen in person, sharing a smirk, Blair with her curtain of dark hair, Morgan with his tortoiseshell frames.

I exit Instagram, curling on my side. The post was not the comfort or closure I expected. I bet Blair's in bed, too, thumbing through those photos, wondering how it's possible she and Morgan will never take another. I bet she's buried beneath blankets; I bet they're not enough to warm her—and I ball up tighter at the thought.

I remain like that until my laptop dings with an incoming email. It's Marilee, writing from her Just Say Yes address. The subject is three words: Message from police.

Bolting upright, I open the email. Someone from the station tried to reach me at work, Marilee relays. They told her I can pick up my phone at my earliest convenience.

My stomach drops at the thought of her fielding that call. I can only imagine the questions it sparked.

Still, this is good news. If the police are returning my phone, then that means they know it doesn't implicate me.

But when I arrive at the station a half hour later and give the receptionist my name, she doesn't hand it over right away. Instead, she dials an extension, and in a few minutes, the detective from the other night steps into the lobby to greet me.

"Ms. Lachlan," he says, "thanks for coming by. Would you mind answering a few more questions while you're here?"

"Oh. Um. I thought—"

"You can retrieve your phone on your way out. Sophie will keep it safe." He nods over my shoulder at the receptionist, then opens a door and gestures for me to enter.

There's something familiar in his expectant expression, and I'm nagged once again by the feeling I know him from somewhere. Or maybe it's simply because we just did this, only forty-eight hours ago. I follow him down a hallway, into an interview room that's nearly identical to the one we used before, and as Jackson and I sit down across from each other, the blaring lights cover me like a rash.

He notes our names, the date, and time "for the sake of the recording" and reminds me I'm free to leave whenever I'd like, same as the other night. Then he offers a tight-lipped smile, his tone becoming more casual.

"I'm sure you'll be glad to have your phone again." He leans back in his chair. "It's hard to be without one these days. Unless—do you happen to have another at your disposal?"

"Another phone? My parents have a landline, if that's what you mean. I live in the apartment above their garage."

"I'm thinking more along the lines of"—he pauses, as if searching for his next words—"a prepaid phone. Do you have one like that?"

"You mean a burner?"

Jackson shrugs. "Some people call it that."

"I don't have a burner. Why— Was Morgan in contact with someone who did?"

"I'm just curious," he says—which isn't a no. Beneath the table,

I pick at my nails. If the woman Morgan was dating used a burner, they can't rule me out as the Rosie he might have texted or called.

"You can search my apartment," I say, and I immediately hear Nina hissing in my head: *Are you serious? Get a lawyer!* "You won't find a phone like that."

"That won't be necessary right now, but I'll let you know if we plan to take you up on that offer. In the meantime, I'd like to talk to you about the list in your phone."

I stiffen—and if my heart weren't on a delay, it would knock. "The list?"

"In your Notes app. It appears to be . . . facts. About Mr. Thorne."

I maintain my gaze, even as I want to bury my head in my hands. Nina was right; I should have asked for a lawyer before surrendering my phone. But I was only thinking of how it would exonerate me, my mind too blurred by Morgan's blood to think through all the pieces of him I'd stored in there.

From the way Jackson's watching me now, it's as if those pieces are body parts.

"I got the idea from TikTok," I say. "Some woman's video. About a list her boyfriend showed her in his phone that he'd been keeping since their first date. Things he learned about her. Things he didn't want to forget. Things he could use later for gift inspiration. I thought it was a good idea." I try for a casual shrug. "That's all it was."

"But you said you never dated Mr. Thorne. If that's true, why would you need a list?"

"I had a crush on him," I admit—because surely a crush is better than the alternative. "I was hopeful that a list like that would be useful one day. So I wrote down info I gathered on social media—likes, dislikes. And I wrote down things he told me in our messages."

Jackson's silence is calculated. He's trying to coax me into saying more. I resist for only a few moments, his quiet creating blanks I don't want his mind to fill.

"I get that it isn't . . . normal," I say. "But it isn't evidence of anything either. And what about my fingerprints? You checked them against the knife, right? So you know I never touched it. You know it was someone else."

"The knife was wiped clean. So far, we're unable to prove who did and didn't touch it."

Damn it. I should have expected that. "Well, what about the emails? The ones where Morgan was telling a friend about this other Rosie. They must have clues in them that could lead you to that woman."

It's only as I say *that woman* that I realize what I really mean: the killer. Because didn't Jackson tell me she was there that night, that Morgan was in the middle of an email draft about their "encounter"? One that was "confrontational"? It sounded like the woman was gone before Morgan started the email, but maybe she wasn't done with him. Maybe she came back. Maybe she picked up a knife.

A chill scampers up my spine. I ball my hands in my sweatshirt sleeves. But this theory clarifies nothing for me. It only compounds the questions I already have.

"We're conducting a full investigation into the emails," Jackson says, a response that's intentionally elusive. "In the meantime, I want to get your thoughts on something. It's pretty strange, isn't it, that Mr. Thorne was both corresponding with you via DonorConnect and, at the same time, seeing a woman named Rosie with pink hair? You have to admit it's quite the coincidence."

He leans on *coincidence*, weighting the word with irony.

I blow out a frustrated breath. "It *is* a coincidence."

"What if it's not?"

I open my mouth to argue again, but Jackson keeps going.

"Can you think of anyone who might try to appropriate your identity?"

The question freezes me, my mouth left gaping. "What do you mean?" I finally say.

"In his emails, Mr. Thorne said he met Rosie at Sweet Bean Café, which is right next door to your workplace, correct?"

It takes me a second to nod. He met her at Sweet Bean? But that's where I met him, too. Well, no: it's where I *saw* him, and maybe would have met him, had Marilee not texted me to return to the store.

"We spoke to the staff who was working there that evening. Unfortunately, there are no security cameras—the owners are a little old-fashioned—but one of the baristas said she saw you there. Apparently, you're a regular?"

I don't answer—only squint at him. Morgan not only met the other Rosie at Sweet Bean, but on the day I saw him there, too?

"The barista remembers informing Mr. Thorne and his companion that the café was closing, which corroborates a detail from his email. But she said that the pink-haired woman at the table with Mr. Thorne was *not* you. That, in fact, you had left hours earlier."

I shake my head, the information like a riddle. "I— So. What are you saying? You think someone followed me to Sweet Bean and—pretended to be me?"

He answers my question with one of his own: "Do you have any reason to believe that someone in your life might do that?"

"No. I can't— It doesn't make sense."

Why would anyone pretend to be me? And not just that: Why would this woman use my identity to date Morgan and then kill him?

An answer flashes—*she's framing me*—but the idea is absurd. Why would she want to? How would she even know she could? Besides Nina and the people at DonorConnect, nobody's aware there's a connection between me and Morgan in the first place.

"Maybe the barista was mistaken then?" Jackson suggests.

"No. Morgan *was* there. I saw him at a table with—"

I catch myself before saying Blair's name.

"A woman. A friend, I guess. She had dark hair. Not pink. But I was only there from like five thirty to six. I went back to work to meet a bride for a consultation and was with her until closing at eight. I can send you her information, if you want."

"That would be helpful, thank you."

"Sure," I say, before wondering *why* it's helpful, why I still have to prove I've never even met Morgan, especially since: "This woman—the one who called herself Rosie. That's your primary suspect, right? I mean, you said Morgan wrote about seeing her the night he was killed."

Jackson pushes his lips to the side, as if considering whether to answer me. "We're looking into all possibilities, with the most likely scenario being that the perpetrator was someone Mr. Thorne knew."

And I barely did, in the end. I'd only just scratched the surface of who he was, who we might have been together. Even on that last day, I was more preoccupied with Daphne's poetry than—

"Any chance this could be related to his wife's death?" I ask. "That was only a year ago, so—"

"Her death was an accident. Why exactly would that be related?"

I'm about to answer, but then I reconsider. I don't like the way his eyes have narrowed on me again, as if everything I say is a secret code encrypting my culpability.

"I just mean," I try, "with two brutal deaths in the same house, in the span of a year, it makes me wonder if there's a connection."

Jackson hums an acknowledgment. "I'll tell you what, Ms. Lachlan." He leans forward, just a bit, erasing a breath of space between us. "Why don't you let me worry about connections."

He stands, our interview apparently over, but his gaze never leaves my face. In the silence, his implication pollutes the air: connections like Daphne's heart in my chest, my correspondence with Morgan, the list in my phone.

Jackson opens the door. "Thanks for your cooperation. We'll be getting the results back on the hair analysis any day now, which should help clarify some things. In the meantime—" He waves me on to the hall outside. "It's in your best interest that you remain reachable."

In other words: don't skip town.

My eyes burn as I return to the lobby. As I retrieve my phone from the receptionist. As I walk out of the station and back to my car. I should be relieved. He found nothing truly incriminating on my phone, and the barista told him I wasn't the pink-haired woman with Morgan. But Jackson's demeanor makes it clear: even though he raised a new theory—as disturbing as it is inexplicable—that someone's been impersonating me, he hasn't eliminated me as a suspect. And the fact that he's thinking it at all—that I could have stabbed Morgan, right through the heart, when his heart was the thing I'd hoped could heal mine—feels, in some strange way, like being called *crazy*. Like my mind is so warped with wanting I've done things I don't remember.

Sitting in my car, the engine still off, I try to steady myself before the drive home. But after a few moments of measured breathing, the hair on the back of my neck begins to prickle.

At first, I assume it's Jackson's questions, still strumming my nerves—but as the sensation remains, I register the prickle for what it is: the feeling of being watched.

I look around, searching the parking lot, the tree line, even the back seat of my car, but I see only a dusk-drenched sky, only puddles of light from the lampposts.

Even still, squinting through the windshield, part of me expects to find a flash of pink. A woman with my body, my face, emerging from the shadows.

———

I'm home for only three minutes before there's a knock at my door.

"Rosie, what is going on?" Mom demands when I open it. She barrels into the apartment, Dad hanging back a bit behind her.

"Hey, Rosie girl," he says. His voice is soft like it was in the hospital, those weeks on the transplant list, when he spoke as if even a greeting could break me. He winces as he steps over the threshold.

"Dad, you shouldn't have come up here." He's reached the point with his hip replacement that he can do stairs by himself, but it's still a discomfort I'd rather he not waste on me. "I would have come down to you guys, why didn't you just—"

"Call?" Mom says. "Believe me, we've tried. Several times." She gestures to my phone on the kitchen table. "I assume that thing works?"

I tap its screen to wake it, but it remains black. "They must've turned it off," I mutter to myself, but Mom catches the words.

"They? Who's they?"

I stall by switching on my phone, studying the Apple icon, but I'm too exhausted to come up with a lie. "The police. They've had it the last couple days."

And yet, I find I've only missed two texts. Both are from Edith, the first arriving yesterday, the second almost twenty-four hours later, when she didn't receive a response.

Morgan Thorne is DEAD?!

Hello? Are YOU dead??

I set the phone face down on the table before looking at my parents. Mom stares at me, bug-eyed. Dad's gaze drops to the floor.

"Excuse me?" Mom says. "Care to explain why *the police* had your phone?"

I ease out a sigh. I didn't want to do this. I thought it might be handled by now. But I don't know how to explain without telling them the truth. Heat flushes my cheeks as I offer a truncated version: connecting with Morgan on DonorConnect; our string of messages; his offer to meet in person; his open front door; his body, his blood, on the kitchen floor. I don't mention that I'd figured out Morgan's identity, his address, all on my own. I don't mention Rosie, either—the one who might be masquerading as me—or the pink hairs she left in his hand. I'm alarming them enough as it is, and from Mom's rapid blinking, her stuck-open mouth, it's clear that those other details could give her a stroke.

Silence swells when I finish speaking, the air growing thick.

Finally, Mom turns away from me to walk to the living room, where she drops into an armchair. I follow Dad as he trails behind her. He places a hand on her shoulder and squeezes. Neither of them look at me.

"The police think you did it," Mom says. A statement. Not a question.

"No," I lie—because, soon enough, they won't.

"That's why they took your phone."

"No, I gave it to him, it was my choice. I wanted him to have it so he could eliminate me as—" I stop.

"As a suspect," Dad finishes for me.

"Which they did. They did eliminate me." I wave my phone in the air. "They gave it back. I'm in the clear." The lies pile up, but it's better than making them worry. I've put them through a lifetime of that in the last eighteen months alone.

Dad moves to the couch, then reaches for Mom, who laces her fingers with his, squeezing them tight. I stare at those hands, linked for all my life—while they watch TV, while they browse a bookstore, while they ride in the car. Every time they drove me to my post-op checkups, their hands clasped across the console were as much a comfort to me as a reminder of how empty my own hands were.

"You don't look right," Dad says, and Mom's nod comes fast.

"You're a mess," she agrees, always blunter than Dad. "Your eyes are bloodshot and swollen. Your hair—" I touch the back of my head, defensive, but my fingers stick in knotted strands. Shame washes over me; I didn't even brush my hair before heading to the station. "You went to work like that today?"

"Only for a few hours. And then I— I've been in bed a lot and—"

"Because of your heart?" Mom asks, voice pinched with panic.

"No, no, I've just been having trouble sleeping."

"Oh, Rosie, not again. Do you want some of my pills? The doctor said they're fine to take with your meds."

I stiffen at her choice of words: *Not again.* Just like Nina, she's trying to lump the past with the present. But my history with insomnia is so unrelated to what's happening now that it's absurd of her to even mention it.

"I saw a dead body, Mom! And not just any dead body. The body of a man I . . . had a connection with. A man I cared about."

"Rosie." My mom breathes my name, and there's so much disappointment in it. Right away, I hear the echo of things she's said to me before. About my early symptoms: *You're making yourself sick.* About my grief after breakups: *When are you going to turn this around?* Like my broken heart was a shirt I was wearing backward. A quick, easy fix. I brace myself for a statement that will sting just as much. But what she says stuns me instead.

"Was this man really corresponding with you?"

"What? Of course he was." I glance at Dad, wanting to share a baffled look, but he seems unsurprised by the question. As if he was wondering it, too.

"Why would you even ask that?" I say.

Mom stares at me, exhaustion creasing her eyes. "The way you're talking about him. This connection you say you had. Did the two of you really have a relationship of some sort? Or was it—" She looks up at Dad, who nods slightly, before completing her thought: "Was it like Brad?"

My reply whips out. "Brad and I had a relationship." She jolts from the lash of it.

"Yes," she says after a moment. "But you know what I mean. The relationship wasn't . . . what you thought. For god's sake, you rushed out to buy that wedding dress and—"

"I know, Mom," I cut in, tone still sharp.

She's telling me this as if I've forgotten. As if I wasn't kept awake, for months after, reliving the horrors of that dress.

She leans forward, her gaze digging into me, pointed as a harpoon. "Rosie," she says, and I feel it coming: another thing I remember too well. "That poor man never even proposed to you."

CHAPTER TWELVE

'm not crazy.

This is crazy, Rosie. You—you're crazy.

But there were things that Brad wasn't meant to see, to know. Things that were never meant to get back to him. And it's not like we hadn't talked about forever. Five months in, he suggested it. We were on the couch, our fingers lazily interlacing, when he said, "I could sit like this forever. Just you and me." I held my breath, expecting him to walk the comment back, like all my boyfriends had before, any time they stumbled into discussions of the future, any time they sounded more serious about me than they'd intended. But Brad doubled down. "Couldn't you?" he asked when I didn't answer. And then, in a moment of vulnerability, he added, "Don't you want that for us? To be together forever?"

I kissed him sweeter, then deeper, than I ever had, and when our lips separated, I answered: "Yes."

After that, I started leaving my things at his apartment, instead of relying on an overnight bag. A toothbrush in his medicine cabinet. Face wash beneath the sink. A loofah in the shower. Change of clothes in his bottom drawer. Every time he noticed another item, he looked, if only for a second, like the men I'd loved before: cornered and concerned. But he never said anything, never told me I'd gotten the wrong idea, that my stuff, my life, wasn't welcome beside his.

Around that time, I was working a bridal convention and chatted with a woman from a new event space that was already booked two years in advance. When I practically swooned at her description of the venue—converted from a former library and leaning heavily into the theme—she asked if I was dating anyone (yes), if it was serious (forever is serious, so yes), and encouraged me to schedule a tour; *If you like what you see, it's best to get your name in now*, she said with a shrug. But my visit ended up being much less casual than she'd made it sound. There was paperwork involved, asking for both my name and the groom's, for our preferred aesthetic, the estimated size of our party. I kept glancing over my shoulder as I filled it out, but still: I felt an unprecedented thrill, listing Brad as my fiancé.

What I didn't know was that the owner of the venue was married to Brad's friend from work. A couple days later, at happy hour, the friend congratulated Brad on "the engagement," told him his wife would love to host our wedding.

Brad sped from the bar to my apartment. He burst inside and demanded an explanation, his face flushed, his eyes wide and wild. My own cheeks flared with heat as I scrambled to sound reasonable. I told him I'd toured the venue for work so I could recommend it to customers or warn them away. I did it "undercover," I said, to get the full effect, and I only used his name as the groom because it was the first that came to mind. Still, I promised to call the owner the next day to come clean and apologize.

We left it at that. But over the next few weeks, I felt Brad drift. He scrolled through his phone on the couch while I waited for him in bed; he was slower to text me during days spent apart, if he even texted at all; he forgot to cancel our dates when he ended up working late, so I'd be sitting at my front window, hair curled, waiting for his car to pull up.

In all those moments, I swallowed down the hurt I felt. I pretended I was fine, that I hadn't noticed the changes, because I was afraid if I pushed him on it, I'd only push him further away. Instead, I held on to the words he said to me in the beginning: *You're the most amazing woman I've ever met. You're so special.* Held on to the question he'd asked me, not even a month before: *Don't you want that for us? To be together forever?* I clasped my hands around the hope of it—that, in asking me that question, he meant he wanted me forever too.

But then, only three weeks after the venue debacle, Brad walked in to find me wearing the dress.

I'd first put it on earlier that day at Just Say Yes. It's a thing we do sometimes—try on new inventory, snap photos for social media—but the second the satin and lace slid against my skin, its beaded bodice glittering, I knew I needed the dress.

Not wanted. Needed.

I'd tried on dozens before, but in this one, I saw myself as I never had: radiant. Like it was me, not the lights above us, that made the gown shimmer. It was such a contrast to how I'd felt the last few weeks—dull and diminished, easily overlooked. But in that dress, I commanded attention. I glowed.

Even Marilee saw it. "Wow," she breathed. "It was made for you." She stepped back, took all of me in. "Look what it does to your eyes. They're like lightbulbs."

I pictured Brad, then, standing at an altar, his own eyes brightening at the sight of me. I pictured a portrait of us, one to replace the stand-in I'd perched on my parents' hutch, one where we'd be facing each other, me in that dress, him in a tux, our gazes twined and twinkling.

I purchased the sample. Took the dress home that day. Stood in it at my bedroom mirror, holding the gown closed in the back—unable to fasten its delicate buttons on my own—and smiled at myself until my cheeks grew sore.

If only Brad hadn't gotten out of work early that afternoon. If only he'd texted first and I'd had a warning. But he was buzzing from a successful presentation in front of his CEO. He headed straight to my apartment to celebrate, used the key I'd given him (though I'd never received one in return), and stepped into my room, already undoing his tie. I didn't hear him come in—I'd been blasting Florence & the Machine's "Cosmic Love" on repeat—but I saw his reflection in the mirror, the shocked expression that quickly curdled into something like fear.

Even after all this time, there are days I look at my reflection and don't see my own face; I see his, frozen in that moment, lips curled with revulsion.

I dropped the hand that held the gown together, the fabric in the back now gaping, almost grotesque, like a fish split up the middle.

"I'm going to return it!" I blurted, a lie I realized, two seconds too late, was a mistake. There had still been a chance, maybe, to convince him that this, too, was just for work—I'd been test-driving a new designer, prepping an Instagram post. But now he knew the gown was mine.

"This is crazy, Rosie. You—you're crazy."

He tripped over himself to get out the door, flinging more words over his shoulder: "I can't, this is too much." But I didn't give up. Even when Nina was there, holding me on my floor, her sweater itchy against my still-bare back, I was leaving Brad voicemails, texting him explanations, begging for a second chance.

> Please, come back. Let's talk.

> It's not what you think, I promise.

> The dress just spoke to me.

I couldn't bear for it to end with a misunderstanding. Not when, in the beginning, it felt like no one had ever understood each other as well as we did. I couldn't endure his silence. Not when we'd once had so much to say to each other—even living, at the start, on separate continents—that our video chats wore down the batteries in our devices.

For weeks, I tried to reach him, reach back to who we'd been in the past. It was only once I gave into it, finally set down my phone, finally faced the pitch-black cave of my future, that Brad acknowledged my existence.

> I miss your face. Come over?

I knew then that he understood; I wasn't delusional, wasn't planning some wedding he hadn't consented to yet. And when he kissed me that night in his doorway, hungry for me in a way he hadn't been in weeks, I knew that the distance, the silence, was over, that we'd go back to the way we were meant to be. Electric. Inseparable.

Brad seemed to know that too. My toothbrush was still in his medicine cabinet, kept like a promise, and in the morning, as we kissed goodbye, he made another: *We should do this again. I'll text you.*

On the second day of waiting for that text, I baked him his favorite cookies. I was already making a batch for our seamstress's birthday— oatmeal raisin were her favorite too—but I baked extra for Brad, still giddy from the night we'd reconnected, and dropped them off at his house so he could find them when he got home from work. Instead of leaving them on his front steps, where squirrels might claw at the plastic wrap on top, I pulled open his garage door and placed the plate on the concrete floor.

Left you a surprise, I texted, and though I waited all day for a response—a picture of him digging into the cookies, an invitation to come share them with him—nothing came.

For five more days, my phone sat silent by my side. I turned off notifications from everyone except for him, because the false alarms, the false hope, became more than I could take. I convinced myself that something had happened to him, because you don't text someone you miss their face, don't kiss someone like you're starving for their taste, don't nuzzle *you're amazing* against their neck as you're peeling off their clothes, and ignore their every text and call.

But then there was the pint glass, shattered on my kitchen floor. The shard cutting my palm. The frantic drive to check on Brad. Blood on my steering wheel. Blood on his front steps.

"I'm not crazy," I tell my parents now.

"Nobody said you are," Dad says. "But I think we should probably call Rich Silverstein."

My head snaps up at the name. His college roommate. The lawyer.

"For what?" I ask, still stuck in my memories, unable to think of that man in any other context than the one involving Brad.

"What do you mean 'for what'?" Mom says, incredulous. "You're a suspect in a murder investigation."

The sentence is like cold water on my face. For a moment, I'd actually forgotten about Morgan. Forgotten there was a whole other life I'd hoped to live that had nothing to do with Brad. Why haven't I learned? Me and hope are a dangerous pair. I'm always cupping it like a firefly in my palms, surprised when I squeeze too hard and its light goes dark.

"I told you, I'm not a suspect." I hold up my phone again, willing it to prove something.

"As a precaution then," Dad says. "Maybe we should just have Rich take a look at those messages you sent the man. He said to reach out, if we ever need him again."

I close my eyes, shake my head. This wouldn't be the first time Rich Silverstein looked at my messages. He once pored over them in my parents' dining room, reading every word I'd sent to Brad in the last month. Because I didn't stop reaching out. Not even after I sobbed on his steps, my blood-streaked keys in my hand. Not even after he told me to go home, we were done, I was crazy. I kept texting, kept emailing, because I didn't understand how quickly we went from forever to never.

There were stretches of days when I'd be strong, wouldn't contact him at all, but then it would come to me: the words I was sure would inspire a response. Make him see I wasn't crazy. I was just in love. In loss. In limbo. Because if he'd texted me out of the blue once before, who was to say he wouldn't miss my face again? Wouldn't, despite my "crazy," invite me back into his bed?

> I'm still so sorry about the way I showed up that night—bleeding and crying. I'm sorry about texting you this many times. But every time you don't respond, I start to question every memory I have of us. Because just two weeks ago, you told me you missed me. You cupped my face in your hands and you kissed me all the way to your room. And I don't know how to reconcile the two—intimacy and silence.

Rich Silverstein read those words. My stupid, futile words. Shame rushes through me, remembering how he printed them out and frowned at the pages, highlighting phrases as he read.

Dad had called Rich to consult about the response I finally did get from Brad, which came not as an email or text—but as a harassment prevention order.

Mom read my messages, too, sweeping up each page after Rich set it aside. "I don't understand," she said to me. "You're a grown woman, Rosie. And Brad has clearly moved on. So why do you sound so—so desperate here? Why can't you just let him go?"

I sat mute in my chair, staring into their living room, straight at the empty space beside the frames on her hutch. Time and time again, I failed to fill it permanently. Only left it looking blanker than it had before.

I saw Brad only once more after the order was issued: at the hearing—where his gaze swerved from mine; where his lawyer kept mentioning my blood on his stoop, even showed the judge photos of the drops I left behind, the cookies I left in his garage, and a copy of the paperwork in which I'd listed Brad as my fiancé.

My parents, there that day to support me, held hands the entire hearing, their knuckles whitening each time Brad's lawyer spoke.

In the end, the judge sided with Brad. The order was extended. And Brad's smile smacked me like a gavel.

When I returned from court, I crawled back into bed and stayed there as much as I could. At first by choice—cocooning against the grief and humiliation—and then, soon after, by necessity, when a simple shower was enough to leave me breathless, when my chest was so tight it felt like my lungs had shrunk.

I feel that way now, too, as Dad stares at me, waiting for a response. I rub my sternum with my knuckles, trying to loosen my airways, and I meet his gaze, which wells with worry.

"Fine, call Rich," I tell him. "Let him know what's going on, just in case. But believe me, if there was anything incriminating on Donor-Connect, I'd have been arrested by now."

My parents don't nod. Don't show any sign of feeling assured. The lines between their brows only deepen, twin trenches of concern and—something else. Because the way they're looking at me now is not so different from the way Brad did, that night on his front steps, that afternoon in my mirror. Not so different from Nina, either, a couple nights ago in her car. I see them doubting everything I've said, I've done. Even with their mouths closed, I see *crazy* on the tips of their tongues.

CHAPTER THIRTEEN

"I want him to die. I want his heart to literally stop beating."

I look up from my phone, frown at my office door, which a woman's voice has breached.

"Like, if he doesn't stop breathing, what's even the point?" In her pause, I'm the one who stops breathing. "Do you think this dress will make him do that?"

I exhale, massage my forehead, picture the bride preening in front of her friends.

"Definitely!" one of them chirps.

I'm operating on only a couple hours of sleep, but I'm determined to work my entire shift. My hair is curled, I'm wearing heels, and I waved at my parents as I left the driveway this morning, my mother's face flashing between the curtains she'd just flicked open. I may not be helping any brides at the moment, but my fingers have the tell-tale indents of hauling gowns to dressing rooms, the hangers having pinched my skin like talons.

I'm doing my best. Even if that means I've had the same spread-sheet open for ten minutes, its cells untouched. Even if I'm more preoccupied by social media than the bride out front who wants a dress that kills.

My phone's on airplane mode so I can check the Instagram Story Blair just posted without her finding my name among its viewers. It's a post she's shared from Burnham Bookshop; they'll be hosting a "community gathering in memory of Morgan Thorne" tonight on the town green, and they've billed it as "a chance for his fans and neighbors to grieve together and honor his work." Blair shared the post without comment, giving no indication of whether she'll be attending, but I can't imagine she will. It seems excruciating, standing among strangers as they mourn a man they didn't actually know—when Blair, by Morgan's own admission, knew all his secrets.

I swipe to my text thread with Nina, even though I checked it only minutes ago. No new messages. No typing bubble. I texted her last night as soon as my parents left, letting her know I had my phone back, sending her proof of life. That message sits at the bottom of the screen, unanswered. Maybe she was working last night? We haven't been in touch enough lately for me to know her schedule like I usually do. Still, even if she did have a shift, it's odd she wouldn't respond to me when she left the hospital this morning. That's usually her first order of business—catch up on all the inane texts I've sent her: complaints about customers, cute pictures of Bumper, funny memes that feel like us. Now I'm worried that her silence is intentional, that she's retreating from me, still uncomfortable about our conversation in her car.

I know she and my parents don't think I'm a suspect the same way the cops do, but they're clearly concerned I misjudged something. They think my bad habits—wanting love, wearing my Rosie-colored glasses—have led me into trouble again. And maybe Nina doubts there's even a second Rosie; maybe she thinks it was me all along, the woman who's been dating Morgan. I lied to her about writing to him; can I really blame her for wondering what else I've lied about?

I should have asked Jackson more questions last night. Too stunned by his suggestion that I have an imposter, I didn't even inquire about Other Rosie at all. But if I knew what Morgan wrote about her in the emails Jackson referenced, I'd have something concrete to share with Nina, something she might scramble to respond to. Oh my god, that's CRAZY, she'd text—meaning Other Rosie, not me—and we'd work together to uncover the identity of the woman who's stolen mine.

I toy with the idea of DMing Blair. She's got to be the "friend" Jackson said Morgan was emailing; at Sweet Bean, she teased him about his novel-like messages. Maybe I could explain my connection to him, ask if—as Morgan's best friend—he'd told her anything about a woman named Rosie, and hope she believes me when I swear I'm not the one he meant. But when I open the app again, I'm still on her story, and I see she's added another. I tap to read it. She's shared the post about the bookstore's "community gathering" again, but this time, she included some text: Thanks to @burnhambookshop for hosting this event tonight. I wasn't sure if I was up for this, but I've decided that crying at home is getting me nowhere. I want to be around people who care about him too.

I nod at the caption, as if the words were meant for me alone. Because crying at home hasn't gotten me anywhere either. Neither has hiding in my office between twenty-minute bursts of work. Morgan's still dead. There's still a woman out there using my name, wearing my hair. And if I'm going to find out who she is and what she wants, there's only one other person I can try. So if Blair's pushing herself to go to that gathering tonight, then so am I.

The town green is strung with stars. Twinkle lights crisscross from telephone poles to trees and back to streetlamps, a sparkling ceiling above the festivities. And I do mean festivities. I expected something hushed and somber, hands cupping candles, heads bent in contemplation, but even before I step onto the green, I'm struck by a wave of laughter and chatter. It froths toward me, sucking me in like the pull of a tide.

I scan the crowd for familiar faces but come up empty. I thought I might see Edith here, but I'm actually relieved not to find her. I still haven't responded to her shell-shocked text about Morgan's death—unable to pretend I'm clueless about it, unable to confess I'm more informed than I'd ever want to be—and any conversation I'd stumble through with her would only distract me from the one I came here to have.

All across the lawn, people sip from plastic cups, clump together in groups, clutch books beneath their arms. I catch the spine of one—*Someone at the Door*—and a memory flickers. No, not a memory. Not mine, anyway. It's Daphne's, her poems so vivid I still see the images of the night her sister died: chipped paint on her front door, a gloved hand reaching through broken glass for the dead bolt. It hits me again; I never got to confront Morgan about what he did to her, never got to hear his perspective on what Daphne called "theft" in one of her poems.

I pull in a queasy breath, step deeper into the crowd.

The owner of Burnham Bookshop moves from group to group, attempting to pass out candles, but people barely register her presence. One woman throws her head back, slaps her friend's arm, and cackles, a sound that chills me, despite the humid evening. There's something almost vulgar about the atmosphere, much more celebratory than somber, as if we're at a book launch instead of a memorial.

The air ripples around me, hazy as a dream. I weave across the green, picking up snippets of conversation, each more dizzying than the last.

"—snagged one of the only signed copies they had in stock this morning. Do you think it'll be worth something now?"

"—never read him, but my sister's obsessed. I'm honestly just here to make her jealous. Speaking of which: let's take a pic—"

"—the chief of police. He's a family friend, and he assured me the community is not in danger; this was a targeted attack. Which is a huge relief. I have *kids*. But it does make you wonder: What could this man have done to deserve that kind of violence?"

When I emerge from a particularly tight knot of people, I think I see a ghost—Daphne's—lurking at the edge of the green. I freeze, midstep, then blink the phantom into focus. It's Blair, standing beneath a streetlamp, the light emphasizing the shine of her dark hair.

Her arms are crossed as she glares at the crowd, and it's there in the pinch of her face: this isn't the reverent event she expected either. She's got one foot on the curb behind her, as if she's thinking of leaving, and as I get closer, I see what her makeup has failed to mask—bloodshot eyes, puffy skin. The same features my mother noticed on me last night.

"Excuse me?" a voice booms across the green. "Could I have your attention for a moment?" I turn to find the bookstore owner tapping a microphone.

She thanks everyone for coming, mentions that, although she sold out of Morgan's books at the store this morning, she'll be getting more in stock soon and is happy to take orders in the meantime.

"As a reminder, we're also collecting donations tonight to Page Turners, a literacy program Morgan supported," she says above the crowd, which is already back to murmuring. Sensing she's losing them, she encourages people to talk to one another about their favorite Morgan novel. Laughter snakes through the crowd at the suggestion, and that's when I realize what this night really feels like—not a book launch, but a book club, one where the author's work gets pushed aside in favor of juicy conversation.

I'm about to turn around, look for Blair again, when someone taps my shoulder. I spin and then startle; Blair is two feet away, staring at me—or at least my hair.

"You're Rosie," she says. "Aren't you?"

"Oh. Yeah. H-hi," I stammer. After only seeing her on social media—besides that day in Sweet Bean—it's strange to be addressing her directly. Even stranger that she's addressing me.

"So you're the woman Morgan was seeing."

"Oh," I repeat. "I'm actually, uh—" I fumble for how to explain, and in my hesitation, she steps even closer.

"I'm Blair. His best friend. I figured you'd be here tonight."

There's something dark in her expression, like I'm a threat, and I realize she's probably made the same assumptions I have—that the woman from Morgan's emails could have been the one to kill him.

"No, I'm a different Rosie!" I say, and Blair squints at me. "My name *is* Rosie, Rosie Lachlan, but I've never even met Morgan in—"

"Your hair's pink," Blair cuts in, her tone like a lawyer calling *objection*.

"I know, but I can explain that. Well, actually, I can't. But maybe you can help."

Her eyes rake across my face like nails. "Start making sense."

"I have Daphne's heart," I blurt, since that's where my connection with Morgan begins.

Blair's face convulses with confusion, so I hold out my MedicAlert bracelet, then rush ahead, sharing the story that's becoming well-worn, the details softening like clothes after too many washes. It's all less vivid than the first time I told it, less mine. Still, I describe my transplant, my messages with Morgan, and with every sentence, Blair's brows sink deeper. I speed up, admit that, even though I figured out Morgan's identity from the start, I kept that from him, kept my own a secret too. Finally, I conclude with Jackson's imposter theory and the fact that whoever Morgan was seeing left strands of her hair at the crime scene.

"I submitted a hair sample," I say, "to prove it won't match."

Blair stares at me like the hair at issue is porcupining around my

head. Then she spits out a question that yanks us back to the beginning: "*You* had a heart transplant? With *Daphne's* heart?"

She says it with something like disgust, as if I took it intentionally.
Hunted Daphne down to be my organ donor. As if I wanted Morgan,
even back then, and found some way to kill his wife, save my own
life, and seduce him all at once.

I don't answer her with words. Instead, I step closer to the street-
light and tug on my collar until she sees the tip of my scar. She drags
her gaze along it like a scalpel.

"Morgan didn't— This is the first time I'm hearing about Donor
Connection or whatever," she says—and I feel the sting of that, prick-
ing my exposed skin. "He said he met you in a café."

"We're two different people," I reiterate. "The Rosie he met in the
café and the Rosie he talked to online."

"But you both have pink hair? Do you realize how crazy that
sounds?"

I inhale slowly. "Like I said, the detective thinks the other Rosie
was impersonating me."

"Why would she do that?"

"I honestly don't know. I don't understand why I'm a part of this.
I was only talking to the cops in the first place because I was the one
who called 911 about Morgan, but then suddenly—"

"Wait. *You* were the one who found him?"

"Oh. I— Yeah, but—"

"Let me get this straight. Morgan was dating someone named
Rosie, and then *Rosie*"—she points at me—"called the cops to tell
them he was dead. And now you're telling me that *Rosie*"—she jabs her
finger again—"is also Daphne's heart recipient. Which is something
Morgan never mentioned."

"I did find his body," I say, and I explain that, too: Morgan's invitation to meet, the open front door, Sickle slipping out. I even pull
up the sleeve of my jacket to show her the scratches from Sickle's

claws—realizing too late that she might see them how the cops do: scratches from Morgan, maybe, as he defended himself from a knife.

But her expression actually changes at that—not screwing tighter with distrust, but loosening. She holds out her own forearm, where there are scratches that look just like mine.

"My fiancée and I are adopting the cat," she says. "I've known that thing its whole life, but it still acts like I'm a stranger."

I smile a little, in solidarity.

"There are two different Rosies," I tell her for the fourth time. "Before that night, I'd never stepped foot in Morgan's house—and I definitely didn't go on dates with him. Look, I can show you our DonorConnect messages. To prove I knew him only through that."

I pull up the thread, thrust it toward her a little too close. She steps back, taking the phone from me, squinting at the screen. I watch her skim, scroll, then slow her pace. After a couple minutes, her eyes tick from the phone to my face and back to the phone.

"He never mentioned he was talking to the person with Daphne's heart," she tells me again, and this time, she's the one who seems stung.

You know all my secrets, he told her that day I saw them in Sweet Bean—but I guess he kept me as one.

"The cops checked my phone against the one Morgan had for Rosie. It's not the same number. I never spoke to him on the phone. I never even spoke to him in person. That's what I was on my way to do that night. I actually . . . I wanted to confront him."

It's the wrong word to use. Blair's head snaps up from my phone, her gaze pointed again.

"Confront him about what?"

Somebody's laughter cuts between us, a reminder we're not alone.

I lower my voice. "I recently read some of Daphne's work, and he . . . It seemed like they had kind of a volatile relationship? That he stole parts of her past and used them in his books?"

Blair scoffs.

"What?" I ask. "Is that not true?"

"It's one truth. But writers do that all the time. It's called inspiration."

"Daphne called it an invasion." I remember that phrase from one of her books: *What you call inspiration feels like invasion.* "In her poetry, she said it was theft."

"Yeah, well. Daphne said a lot of things."

"What does that mean?"

Blair huffs out a frustrated sigh, hand lurching forward to return my phone. "Daphne was . . . not well. She went through a lot as a kid, so half the time, she pushed all her anger and grief and fears of abandonment onto Morgan and took it out on him. The other half, she'd just trauma-dump. Like he was her therapist, like he was somehow meant to fix it. So when he wrote about it, he was just trying to turn her story into something that *ends*—because it never ended for Daphne. Which means it never ended for him."

There's a name for what Blair's talking about, a term I recall from a psych class I took in college: secondhand trauma. It means that Daphne's past rubbed off on Morgan, that in hearing what happened to her, he felt the effects of it himself. Felt, in a way, like it had happened to him. And if that's true, he might have seen it not as stealing Daphne's story but as making sense of his own.

"But," I say, "he made it sound like Daphne only lashed out at him once she saw her past in his work. It seems like *he* triggered *her*, more than the other way around. And in Daphne's poems, she made him seem . . . hungry for her trauma. Like it fed him as a writer."

Blair shrugs. "They both had their own perspectives. I'm just telling you what he told me."

I'm tempted to push it, ask more about Daphne and Morgan, but as much as their marriage remains a mystery to me, it's not a mystery I'm meant to solve anymore. Not when there's another that's much more urgent. More threatening.

"So, the woman Morgan was seeing," I start. "The cops said she was at his house the night Morgan died. They also said he was drafting an email to a friend, describing what happened between them, presumably after the woman left, but—"

"He was?" The question shoots out of Blair, her eyes wide with longing, desperation. My shoulders sag, only now seeing how sad it is: she never got to read the final message her best friend meant to leave her. Didn't even know it existed until now.

"Um, yeah." I keep my voice soft. "But the draft, it—he never finished it. So, what if she came back? The other Rosie. Because the detective made it sound like she and Morgan argued about something, and then the next thing anyone knows, he's dead."

I give Blair a moment, watch it sink in. Her gaze drops to the ground, her cheek hollowing as she bites the inside of it. She shakes her head, exhales an angry, airy laugh, and when someone on the lawn shrieks to their friend, "It's so good to see you," it feels like they're interrupting a funeral.

"Jesus," Blair says, before looking back at me. "And so—what? You think this"—she pops up air quotes—"'other Rosie' is framing you or something?"

"I don't know. Maybe. All I know for sure is what I've learned from the detective: there's someone out there who dyed their hair the same color as mine and used *my* name with Morgan, all while I was writing to him online. And there's a witness who says the pink-haired woman she saw with Morgan is *not* me."

Blair straightens at that. Scans me up and down. "What else have the police told you? Because they're not telling me shit."

I try to think of something I haven't already shared. "The phone the woman used with Morgan was a burner."

Blair scuffs out a sound—half laugh, half groan. "Of course it was. I told him from the start that something seemed off about her. That she was a walking red flag. And now . . ." She bites her lip, shakes her head again. She doesn't need to say what *now* is. *Now* is this gathering. *Now* is our bloodshot eyes.

"So you believe me?" I ask, noting the pronouns she used: *her* instead of *you*. "You believe there's another Rosie?"

She appraises me awhile, lip still caught between her teeth. "Fuck it," she finally says. "Maybe? I don't know. But I need to know what happened to Morgan, and if you *are* telling the truth, you might be the only one who can identify the woman he was seeing. Morgan didn't even know the most basic details, like her last name or where she worked. And if she really was impersonating you"—there's a sarcastic edge to *impersonating*, like she can't believe she's entertaining the theory—"then she's got to be someone you know, right?"

I'm slow to nod, holding myself stiff to suppress a shiver.

"So here." Blair pulls her phone from her back pocket, swipes and taps at the screen before handing it over. "Those three emails at the top of the folder are the only ones where he mentions Rosie. We never got a chance to talk about her in person."

I stare at the screen. "You're letting me read your emails?"

Blair waves an impatient hand. "This is what you want, too, right? To find out who she is?"

It is. But it's terrifying, too. I'm on the verge of learning about the woman who already knows so much about me.

My palm trembles beneath the phone, but I grip it tight to steady myself. Taking a breath, I prepare to dive in—just as a group of women burst into laughter a few feet away.

"Wait." Blair snatches back the phone, her nails scraping me in the process. Her eyes, slitted and suspicious, sweep the crowd. "I hate these people. And I don't want them to overhear anything they could gossip about later. We should do this somewhere else."

"Oh—right," I say. "That makes sense." I picture us sitting at Sweet

Bean instead—there'd be something eerie yet strangely right about reading the emails in the place where Morgan met Other Rosie—but the café is usually closed by now.

I scan the street, thinking of other options, then suck in a breath.

A head of pink hair peers at me from a parked car.

"What?" Blair says.

I squint into the distance to watch the head move. Only it's not a head anymore. It's just the sleeve of someone's coat. As someone jumps in the passenger seat, the driver's pink elbow peeks out the open window.

"What?" Blair repeats, sharper this time.

"Nothing," I say. "Sorry. Just—follow me. I know where we can go."

CHAPTER FOURTEEN

"You brought me to your *house*?"

Blair gapes at it like it's haunted, like gauzy figures stand at the windows, watching us through the glass.

"I live in the apartment over the garage. The house is my parents'."

She spins toward me, and the look she gives me is uncomfortably familiar. One that means I've gone too far.

"You wanted privacy," I explain.

"I meant like a coffee shop or something. Not your *house*."

She emphasizes the word like it's the most ludicrous thing in the world, welcoming a stranger into your home. But she doesn't feel like a stranger to me—and not just because I've combed through her photos, clocked all the ways she's changed since she first met Morgan in college. There's something in Blair I recognize: the kind of pain that gnaws at you like an infestation, weakening you from the inside out. She's trying to hide it—stiff posture, clenched hands—but I know she feels close to crumbling.

"A coffee shop wouldn't be private," I say, "and my house was in walking distance."

She glares at me through the darkness, shifting her weight as if she might bolt. "For all I know, you could be the one who killed Morgan."

I frown at her. I thought we'd moved beyond that. "Do you really think I killed him?"

"I don't know, I met you like ten minutes ago."

"But you asked me to read his emails," I point out.

"Yeah, maybe this was a bad idea."

I draw closer to her. "No, I think it was the right one. I think we're each other's only lead."

She bites the inside of her cheek, head slightly shaking as her eyes veer up the street.

"Please." I touch her arm. She looks at my hand before dragging her gaze to mine. I let go. Take a step back. "The police may have told me more than you, but they're not telling me much. Nothing makes sense, I've barely slept in days, and I have to know who this other Rosie is. I have to know why she did this. To Morgan *and* to me. I have to—"

I stop as pressure builds in my chest, like a sob is stuck there. I rest my palm against my heart, focus on breathing until the strain subsides.

As Blair watches me, her expression inches from wary to almost worried. "You okay there?"

I nod, measuring another inhale.

Blair nods gently in return, then scrapes out a chuckle—dry and a little bitter. "You know, you're the first person I've seen in the last few days who looks as shitty as I feel." She shifts from foot to foot again, bouncing on her knees. "Fine, let's go inside. I had a giant latte before I left and I've had to pee for like an hour." She marches up the driveway, and I stutter into step behind her. "And while I'm doing that," she adds over her shoulder, "you can start reading the emails so we can nail this pink-haired bitch."

Once inside, I point Blair to the bathroom. She heads there after handing me her phone, open to the messages, and I drop into a chair at the table, exhaustion hitting me all at once.

Beside the fruit bowl, there's an orange prescription bottle I don't remember leaving there. Reading the label, I see it's not one of mine; it's Mom's. The sleeping pills she offered to let me borrow last night, accompanied by a note: *To help you feel better.*

But sleep is just an opportunity to dream. And right now I'd only have nightmares.

Pushing the bottle out of the way, I turn to the emails on Blair's phone—and right away, Morgan's words knock me sideways. It's like reading an alternate version of my life, one where I did orchestrate that café meet-cute I fantasized about. When Morgan describes the exact shade of Other Rosie's hair, I can't believe how similar it is to my own: *like a cherry blossom.* She even bought a Danish, *my* go-to order at Sweet Bean. Then again, that's most people's go-to order, the pastries so popular they've been featured on the Food Network. Still. It feels like another violation.

But as I read on, the feeling branches into other, more complicated ones. I'm torn between being unnerved by this woman—and strangely drawn to her. I enjoy her sense of humor, her quirky little quips. If I didn't know any better, I might actually laugh at her banter with Morgan. Instead, I feel a jab of jealousy at how quickly she captivated him.

Then I reach the point in the email when Morgan mentions Daphne, and any envy or endearment instantly dissolves.

I've always known it's a risky thing, letting women get too close to me. You're the only one, Blair, who knows the real me and somehow hasn't suffered for loving me.

I continue reading and struggle to balance it all: details I'm collecting about Other Rosie—she likes *Friends*, same as me, but same as millions of other people, too—and my mind's furious whirring at Morgan's more unsettling lines. I think she sensed something in me. The darkness like a storm beneath my skin.

"Find anything?" Blair asks, reentering the room as I finish the first email.

I shake my head, gesture for her to sit. Then I dive into the second message, where Rosie leaves a note for Morgan in his mailbox, setting up a date at the park. Morgan watches her there before he approaches, hoping she'll worry he stood her up. They joke about birdbaths. Bugbaths. Morgan says he's—

My breath snags in the back of my throat.

I've been preoccupied with ideas for my next book. I think it'll be about a woman who had a heart transplant. She connects with the husband of her heart donor

I look up midsentence. "He was writing about me?"

"Apparently," Blair scoffs, and I can't tell if her irritation is directed at me or Morgan. "But he never told me you were a real person."

I slump back in my chair, the air knocked out of me.

He says in the email, I'm still waiting for the protagonist to take shape. Is that all my messages were to him—inspiration for a character? When he asked if we could meet in person, was it only so he could study me up close? See the pink, puckered skin between my breasts, then describe it in a book?

My scar aches at the thought, and as I rub it through my shirt—*my* scar, mine—I read the lines that follow, where Morgan sketches Other Rosie as a character too. Her hair. Her contradictions. He ponders what he could do with her, wonders at the darkness she's endured—the same thing that once drew him to Daphne.

I touch my knuckles to my lips, push back against a surge of nausea, but at the start of the third email, he references my story again: I think there's something there. Something with all sorts of twisted potential. I read the sentence twice, my eyes stuck on twisted. Stinging with it.

Across the table, Blair's gaze presses on me, impatient. I force myself to continue.

Morgan invites Rosie to his house, shows her his library, and even though I'm supposed to be scrutinizing her gestures for something familiar, I can't help but dwell on his references to his wife instead— each one pinpricked with guilt. He insists he's done punishing himself over her: It doesn't change what happened that night. He recalls how, at Blair's encouragement, he removed all pictures of Daphne so she'd stop accusing him from the frames. Even when Morgan kisses Rosie—something that, only minutes ago, might have felt strangely like a betrayal—he alludes to Daphne's death, thinking of Rosie's skull as something he could crush.

Dread curdles inside me as I near the end of the email. Rosie scrambles out the door, and Morgan panics that she knows something, that she's scared he hurt his wife. I shouldn't have let her leave, he says. A sentence that growls with aggression.

For the first time, I wonder: If Other Rosie did kill Morgan, is it possible she was defending herself? Possible that, had she not stabbed him, she might have been the second woman to end up dead in that house?

"So?" Blair says when I set down the phone. "Did you find anything?"

I shake my head, staring at the screen until it blurs. "Not about Rosie." I choose my next words carefully, conscious that I'm speaking to someone who loved Morgan—and knew all his secrets. "Blair, is there any way . . ." I trail off. Try again. "Do you think it's possible Morgan killed Daphne?"

Her eyes flash. "No!"

"He said he wanted to prove he can care about a woman without it ending in bloodshed."

"That doesn't—"

"He freaked out when he thought Rosie was suspicious of him.

And every time he so much as mentions Daphne, his tone sounds really guilty. He said after she died, he looked at her pictures and only saw her blaming him. What else could all of that mean—other than he did something to her?"

"It means the opposite!" Blair snaps. "It means he did nothing to her. Nothing!" She slaps one hand on the table, so hard I feel the vibration under my elbows. But just as quickly as her muscles tensed, they loosen on a sigh. "That's why he felt guilty."

With a grunt, she tilts forward, massaging her temples, eyes plastered to Mom's prescription bottle without seeming to see it.

"He was writing when she fell," Blair says. "In his office down the hall. He told me he heard some noises in the bathroom, like a giant thud, but he—he didn't pay much attention to it. He was writing," she says again.

Blair reaches for the orange bottle, absentmindedly tipping it back and forth. As Mom's pills rattle inside, it sounds like teeth chattering.

"He went to refill his water at the bathroom sink, like an hour later. That's when he found her."

I sit up straight. "An *hour*? He heard a crash in the bathroom, and instead of checking to make sure his wife wasn't hurt, he just ignored it so he could *work*?"

"You don't get it, that's just how Morgan was. Once he was in the zone or whatever, he had to keep writing. He couldn't just *stop* or he might lose those words, his train of thought. And he had deadlines, contracts, he—"

"His wife was dying on the bathroom floor," I say, and I'm surprised how steady I sound.

"He didn't *know* that, though. It never occurred to him that the crash he'd heard could mean she was hurt."

But how could it not occur to him? I hear so much as a thump in the distance and panic it's one of my parents, my mom tripping over a rake in her garden, my dad falling on the steps up to their house, his new hip blasted out of place.

"Look," Blair says. "Daphne and Morgan weren't, like, in the best place when she died. They'd been fighting a lot."

My eyes widen, prompting Blair to charge ahead: "Oh stop, I don't mean it like that. She just kept randomly getting upset with him. Especially when he wrote. Like, one time, she burst into his office, slammed his laptop shut, *while he was working*, and started yelling at him. Completely out of nowhere."

Dimly, I remember that incident from his messages. He said Daphne demanded he look at her, and when he did, he saw only a stranger.

"That doesn't sound like something that happens 'randomly.' 'Out of nowhere,'" I say, emphasizing Blair's words.

"With Daphne, it was. Although—in her defense, I'm sure it can't be easy, watching your husband sell millions of copies of his books while yours are published by some tiny press no one's heard of. And Morgan did say she was sensitive about him taking inspiration from her childhood. So I think when he was in his office for a long time, completely locked into his writing, Daphne just got—I don't know: worked up."

"Did you ever actually ask her about it, though? About why she kept getting upset?"

Blair fires off a quick, staccato laugh. "Uh, no. Daphne and I didn't talk like that. I tried to be her friend, but she always got, like, agitated around me. I don't know if it was a gender thing—like she was threatened by Morgan's best friend being a woman—or if it was just because I'd known him so long and barely blinked when he was being . . . difficult. Because he actually could be kind of a dick. But that's fine, I can be kind of a bitch. Either way, most of what I know about Daphne comes from Morgan, and he always talked about her"—she curls her fingers into air quotes—""unhinged outbursts.'"

Unhinged. A more palatable word for crazy. But no matter what Morgan told Blair, no matter how Blair defends him out of loyalty and love, if Daphne got "upset" sometimes, she had her reasons. I'm rattled enough just from Morgan thinking of me as research; I can only imagine how betrayed Daphne felt whenever he embedded her trauma in his books.

"Couldn't he have been lying?" I ask. "About what happened the night she died. From just the handful of messages I exchanged with him, I know he lied sometimes—so how do you know what he told you was the truth?"

"Because I know him," Blair says, her tone as barbed as her gaze.

"Yeah, but—"

I thought I knew him too. Not like Blair did, obviously—Morgan and I talked for only a few weeks compared to their years of friendship—but I saw him, saw our future, so clearly in my head that, for a while at least, I believed the fantasy would only be sharpened by reality, not shattered altogether. Even when I spoke to Piper, who actually knew Daphne, knew the effect that Morgan seemed to have on her, I dismissed most of what she said. But I don't think I can anymore. Which means other things she said might have also been true.

"I spoke to a close friend of Daphne's who said Daphne was scared in the days leading up to her death." There was that reviewer, too—a former student of hers who described Daphne as troubled, distracted, like she hadn't been sleeping.

"Scared?" Blair cocks her head, frowning. "I don't know about that. I guess she was . . . more upset than usual?" Her shoulders lift as they curl forward—half shrug, half wince. "But I think that was my fault, actually. There was this night when Morgan and I were supposed to go out for a drink, but he was still working when I picked him up, so for a few minutes it was just me and Daphne, standing there awkwardly, this air of hostility just . . . wafting off her, like always. So just to say *something*, just to fill up that angry silence, I was like, 'Hey, what do you think of the sequel?' And how was I supposed to know he hadn't even told her about it?"

I shake my head. "Sequel?"

"To *Someone at the Door*. He'd just signed the contract for his next book, right before Daphne died."

I reel back in my chair. It shouldn't surprise me; Morgan's debut was his most successful novel. There's been demand for a sequel ever since the film adaptation leaned into the story's loose ends. But Morgan must have known it would hurt Daphne. He must have known, in publishing and promoting his new book, the old one—with its haunted title—would be everywhere again.

"And Daphne was not happy about it," Blair says. "She marched up to Morgan's office and I could hear her yelling at him. Crying. Demanding to know what the book was about, what other"—Blair tosses up air quotes again—"'scraps of my life' he'd be using in it." She crosses her arms, scoffing. "It wasn't going to have anything to do with her. But she freaked out all the same. Barely gave Morgan a moment of peace."

And still, he kept writing it. Even on the night she fell, the night she died, he kept writing a story he knew Daphne feared.

"So, are you done," Blair says, "acting like my best friend could be a murderer?"

I manage a nod. Swallow saliva that's turned acidic. Morgan wasn't a murderer, no. But he wasn't the man I'd pinned my hopes to either.

"Great." Blair leans forward, sliding her phone from my side of the table to hers. "Now: What about Rosie? Did you recognize anything?"

"No. Sorry."

Blair groans, leaning back in her chair. "Well, it has to be someone you know. It's usually the people closest to us who hurt us the most."

I nod, because I'm still seeing Daphne on the bathroom floor, her skull cracked from a fall Morgan heard—and didn't give a second thought. I see the rings on their fingers, in sickness and health. I see how close I came to falling for a man who would break a vow like that.

And if that's how he treated his own wife, I can't help but wonder who else he's hurt with his behavior. And who would want to hurt him in return.

"So is there anyone who has, like, a grudge against you?" Blair asks. "Someone who would *want* to frame you?"

I shake my head, the line between Morgan and his killer becoming even more difficult to see. Because it's one thing for someone to want revenge on Morgan. But why would they make me a part of it?

"Not that I can think of. And the only ones who even know about my connection to Morgan are my best friend and DonorConnect itself."

"Okay, so maybe it was your friend."

I almost laugh. "It's not."

"Maybe she pretended to be you for some reason and—"

Now I actually do laugh, the sound so sudden it cuts Blair off. Even if Nina had the inexplicable desire to throw on a pink wig, date Morgan Thorne, cheat on her husband, whom she loves more than anyone—when would she have had the time? Her life is a closed circuit of hospital, home, and the occasional thrift store.

The thought squeezes my laughter into a nearly hysterical pitch—until it stops as quickly as it started. I slump back, overwhelmed with weariness.

"No," I say. End of subject. I hold Blair's gaze, determined not to break it. Her brow wrinkles as we watch each other, and after a few moments, she rolls her eyes, stands from the table, and pockets her phone.

"Okay then, I guess we're done here." But instead of turning for the door, Blair leans forward, tapping the note Mom left me: *To help you feel better.* "What is it, Valium?" She nudges her chin toward the prescription bottle, its label facing me.

"Sedatives. My mom wants me to take them. I've been struggling to sleep since . . ."

The phrase dangles for only a second before Blair nods. "Yeah. Me too," she says. "Must be nice, though, having a mom who actually cares."

I look away, remembering Morgan's comments about Blair's mother, that day I eavesdropped at Sweet Bean. Even in the emails I just read, he said her mom intentionally sabotaged Blair's appointment for her wedding dress.

"Sorry," Blair adds. "That's bitter of me. I just—haven't received so much as an acknowledgment from my parents about Morgan. I left them a voicemail, but—" She shrugs.

"I'm so sorry," I say. "That's a terrible thing for family to do."

She chews her lip, staring at Mom's note. "Morgan was my real family." She blinks hard and fast. "I'll never stop fighting for him."

When she opens the door to leave, muggy air rushes at me, almost stifling. Blair pauses in the threshold, meeting my eyes again—only this time, there's a warning in hers.

"You should probably be careful," she says. "If this Rosie woman really did pretend to be you *and* killed Morgan? There's not much else she won't do."

CHAPTER FIFTEEN

I've returned to work on only three hours of sleep—more than I got the night before, but nowhere close to enough. I didn't take Mom's pills. I thought about it, even went so far as to dump one into my palm, triple-check they were safe with my meds. But in the end, it didn't feel worth the risk, adding another drug to my system, synthetically slowing my heart.

It was two in the morning when I realized my mistake. It wasn't just Morgan's body I couldn't stop seeing anymore; it was Daphne's, too, splayed on the bathroom floor, the white marble tiles rimmed with red like bloody teeth. I even heard her whisper. *Morgan. Help me. Please.*

More than anything, that's what kept me awake: the voice and words I imagined so easily. They resonated somewhere deep, a vibration in my bones. I knew it wasn't the same as what I went through; Brad's neglect never endangered my life. Still, I couldn't help but hear myself in those pleas, Daphne and me calling to men who promised forever—then left our pain unanswered.

"I already gave you my card," someone says to me.

I look at her—twentysomething, polite smile. My hand is

outstretched for payment, but the screen says her card has been approved. It's on the counter, beneath my other palm.

"Sorry." I pass it back to her, then print out the receipt that itemizes the customizations on her gown. I had to bite my tongue when she rattled them off to me earlier, too tempted to rein in her excitement: *If you need to work so hard to make it perfect, it's really not the one.* Then again, my gown was flawless in fit and style, and it might hang, unworn, in my closet forever.

After the bride leaves, I head for the door myself. I was smart enough last night to build a pick-me-up into this day. As soon as Blair left, I texted Nina, asking if she'd be free for lunch. She was slow to write back, which kept me staring at my phone, bargaining with it to chirp out her reply, but when it finally came, she proposed a Sweet Bean date, only steps from the store, so we could "maximize our time together." Seeing that text settled something in me that had felt unsteady since Nina first picked me up from the police station. She not only wants to spend time with me again; she wants to spend as much as we can.

I practically skip to Sweet Bean, exhaustion be damned. I'm reaching for the door handle when something compels me to stop midstep. Someone's gaze leeches onto me. I feel the bite of it. The slow, persistent suck.

I don't have time to look around before arms grab me from behind.

"Hey."

I relax at the sound of Nina's voice, then spin around to hug her. Her grip is as tight as mine, and I'm sure now: I only imagined the distance between us. Maybe even misread her expression in her car the other night.

"Danishes for lunch?" she asks as we part.

I hiss in a breath through my teeth. "I think I'm going to be strong and go with a sandwich. I need more than sugar if I'm going to make it through the day."

"Wow, such an adult. I pick sugar. They better have a raspberry left."

As we wait in line to order, I listen to Nina gush about an antique bench she just bought, comforted by the giddy rhythm of her voice. But it's only a minute before my eyes drift toward the table where I first saw Morgan. It isn't difficult to place him there, or to picture the pink-haired woman he collided with. I see the back of her head, bobbing with laughter, see Morgan smiling across the table, his canines sharper than they look in pictures. The sky dims, rain taps against the window, and the barista approaches the couple to tell them they're closing. They stand up, Morgan gestures for Rosie to go first, and as she turns, I hold my breath.

But her face is a blur of skin and pastel hair and Nina's nudging me forward in line.

Once we collect our order, we carry it to a table outside. We take synchronized bites of our food, mirror images of each other, and I smile at how normal this is. How safe. But as soon as Nina puts her Danish down, clapping crumbs off her hands, her demeanor changes.

"So," she says, back stiff, shoulders square.

She grills me about the last few days and what I've heard from the police. I hold back a sigh. I'd hoped our lunch could distract me from Morgan, provide a reprieve as restful as a nap, but it was unrealistic to think that Nina wouldn't question me, that she didn't agree to these plans just so we could talk it out in person.

I fill her in on all of it, and the longer I speak, the tighter Nina squints. Her eyes widen only once—"He just kept *writing*, Neens, he never even checked on her, and Daphne was in there dying"—but they shrink again when I tell her Morgan's emails turned up nothing useful on Other Rosie.

"So you agree with that detective?" she asks. "You think someone's impersonating you?"

"They have to be, right? Otherwise, it's too big a coincidence."

"But"—Nina rips off a piece of Danish—"why would anyone *want* to be you?"

I fall back as if pushed, struck by the implication. "Okay, ouch."

"No—" She waves the pastry in the air like she's erasing her question. "I didn't mean it like that. I meant: What motive would someone have? Why do you think they'd want to frame you?"

I shake my head, still dazed by her original wording. "I don't know."

She watches me while she chews. "What about a lawyer? Did you find one?"

I'm saved from answering when someone says my name. Over Nina's shoulder I find two women approaching. One is tall with honey-colored curls; the other is running her fingers through her white-blond hair, as if to neaten it just for me.

"Hey!" I greet Piper and Edith, but my gaze is fixed on the latter. She looks a lot better than the night I met her in Just Say Yes. Her face is unmarred by tears, her mascara unsmudged, but there's still something heavy in her features, her smile weighed down by weeks of grief.

"Looks like you had the same idea as us," Piper says, gesturing to Sweet Bean before homing in on Nina. "Hey! Good to see you! It's been years, right? If you don't count Facebook. How are you doing?"

"Good, how are you?" Nina's polite but impersonal tone tells me that she, too, has few memories of Piper from high school. I wonder if she remembers she's one of the girls I caught mocking Winnie, the freshman Nina and I befriended soon after.

Piper points at Nina's half-eaten Danish. "I'll be great if you tell me you didn't get the last raspberry."

"You're in luck. They just put out a fresh batch."

"Oh thank god. I'm hoping for almond, too."

I turn my focus back to Edith. "I'm sorry I've been MIA."

It's not just the text I never answered: Morgan Thorne is DEAD?! Even before that, I'd already failed her. I'd promised to take Edith out, to help her through her heartbreak, but I didn't follow through, too consumed by Morgan and Daphne and what I'd hoped would be the end to heartbreak of my own.

"How are you holding up?" I ask.

Edith nods, attempting optimism, before succumbing to a shrug. "I'm okay." Her eyes shift toward Nina, who's watching me expectantly.

"Oh, sorry. This is my best friend, Nina. Nina, this is Edith."

They exchange hellos and nice-to-meet-yous, but Nina still seems to be waiting for something. "I'm sorry, did you go to our high school too?" she asks after a moment.

"No, I work with Piper." Edith scratches her neck, the skin instantly reddening beneath her nails. "And I was a customer of Rosie's."

"Oh, are you getting married?" Nina asks brightly.

I stiffen, opening my mouth to deflect, to save Edith from the agony of that question, but she answers right away.

"Uh, no. Not anymore. My fian— My ex-fiancé called it off, actually. And Rosie told me she'd been through the same thing. So we've been texting."

Nina whips back toward me, her gaze like a slap. "Did she now," she mutters.

I sip my water as heat rushes to my face. It takes me too long to swallow. "Yeah, I told her about my wedding gown. The one I never got to use." I try to keep my expression neutral, willing Nina to play along with the assumption Edith made the night we met.

Nina looks at me a beat longer, letting me sweat, before glancing up at Edith. "I'm really sorry. That must be so hard."

"Thanks," Edith says, fidgeting with the strap of the tote bag that bulges at her side.

"You're not the friend who was seeing Morgan Thorne, are you?" Piper asks Nina.

My cheeks flare hotter as Nina jerks back in surprise. "Me? No.

Rosie's been . . ." She trails off, her attention steering back to me. "I'm confused."

"Oh. Sorry," Piper says, but from the way she drags her gaze between the two of us, I can tell she didn't miss it: Nina's emphasis on my name. "Rosie told Edith she had a friend who'd just started dating Morgan Thorne."

"Before he died," Edith adds. "Oh—obviously." She shakes her head at the unnecessary clarification, balling her fists into the sleeves of her jacket, an almost childlike gesture of self-consciousness. "You wanted to, like, vet him for her, right?" she asks me before addressing Nina again. "And Piper was close with his wife, so—"

"So I agreed to speak with Rosie," Piper cuts in, and now her tone is sharp. She studies the disappointed slouch in Nina's shoulders, the nearly visible tsk on her tongue. Then she narrows her eyes at me, clearly knowing I lied.

The realization rolls through Edith, too. "Wait. Were *you* the one seeing Morgan?"

I bite my lip. "Not exactly. I did lie about the friend thing, though. I'm sorry."

Edith looks at me as if through a film of fog, unsure what she's seeing. "'Not exactly'?" she repeats. "I don't get it. Why would you pretend it was your friend?"

"That's a great question," Piper chimes in. "You could have easily said, 'Hey, I just started seeing Morgan Thorne and I'm curious what—'"

"No, I wasn't seeing him. I never even met him."

Piper's mouth is frozen around the word where I cut her off. "O-kaaaay," she finally says. "You understand that's worse, right? You met with me under false pretenses because you, what, wanted information on him? That's really creepy. Especially considering he turned up dead."

"Piper," Edith says. "That has nothing to do with this."

"We don't know that." She spins on her heel toward Sweet Bean's door, hooking her arm around Edith's elbow. "Come on, let's go."

Before they disappear inside, Edith slips a glance at me, her face still crimped with confusion—and something like betrayal. Now that she knows I deceived her, I won't be surprised if she never texts me again.

It shouldn't hit me as hard as it does. I barely knew Edith in the first place. But she trusted me with her deepest pain, believing I lived it, too, and I took advantage of that connection—just to get closer to Morgan. Guilt rocks through my stomach, making me push my plate away.

"Why do you keep lying?" Nina asks.

I stare at my unfinished sandwich. "I don't know."

But that's not true. It all boiled down to the same instinct—trying not to seem crazy. That's why I lied to Nina, letting her think I'd stopped messaging Morgan, stopped obsessing over his Instagram, his house. It's why I lied to Edith, too, letting her think my fiancé broke off our engagement, instead of admitting I once bought a dress without even having a fiancé in the first place. And if I'd told Edith, told Piper, the real reason I went digging for info on Morgan, I can only imagine the calculations they would have made, the conversation they might have had with each other: *This Rosie woman sounds like a stalker.*

Still, if I was so afraid of people hearing the truth and believing I'm crazy, doesn't that mean I believed it too?

My skin prickles, and I feel it again, the pins-and-needles aware-ness of being watched. But whether it's Nina studying me from across the table, or Piper and Edith from inside, I don't know. My gaze is stuck to my plate. I can't so much as glance at my best friend. She knows me too well, reads me too easily, and her eyes might as well be mirrors the way they reflect it all back: my questionable actions, my unhinged decisions. I can't see her without seeing all of me.

"You know, part of me isn't even sorry Morgan's dead," she

says—and that forces my attention. Nina finishes her Danish in a bite so big I'm worried she'll choke on it. She chews for a long time, her sentence lingering like smoke. Finally, she swallows it down. "I know you're not supposed to say things like that. But it just scares me, thinking of what might have happened, had you kept going down that path with him."

"You mean, like—what he would have done to me?"

I see the danger now, clear as headlights on a midnight road. Morgan made space for my darkness, invited it in. But he did that with Daphne, too—only to use it against her in the end. A woman's pain just research for him.

"No," Nina says. "I'm scared of what *you* would have done."

I tilt my head. "Me?" But before she can elaborate, I notice a police cruiser winding through cars in the parking lot. Nina spots it, too, and we track its movement to a space in front of Just Say Yes. When Jackson Dean steps out, I stand so quickly I rattle the table, toppling our waters.

"Rosie!" Nina says, diving for napkins.

"Sorry." I dump my own onto the pile, but I don't stick around to help. I stumble through an apology, tell her I'll text her later, because right now, Jackson is walking into the store and there's only one person I can imagine he's here to see.

CHAPTER SIXTEEN

I'm steps behind the detective, but he's already talking to Marilee by the time I rush into the salon.

"Oh, she's right here, actually," Marilee says, and Jackson turns to me with a nod of acknowledgment.

"We can speak in my office," I blurt, louder than I intended. A bride and her friends pause at a rack of dresses to look me up and down. Jackson cocks an eyebrow, while Marilee stares at the badge on his belt, no doubt remembering the message she passed to me from the police just days ago.

"That would be great," Jackson finally says, moving aside so I can lead him to the back.

Questions cluster as I walk. Why is he here? Why didn't he call first, request I come to the station? His steps behind me are soft and unhurried, but is there something urgent about this visit?

I open the door to my office. The space is small enough when it's just me in here, but as soon as Jackson joins me, the walls close in, the boxes stacked against them threatening to crush us. I push in my chair as far as it will go, trying to make more space, but we're still barely three feet apart.

"Nice," Jackson says, chuckling at the wall behind my desk, where there are printouts of baby chicks wearing cupcake liners as skirts. "I saw that online once. This one is *not* having it." He points to the chick I always think of as Grumps, his ornery face puffing out above the skirt. "This one, though." His finger moves to my favorite, the chick who looks proud, like she's modeling the new spring collection of baking cups. "She's the star."

"Yep," I say, suspicious of his warmth. He must be trying to get my guard down, or maybe he's savoring the moment before he shares some unnerving update. Maybe Other Rosie did more to ensure I took the fall. Maybe she planted something of mine at the scene, made sure the evidence was so stacked against me, the cops would have no choice but—

"The results on the hair came back. It's not a match."

I blink at him, silent. My insomnia must have gummed up my brain, because I have to replay his words before I process what they mean.

"I'm not a suspect anymore?"

"I didn't say that. I just wanted to let you know and follow up with—"

"But you don't think I'm guilty. Otherwise, you would have called me to the station, right? And something else is—" I focus on his expression. "You're looking at me differently."

It's too forward. Too much. But it's also the truth. His eyes are the gentlest I've seen them—aimed at me, but not sharpened.

And that's how it finally clicks, the reason I've had that vague, intermittent feeling I know him.

"You're Winnie's brother, aren't you?"

It helps that I just saw Piper, whose presence sparked thoughts of the girl, but now that I've made the connection, it's more than Jackson's eyes that remind me of her. It's the straight slope of his nose, his thick brows. And god, his last name. Of course—Winnie *Dean*.

Jackson's face opens with surprise. "You know my sister?"

"I was a senior when she was a freshman, but I hung out with her that year."

I gave her rides home when it was raining. Chatted with her at school dances. It wasn't charity; I genuinely liked her. She was funny, baked the best cookies, and made impeccable playlists.

"*You're* the senior? Wow. Okay." Jackson shakes his head as if dazed. "I was in college when Winnie started high school, but whenever we talked, she always brought you up. I'm pretty sure she referred to you exclusively as 'the senior who thinks I'm cool.'"

I laugh. "She was a sweet kid. How's she doing?"

"Really good. She's in Boston, training to be a vet tech." He searches my face before he continues. "You know, I've always been glad she had 'the senior' during that time. She became a new person after meeting you. More comfortable in her own skin. So: thanks for that."

"You don't have to thank me. She was my friend."

He rocks on his heels, returning his gaze to the wall. Then he clears his throat, as if uncomfortable with the turn our conversation has taken. Still, maybe it will help; maybe my connection to Winnie, his gratitude that I took her under my wing, will sweep away any remaining suspicions he has of me.

"So whose hair is it?" I ask. "Now that you know for sure it's not mine."

"We're working on that."

"But this corroborates your theory, right? That someone was trying to look like me?" Nina's voice zips through my head: *Why would anyone* want *to be you?*

"We're investigating all possibilities," Jackson says, back to evasive, professional. "But in the meantime, it would be helpful if you could give me the names of everyone who knew you were corresponding with Mr. Thorne."

"Nobody. Just DonorConnect. My friend knew we'd exchanged a couple messages, but that's it."

Jackson pulls a notebook and pen from his pocket, opens to a blank page. "What's your friend's name?"

"Nina Burke. But it's not her. Her hair isn't pink, for one thing, and—"

Jackson raises his pen like a finger to stop me. "It appears the hair was colored with the kind of dye that washes out easily. Likely with a single shampoo."

I frown at that. "So you think this person was just . . . dyeing her hair every time she saw Morgan?"

"It's possible."

The effort that would take. It only reiterates Other Rosie's commitment to fooling Morgan. To being me. I shake my head at the absurdity.

"Okay, well, one: Nina doesn't have time for that, or for living a double life. She's an ER nurse who mostly works nights. Not to mention she's happily married. And two: she'd have absolutely no motive to infiltrate Morgan's life and pretend to be me. She was the one who wanted me to *stop* talking to Morgan."

Jackson arches a brow, intrigued instead of deterred. "And why is that?"

I press my lips together. This is the second time in twenty-four hours I've had to argue against Nina being behind this, but Jackson and Blair don't know how long she's loved me. Or how well. At her wedding, she dubbed me her Sister of Honor, "because you've always been family." When Brad left me crumpled on my bedroom floor in my wedding dress, Nina smoothed my hair, swept my tears off my cheeks, without even asking why I had the dress in the first place.

"She thought it was weird," I tell Jackson, "for me to start a relationship with the husband of my heart donor. She didn't want me to get invested in such a complicated situation because she knows I get . . . attached to people." I hear my mistake right away, even before Jackson glances up from his notepad. "I tend to throw myself into relationships headfirst. Or, heartfirst, I guess. I kind of leave my head behind." I laugh, but the sound is awkward, rattling like a cough in my throat.

"What does that mean, exactly? To leave your head behind. You do things without thinking, or"—Jackson twirls his pen in thought—"you do things without remembering?"

An ache pulses in my forehead, like the edge of a hangover. "I just mean: love isn't logical."

"And you were in love with Mr. Thorne?"

"No, I'm saying Nina knows how it was for me with men in the past, so she—"

"And how was it? With men in the past."

Even though he interrupted me, his tone is not forceful or unkind. He sounds almost casual, like someone on a date inviting me to share my romantic history.

"I just . . . go all in with the person," I tell him. "And I usually end up hurt."

Jackson's pen races. "Is that what you'd say your list was? Going all in?"

I frown until I register the reference: my Notes app filled with details about Morgan.

"No, I— I hadn't done that before."

"I see you had a harassment prevention order filed against you." His eyes rise from the page. Latch onto my face. "Can you tell me about that?"

Shame rushes through me, hot and prickly. Rich Silverstein assured me the order wouldn't appear on my criminal record, but I should have expected a cop to find it with minimal effort. How much has Jackson seen? The transcript of voicemails and texts? The photos of blood on Brad's steps? Does he know that, even when Brad wouldn't speak to me, I told him in an email I'd love him forever?

"It— That was— It was a bad time for me, a-and—" I stammer, then stop. I've already shared too much. Ever since Jackson entered the store, I've handled this completely wrong. "I don't think I should discuss that without my lawyer present."

Jackson nods, unsurprised, then taps his notepad. "This friend of yours. Nina Burke. That's Burke with an *e*?"

"Yes," I answer, before realizing why he asked. He's going to question her about me. Because even though his sister liked me, even though my hair and phone number don't match what they've connected to Morgan, there's a court order in my past, a list of facts in my apps, that keep him from crossing me off his list. I set my hand on my desk, weary and woozy, and I wonder who else he'll talk to. If Brad's contact info is somewhere in his notebook.

The ache in my head knocks harder. Exhaustion presses on me, my eyelids like iron.

"One last thing," Jackson says. "Did you know that Mr. Thorne was working on a book about a woman who had a heart transplant?"

I wince like he's pressed on a bruise, and I see him catch that this isn't news to me. Still, I don't understand how it's relevant. Unless he thinks it could somehow be motive? That I'm so unstable I'd murder a man for using me as research?

"I didn't find out until yesterday," I say, "when Blair Hawkins showed me some of Morgan's emails."

Jackson stops writing in his notebook to look at me. "You've been engaging with Mr. Thorne's friends?"

He says *engaging* like it's on par with stalking.

"No. Just Blair. And she approached me. She thought I was the Rosie from Morgan's emails, and I explained the situation. We're trying to figure out who that woman is. Because we both think she killed him."

Jackson's stare pierces through me, pensive and persistent, until he slaps his notepad shut.

"Thanks for your help," he says. "That's it for now."

The abruptness unmoors me for a second. "Uh, okay," I say as he opens my office door. I scurry behind him, conscious of the eyes that follow us to the front of the store—Marilee's among them. I'm not sure how I'll explain why the police keep contacting me.

"Will you update me?" I ask, trailing him outside, straight into sunshine I have to squint against. "If you find a match to the hair?"

He opens the door to his cruiser, then sets one hand on his hip, the other on the roof. "I'll be in touch as needed. But, Rosie," he says, and it's the first time he's done that: ditched the "Ms. Lachlan" without my prompting. "I'd advise you to watch out for yourself. It's appearing more and more likely that someone went to great lengths to pretend to be you."

It feels like whiplash, the jolt from his scrutinizing questions to something more like concern. His warning even echoes Blair's from last night.

"So you think she's a threat," I say. "The woman Morgan dated. Which means you agree she could have killed him, right?"

Jackson resumes his stare, and in this light, it's hard to tell if it's just the sun that has him narrowing his eyes again.

"I don't know what happened to Mr. Thorne," he says. "But I'm doing everything I can to find out."

He taps the hood of his car in goodbye, and just like earlier, I become aware of someone's gaze. This time, I catch the culprit. Two culprits, actually. Piper and Edith have exited Sweet Bean and are standing on the sidewalk, taking stock of the scene: me speaking with a detective; him squinting at me, emphasizing his effort to catch Morgan's killer.

As Jackson settles into his cruiser, Piper pitches her lips toward Edith's ear. "Oh my god, see?" she says, not bothering to lower her voice. "Even the cops think she's involved."

I miss Edith's response beneath the rumble of Jackson's engine, but as Piper steers her into the parking lot, Edith peers back at me over her shoulder, same as she did when entering Sweet Bean—only now, she doesn't look at me like I've betrayed her.

She looks at me like I'm dangerous.

CHAPTER SEVENTEEN

I wake the next day in my wedding dress.

I'm lying on my stomach, and before I even open my eyes, I become conscious of beads biting into my fingers. I adjust my legs and there's a swish that sounds like dressing rooms, bridal risers. I scratch my side and my nails catch on lace.

I roll over, jerk upright. Take stock of myself. I'm on top of my bed, the fabric my only blanket. If someone were to walk in right now, they'd walk right out, leave me in this gown for the second time—because why am I in it? Why am I dressed for a wedding to no one?

The night comes back to me in slivers: my reflection in the mirror, trying not to see Brad's face behind me, the face that kept me awake long before Morgan's or Daphne's ever did; my arms twisted around my back, grappling with the buttons before I gave up; my complexion so pale it was difficult to tell where the gown ended and my skin began.

Before that, though. What compelled me to step into the dress at all?

I return to the moment I got home last night, texting Nina one-handed as I struggled with my key in the lock. I warned her Jackson might approach her, might have questions, but shared the good news, too: my hair was not a match for the ones in Morgan's hand. As I walked inside, willing her to respond, my phone was the only light leading me on. Then there was the glow of the open refrigerator as I reached for the orange juice, mixed it with my meds, and swallowed the bitter mouthful.

I stayed like that, in semidarkness, letting my phone point me to my bedroom, getting ready in the bathroom with only the night-light. I wasn't taking any chances. I'd worked long after closing, making up for lost time, making myself so tired my eyes actually ached, and now that I was this close to my bed, I worried if I turned on the lights, my body might be yanked from the drowsiness that felt as powerful as a drug.

That's why I didn't think I'd need Mom's sleeping pills. I assumed I'd slip between the sheets and drop into a dreamless sleep, as good as being blackout drunk.

But faces swarmed me again. Not Morgan's or Daphne's. Not Brad's, either.

Edith's. The fear beaming from her eyes when she clocked a cop's suspicion of me.

Jackson's. The curl of his lips teetering between smile and smirk.

And worst of all, Nina's. The cool appraisal of her gaze. Her glances like paper cuts.

I heard her voice, too: *I'm scared of what* you *would have done. Why would anyone* want *to be you?* And it was those lines that had me launching out of bed, flicking on the lights, chasing all the faces away.

I retrieved Mom's pills from the kitchen and gulped one down. Then I opened my closet for my favorite sweatshirt, an extra layer of comfort against the chill of Nina's question, and saw my wedding dress instead.

It was still in front, free of its garment bag, from that day last week when I'd pulled it out to daydream about a second chance—for me and the dress. But as I looked at it last night, I didn't see an aisle lined with candles, a man in a tux, or feel the phantom grip of a hand on my waist. I saw only how gorgeous the gown was. Felt only what a shame it was I might never wear it.

I stroked the lace and remembered what the dress had done for me that first time I put it on at Just Say Yes. Even though Brad had been distant for weeks, even though I'd felt him prying my fingers off his, one by one, the dress made me feel buoyant—like if Brad did set me adrift, I would float instead of sink. At the same time, it made me see myself as someone worth being tethered to, and standing in my room last night, the echoes of Nina's words still in my head, I became desperate for that feeling again. I wanted to look at my reflection and see someone I loved.

The problem was: it didn't work. The gown looked like a costume. I stood at the mirror and saw only an actor.

I don't remember lying down or closing my eyes. But Mom's pill must have knocked me out before I had a chance to remove the dress, because now I'm here on my bed, blinking against daylight, which bounces off the gown like sun off snow. It's so blinding it takes me a few seconds to read the time on my bedside clock—and then I gasp.

It's the middle of the afternoon.

I scramble for my phone, find texts from Marilee, asking when I'm arriving to work, then if I'll be arriving at all. I rush to respond, typing out apologies, instructions, additional apologies that pile up in blue bubbles. Then, turning the phone face down on my bed, I focus on getting my bearings. I finally slept—which is good. And sure, it was longer than I expected, but maybe that's what I needed. I haven't slept so deeply and thoroughly since recovering from my transplant, and even then, there were always interruptions, my parents waking me on a rigid schedule to make sure I took—

My meds.

I slept through my morning dose.

I try to stifle a surge of panic. It's fine, I'm fine, I know the rules. It's still more than four hours before my regular nighttime dose, so

I can take the missed one now instead of skipping it altogether. The delay just makes me nervous, like my body has noted my carelessness, and now it's counting down the minutes until it can reject my heart.

I propel myself out of bed and almost walk to the kitchen without taking off the dress, framed by the windows like a bride in her wedding portrait. Stopping at the threshold of my room, I slip the cap sleeves off my shoulders and undo the zipper at the top of the skirt. I should be able to shimmy right out, but the bodice stays in place. I pivot my back toward the mirror, craning to see if the lace is caught on something—and I freeze. Because the lace isn't stuck or snagged.

It's buttoned.

But that isn't possible. I have never been able to button the bodice myself. That's why Brad saw me that day with the dress gaping open. That's the whole symbolic point of buttons on wedding dresses; a bride cannot manage buttoning or unbuttoning them on her own, so she needs someone close to her—a parent; a best friend; or, at the end of the night, a partner—to do it.

I rub my eyes, trying to scrub away the grogginess of the sedative. I blink and blink and twist back to the mirror, but still, the bodice is buttoned. Not completely. Not all the way to the top. But higher than I can reach.

Was someone here while I slept? Did Mom come up to see me after hearing I was a no-show at work? If she did, I can't imagine why she'd button the dress. One look at me and she would have gasped so loud it woke me up, would have called my dad in to witness my new low: *Look at her, look what she's wearing. What is she* doing? *What do we do?*

But who else then? Nina has a key. She's let herself in plenty of times—to leave me baked goods or thrift store finds. That was usually while I was working, never late at night, sure, but maybe she saw my texts, assumed I couldn't sleep again, and wanted to talk about it in person, same as she had earlier in the day at Sweet Bean.

I grab my phone, open our text thread, and am halfway through asking if she stopped here last night when I realize she did respond to my messages. Just after midnight.

> Yes, the cop talked to me. And I'm sorry, Rosie, but I think I need a little break.

I reel back. A break from what? From me?

I'm erasing my half-formed text to ask for clarity instead—What does that mean? A break for how long? What would that even—but I stop midquestion when I realize something else: I didn't have a notification about this message when I woke up. Which means I must have read it when it came in last night. Except I have no memory of that. Same as I don't remember the transition from standing in front of my mirror to crawling back into bed.

And if I don't remember those things, is it possible I don't remember buttoning the dress? I contort my arms behind my back to confirm I'm physically incapable of doing it, and it's true, I can't get enough purchase on the tight loops to unhook them. Still, my fingers can just scrape the highest of the buttons. It's awkward, my arms instantly ache with the effort, but apparently it is feasible that, with a lot of concentration and very nimble fingers, I might have been able to fasten them myself, even if I can't undo them now.

Would I have had that, though—focus, dexterity—late at night, when I was already so exhausted, when Mom's sedative was dragging me toward sleep?

At the thought of the drug, I'm jolted back to the fact that I still haven't taken my meds—and despite my confusion, despite the bodice feeling tighter by the moment, my priority needs to be protecting my heart.

The dress rustles as I hurry to the kitchen, the train lagging behind me, dragging along a floor I haven't cleaned in days. I try not to think of the dust that might be latching onto the fabric—not only because I need to focus on the task at hand, but also because it's futile, worrying about dirt on a dress I might never wear again.

Why would anyone want to be with you?

I stop, holding my orange juice. It's the question Nina asked me yesterday, but my mind has revised it to add a single word, and now the bodice pinches like a corset.

I squeeze the cyclosporine from the syringe, stir the liquid together. What does it mean when your best friend needs a break from you? Nina and I have never taken a break. Even when we went to separate colleges, we were in constant contact with each other, texting updates from the parties we went to, sending pictures of the campus squirrels we'd become obsessed with. Taking a break from her feels like taking a break from eating. It simply isn't sustainable.

I raise my glass to my lips, and it's just as I tip my head back that I notice something I rushed past before: my apartment door. It's open.

The medicine pools in my mouth, bitter as gasoline, but I'm slow to swallow it, my muscles frozen as I stare at the door. Once I choke it down, I force myself to creep closer. It's open only a couple inches, but it's enough to reveal that my keys are stuck in the lock on the other side. I wrench them free and shove the door shut.

This must be another thing I don't remember—leaving my keys in the lock, leaving the door just slightly ajar. It's irresponsible, but I've done it before, when bringing in groceries, when talking on the phone, times when I wasn't even half as tired as I was last night. And I'd certainly been distracted when I got home yesterday, glued to my screen as I texted Nina.

But as I brace my back with one hand, the buttons of my dress like vertebrae along my spine, I can't help but wonder if I did close the door—and someone outside saw the keys left in the lock. Used them to enter my apartment.

"Hello?" I call.

Silence answers.

I inch open a kitchen drawer, slide out a chef's knife, wincing at the snick it makes against the other cutlery.

"Hello?" I repeat, gripping the knife with both fists, more like a baseball bat than a blade.

I open the kitchen closet, the pantry, even knowing the spaces are too shallow for hiding inside. Sweat dews on my forehead as I tiptoe back toward my bedroom, the swish of the dress impossibly loud. From the doorway, I see there's no one in my open closet, nothing but boxes under my bed. When I edge into the bathroom, I yank the shower curtain back and slash forward with the knife.

Only for an instant do I think of Morgan—the blade in his chest so similar to the one I'm clutching—because then I'm leaning against the wall, my breath speeding in and out.

There's no one here.

My relief is only momentary. Just because I'm alone right now doesn't mean I was alone all night.

I think of the warning I received from both Jackson and Blair: that if Other Rosie went so far as to take on my identity, who knows what else she would do. Was it her, slipping into my apartment, fastening my dress in the night? The thought ices the sweat on my skin.

But I still come back to why. *Why would anyone* want *to be you?* No—not that. I knead my forehead against the intrusion, tap my knuckles against my skull to call forth the real question. Why would Other Rosie bother with the buttons at all?

It must have been a message. She wanted me to know she'd been here. That she knows where I live. Knows how to get inside my head.

I set the knife on my dresser, grab my phone off the bed. I need to call—someone. The police. Jackson. But that instinct withers as I play out the conversation in my mind: *I think Other Rosie broke into my apartment last night. Well, not broke in exactly. I left my keys in the lock outside. But I'm pretty sure she was here because someone buttoned up the wedding dress I was sleeping in—*

I stop right there. Almost laugh at how bizarre it sounds. Jackson might already know the whole story of this dress; it came up in court, Brad's lawyer presenting "the timeline"—the venue visit, my deceitful answers on the paperwork, the dress I confessed to purchasing once Brad caught me in it. One man has already called me crazy for wearing it; I can't deal with Jackson thinking it, too, then adding it to his list of reasons to keep an eye on me. And if he came here—to investigate the scene, ensure my safety—he'd find me still in the gown, because I can touch the highest button, but unlooping it remains impossible.

Who else can I call? Not my parents, even though they could be here in seconds, free me of the dress they'd be alarmed to see I haven't sold by now. I can't exactly go knocking on neighbors' doors either. That leaves the person I always call, the person who always comes, and I'm already pulling up her name in my Favorites when I remember—again, fresh pain sizzling through my sternum—she asked me for a break.

My thumb hovers above the screen as I spin through everything Jackson might have asked her. *Can you tell me why you didn't think it was a good idea for Rosie to communicate with Morgan? Is there something about her behavior that made you wary of her contacting him?* His questions must have made her reconsider my actions, my obsessions, all the messes of mine she's become accustomed to in loving me this long.

Why would anyone want to be you? Why would anyone want to be with you?

I turn to the full-length mirror. The dress looks better now that it's buttoned—the bodice doesn't gape around my torso; the sleeves don't slip off my shoulders. But *better* isn't the same as *right*. I look nothing like the brides at Just Say Yes, the ones whose smiles light up like neon, the ones whose friends and family buzz around them, bright as bulbs themselves.

Even worse, I see something now I don't remember noting last night: the sweetheart neckline accentuates my scar, drawing the eye right to it.

When I bought this dress, I had no idea that, soon enough, I'd have a scar to hide. Didn't know a lacy high neck would be better. Couldn't conceive my own heart would try to kill me. Nina always says I shouldn't mask it, shouldn't limit my wardrobe to crewnecks or boatnecks; I should be proud of what I've survived, proud I'm still here. She doesn't understand that showing it off means showing how bad, how defective, my heart actually was.

But now, in this dress, it's all anyone would see, the pink ridge of skin that's both the toughest and tenderest part of me.

I can't stop staring at it, gruesome against the elegant lace.

Is that the spot where they'll cut me open again, if I'm lucky enough to get a second transplant? My chest flares with fear: hospital beds, beeping monitors, bruises from IVs. And unlike last time, my parents older, if even still alive, unable to stay by my side. Nina with children she has to care for, family taking priority over friends. No hand committed to holding mine. No one but nurses to give me sporadic company.

My scar stares back at me in the glass.

I claw at the back of the dress again, but the loops are tight, the buttons tiny, and I'm still unable to manage them. I pant with the effort, face flushing an ugly red. For a moment, I consider picking up the knife again, sawing at the fabric until I can rip the whole thing off.

But then sunlight winks off the beads, and I'm reminded of an image I had when I first bought the dress: the bodice shimmering in sync with a diamond on my finger. A ring from someone who wanted to be with me forever. To rip the dress now would be to tear that hope in half.

I do not cut the fabric.

Instead, I watch the mirror. And for a long time, I'm trapped by my reflection, trapped by the gown, with no one here—not a partner nor parent nor friend—who can help to get me out.

CHAPTER EIGHTEEN

Marilee's the one to free me.

I have to wait until she leaves work, hours I spend in front of *Gilmore Girls*, sweatshirt zipped over the bodice of my dress, blanket over the skirt. Episodes play on, bleed into the next, and suddenly, it's winter in Stars Hollow when I could have sworn it was just the end of summer. I haven't really been watching. My eyes keep darting to my door, checking for flashes of pink hair in the windows. Or maybe not pink anymore. Jackson said the dye was easily rinsed. Other Rosie could look like anyone now.

When Marilee arrives, she doesn't ask questions. I think she sensed my shame through the phone—the strained, whispery way I spoke—so she simply gets to work. She's brought the crochet hook we use at the salon, a tool that simplifies the task. As soon as the final button is undone, I breathe like someone emerging from underwater. Then Marilee hustles out the door, her goodbye a bit too chipper, her secondhand embarrassment evident in her blush.

I toss the dress into my closet. I slide on clothes that feel more luxurious than satin and lace ever could—yoga pants that hug my legs, a shirt so soft it's buttery—and head to my parents' house to pick up Bumper for his walk.

They don't seem to suspect anything. Dad's watching TV, Mom's scrolling on her iPad. But they greet me with wary, watchful looks, as if worried I'll spring something new on them, announce I'm on my way to the police station for another round of questioning.

"Did you take those pills I left for you?" Mom asks.

I bend down, bury my face into Bumper's fur. "Yeah, thanks."

"And they're helping?"

I can still feel the buttons studding my spine.

"Yeah, thanks," I say again, and when I straighten, winding Bumper's leash around my wrist, I consider asking if they saw any shadows last night as someone passed their house to get to mine. But they don't even know about Other Rosie—that's one of the details I spared them when relaying my connection to Morgan—and to explain now would only compound their horror, have Mom insisting I call the police. And then I'm right back where I dead-ended last time, faced with explaining to Jackson that I slept in a wedding gown.

I take a different route with Bumper, the opposite direction from Morgan's house. He keeps planting his feet, insisting on turning back to the path he's used to, and I feel that tug in a deep, visceral way. "No," I tell him. "Come on." I rub the scruff on his head and he relents into a reluctant trot. I keep my headlamp turned on, a third watchful eye to ward off anyone else's.

It isn't long after I drop Bumper off that I see my parents' lights go out. I peek through my living room curtains, scanning their house and the driveway between us. They'll be heading upstairs now, off to bed, and there's a coziness to that—the certainty of sleep—that feels impossible to me. I check my lock for the fourth time since getting home. I check each room and closet again. I'm alone here, and it'll stay that way—a mantra I repeat to myself as I mix my next dose of meds.

One last glance at the door, and I shut off the lights in the living room and kitchen. Then I head to the bathroom, hopeful that the ritual of face washing and teeth brushing will lull me into something like rest. I bend over the sink, splash water onto my cheeks, and when I stand upright again, I catch myself in the mirror—still wearing the dress.

I gasp and it's gone. I'm back in a shirt that's not even white.

The gray cotton shouldn't have glitched to beaded lace. But I saw it. A lingering vision from earlier today. Or evidence I can't trust my own mind. After all, I'm still not positive it was somebody else who buttoned the dress.

I meet my gaze in the mirror, toothpaste frothing over my lips as I think it through. It would be such a risk, Other Rosie entering my apartment. What if I'd woken up? What if I'd clawed at her, called the police? And if she wants me to go down for Morgan's murder, it makes more sense for her to take something from my apartment—something she could plant in Morgan's house—than to leave proof of her presence behind.

I reach around my back for the hundredth time, miming the act of buttoning the dress. I've gone back and forth all day: I could do it; no, I couldn't; it's difficult but possible; it's difficult *because* it's impossible. Now, with my muscles more relaxed, I see once again how I might have done it. I consider, too, that if it had been someone else—someone trying to threaten or simply scare me—they'd likely have buttoned it all the way to the top. But the dress was still open a little, as if the person fastening it grew too tired to finish, then slumped right onto the bed.

That's not much comfort, either—that I've done some things I don't remember.

Back in my bedroom, I plug my phone into its charger, pull back my blankets, then shuffle across the carpet to the light switch by the door. Before I can turn it off, something lures my attention past the threshold, toward the kitchen, where the darkness seems to shift. I squint into it, then slide my hand up the wall outside my bedroom until it reaches the switch out there. I flood the room with light—and stumble back a step, blinking against another glitch.

Black mask, black clothes, a knife; *someone at the door*.

But this image doesn't change. And I know it's real when the person charges forward.

I can't even suck in a breath before their knife slashes at me. I lurch out of the way, rocket toward the door, and am yanked back so hard I crash onto the kitchen tile. I don't have an instant to recover before the blade plunges toward my chest. My arm leaps up by instinct, and the knife slices across my skin.

We both look at the blood—them through their ski mask, me through stretched-wide eyes. I don't feel the pain of it yet, but the color is so shockingly red my mind spurts toward Morgan, dead on his kitchen floor.

I push up against the intruder, and they push back with one arm, knife arcing in their gloved fist. It grazes my shoulder, and as they pull back to stab me again, I grab their wrist with both hands, hold it away from me, and twist in opposite directions. It's a desperate, juvenile move, the kind of injury my sister and I would give each other as kids, but I squeeze so tightly they let out a huff of surprise before the knife clatters to the floor.

We scramble at the same time, skidding through my blood—them for the weapon, me to stand up—but we're tangled in each other; our flailing limbs send the knife skittering away. As they reach for it again, I run for the door—which is still locked. I only have time to flip the dead bolt before an arm clamps around my neck, dragging me backward, wrenching me down. Then I'm jammed between their legs, my back pressed to their chest, their breath pulsing against my ear.

My throat grates against the choke hold, releasing a sound like static. I try to rake at their arm, but my muscles slow as if moving through sludge. As my attacker squeezes tighter, my eyes pop. My skin feels like cellophane wrapped around my skull.

The air thickens, too solid to sip. As my vision narrows, black dots spattering the edges, I see a scuff on my attacker's black boot that looks like half a heart. Even in my dimming consciousness, I'm reminded of the friendship necklaces Nina and I wore in middle school. The gold heart sawed in half. Each piece jagged and incomplete without its companion.

My mouth gasps for air that doesn't come. I hear thumping then— my heart, Daphne's—and the arm lets go.

I crash back as they jump up. Oxygen rushes into me like water. I curl against the tile, coughing, sputtering, while the attacker pounds across the kitchen, out the door—and collides with someone on the landing.

"Oof— What— Hey!" A woman's voice.

That thumping again. Quicker than before. Because it wasn't my heart I was hearing. It was the clomp of feet up the stairs.

"Oh my god—Rosie!" the woman calls from the door, her voice muffled by my coughing. As she rushes in, drops beside me, I'm not sure if it's Mom or Nina or—

Edith. My eyes spring wide when I see her. Her hair dangles over me; her own eyes bulge with alarm.

"What happened?" Her hands hover over my body, assessing the damage.

I grab her arm. "They—" But I can't get more out. That single word scrapes my throat.

"It's okay," Edith says, her sleeve smudged with my blood. "First, just— Where are the towels?"

I let my head fall back instead of answering. She scurries out of view and returns with a dishcloth, which she wraps around my wound. Red blooms through the white, and my heart is actually thumping now— hard and fast, belated adrenaline. The cut on my arm throbs to its beat.

"I don't think you, like, severed an artery," Edith says, holding the towel tight. "But you definitely need stitches."

"Their knife—" I force out, gesturing to the blade that slid beneath the kitchen table.

"Shh, it's okay," she says again before placing my hand on the cloth. "Put pressure on this. I'll call 911."

Edith rummages through the tote slung over her shoulder, and I focus on the rhythm of my lungs, swelling and compressing like an accordion, wheezing out some still-strangled notes.

Beside me, Edith mumbles into her bag: "Where is it, where the hell is my phone, why do I keep so much stuff in here." She pauses, eyes lifting to lock onto the wall, then palms her face. "I left it in my car!" She drops her hand, which has left bright red smears on one cheek, like only half of her is blushing. "It's fine, I'll use yours instead."

She scans the kitchen, the living room, for my phone. I lift my bloody arm toward my open bedroom, but the thought of her car, her phone left inside it, makes my limb fall limp.

"How did you get here?" I ask, voice gritty. I prop myself up on my elbows, pushing through my weakness, fighting a wave of dizziness.

Edith stands up, still combing the counter, the end tables, for a phone. "What do you mean? I drove."

I shake my head. That wasn't what I meant. "How did you know where I live?"

And why is she here, at this exact moment? Right when I needed her. Right as my attacker sprinted away.

She stops searching to look at me. "You put your address on the note."

"What note?"

Did I message her something I don't remember, right around the time I might have been buttoning my own dress? But no. I *didn't* button my dress. I was right to suspect Other Rosie; my intruder proves that, slipping inside without me hearing a thing. Except my door wasn't open tonight. My keys weren't in the lock.

"The note you slipped under my door telling me to come over."

My thoughts skid on her answer. My hand loosens on the towel.

"I didn't leave you a note. I don't even know where you live."

Edith frowns. "What?" She watches me a beat longer, waiting for me to explain something I can't. "But— I have it right here. Hold on."

She fishes through her bag, shoving items aside, pulling out a glasses case, a crushed granola bar, sunblock. With a grunt of frustration, she kneels on the floor, dropping those items beside her. I look into the bag myself, as if I'll instantly find the note that's eluding her, but the piece of paper is lost in a clash of objects. Makeup bag, wallet, hair spray, charger, Tylenol—

"Ah! Right here!" Edith plucks out the note, thrusting it into the air, the paper already spotted with her fingerprints.

It should nauseate me: more of my blood. Whirls of rusty red. But I hardly even look at the note, don't bother to scrutinize its words. I'm stuck, instead, staring into Edith's bag at the bottle of hair spray, which was nudged a little when she grabbed the paper. And now that I see the name of the product, the color of its label, I see it isn't hair spray at all.

It's hair dye.

And the shade is Pretty in Pink.

CHAPTER NINETEEN

"I t was you."

Edith cocks her head, still holding the note in the air. As her white-blond hair grazes her shoulder, nearly colorless, I see how easily the dye would have masked it.

"What was me?" she asks.

I snatch the bottle from her bag, point to the label, blood trickling down my arm. "You're the Rosie that Morgan was seeing."

There's a moment in which her face is blank, looking at the bottle without recognition. And it's a moment of hope, a moment in which I didn't welcome someone into my life who tried to destroy it. A moment in which I'm not some stupid girl who sees connection where there's actually danger.

But then Edith closes her eyes, inhales slowly like she's counting the seconds—and exhales with a nod.

When she takes the bottle from my hand, I barely feel it go.

"Why?" I ask, the word so pained it's like I had to squeeze my windpipe to squeak it out. It's not enough, doesn't articulate my question. Edith and I barely know each other. So why would she pick me to impersonate, me to pin it on?

Instead of answering, Edith chews her lip. "That cop I saw you talking to—does he know about the Rosie thing?"

"Yes. From Morgan's emails."

She perks a bit. "He wrote emails about me?" She sounds so flattered—until fear flits across her face. "Oh god, what if the police—" Her gaze slams onto my arm. "Keep pressure on that!"

With her free hand, she presses the towel to my wound. I wrench away from her.

"Why did you do it?" I swallow through the pain in my throat. "Why pretend to be me?"

"That's not what— I didn't think—" She stops, seeming to gather herself. "I just met him one day. At Sweet Bean. We crashed into each other, completely by accident, and—"

"*Was* it an accident? Because I was there that day too. The cops said a barista saw both of us. Two pink-haired women, at different times. So were you following me?"

"No!" Edith looks scandalized by the suggestion. "I only picked Sweet Bean because you'd recommended their Danishes for dinner when we met. And then I just—bumped into Morgan. I'd never seen him in person before, so I got kind of nervous, and when he asked me for my name, I-I don't know."

She pushes out a sigh, and when she speaks again, her voice is low and warbly. "I didn't want to be Edith, the woman whose fiancé would dump her. The woman who'd been crying into frozen dinners all week. I wanted to be anyone but myself."

She pauses, and despite my confusion, my alarm, I can't help but think of the weeks after Brad. Times I caught my reflection in the mirror. Times I was tortured by the dark pockets beneath my eyes, the pillow creases scarring my cheeks, the nests of hair on my head. It terrified me, because I saw in that mirror what I knew Brad had seen: a woman worth leaving.

"So you lied to him," I say, shaking off that image. "You gave

Morgan a fake name. Hid your real identity the entire time you were seeing him."

Anger pushes out the words, but as soon as they're spoken, I feel ashamed, too. Because if I'm angry at Edith for deceiving Morgan, then don't I need to be mad at myself? I hid my own identity from him—per DonorConnect's guidelines, sure. But message after message, I pretended I had no clue who he was, either, even though, night after night, I'd paused outside his house, peering through the windows.

"I didn't set out to lie," Edith says, "but when he asked me for my name, I just kind of . . . blurted out yours instead."

"Why *my* name?"

She wipes at tears I didn't see spill. "Because you were kind. And interesting. You seemed so sure of yourself. So uniquely *you*. And you were someone who'd survived a massive heartbreak just like mine. You were on the other side of it, and . . . I wanted to be like that."

I blink at her. The pain in my arm ebbs to less than an ache, as if the blood is seeping back toward the cut. *Why would anyone* want *to be you?* Nina asked. And all along, Edith had an answer. I'm kind. Interesting. Uniquely myself. But—that's not even true. It was a brief, fleeting thought, back at the beginning of all this, but didn't I consider dyeing my hair to look more like Daphne? I was willing to blacken the brightest part of myself, a part I actually loved, just to look like someone a man—a stranger, really—had been attracted to.

"That's why I dyed my hair, too," Edith adds, shaking the bottle like she might spray it on again. "The night we met, you talked about changing hairstyles, how it can separate you from the person you'd been before. And I *loved* your hair. I thought it could be"—she gives a shy shrug—"a fun new look for me. Something that would stop me from seeing my same old self. So I got this." She rolls the bottle between her hands, staring at the label. "Just to try it. I'm not bold like you, I couldn't commit to something more permanent without seeing how it looked on me first. But then I met Morgan like that, and he complimented my hair, so I had to keep dyeing it every time I saw him."

Had to. The phrase hits my ear like a wrong note. She believes she *had to* keep dyeing it, believes it was the only choice, just because Morgan liked it.

I grip the towel tighter, the pain cracking open again, distracting from the off-key sentiment I know too well.

"You're acting like it was an accident," I say. "Using my name. Dyeing your hair like mine. But you took it way too far." I glance at the blood on the floor, the red on my nails like chipped polish. "Why did you send someone to attack me?"

"What! I didn't!"

"Were you here last night? While I was sleeping?"

"What?" she says again. "No. This is the first—"

"You buttoned my gown."

I state it as a fact, but the bewilderment on her face, the flash of *what a crazy thing to say*, is enough to convince me I'm wrong. It wasn't Other Rosie—Edith—who snuck into my apartment and fastened the dress. It was whoever broke in tonight, cutting me with that knife, choking me from behind. The person Edith knew, somehow, to save me from—her timing too precise to mean she's not a part of it.

My eyes latch on to the blade beneath the table, close enough to grasp.

"I don't know what you're talking about," Edith says, "but I had nothing to do with what happened here tonight. I have no reason to hurt you!"

"What about Morgan? You had a reason for hurting him?"

I shift my weight to the right, the direction of the table. Edith doesn't seem to notice, even as she gapes at me.

"You think *I* killed Morgan? How— Why—"

"I know you were there the night he died." I slide another inch.

"There were pink hairs found in his hand at the scene. And they weren't a match for mine."

Edith's knuckles whiten around the spray bottle.

"The police are looking for you," I say.

I glance at the knife, just a few feet away, but now I'm not sure that's the right move. I should be running for my phone or running for the door. Scrambling for a weapon, when I'm already injured, might only leave me vulnerable again. And is that really the answer—more blood on a kitchen floor?

"No, no, no," Edith mumbles through my hesitation. "I swear that wasn't me. I mean, yes, I went to his house. But I didn't *kill* him. God, I— I only went there that night to ask him about Daphne."

My muscles, poised to spring up, freeze instead. "What about Daphne?"

"I don't know—everything, I guess!" Her gaze falls from mine, her cheeks flushing. "You have to understand, I was so . . . hopeful about us. I mean, the sparks that first night at Sweet Bean— I didn't think I'd feel sparks ever again, let alone so soon after my fiancé."

She squeezes the bottle of dye like a stress ball, clenching and unclenching. "I made sure to be cautious. I've been burned—badly— and I'm not even close to ready for a new relationship. But I felt like I *needed* to see him again. Because feeling that . . . that *zing* with him was the only thing that had truly helped me in weeks."

She loosens her grip on the dye, cradling it in her palm. "Morgan made me feel— I don't even know what to call it. It's just, he could have had any woman he wanted, but he sat there in Sweet Bean with *me*. Shut the place down with *me*. Said he wanted to do it again with *me*."

Despite myself, I nod, because I know the feeling she's talking about. Through messages alone, Morgan made me feel intriguing and funny and important, even repeating my own lines back to me, admiring them in a way that made me admire them too. Sometimes, those messages were more like mirrors, showing me reflections I

hadn't seen before, so that as I fell for him, it was a little like falling
for myself.

It was like that with Brad, too. His piles of pretty words. *Amazing.*
Beautiful. Special.

"Then you texted me about those rumors you'd seen online,"
Edith says. "About Morgan maybe killing his wife. And obviously
that freaked me out, but I still met up with him anyway, because you
said your friend had just gone out with him." She pauses, pointedly,
to acknowledge my lie. "Hearing that made me feel like I already had
to win him back. So we met at the park, and it was just like the first
time. Sparks I swore I could see."

"That's when you gave him your number," I recall from the emails.
"Except the detective told me it was a burner."

I let the implication charge the air. You don't use a burner unless
you want to leave no trace, no connection to the person you're calling.

"Okay, I see how that looks," Edith says. "But I didn't get that for
Morgan. I—" Now her cheeks darken, from pink to red. "I got it so I
could call my ex."

She dips her head to stare into her lap. "Those first few weeks, I
missed him so much it felt like I couldn't breathe. I thought if I had
a second phone, I could still call him—hear his voice if he answered,
hear his voicemail if he didn't—without him knowing it was me. It
was stupid, I know; I only did it a couple times. But I still had the
phone in my bag when I was with Morgan, and like I said, I was
nervous about the rumors you'd heard. I wanted to keep seeing him,
but I figured I should be careful. Maybe it was overkill, maybe it
wouldn't have mattered if he knew my number, but I haven't exactly
been thinking my clearest the past month or so. It's like I was drawn
to Morgan and . . . scared of him, all at the same time. And not just
because of the rumors, but because, when you've just been burned,
relationships—sparks—are scary."

With her free hand, she flicks out her fingers—*sparks!*—the way you would when shouting *Boo!*

"It was hard to know what to think of him. On the one hand, he seemed like a good, regular guy. Like, when he told me he's still friends with one of his college girlfriends, I thought: okay, if someone dated him and found him worth sticking around for, he can't be that bad."

She shakes her head at her own flimsy argument, even though part of me gets it. Morgan and I never got to the requisite exes conversation—beyond what I shared of Brad—but I bet it would have comforted me, too, his old girlfriend keeping him close. Because it means something, doesn't it, when a woman vouches for a man?

"But it still nagged at me. The whole Daphne thing. So I looked into her, into him. I read Daphne's books at the library. I found this interview of them together online and something just didn't seem *right*. I talked to Piper, too, to get her take."

I drop my gaze to my arm, reposition the towel to a less saturated section. Edith might not have been stalking me the day she met Morgan in Sweet Bean, but she's certainly followed in my footsteps since then. Even if she didn't know it.

"But still, I kept going back and forth. And Morgan kept . . . wanting to see me. And I can't explain to you how intoxicating that is. It had been so long since I'd felt wanted. *Pursued.* Because things with my fiancé— I'd felt for a while that he was having second thoughts. That he was halfway out the door."

She bites the inside of her cheek, bracing against the memory, but it's visible on her face—the raw nerve she's gnawing. "Anyway. I finally decided to just ask Morgan about Daphne in person. Which is why I was there that night. *Before* he died."

I stretch my neck against the pain still ringing it, shocked at the timing of it all. Not only did Edith and I embark on the same investigation, but we ended up in the same place, on the same night: right at Morgan's door. If I'd arrived just a little bit earlier, I might have seen her there.

"But I didn't kill him," she reiterates. "If anything, I wanted to *start over* with him. I wanted him to tell me the truth about Daphne, assure me that everything I'd seen and heard meant nothing, and in return, I was going to tell him the truth about me. That I'd given him a fake name. A fake number. But before I could get into it all, he just—kissed me. A shut-up kind of kiss. Like he knew he wouldn't like what I was going to say. And I don't know, maybe he ran his hands through my hair and that's how my— I don't remember. It was our first kiss, so I kind of—"

"What? No, it wasn't. Your first kiss was at the park."

"Um. Nooo . . ." She stretches out the word until it tilts toward a question. "It was at his house."

"He wrote about it in his emails, Edith. You kissed at the park. In his library. In his bedroom—that was the time he squeezed your hand too hard and you freaked out and left."

"Squeezed my—" She squints at me like she's having trouble understanding. "We did meet up at the park, but we didn't kiss there. He gave me a tour of his house and showed me his library, his bedroom, but when I peeked into the master bath, he grabbed my hand and yanked me backward. *That's* what freaked me out. He claimed he didn't want me to see 'the mess in there'—and I don't know, maybe that's all it was—but of course I thought of Daphne. Dying in that bathroom, just a few feet away. All the rumors about Morgan killing her."

"Wait— But— Why would he write about kissing you all those times if he never actually did?"

"I have no idea. That's really weird."

My head spins to make sense of it. Morgan told Blair his emails were a way to record and shape the events of his day. Now they seem like fiction, molded from moments of inspiration, Edith and I merely characters to him. Stories he believed were his to tell.

It makes me wonder what else he lied to Blair about.

"What happened when you confronted him about Daphne?" I ask.

"He got pissed at me, just for *asking* about his wife. His eyes like . . . flashed. I swear they were *bright* with anger. And it scared me. So I left."

I search her face for a tell, a flicker of deceit, but she doesn't so much as blink.

"And you didn't go back?" I ask.

"No, I swear. I didn't even know he was dead until two days later. I wasn't working that weekend, so I mostly stayed in bed, off my phone, feeling depressed."

There's something in her expression that's familiar to me. Just like I recognized the desperation and despair on her face when I first saw her through the glass at Just Say Yes, I recognize the agony of being misunderstood. Of not being believed.

But maybe that's desperation, too. A frantic need to spin a story.

"Why are you *here* then?" I ask. "At the exact moment someone was strangling me."

"I told you—this note." Edith picks it off the floor beside her, holds it out for me to take, but I don't dare touch it, don't smudge it with prints of my own. I lean forward to read.

I spoke to the police. I know about you and Morgan.
Come to my apartment at 10:30 tonight. 35 Carver Lane
(above the garage).
—Rosie

CHAPTER TWENTY

The message is typed, the paper the size of a cell phone. I read it a few times, but it might as well be calculus for all the sense it makes. Even my name looks like an equation, and as I stare at it, a chill skitters over my skin. My wound pulses beneath the towel.

"You were talking to that cop outside Sweet Bean yesterday," Edith says. "And then this note was under my door today. So I thought the police must know Morgan had been seeing a 'Rosie' and they questioned *you*, but you—" She shakes the note. "You figured out it was me."

I think of the fear I saw stamped onto her face when she caught me with Jackson in the parking lot. I assumed it meant she was scared of me, scared I was a suspect in Morgan's murder, but now I know: she was afraid of becoming one herself.

"I didn't write that note," I tell her. "I didn't know you were the other Rosie until I saw that hair dye in your bag."

She frowns, gaze darting between the bottle in one hand and the note in the other. "Then who did write it?"

Goose bumps lift the hair on my neck. "I don't know."

Edith's lips move in silence as she reads the message again.

"Maybe . . ." she starts—then stiffens. Her eyes sweep the room, pausing on the puddles of blood, the knife beneath the table. "Maybe whoever attacked you is after us both. Someone lured me here tonight, right as you were hurt. Maybe they wanted you to think I was guilty. Of hurting you *and* Morgan. Do you—oh god, do you think it was Morgan's killer who did this?"

Yes. Or at least I *did*. I never had time to articulate the thought, but in those ragged seconds of scrambling for safety, for air, I must have assumed the person in black was Other Rosie. But now that I'm looking at Other Rosie, who's adamant she had nothing to do with the attack—on me or Morgan—I don't know who else that leaves.

Edith squints at the note. "Morgan and I never met up with anyone else. Never even took a picture together that he could show someone. So how did this person know there was a connection between me and Morgan in the first place? And how did they connect *you* to me and Morgan? How did they know you'd spoken to police? How—" She drops her head, lets out a defeated breath. "I don't understand."

"I don't either," I admit, queasy from her questions. "So let's call the cops and they can sort this out."

"But—" Edith's eyes swell with panic. "You said they have my hair! That it was in Morgan's *hand*! I'll look insane—I used your name, dyed my hair like yours. They'll think I killed him!"

I don't doubt the possibility of that. But I see no other way to untangle the knots of this night or to keep myself safe. Because whether or not Edith had anything to do with it, someone broke into my home and assaulted me.

I try to stand, but the movement leaves me dizzy. I don't even make it to my knees before a sharp, shrill sound forces me to pause.

It's sirens. They're piercing the room. Lights, red and white, carve the dark outside.

I jerk my head to Edith, find her frozen in those lights, and we hold each other's gaze as car doors open and close, as footsteps pound up the stairs.

"Ms. Lachlan?" a woman calls, and it's only now that I notice my door is ajar. Two officers rush inside—followed by someone I recognize.

"Rosie," Jackson says, darting between his colleagues to crouch beside me. He scans the towel on my arm, the stains on the floor. "What happened?"

"I— Someone—" I try to answer, overwhelmed by the swarm of police and the EMTs who have slipped in behind them. One of the officers wields a flashlight, slashing it across the walls. I blink against the beam, then focus on Jackson. "How did you know something happened?"

A crease bisects his brows. "From your text to 911."

"My what?" Over Jackson's shoulder, Edith and I share a bewildered glance. "I didn't text 911. I was about to call, but—" Jackson stands to make room for the paramedics. One pauses to read my MedicAlert bracelet before unpeeling the towel from my arm; the other assesses the tear in my sleeve where the knife grazed my shoulder. They both reach into bags at their sides, extracting wipes and gauze, but I return my attention to Jackson. "Are you sure it wasn't my parents who texted?"

I look at the door again, as if I'll find Mom and Dad surging through it. But if they'd seen something—the shadow of my intruder, a glimpse of our struggle through a window—they would have never waited for the cops to get here before coming up themselves. Not to mention: A text? I didn't even know you could text 911, so I doubt they would either.

"The texter identified herself as Rosie Lachlan," the male officer says.

Edith's inhale is sharp. "Just like on the note."

"What note?" Jackson asks, studying Edith. His eyes narrow as he catalogs the details: smears of blood on her face, red fingerprints on the paper in her hand, and cradled loosely in one palm—the bottle of pink hair dye.

"It wasn't her," I spit out, the certainty of it smacking me in the face. Because even though her timing tonight was eerily perfect, even though I have no idea who wrote the note that led her to my door, I do know one thing: neither of us contacted 911.

Which means Edith might be right. Someone's targeting us both.

In the end, though, it doesn't matter that I believe her. The cops arrest her anyway.

———

"What the hell happened? Are you okay? Is it your heart? What's that bandage for?"

I've been awake the entire night—receiving treatment at the ER, giving Jackson my statement, having precautionary EKGs and CT scans—so when Nina barrels through the privacy curtain of my room, shrieking questions at me, I'm slow to process them.

"What are you doing here?" I ask instead. "Did my parents call you?" I glance at the clock: 6:42 a.m. Mom would never call someone before eight, unless it's life or death.

"Uh, do you really not remember I work here?" Nina says. "Oh god, was it a head injury?"

"No, I just didn't see you anywhere, I assumed you were home."

"Why is your voice like that? Tell me what happened. Unless— Is it hard to talk?"

I shake my head. I still sound husky, but it only hurts to swallow, not speak. I give the monitor beside my bed a reflexive glance to check my vitals, and as it beeps its steady beat, I tell Nina about the attack. Her eyes snap wide at first. Then instinct overrides emotion and she shifts into nurse mode. She places gentle, probing fingers on my injuries as I describe them. She even peeks beneath the gauze on my arm to check her colleagues' work in stitching me up. When she's satisfied, she sits on the side of my bed, shaking her head in shock. I've just gotten to the part where I found the hair dye in Edith's bag.

I relay the story for Nina the same way I did during my statement—insisting on Edith's innocence and excluding one important detail: the buttoned wedding dress.

"I accidentally left my door unlocked the night before," I say, because it's true. "And when I woke up, I had a weird feeling like someone had been in my apartment while I slept." Also true. "So I don't think last night is the first time they were there."

Nina follows up exactly as Jackson did: "Why didn't you call the police about that?"

"I didn't have any proof."

She scowls before launching into another question. "Was your door unlocked last night too? I can't imagine you'd overlook that two nights in a row, but . . . how did they get in?"

"My door was definitely locked, I checked like twelve times. I checked the whole apartment, too, and I was completely alone—until suddenly I wasn't. But the cops said there was no sign of a forced entry, so I have no idea what happened."

When Jackson mentioned that phrase—*forced entry*—my mind sprang to Daphne. The dark figure on her porch. The hand punching through glass to reach the dead bolt inside. I stopped hearing him for a second, stuck on how uncanny it is that Daphne and I have both lived through an intruder, but then my chest tightened at that thought, as if protecting her heart. Because even though I'm shaken by what happened, even though I shiver just thinking of where my intruder might be now, I didn't lose anyone in the attack. If anything, it brought someone back to me. My best friend, who only two nights ago wanted a break, is by my side again, stroking my hand.

"No forced entry," Nina mumbles to herself, "but the door was locked." Her brows knit tighter. "I don't like this."

"Really? That's weird, because I *love* it."

She laughs, softly at first, then harder than the quip deserves—but it's a necessary release of tension. When she stops, her face is more relaxed, a smile idling there, and I'm surprised by her change in demeanor. In a matter of seconds, she's gone from concerned to calm. Almost carefree.

She looks around the room. "Wait, you've been here all alone? Where are your parents?"

"You just missed them. They went to let Bumper out and my mom wanted to"—I pause, no easy way to say it—"clean up the blood in my apartment before I go home. They'll be back soon. They're my ride."

"God, this must have been so hard for them," Nina says, "seeing you like that. Watching you get rushed here again." She rubs my knuckles, worry returning to her eyes. "Hard for you, too, I'm sure."

"They took it . . . surprisingly well, actually. I mean, they were upset, and they want me to stay in their house for now, but . . ." My attention drifts past Nina to where my parents sat for much of the night.

"But what?"

I don't know how to describe it. Just like Nina, there was something newly unburdened about their expressions. They were horrified by what had happened to me—while they were sleeping next door, no less—but they were a little lighthearted too. They joked about the nurse's shoes, which were "inappropriately vomit-colored," according to Dad, but the last time we were in the ER together, when my own vomit had been clumped with blood, their demeanor was solely somber, humor itself the inappropriate thing.

And maybe that's the difference. Our previous ER trip was the beginning of what could have been the end, the moment we knew I was sick. But this time, all I need are stitches and bandages. No transplant lists. No indefinite hospital stays.

"I think they're just glad it wasn't my heart," I tell Nina, checking the monitor again.

She nods in agreement, her eyes landing there, too. We sit in silence that feels like a vigil.

Nina breaks it first: "So do the cops have any idea who did it?"

"Not yet." I swallow what feels like sticks instead of saliva. "Jackson said—"

"Who's Jackson?"

"The detective. Didn't you say he talked to you?" I know she did. She mentioned it in the same text where she asked me for a break.

"Yeah, but I'm not on a first-name basis with him."

"He's actually— Remember Winnie Dean? He's her older brother. Isn't that a weird connection?"

Nina's eyes twitch for a second, almost a squint, but she doesn't respond.

"He told me they'll fingerprint the knife, but the person had gloves on, so I'm not holding my breath. He also said they're going to talk to all my neighbors, see if anyone saw anything, if there are cameras they can pull footage from."

"Well, *you* saw the person. So let's start simple: Were they built like a man or a woman?"

Jackson asked the same question, of course. Once again, I try to concentrate on the memory—hands clawing for the knife, the crook of an arm crushing my neck—before rebounding fear slams shut the scene.

"It could have been a tallish woman. Or it could have been a man on the shorter side. Honestly, it happened so fast I barely got a chance to look at them. The only distinguishing feature I noticed was this scuff on their boot that looked like half a heart. And I think— I think they're the same person who killed Morgan."

Nina straightens. "Did the police say that?"

"No, but whoever attacked me has to be the one who lured Edith to my apartment. And probably the one who texted 911. I think they wanted Edith to be found at the scene so the cops would have to investigate her. Then they'd figure out Edith's connection to Morgan and—"

"Wait, that text. Could the cops tell whose phone it came from?"

"Jackson said it was unregistered. He promised they'll keep looking into it, but— I'm worried he doesn't see it like I do: that Morgan's killer is still out there. He seemed pretty satisfied, finding Edith with that bottle of hair dye, like he was catching her red-handed."

"Pink-handed," Nina offers.

"And I get that it looks bad, the strands of Edith's hair in Morgan's hand. But someone else must have been at his house that night—*after* Edith left, and *before* I got there. And whoever it was, they're setting Edith up to take the fall."

"But wouldn't there be an easier way to do that?" Nina asks. "The note, the 911 text, the timing of the attack—it's all so complicated. Couldn't they have just dropped an anonymous tip that the cops should look into Edith? Why would they work so hard to hurt *you* in the process?" She glares at my bandage.

"They must have known—somehow—about me and Morgan, just like they knew about Edith and Morgan. So maybe they're—" I grapple for the right words. "Punishing us? For dating him?"

"You weren't dating him," Nina says.

"You know what I mean."

"Not really! And I think you're being awfully generous to this woman, who—let me remind you—dyed her hair like yours and started using your name. That's crazy! And Edith could have easily written that note herself. She could've even texted 911 one second before she came through your door. She probably figured it was only a matter of time before the cops tied her to Morgan, and she wanted to make herself look innocent by orchestrating what *seems* like a setup and— God, I don't know."

Nina rubs her forehead at the effort to implicate Edith. I understand the mental knots she's tying. It's not exactly normal, meeting a man and giving him some other woman's name. But I also recognize the impulse behind Edith's choice, which she made while reeling from loss. It does something to you, watching the person you love, the person who said they love you, leave you behind. It makes you suspicious of yourself, makes you question everything you did, everything you are, searching for the flaws that caused the pain—and you'll find them everywhere. In memories. In mirrors. So what's a new name, other than a chance to reinvent yourself? To wipe the glass clean in the hopes of seeing a different reflection.

This is something that Nina, who's never been dumped, just can't understand. But Edith and I know: breakups are more than heartache. They derail the life you thought you had—which only throws everything else off track. Your plans for the future. Your routines. Your sense of worth. Even once the dust settles, you're left with disorienting fog. Internal chaos. And what's a person to do with that? Maybe they dye their hair. Or drive to their ex's house. Maybe they pretend to be someone else. Or call the same number, over and over, because the unanswered ring is better than silence. And maybe sometimes what looks like *crazy* is just an attempt at taking back control.

"The point is," Nina continues, "I wouldn't trust a thing Edith says. That girl gives me the creeps. Look: goose bumps."

As she pulls up her sleeve to show me, I register the outfit she's wearing. Jeans and a thin sweater—not her hospital scrubs.

"Why are you in regular clothes? Didn't you say you were working?"

Nina yanks her sleeve back down. "No. I didn't say that."

"Then how did you know I was here?"

"I checked my phone. We share locations, remember?"

Sure—to track each other's ETA when we're meeting up, or for safety reasons, in case I'm ever out somewhere and don't come home. But how did Nina know to check it this morning?

"You said you wanted a break," I remind her, because I'm not sure *why* she'd check it, either, not when she'd asked me for space.

"Yeah, well, that's because that detective requested a hair sample from me, based off things *you* told him. He questioned me for like an hour, obsessed with where I was the night Morgan died."

My eyes widen at that, but she gives me no chance to respond.

"You roped me into this whole thing—the murder of a guy I never even met—and I just . . . I needed a minute. But that doesn't mean I didn't want to make sure you were okay and not, like, dead in a ditch somewhere. Or"—she gestures to the room around us—"having a problem with your heart."

Part of me is comforted by her answer, the fact that she cared about me even when she wanted distance. But another part is still confused.

"Why were you looking for my location at the crack of dawn?"

"I woke up and couldn't get back to sleep, so I got on my phone and checked." Nina shrugs. "It's just habit lately."

My frown deepens. "It's habit *lately*," I repeat, emphasizing her word choice. "Since when?"

She purses her lips, toggling her head from side to side, as if counting up the days—or whether she'll tell me the truth. Then she heaves out a sigh that sounds like surrender. "Since I picked you up from the police station."

I take a moment, sifting through that answer. "So you mean you've been"—I swallow through the pain in my throat—"making sure I was safe?"

Nina nods, but it's too slow to be convincing. As her eyes stray from mine, slippery with guilt, something clunks inside me. I look at my monitor, expecting to see a break in the beat of my heart.

"Or do you mean," I ask, dragging my gaze back to Nina, "that you've been checking up on me since then because that's when you learned I was a suspect?"

She understands what I'm really asking. I know it from the way she throws up her hands: a defensive gesture. "I was just worried, okay? I know you'd never intentionally hurt someone, but—"

"But what? You thought I *accidentally* killed Morgan?"

"I didn't know what to think! You went to Morgan's house that night without him explicitly inviting you over. That's not a normal thing to do, Rosie. And then you went inside with the cat, so I thought: maybe Morgan freaked out at seeing a stranger in his house and fought with you and you grabbed a knife in self-defense. I don't know! I was ninety percent sure you were innocent, but—" She stops, leaving a silence so loud it muffles the beeping on the monitor.

"But there was still that ten percent," I finish for her, voice even raspier than before. Pain slashes through my arms, as if the knife is still cutting me.

"Look," Nina says, "it's all sorted now, right? The hair in Morgan's hand was Edith's, she really did use your name, and you obviously didn't attack yourself last night. So: case closed. You didn't kill Morgan."

It's there on her face again—that lightness, the release of a weight she's been carrying. The same expression my parents snuck at each other from their chairs. And it finally clicks for me what I've been seeing: relief—not just that I'm okay, but also that I'm not. Because only now, now that I'm a victim, do the people I love most believe I'm innocent.

"I'm sorry, okay?" Nina says to my silence. "I don't mean to upset you. But let's not pretend you don't have a history of acting before you think. You once drove with a *bleeding hand* to your ex's house."

"Because he wasn't answering his phone! And I couldn't deal with the silence after—"

"The silence *was* his answer! Which you would have realized if you would just see things as they really are for once, instead of how you *want* them to be. I mean, god—instead of talking to Brad about your relationship when you noticed him being distant, you bought a wedding dress. A wedding dress! And then when he texted you out of the blue to tell you he missed you, you convinced yourself it meant you were getting back together. But it was a booty call, Rosie. Not a declaration of love. Because if he really loved you, he would have respected you enough not to sleep with you one night and ghost you the next."

Nina stops to catch her breath, her words having burst out like a sneeze she'd been trying to hold back, and even though I've barely spoken, my breath feels ragged too.

She's never criticized me this explicitly, never spoken about my wedding dress like it's a symptom of some sickness I didn't know I'd contracted. And worst of all, she's never questioned the one thing I held on to—that whatever else happened with me and Brad, he *had* loved me.

The last few minutes are too much to process, a one-two punch of Nina's doubt and disapproval. I touch the bandage on my arm, then rub my neck, but I can't pinpoint the pain I'm feeling. It pumps through my body like blood.

"You have your Rosie-colored glasses," she continues, softer, slower. "And sometimes they get you into trouble. You miss what's right in front of you."

Nina gives me a gentle smile, expecting a response, I think. But I can only stare at her, the person right in front of me, wondering if I've been seeing her clearly or with a pretty tint.

"Okay, hon," a voice says, coming through the privacy curtain. It's the nurse who took over at six a.m., who gave me crackers and water before leaving to get my discharge papers. "Let me just go over this with you real quick and then—oh. Nina. Are you working right now?"

"Nope, not stealing your patient or anything." Nina stands from the bed, turning her smile toward her colleague. "Rosie's a friend of mine." She grabs my hand and squeezes, but my muscles won't return the gesture. "My best friend, actually."

"Oh! Look out for her then, okay?" the nurse says. "She's had a rough time."

"I definitely will," Nina says.

As the nurse unhooks me from the monitor, she and Nina chat over my head. I don't hear them, though. I'm still absorbing Nina's critique.

They get you into trouble. That one sentence is doing double duty: an explanation for the ten percent of Nina that thought I could have killed Morgan, and a warning that I'm wrong to believe in Edith. That I'm just not seeing her right.

But right now, I'm seeing her in handcuffs at the police station, bearing the brunt of Jackson's suspicion. I'm seeing her struggle to explain it: why she used a different name with Morgan, why she dyed her hair each time she saw him. I'm seeing Jackson write her off as some crazy woman, as if he's never been driven by hope or fear, as if his heart never tugged him down paths that others might question, as if our hearts are led by logic at all.

The nurse reads aloud my discharge instructions. I nod along but focus on other words instead: *You miss what's right in front of you.*

I've definitely missed something. Someone knows more about me and Edith than they should; someone knew how to set that trap for her, how to get inside my locked apartment. But first and foremost: they knew I had a connection to Morgan.

It might be someone I know myself, someone I assumed was harmless—until these bandages on my skin, the cuffs on Edith's wrists, proved they weren't. And even though it hurt when Nina questioned and criticized me, she's given me a path to follow the second I'm released.

Because they're still out there, the person responsible—for Morgan's murder, my attack, Edith's arrest. And if I'm going to find them, I need to stop seeing what I want. I need to go back, retrace my steps, and see what—or, in this case, who—is really there.

CHAPTER TWENTY-ONE

've got my laptop open to DonorConnect, a notebook open to a fresh page, and Daphne's poetry beside me on the bed. Everything's worthy of investigation—every message I've received, every scrap of research I've done, since my life intersected with Morgan's. I'm fresh off six hours of sleep, which my body and Mom demanded almost as soon as I got home, and now, I'm ready to review these past few weeks with clear, unbiased eyes.

At my parents' request, I'm back in my childhood room. I don't mind it; Bumper's snoring at the foot of the bed, taking over as my new nurse, and earlier, I was barely able to gather my stuff in my apartment without having a panic attack, without seeing a figure in dark clothes in my peripheral vision. Mom had done her best with the floor, but there was a rusty shadow on the tile that she said she'll need stronger products to remove. It made me wonder about Morgan's floors, all that beautiful hardwood—if even now, his blood is cemented in the seams between boards, keeping the secret of whoever sent it there.

Bumper rolls onto his side, a comforting weight on my feet that pulls me back to my surroundings, and I focus on the white walls to stop seeing so much red. But the longer I stare at the paint, clean as my new bandage, the more I realize there are things that haunt me here, too. The pillow I'm leaning against is the same one I cried into when Noah, my high school boyfriend, broke up with me two days before prom to take someone else as his date. The candle on the nightstand is the only gift Jared from college ever gave me—a last-minute purchase at CVS after he forgot my birthday. The closet stores the dress I wore to my sister's wedding, the night I hoped Gabe would whisper in my ear while dancing, tell me I looked beautiful, but instead he left after cocktails because "weddings aren't my thing."

Each of those men had claimed they loved me. They muttered it in the back seats of cars. Moaned it during sex. Tossed it over their shoulder on their way out the door. But now, years later, Nina's in my head, making me wonder—even as I consider the flaw in her logic. Because the more I think of Brad's "disrespect," his "booty call" text—I miss your face—the more I remember how happy it made me. And wouldn't disrespect feel horrible instead, the way it did when I was dumped before prom, pity-gifted a candle, abandoned at my sister's wedding?

Then again, the happiness from that text was temporary, drained out of me as soon as Brad went radio silent, and now I'm remembering the hours *before* he sent it.

It had been a week since I'd last tried to reach him, and as I took myself for a crisp November walk, trying to feel something other than sad, I was struck by the sunset spread out above me—a perfect swirl of pinks and purples. It stopped my breath for a second. It showed me something vital, that all the beauty in my life hadn't ended with my relationship, and I felt such a profound rush of hope that I snapped a photo of that sky and made it my profile picture on Instagram, re-placing the one of me and Brad. But it's like he sensed my moment of peace—or just noticed I'd swapped out his photo—because it was only hours later that he sent that text, and it would be months before I felt anything like serenity again.

I can't imagine doing that to someone I care about—baiting them with affection just to let them dangle indefinitely on that hook. So maybe Nina's right. Maybe I've been wrong about Brad. About all the men before him. I know the sound of love on somebody's lips—even in our final nights together, Brad mumbled *love you* in the dark—but maybe that's not the same as seeing that love. Maybe, after all this time, I don't know what it looks like at all.

"Stop," I scold myself, startling Bumper. I lean forward to stroke his head, then pull my computer onto my lap. I'm not supposed to be investigating my own past. Not my distant one, anyway. I'm supposed to be looking for someone I missed, someone with a reason to hurt Morgan—and by extension, Edith and me.

I start with DonorConnect, searching Morgan's messages for people in his life besides Daphne and Blair. But I strike out in the first few, and in the fourth, there's only a vague, passing mention of students he once had.

It's around then that he calls Daphne *unhinged*. She gave so much of her mind to her students, he hypothesizes, that it's no wonder it ultimately fractured. He says he encouraged her to see a doctor after she became, in his perspective, disproportionately upset he wouldn't share his drafts with her, and his words grate on me now. Daphne was only reacting to Morgan's pattern of using her past as plot, terrified it might happen again—especially once Blair told her he was writing a sequel to *Someone at the Door*. So her mind wasn't broken; it was battling for control. Control of her own narrative. Control of the emotional chaos he'd caused.

And yet, only two paragraphs later, he claims he loved her. But over and over he'd capitalized on her pain, then downplayed what he'd done. I remember his justification from one of Daphne's poems:

There's no copyright on trauma, a sentence that's both an admission of guilt and a dismissal of the charge.

How can that be love? If Nina were here, I think she'd call it something else.

I'm about to give up on the messages, but the thought of Nina makes me look again. She said I miss what's right in front of me—and she's right; I haven't been careful enough while reading this last one, too caught up in finally seeing Morgan clearly that I forgot to check for anyone else.

On my second read, it pops to the foreground: the reference to Piper. Well, to Daphne's "new friend," whom Morgan believed was responsible for some of Daphne's agitation at the end, but I've known from the start that it's Piper. Piper with her distrustful face and disdain for popular authors.

But also—I straighten against the headboard—Piper who knows Edith. Knows me.

Piper who believes Morgan killed her friend.

If my heart weren't on a delay, it would be picking up speed. Instead, there's a steady calm inside me as another connection clicks into place.

Piper was there, a couple days ago, on the sidewalk at Sweet Bean. She saw that I "spoke to the police," just like was referenced in the note left under Edith's door.

I grab my phone, unsure what I'm intending to do with it. Call Jackson? Tell him to look into Piper? It's too soon for that; I have no proof—and he already thinks he has some against Edith.

The moment of indecision gives my epiphany a chance to falter. Because if Piper wanted revenge against Morgan, why would she wait a year after Daphne's death to get it? And why would she set up Edith to take the fall? The two of them are friends and—

"Stop," I say again, because that last thought was courtesy of my Rosie-colored glasses, making me assume Piper wouldn't hurt someone close to her. But I've spoken to the woman only twice; I don't actually know her at all.

I reach for Daphne's books, leafing through them for any reference to Piper, a friend, anything, before remembering that the collections predated Daphne's relationship with her. The only poem I've read that might have overlapped with their friendship is the one on the postcard—Daphne's last, according to the bookstore owner.

I pull it out and read it again, just to be sure I haven't missed anything. But it's the same story I already know about Morgan: *You've robbed me again and again. Siphoned my love. My likeness. You won't stop until there's nothing left.* Still, I stare at the lines. *Siphoned my likeness.* It almost sounds like what I could have said about Other Rosie.

No, not "Other Rosie" anymore. Edith—who's probably still being grilled at the station.

I push aside the books, determined to keep researching Piper. I'll just have to do it the old-fashioned way. Through social media.

I start with Instagram. A few Piper Bells come up, but from their profile pictures alone, it's easy to rule them out as the one I know. I grunt as I clear the search bar—and that's when I see Blair's name instead, at the top of my recent results.

I hesitate for only a second before deciding my next move.

If Morgan referenced Piper to me, a person he barely knew, he might have spoken with Blair about her more at length.

I send her a message.

> Hey, I hope you're doing okay. A lot has happened since we spoke the other night. Someone's been arrested for Morgan's murder—but I'm positive they didn't do it and I'm still trying to figure out who actually did. Did Morgan ever talk to you about a woman named Piper Bell? She was one of Daphne's friends.

Tapping out of the chat window, I'm returned to Blair's profile, where Morgan's face fills half the frame of a new post. She's added another set of pictures, and I can't help myself. The desire to look is a hard habit to break, even as the sight of him—Daphne's *smiling swindler, blue-eyed betrayer*—leaves me a little nauseous.

The first photo is recent, given their hairstyles and Morgan's glasses, but as I keep swiping through them, I watch the pair age backward, as if Blair's trying to move Morgan further and further from the year of his death. Their hair gets shorter or longer; their skin gets smoother—but the evidence of their closeness never changes. In the final photo, they sit on their college green, a pillared library hulking behind them, and they tilt toward each other, laughing in a way that's reminiscent of pictures of me and Nina. Not for the first time, I imagine the immensity of Blair's loss. The love of a best friend is purer and steadier than any romance I've ever had, and I wonder now if I, too, have lost that, if things will ever be the same between me and Nina now that I know there's a percentage of her that thinks I'm capable of murder.

A chime on my phone cuts through the thought—Blair's responded.

> Wait what?? PIPER BELL was arrested for Morgan's murder?? Where did you hear that? It's not in the news and the cops won't give me updates!

> No, sorry, it was someone else who was arrested. A friend of mine.

> I TOLD YOU

Blair's reply calls back to our first conversation, when she cast suspicion on Nina as the only person who knew my connection to Morgan.

It's not worth it to correct her, to waste time explaining Edith's part in all this.

> My friend is innocent. You have to trust me. Someone else did this, and right now I'm trying to find info on Piper. Morgan told you about her?

Blair's all-caps use of her name certainly seems to suggest so.

A couple minutes pass without a response, and I see her staring at her phone, mulling over whether to "trust me" when I'm basically a stranger to her. Finally, she answers.

> No. I had no idea Morgan OR Daphne knew her. Maybe we're talking about different Piper Bells?

Without a picture to pull up, I offer the only details I have.

> She works at the Burnham Library. Curly blond hair.

> Jesus, YES. She moved to a rental down the street from me like six months ago. I've gone to her house a few times for drinks. You think SHE'S the one who killed Morgan?

For a few moments, I'm unable to respond, too stunned by the strangeness of it: Piper moving so close to Blair, spending time with the friend of the man she believes killed hers. It could just be a coincidence—Piper might not even be aware of Blair's connection to Morgan—but there's something prickling at me, telling me to treat this like a lead.

> What's Piper's address?

> Why? Are you going to go talk to her?

Actually, I'm wondering if Blair's neighborhood is close to Morgan's—because that could maybe explain it. If Piper wanted revenge against him, then maybe she rented a place nearby, where it would be easier to watch his every move.

Without waiting for my answer, Blair sends another message.

> Because if you're going to confront her, then come get me first so we can go together. Morgan is MY best friend and I'm tired of being in the dark.

I hesitate, considering the request. It's not exactly smart to knock on Piper's door, question her in her own house, and put her on the defense—especially when I'm already worried she might have attacked me—but with Blair as backup, Blair who told me she'd "never stop fighting" for Morgan . . .

> Okay. Send me your address and we'll talk to her.

CHAPTER TWENTY-TWO

The address Blair gives me is several miles from Morgan's house—not exactly close enough for Piper to keep tabs on him. As I climb the porch steps, the front door opens, and a woman steps out in leggings and a T-shirt. She startles when she sees me but quickly recovers.

"Are you Rosie? Blair mentioned you were stopping by. I'm Vanessa. Nice to meet you."

I return the greeting and shake the hand she offers, wondering just how much Blair mentioned, if her fiancée knows we're about to confront a possible killer.

I'm guessing not by how unbothered she seems as she flits by me toward her car. "Sorry, I'm late meeting a friend at the gym! Blair's inside, though. You can go on in."

I face the door she's left open and it's impossible not to flash back to the door I found ajar at Morgan's house, on a night just like this, the sunset bouncing off the windows, keeping me from seeing what's inside. I hesitate on the threshold, legs locked by that moment before the horrors began, until Blair calls out to me: "Come in before you let the damn cat out!"

I rush into the house and find Blair scooping up Sickle, who struggles in her arms. When I close the door behind me, she lets him jump to the floor and dash down the hall.

"He hates me," she says. "Do you mind taking your shoes off? We had our floors redone last month and we're still obsessive about them."

"Sure, but—aren't we going to Piper's?"

"Not until you tell me why you're suspicious of her in the first place. I'm not going in there, guns blazing, until I have all the information."

I hesitate. "Are you actually planning on bringing a gun?"

"It's a figure of speech, Rosie."

"Oh. Right." I slip off my sneakers, placing them on a tray that's cramped with flats and heels and boots.

"Sorry, I'm kind of a shoe whore," Blair says. "And terrible about putting them awa— Whoa, what happened?" She points to the bandage on my arm.

"What happened," I say, "is the reason I'm suspicious of Piper. One of them, at least."

At Blair's raised brow, I explain what she needs to know: Piper's hatred of Morgan, her conviction he killed Daphne, her connection to me and Edith—who, I add, was Morgan's Rosie, "and even though Edith lied to him, I don't think she killed him, because . . ." The intruder. The attack. The setup for Edith's arrest. It's on my last few sentences that my voice begins to rasp. I struggle to clear my throat and touch my neck at the grating pain.

"Jesus," Blair says. "That Edith-slash-Rosie thing is fucking weird. And nothing you've said is really *evidence* against Piper, but I guess . . . she does connect a lot of the pieces. I had no idea she was friends with Daphne." Her face bunches in anger. "If she really is the one who killed Morgan—I waved to that bitch just yesterday!"

I only cough in response, and Blair leans back, as if I could be contagious.

"Do you want some tea or something? I have this honey chamomile kind that's good for throats. And I guess we should probably . . . figure out a strategy for double-teaming Piper."

My words come out smoother, but still a bit strained. "That would be great, thanks."

"Sure. I'll be back. Sit if you want."

As she heads to the rear of the house, I move deeper into the living room, where there appears to be a project underway. Empty picture frames and matting are laid out on the love seat, photos spread along the coffee table. Blair's creating some kind of memorial for Morgan, selecting pictures to display, and it's like her Instagram has come to life. I even recognize the photo I looked at earlier, the one of the two of them on their college green. But this version is larger, not cropped like it was online, and it allows me to see a new detail at the bottom of the frame: Blair and Morgan are holding hands.

I squint at their fingers—tightly knotted—then study an adjacent photo, which appears to have been taken on the same day. In this one, their hands are still clasped, but now Blair's head is tipped onto Morgan's shoulder, her face almost dreamy as she gazes up at him.

It's an expression I've never seen her wear in other pictures or in real life. It's so much softer. Sweeter. Completely unguarded. And as close as Blair and Morgan have always seemed in photos, there's something else that's different about her expression here.

It's not the way you look at a friend.

A memory prods at me. Last night. Edith and me on my kitchen floor. What was it she said about Morgan? *He told me he's still friends with one of his college girlfriends.*

I pick up the picture, look at their grip on each other, and it's obvious: Morgan was talking about Blair. They were a couple once.

I circle the table, scouring the other photos for evidence of romance. I lean closer to inspect body language, hand placement, as questions spring up. How long did their relationship last? When did it go from love to friendship? Who was the one to officially end it?

The pictures offer no answers. All I see are the ways Blair has changed over the years, even more than Morgan, whose hair is simply shaggier in some photos. But Blair transforms. In their college days, she sports a platinum pixie, which she then grew out into something more wheat-colored and shapeless. Then there's a sleek blond bob. Then, in sharp contrast to her lighter hair and barely there makeup, there's her current look: bold eyeliner; heavy mascara; long, dark hair. A look that's less like the woman Morgan dated in college—and more like the woman he married.

You've robbed me again and again.

My body tenses, Daphne's words booming through my head.

Siphoned my love. My likeness.

I hold myself still as the line reverberates. *My likeness. My likeness.* Earlier today, there'd been something there, reminding me of Other Rosie. Of a person who'd appropriated my identity. I thought I'd been applying the poem to my personal experience. But maybe—

You won't stop until there's nothing left.

My hand is frozen around the photo of Morgan and Blair, my gaze stuck to the ones on the table. And now it's Piper's words that return to me, from the library the day we met. She said Daphne was "freaked out," and she was sure it was because of Morgan. In a way, Blair corroborated that, suggesting Daphne's behavior was about the sequel Morgan was writing. But as I stare at the photos of one woman who looks like another, a new theory emerges, souring my stomach: What if Daphne's agitation wasn't about Morgan at all?

What if Daphne was afraid of Blair?

"Okay, I'd let this steep a few minutes, but here you go."

I whirl around as Blair reenters the room, holding out a mug to me, a tea bag draped over its lip. Her eyes flick from my face to the picture clenched between my fingertips.

"These photos," I say. "You— Did you—" My words stumble as my mind keeps churning, working toward something it hasn't articulated yet. I start over, back at the beginning. "You dated Morgan?"

"Uh, yeah," Blair says, arm still extended to offer the tea. "Why, is that a problem for you?"

"And then you changed yourself, years later, to look like Morgan's wife."

Blair's face is blank. But when she sets the mug onto an end table, she's ungentle enough that liquid sloshes over the rim. "Daphne Thorne did not have a monopoly on dark hair."

"You were still in love with Morgan, weren't you?"

"What?" She shakes her head like it's a non sequitur.

"You tried to be more of what he wanted. More of *who* he wanted."

The disgust in my voice is as audible as the strain. I clear my throat—because that tone is hypocritical.

"I get it," I add. "I've done it, too."

I may not have dyed my hair or changed my makeup to appeal to a man, but I've altered myself in dozens of other ways. Filling my playlists with indie bands for Brad, memorizing lyrics to songs I didn't even like. Watching hours of monotonous gameplay online, just so I could convince Gabe I was a cool gamer girl. Distressing a Patriots jersey so Tyler would think I wore it every Sunday, saying nothing when he threw an end table after a Super Bowl loss, even though he'd recently told me that girls "act insane" over Taylor Swift.

"You loved him," I say, "so you tried to be like the woman *he* loved. Except—you terrified Daphne with that. She wrote a poem about you. One of her last."

Blair's gaze darkens. "What are you talking about?"

I recite what I remember, paraphrase the rest.

"She sounds like she thought you were going to hurt her," I conclude.

"That's bullshit, I didn't *mean* to hurt her."

I almost miss it. Her tone is so disgusted, so dismissive, that the meaning beneath it almost whizzes right by. But then her eyes jolt wide, as if she's slipped up, blurted a secret, and the confession implicit in her statement bounces like an echo between us.

"But you *did* hurt her," I say, speaking the confirmation aloud.

Blair opens her mouth, her throat creaking without words, her breath sputtering across her lips.

"Look," she finally says, "*she* came after *me*. I was defending myself!"

"She . . . attacked you? When?"

"She wasn't even supposed to be home! I'd made sure she wasn't. I was just going to slip in and out so I could— God, you're going to twist this into something it's not, but: Morgan had mentioned how Daphne had this new . . . scent. A body wash or perfume that made him want her like crazy. Had him pulling her into bed every chance he got."

Blair's lips twist like she's tasted something bad. "He was always doing that to me. Talking about their sex life. Just to torture me, I think. Because—yes, I loved him, and he knew that. And that night I just wanted to see what this"—she rolls her eyes—"magical new scent was. But Daphne found me in her bathroom and freaked the fuck out. She said I'd been stalking her—which is ridiculous! We lived in the same town; I couldn't help if we ended up in the same places sometimes! She accused me of trying to steal Morgan from her, but *she* stole him from *me*."

Blair's breathing intensifies, each exhale heavier than the last.

"Right before they met, he and I had started hooking up again. It had been like ten years since we dated—but that's how strong the pull was between us; it was never really over. Morgan acted like it was no big deal, we were just having fun, but we both knew that was bullshit: it's never casual when you sleep with your best friend. So I thought we'd finally be together—forever this time. Until suddenly he wanted to stop. Because of Daphne."

She crosses her arms, paces a tight line between the couch and table. I take advantage of her distraction, glancing toward the door to gauge the distance.

"And I kept waiting for him to get sick of her, which is what he does. He starts to pick apart the things he once praised. And he *was* getting sick of her. He was sick of her trauma dumping. Sick of her complaining about what he decided to *do* with that trauma. Which was memorialize it. Daphne should have been fucking honored. He never drew inspiration from me."

She pushes out another huff of air. "And it doesn't even make sense—why would she care if I 'stole' him? She was always so tense around him, always so miserable about one thing or another. So why did she even want him?"

It's a rhetorical question, but my mind—eager to dissociate from Blair, from this horrible story that can only end one way—conjures the answer: for some of us, bad love feels safer than no love at all.

"And like I said, I didn't need to *steal* Morgan from Daphne. I just needed to remind him: he'd wanted me before, he could want me again. I could be *exactly* what he wanted. But that night, Daphne went on and on about how I was trying to make her look crazy because she'd figured out—"

Blair stops, eyes locking with mine, and for a second, I think she's reacting to my movements, the way I've been inching from her as she speaks. But then she clenches her jaw, like she's caging her words.

"Figured out what?" I ask.

She hasn't blinked since she cut herself off. Her face is as tight as a held breath.

"It was so stupid," she finally says. "Nothing for her to get so worked up about, just—" She shrugs. "Morgan wasn't actually writing a sequel to *Someone at the Door*. I only told Daphne that to fuck with her. I knew she'd get upset and yell at Morgan and act all crazy and—"

Blair pauses. "Ha. Okay. I hear it. I guess she was right; I *was* trying to make her look crazy."

As Blair laughs, I force myself not to react, but the confession—not stupid; ruthless—zaps me like a live wire, my nerves blazing inside me.

"Not like she needed much help! I saw it firsthand, that night in her bathroom. She admitted to snooping through Morgan's computer earlier that day, looking for his latest contract. She'd seen it wasn't for a sequel. So she went off about that, too. Said I'd been *gaslighting* her, along with all her other accusations: I was stalking her, trying to *be* her, trying to take her place." Blair laughs again, dismissive. "At one point, she even lunged forward like she was going to push me or something. So I pushed her first. Textbook self-defense. But obviously I didn't expect her to crack her fucking head on the edge of the vanity!"

I reel back, staring at Blair—but I can't even focus on her. Instead, the scene solidifies in front of me: the fractured skull, the bathroom tile, the blood. I've imagined it so many times, but only now do I feel like I'm in that bathroom with her. It's all I see—Daphne's body splayed, the white floor slowly soaking red—until the image shifts and I see myself, just a few hours later, the nurses at the hospital prepping me for surgery.

I can't help but go there. Daphne's blood haloing around her head is the only reason mine keeps pumping. I already knew that. Knew I'd have to live with that cruel, convenient equation. But now I'm standing in front of the person who caused Daphne's injury. And I feel it in my heart, which is finally pounding—the loss of a woman I didn't know until she was a part of me. A woman who spun her pain into poetry. Who was never loved the way she deserved.

"You left her there to die?" I ask, barely above a whisper.

"Not *to die*. I figured Morgan would rush in any second and help her. It would have been easy to deny it if Daphne accused me of anything—Morgan trusted my mind way more than hers—but it never even came to that. Because everything else I told you is true. Morgan said he heard a crash in the bathroom but didn't check to see what had happened. And it's not like Daphne was being quiet before she fell; he had to have heard her voice, too. So it's interesting, isn't it, how he completely ignored her? I mean, would he really do that to someone he *loved*?"

No. Absolutely not. But there's no time to dwell on that. I need to get out of here. Away from the woman who pushed Daphne to her death and isn't even sorry.

I'm closer to the door than Blair is, but if she sees me run for it, she could try to pull me back. My eyes sweep the floor, mapping each step I'll need to take. There's about ten feet between me and the way out. I'll have to grab the shoes Blair insisted I remove, but maybe I could . . . go for the mug of tea? Splash the still-steaming liquid in her face and escape while she's—

A grating sound scrapes through the thought. I turn toward it and find Sickle scratching the hardwood, like there's something buried beneath it.

Blair shouts before she leaps at him—"Not my floors, you little shit!"—and that's all the distraction I need. I slide toward the door in my socks, reach down for my sneakers with one hand, grab the doorknob with the other.

And I freeze.

There's a pair of boots beside my shoes. Black leather with laces and thick soles. I've seen dozens of women—and men—in boots just like them, but these are different.

These are ones I've seen so recently. These are ones with a scuff on the toe—shaped like half a heart.

CHAPTER TWENTY-THREE

"**N**ot so fast, Rosie."

I'm still crouched, hand on the door, when I look up to find Blair holding a gun.

She didn't scramble for it. Didn't fumble at a locked cabinet. She must have had it on her this entire time.

She jerks the gun to the left, motioning for me to step away from the door. My hand has already slipped from the knob, too slack to keep its grip. I follow the path she traces, shuffling closer to the middle of the room.

"It was you," I say, "in my apartment. You—" I glance at my bandage, which Blair asked about when I arrived, as if she weren't the one to cut my arm in the first place. "We were gonna go to Piper's, interrogate her about the attack, when the whole time it was you who—"

"Jesus, you're so gullible. We were never going to talk to Piper. I have no idea who that woman is or where she lives. But it got you over here, didn't it?" Her thumb pushes forward—*click*—releasing the safety on the gun. "You should've just let Edith take the fall."

I've never had a gun aimed at me before. The single black eye, staring at me from the end of the barrel, makes it even harder to process what Blair means. I start simple: Piper is not her neighbor. Piper didn't do any of this.

"You killed Morgan," I say. "You murdered your best friend."

"Don't give me that look. I didn't plan to kill him."

"Just like you didn't plan to kill Daphne?"

Blair squares her shoulders. "Yes. Exactly like that."

"Except you didn't push Morgan and cause him to fall. Unless you're saying he fell onto that knife?"

"Shut up, I didn't *want* him to die," Blair spits out. "I love him." Her voice breaks around it, *love*, tears icing her eyes. She sniffs hard, blinking them away, then flexes her finger, nearly touching the trigger.

"Does your fiancée know you're in love with him?" I ask, but in my peripheral vision, I scope for a weapon, a way out.

"It's not like I cheated on Vanessa. I love her, too, you know. I'm not a *monster*. And anyway, when we first started dating, it wasn't even— I just wanted to wake Morgan up. He was so messed up after Daphne died. He needed to see me with someone else, realize he couldn't bear to lose me, too. But he was too deep in his guilt over Daphne. And in the meantime, I fell for Vanessa." Daphne shrugs one shoulder, as if it's so casual, falling in love. "But it's not the same as what I felt for Morgan. Morgan was my home. My family. Better than family, because *he* actually loved me."

"He loved you so much that you killed him?" It's antagonistic, but she seems to be responding to that. This is the woman who stabbed and strangled me. Stabbed Morgan. Shoved Daphne. She clearly likes a fight.

"I was giving him one more chance," she grinds out, adjusting her grip on the gun. "I'd gotten engaged so Morgan would know I was serious—but he called my bluff. Acted all happy for me. Tried to talk wedding plans. It was like a game to him. One of us would have to blink first, and I swore it wouldn't be me this time. But then *Rosie* came along."

She hisses the name. My name. But I know she's not talking about me.

"Right away, he rubbed their relationship in my face, just like he used to when Daphne was alive. It amused him, making me jealous. You saw the emails; he never spared any details. I know every kiss he and Rosie had."

I almost nod—I did see the emails. But according to Edith, none of those kisses actually happened; their first wasn't until their last moments together.

Judging by the pained set of Blair's jaw, the fiction in Morgan's emails is still achingly real to her. And maybe that was the point. *It was like a game to him.* With Blair as the toy.

"Then, when I went to his house that night, Rosie was *there*," Blair says. "I saw her through the doors in the back, kissing him in the kitchen with her stupid pink hair—no offense—and that only emphasized the urgency of what I'd come to do." She runs the back of her wrist across her forehead, wiping invisible sweat, then drops her arm to her side. Her aim on me slackens a bit, slipping from my head to my heart. "I couldn't let Rosie be another Daphne, luring him away from me. But then they seemed to be arguing—she left in a hurry, all upset—and I thought: great, even better timing."

"Better timing . . . to kill him?"

I'm not good at this, provoking her, prompting her to keep speaking. My words sound wooden, coated with a meanness I don't even recognize. Blair blasts me with a cold stare, returns both hands to her weapon—and I wonder if I miscalculated, if this will be the comment that convinces her to pull the trigger and end the discussion altogether.

My eyes dart toward the door, then the wide picture window. It's dark out now, and the living room lamps blaze, allowing the glass to reflect the scene: Blair with her feet planted, shoulders back, pointing a gun at an unarmed woman. It should be easy to see from the sidewalk. Maybe someone walking out there will glance our way and alert the police. Maybe Vanessa will come home early and stop her fiancée. Maybe I still have a chance.

"Hey, get away from there!"

In looking at the window, hoping for witnesses, I've drifted closer to it. I step back, letting Blair steer me with the gun until we've switched positions and she's blocking the door.

"And stop looking at me like that," Blair demands. "You're still acting like I wanted him dead. I'm *devastated* he's dead."

Again, her voice splinters, eyes shining in the light.

"Then how did it happen?" I ask, forcing a softer, more empathetic tone.

She swipes a stray tear. "I told him I was still in love with him, and if he didn't admit he felt the same way, then I really would marry Vanessa. And do you know how he responded? He said, 'Come on, Blair, you know that's just puppy love.' *Puppy love!*" The phrase whips into the air, making me flinch. "Like I was nothing but a kid with a crush. And then he laughed, like I was crazy for thinking the man who called me his best friend, who shared his biggest secrets with me, might actually want to *be* with me, too. And it just—it broke me. My brain. My heart. I don't even remember picking up the knife. It was just there, on the counter, and then it was in my hand. And I—"

She thrusts the gun forward in demonstration. Then she stares at the weapon, almost awed by the memory.

"It felt like instinct." Another tear slides down her cheek, but this time, she doesn't bother wiping it.

Her eyes linger on the gun, her hand. She tongues the tear, now at the corner of her lip. "I pulled the knife out, almost immediately. But that was a mistake. The blood just . . . gushed out of him."

I shake my head, the image appalling—but not aligning with the scene I stumbled upon. "The knife was in his chest when I found him."

Blair nods, pulling in a shaky breath, her gaze unfocused now. "He was suffering. So I put him out of his misery. Put me out of mine. It was a kindness, really. To both of us."

Her arm sinks, as if growing heavy, the gun drifting lower. I move a step away from her. Then another. Somewhere, in the back of the house, there must be another door.

"I told you not to look at me like that!" Blair shouts, freezing my feet.

"Like what?" I ask—anything to keep her talking.

"Like you think I'm demented. As if you're so perfectly sane and stable," Blair scoffs. "Two nights ago you were sleeping in a wedding dress! Why's that, Rosie? I've been dying to know."

I shouldn't feel smacked by another revelation. I always knew the person who attacked me must have been the one to button my dress. But there have been so many pieces to Blair's confession, so many horrors to absorb, that I've been slow to snap the whole picture into place. And I won't let her turn this around on me when she's the one who still owes answers.

"Why were you even there? Were you planning to attack me that night, and then—what? Got distracted by the dress? Decided to freak me out instead?"

"Well, it really was quite the distraction. You were passed the fuck out, in a *wedding dress*, and I'm sorry, Rosie, I just couldn't help it. It was too easy to fuck with you."

I don't know why I'm surprised when she ends the explanation there. This is the same woman who admitted to "fucking with" Daphne. She seems to thrive on manipulation. Power. Maybe that's due to the lack of power she felt she had with Morgan. Or maybe she doesn't deserve to have me rationalize her decisions. Maybe still, even now, my Rosie-colored glasses are on.

"But no, our scuffle in your apartment happened when it was meant to," Blair says. "That first night was just to scope out your place, find the best way in—and what do you know, you gave it to me yourself." She fires off a chuckle. "The key was right in the lock. As if you *wanted* me to make a spare."

She grins like she expects me to applaud her. "And actually, it was you who gave me everything. Not just the key. I'd seen Rosie—sorry, *Edith*—through Morgan's back door, but I didn't know how to find her again. Which obviously I had to—she'd make the perfect suspect. So I went to that stupid gathering at the green, thinking she'd show up, but then: you were there instead. A different Rosie. Not the one I'd seen kissing Morgan—her hair was shorter than yours. And when you couldn't figure out who Fake Rosie was from the emails I showed you? Fine. All I had to do was watch you until you inevitably crossed paths with her."

Watch me. She means stalk, of course. Because that day on Sweet Bean's patio, when we ran into Edith and Piper, I'd felt someone's gaze on me, grazing my face as palpably as a hand. I dismissed it first as Nina's, then Edith's. But it must have been Blair's. She was there, lurking somewhere—just another thing, right in front of me, I missed—and she must have recognized Edith as the woman she'd seen at Morgan's.

"From there, the plan became simple: give the cops a reason to investigate her. They'd take some DNA, find it was a match to the hair *you* told me they found, then assume she was some kind of psycho who murdered Morgan and killed the woman she'd pretended to be while dating him."

My eyes narrow. "Except I wasn't killed."

"Well. Yeah. I didn't get the timing *exactly* right. Edith was supposed to stumble upon a much different scene."

I stare at her until her meaning crystallizes. My hand drifts to my neck, where one night ago, Blair's arm clamped, tighter and tighter, until I couldn't breathe.

"Someone had to go down for Morgan's murder," she adds, "and obviously it wasn't going to be me. Might as well be Edith, who'd twisted him around her little finger, given him new ways to torture me, got him thinking of ways to use *her* in his writing when he'd known her all of five minutes. And you! You're not even grateful, are you? That Morgan saw your story, your transplant, as something worthy of his art. What makes you so fucking special? He never even *met* you. But I told him every cruel thing my parents have done to me, every heartless thing they've said, and I never once made it into his books. And if my pain wasn't enough—if I wasn't enough—then why the hell were Daphne and Edith and *you?*"

She widens her stance, glaring at me down the barrel of the gun. Her finger twitches on the trigger.

"If you kill me," I blurt, "your whole plan will be for nothing. The cops will arrest you anyway."

"I wouldn't be so sure," Blair says. Then she softens her gaze, shifts from smug to scared, speaks in a shaky voice. "It was s-so terrifying, Off-officer. Rosie just—came after me tonight. I had to fight back, but oh god, I didn't want to kill her!"

She imitates a sob. Then the fear disappears as quickly as she conjured it, a tiny smile returning to her lips.

"They'll have no evidence against me. They'll have DMs where I invited you over because I was determined to know who killed my best friend. And—" Her face transforms again, back to the trembling, trau-matized expression from seconds ago. "Officer, I don't understand it. She told me she was suspicious of Piper Bell, but she started accusing *me* of attacking her. I think . . . I think Piper was just a ploy to get to me."

"They'll see you didn't even know Piper. That she's not your neigh-bor. That *you* used her as a ploy to get *me* here."

Blair hesitates—but only for a second. "Don't worry, I'll think of something."

There's a chilling finality to the way she says it, like she's done offering explanations, like she's just as aware as I am that her fiancée could return while I'm still able to talk.

She flexes the hand bracing the gun.

Of all the ways I've envisioned I would die—gasping for breath; cut open on an operating table; boiling with infection; whittled to bone by cancer; alone in a hospital bed, my hands unheld—I never saw it ending like this.

I struggle for one last way to stall: "Did you—" I swallow and try again. "Does Vanessa know what you've done?"

A muscle jumps in Blair's jaw. She opens her mouth to answer—and I lunge for her.

I claw for the gun, slam my shoulder into her chest, feel the stunned whoosh of her breath explode against my cheek.

My life will be shorter than others'—that's the deal I accepted in receiving Daphne's heart—but I can't let it end tonight. Because if I die now, the truth dies with me.

I have no choice but to fight. For Daphne. For Edith.

And for me, too.

Our bodies crash to the floor, and it's a repeat of last night—only this time, Blair and I both scramble for the weapon, and I'm not running for the door. We twist and tumble, gritting our teeth. When she rakes her nails against my bandage, I cry out but I don't let it stop me.

I can't.

I've barely begun my second chance at life, so consumed by fears of a lonely, loveless future. But right now, faced with the desperate glint in Blair's eyes, I know what I'm up against is worse: no future at all.

I reach higher as Blair holds the gun above her head, my hands scrabbling up her arm to her wrist. I graze the gun at nearly the same instant I feel it slip out of reach. Then Blair's fist bashes my side and I fold inward at the flare of pain. She scrambles to slide away from me, but I latch on to her.

"Get off me!" she snarls. "You're not going to—"

Sirens blare through her sentence. We freeze, my hand wrapped around hers, both of us wrapped around the gun.

Lights bounce outside, casting the room in red and blue. The colors dance on Blair's skin—a blush, a bruise. Then footsteps pound toward us, and I scurry off her, just as she points the gun at the door.

Three hard knocks rattle the windows. "Police, open up!"

The gun quivers in Blair's hand. Her eyes blaze as she attempts to steady it.

"Put it down," I warn her.

She shakes her head, mumbling something I can't make out.

"Blair. You have to put it down."

She looks at me then, tears coating her eyes like resin, hardening them into an impenetrable sheen. "No. This isn't fair. None of this would even be happening if he'd—" She blinks in time to two more knocks. "I just wanted him to love me. I just wanted us—"

I never hear the end of her sentence. The door bursts open, splinters spraying out like the air has shattered. Three officers rush into the room, guns pointed at Blair.

"Drop your weapon, now!" one shouts.

Blair doesn't so much as flinch. Her gaze is still pressed to mine. "Everyone's going to say I went crazy. But I wasn't crazy. I was *hurting*." The word scrapes out of her, raw and ragged. "I still am. Right here." She places the tip of the gun against her chest, her heart, and I suck in a breath, just as the police take a synchronized step toward her.

"Ma'am," one starts, "you don't need to do this. Just put the gun down and we'll—"

"Jesus, are you serious?" Blair's head snaps toward the officer. "I'm not going to kill myself."

She slaps the gun onto the floor, and I shield myself, cower away from it, anticipating a blast. By the time I uncover my face, an officer has scooped it up.

"Put your hands in the air," the cop in front orders.

Blair looks at me again, her expression a blend of defeat and defiance.

"I guess it doesn't matter," she says, raising her arms. "I won't be with him either way."

A cop twists Blair's arms behind her back, clicks on handcuffs, then hauls her to a standing position. Another officer kneels down beside me, but her words come to me muffled as Blair is marched outside.

"Sorry, what?" I ask. The woman's face is concerned, her eyes pinched with urgency. She repeats herself, but I still don't hear her, because now there's a voice outside, rising above hers.

"Ma'am, please stay out here, ma'am—"

There's a blur of motion as someone runs into the house—followed by a familiar sound.

"Rosie!"

"Oh my god." I tear away from the officer, struggling to get to my feet, but Nina reaches me first. She falls to the floor beside me.

"What— How did you—" I stumble over the questions, too stunned to see her.

"You weren't at your house. I checked your location and didn't recognize it. I just—"

The cop who tried to stop her outside surges forward to intervene, but the officer nearest us puts a hand on his arm; there's no threat to anyone here.

"—wanted to make sure you were okay. I saw your car in the driveway, saw that woman in the window with the gun, and I called 911, but they said I'd make things worse if I intervened, that she could— She could—"

Nina breaks off, dissolves into tears, and I slump against her chest as she gathers me in her arms. I focus on her warmth, her softness and solidity, unable to articulate my surprise. I hoped for someone to spot us through the window, call the cops just in time, but I hadn't considered it would be Nina. Maybe I should have. This is not the first time I've been crumpled on the floor in her arms.

"They told me to wait outside until they got here," she says. "But I swear if they'd taken even a second longer, I would have knocked that woman to the ground."

A laugh sputters out of me. "I've never seen you knock so much as a fly to the ground."

"I would if it was pointing a gun at you."

"Like a fly-sized gun? Or a regular gun? Because that would be a strong fly."

"Stop." Nina sniffles as she laughs, and I burrow closer to her. I'm dizzy with it all—Blair's confessions; Blair's finger on the trigger; the cops who crowd the room—but Nina keeps me from spinning.

"Do you hate me?" she asks.

I pull back to look at her. "Hate you? You saved my life!"

"But the things I said at the hospital. I shouldn't have talked to you like that. And that ten percent thing? I'm so sorry, Rosie. I didn't *really* think you could kill Morgan. You just want love so badly that it blinds you sometimes." She pauses, biting her lip. "Okay, that sounds like I'm justifying it again, but— I don't know how to put it."

"It's okay," I say. "You're right. It does blind me sometimes."

Or, at the very least, it compromises my vision, my Rosie-colored glasses making everything pink, love-tinged, so they camouflage red flags. Can I blame Nina, then, for doubting me a little? My grasp on reality isn't always reliable. And maybe what really matters is that she knows my flaws and still chooses me as her friend. That even with that ten percent, she tracked me down tonight, believing I was worth protecting.

"It's okay," I repeat, sinking against her, tightening our embrace.

Nina's heart drums against my ear, and it's a beat that never wavers. I tune out the cops, close my eyes against the flashing lights, and as my own heart thumps, I press myself closer to her, listening to all that love for me.

CHAPTER TWENTY-FOUR

"**W**ait, so you just . . . grabbed the gun?"

"Well. I tried to. I wasn't very successful."

"Still! That's so brave! I would have frozen."

I pop a forkful of pasta into my mouth. Edith and I are finally getting that dinner I promised her weeks ago—and we're celebrating, too. It's been two days since the police informed Edith she's no longer a suspect, three since the night Blair was arrested. There's a bruise beneath my rib cage, a twinge when I twist my torso, a scratch on my cheek, and one of my stitches had to be replaced, but despite the stress on my body, my heart is fine. That's what the labs and scans promised, anyway. Over the next two weeks, I'll have my regularly scheduled biopsy and angiogram, so I won't rest completely easy until I get those results. But for now, I'm here, eating delicious food, enjoying Edith's company.

"This means you fought that woman twice," she says. "Both times she had a weapon, and both times you won."

"I don't know if we can call it winning. You saved me the first time, Nina and the cops saved me the second time. I really just"—I shrug—"got lucky."

"Sure, but you're alive," Edith says. "I call that winning."

I chew my pasta, nodding. Because she's right. I've won. Every beat of my heart—of Daphne's heart—is another victory. I not only fought Blair; I stopped her from silencing that heart for a second time.

"Seriously, you're a badass," Edith continues. "Blair was clearly crazy. She would have killed you in an instant. But you went for it."

Out of sheer habit, I wince at *crazy*, even as I understand why Edith says it. Blair killed people. Stalked them. Attempted another murder. Nothing about that suggests she was sane. But Edith's wrong about one thing: Blair didn't kill me in an instant. She could have. She'd hidden that gun on her body with the intention of taking me out. But first, she talked me through her crimes. Laid out what she believed was unimpeachable logic for each one. I don't know if she genuinely thought I'd agree with her actions, or if she simply wanted to unburden herself of all her secrets. Either way, one of the most dangerous things about Blair in the end was that, to her, her story wasn't crazy at all; it was common: she'd simply loved someone.

"I mean, I know I did some problematic things when it came to Morgan," Edith says. "But Blair took wanting him to an extreme."

I just wanted him to love me, she said as the cops closed in. *I just wanted us—*

I never heard the rest of what she planned to say. But I don't have to. That interrupted sentence was a truth all its own. *I just wanted us.*

And there's something else Blair said, right as she surrendered to the police: *I guess it doesn't matter.* As if, after everything she'd done to frame Edith, to escape punishment, Blair realized that her freedom, her future, was useless to her if Morgan didn't love her.

It haunts me, how familiar that feels. After Brad ended things, I caged myself in my bedroom. Darkened the windows. Refused the company of people who cared. Muted all phone numbers except for his, which never lit up my screen. It was debilitating work, turning my pain into a prison, but disturbingly easy, too, because just like Blair,

I'd pinned my happiness on somebody else. And over the years, I'd changed myself, bit by bit, for so many different men that, without one, I had no core identity to fall back on. I became only the absence of them.

It's an uncomfortable fact I have to reckon with, how much I see myself in Blair. But now that I've had my past reflected back to me, I'm hopeful that, in the future, Blair doesn't have to be a mirror. She can be a warning.

"So, to recap," Edith says, "you're brave, you're badass." She ticks the qualities off on her fingers. "And you're . . . beautifully belligerent?"

"I'm *what*?"

"Sorry. I was on a roll with the Bs. It felt like the third thing had to match."

As she laughs at herself, I'm reminded of something I wrote to Morgan on DonorConnect, when I was trying out his Foolproof Trick to Naming Pets: Wait, why do those all start with the same letter? I'm suddenly nervous I only know nouns that begin with B. The memory prickles, but it isn't painful. It's more like recalling a date that started promising before ending disastrously. It feels like a bullet dodged.

"Let me try again," Edith says. "You're brave, you're badass, and you battled a literal murderer. There. *Battle* starts with B."

We laugh together now, even though there's nothing funny about Blair's crimes or how close I came to becoming one. Still, I appreciate Edith's praise.

I've never thought of myself as brave or badass. Truthfully, I've thought so little about my own attributes over the years, too concerned with creating the ones my boyfriends wanted to see. But this portrait Edith's painted of me—someone who battles danger and wins—makes me sound like a woman I'd like to know.

Even more, she makes me sound like a survivor.

Maybe in a dim, distant way, I already knew that. I survived my transplant, after all. But when my cardiologist first informed me I needed a new heart, I didn't think of surviving as something I'd *do*—actively, with intention. I thought of it as something that may or may not happen to me, a thing like the weather, completely beyond my control. But now I think: it was *me* who made a home for a foreign organ. *Me* who swallowed the meds that kept my body from kicking it out. *Me* who endured the side effects, who kept to the schedule of painful tests and biopsies. So, in those ways, surviving *was* a choice, and it's one that, every single day, for more than a year now, I've been brave enough to make.

How strange I didn't see it before. I was too focused on what I'm lacking—a romantic partner, a fail-safe future—that I forgot to notice what I've had all along: myself. A woman who was so strong, so *badass*, she lived through losing her heart.

"Also, I really want to thank you," Edith says. "Most people would've run for the hills after what I did—and I wouldn't blame them. So I'm amazed you didn't write me off. That you trusted me when I told you I didn't kill Morgan. That you actually want to spend time with me, now that it's all over."

I smile, resisting the urge to brush off her thanks, to tell her it was probably just my Rosie-colored glasses that kept me fighting for her. A few days ago, when I was huddled on the floor with Nina, I recognized she was right; those glasses had distorted my vision, convinced me that so many people in my life had been better than they actually were. But at the awe in Edith's eyes, I consider that maybe those glasses aren't always an impairment. I love that I look for the best in people. If I didn't, I might have done exactly what Edith said—written her off as soon as I learned she was Other Rosie. And that means I wouldn't be here at this dinner tonight, discussing it all with a new friend.

I'm realizing, too, that whenever Nina and I have talked about my Rosie-colored glasses in the past, we've always done so as if I've chosen to put them on. A lot of times I do, that's true—or I've just worn them so long it's not even a choice anymore. But there have also been times when people—men I loved—have effectively handed them to me, encouraged me to look through their pretty pink lenses. Those men told me they loved me, then later proved they didn't—proved, like Nina said, they didn't even respect me. But while they were standing there, right in front of me, saying exactly what they knew I wanted to hear, why wouldn't I believe them? Why wouldn't I trust the vision they showed me?

Thinking of it that way, I can't really blame myself for feeling a little unbalanced, a little unstable—yes, a little crazy—once they ripped those glasses off, once I saw the world in all its true chaotic color.

When I focus on Edith again, she's staring into the distance with an almost anguished expression. I follow her gaze to a man at another table, his hand knotted with a woman's. He's stroking her knuckles, smiling at her as she laughs through a story she's telling. For a second, I worry that the man is Edith's ex, that I've taken her tonight to the one place where her still-raw wounds would be clawed back open. But then she says, "I miss that," her voice so brittle it's nearly a whisper, and I understand it's not the sight of the man that hurts her; it's the couple.

"You'll have it again," I say, because I know that's what she needs to hear right now.

But the truth is: she might not. Her last relationship might truly be her last relationship. There's no way of knowing, no guarantees. Love is too fickle and unpredictable for that. Life is too. But either way, I know Edith will be okay. Because even if she doesn't find a romantic partner, she's a sweet, funny person who won't be alone. And at the very least, she'll have me. Which is something, I think. Something pretty good.

———

Two days later, Just Say Yes is quiet. It's a random lull in the afternoon, a two-hour break between appointments, the only sound coming from the back, where Marilee slices through tape to open deliveries that came in this morning. So I'm surprised when a woman enters the store, eyes sweeping the racks of dresses before she approaches me.

"Can I help you?" I ask.

"Um. I'm not sure. I need a dress, but my budget is pretty small. I was just driving by and figured I'd see if you even carry any dresses in my price point."

"Sure, what is it?"

"Four hundred dollars?" She cringes a little, as if worried I'll judge her.

Inwardly, I cringe, too, because our least expensive dresses run around twice that much. Still, I check the computer at the reception desk in case there's a markdown I've forgotten.

"No, I'm so sorry," I say when my search yields nothing.

The woman's shoulders fall, even as she nods. "That's okay, I knew it was a long shot. My fiancé and I are teachers, so money's already tight, but we're saving for a down payment on a house, and even with a small wedding—" She stops, waving in apology. "You don't need my life story. I just saw the window display and couldn't help myself."

I bite my lip, glancing at the computer. I'm not allowed to comp a dress again until September, months from now, but I feel the sting of her disappointment as if it were my own.

"Thanks anyway," she says, turning to go.

"Wait! Hold on."

As she pivots back, I look at her more closely. We're about the same height. Similar body types. It might not be a perfect fit, but—

"There is one dress," I say.

"There is?" Hope springs to her face.

"Yeah—one sec." I open a browser, search for a Casablanca gown from a few seasons ago, plugging in the name and style number I know by heart. When the image pops up, I swivel the monitor so the woman can see it. "Do you like this?"

Her eyes instantly sparkle. Her mouth opens with a gentle intake of breath.

"It's gorgeous," she says. "I love the beading. And the lace." She steps closer to get a better look. "That's really in my price range?"

Behind her, the door jingles as someone enters the store. I see only their shoulder, an elbow, a shoe—another deliveryman, I'm sure. "I'll be with you in a moment," I call, before answering the woman's question about the dress: "Let's set up a time for you to come try it on. And if you love it, it's yours. No charge."

Her mouth opens wider, her brows creased in confusion.

"It was purchased by another customer," I say—which is true. "Her wedding was canceled." Not even close to true. "So she's donating it back to us, for a situation just like this." Soon to be true.

"Oh," the woman says, "I'm so sorry that happened. But that's such a nice thing she's doing! I probably would have just sold it." She chuckles before taking out her phone, opening her calendar. "But yes, I'd love to try it on. Thank you so much. When can I come back?"

As I get her details for the appointment, something bubbles up in me, a strange mix of delight and discomfort. It'll be good to get rid of the dress, even if it's hard, even if it's like letting go of a part of myself. I don't know if I could ever put it on again without remembering the hours I spent stuck inside it, unable to reach the buttons. Even now, just thinking of it, I feel a phantom constriction, like arms are wrapped around me, gripping too tight.

There was a point during these last few weeks when I thought that the gown didn't have to be tied to the past, that it could be a promise for the future instead. But that's a lot of pressure to put on my future—especially when I have no idea how long it will be. It doesn't even make sense to me anymore, the idea that, to make my remaining time worthy, I have to spend it with somebody else. My time is already worthy, just by being mine, and I can use it to do the things I love: laughing with friends, reading good books, listening to Taylor Swift, finding ways to ease people's burdens. And who knows what else I'll discover about myself when I'm not worrying over a relationship or stressing about romantic prospects. Who knows what else I'll become. Even if my worst fear comes to fruition, even if I'm alone in a hospital during my final moments, at least I'll know that I actually lived. That I loved and cherished myself while I did.

"Thanks again!" the woman says. "I'll see you next Thursday." She wags her phone, where she's just input the appointment, and as she walks to the door, she reveals the man who's been waiting patiently behind her.

Jackson.

"Oh—hi," I say, jolting a little. "Did you . . . have more questions about the other night?"

I already gave him a full statement, relaying every piece of Blair's confession, every sentence I could confidently quote from memory. But I'm happy to give more, happy to do whatever I can to ensure there's justice for Daphne.

"No, I actually wanted to check on you," Jackson says, "see how you're doing." My face must twitch with surprise, because he's quick to add, "I was in the area. Well . . . I was next door, eating a cinnamon roll."

He holds up his hand, fingers splayed, as if there might still be evidence of the sticky pastry.

"I know it's none of my business," he continues, dropping his arm back to his side, "but I can't stop thinking— Is your heart okay? I don't know much about transplants, but I imagine the recent stress and physical exertion might have . . ."

His sentence rolls to a stop, a blank he isn't sure how to fill.

"Oh, yeah, it's fine," I say. "Thanks for asking."

I'm touched by his inquiry, the caution and care in his voice. It's a stark contrast to the way he spoke to me the night we first met, when he thought my hair was tangled in a dead man's hand. He was kind to me when he took my statements, too—both after the attack in my home and after the fight at Blair's. His questions were extensive but gentle, sensitive to my recent traumas.

"Good. That's good." Jackson nods, looking past me toward the racks of gowns. "It's a good heart."

"What?" I ask, laughing a little, unsure I heard him correctly.

His eyes meet mine again and they're such a pale but warm brown, the color of cinnamon sticks. It's a lovely, unusual shade, and it reminds me of Christmas, of gingerbread houses, of sipping comfort from a steaming mug.

"That's what my sister always used to say about you," Jackson says, "after you took her under your wing. 'She's got a good heart.'"

I smile at that. Winnie Dean was always so sweet. "Will you tell her I said hi?" I ask.

"Of course." His gaze remains on mine, like he wants to say more, but then he lifts his hand and turns toward the door. "Take care, Rosie."

I watch him go, a little unmoored by the interaction, brief as it was. Outside, he heads toward his car, passing a man and woman chatting together on the sidewalk. The woman laughs, then pauses to drink from her coffee cup, and the man places his hand on her waist, pulling her closer to kiss her forehead.

I turn away, the public moment somehow too private, and try to suppress a twinge in my chest. I place my hand above the ache, feel for the thump of my heart. I count its beats, measure its rhythm, and only let go when I'm satisfied.

Winnie Dean was right. It's a good heart.

I rummage through my purse beneath the counter to pull out my phone. I should do more than rely on Jackson to pass my hello onto his sister. I should get in touch with her on my own. It can be part of my commitment to focusing on myself—making new connections, strengthening old ones, filling my life with fun and friends.

I find her easily on Instagram and kick myself for never having thought to look her up before. A quick scroll through her profile shows me she lives in Boston now, she has a dog she adores, and she still enjoys baking, just like she did in high school. There's a photo from last Thanksgiving where she and Jackson are both in oven mitts, holding separate casseroles. The Sibling Stuffing War continues, she captioned it. Spoiler alert: I won. I click on the comments, where Jackson's added, If by won you mean SABOTAGED, and I smile at the implied hijinks while tapping on his handle.

There are only about a dozen pictures on his page, and the most recent is from late last year. In it, he stands on a lawn that's quilted with leaves, beside a realty sign boasting a Sold banner. The caption is simple and straightforward: Finally a homeowner.

Curious, I zoom in on the house behind him. It's a quaint yellow colonial with a white porch that bears a wooden swing. And above the front door, which is painted a rich emerald green, is—

I squint. Zoom in closer.

Yep. I know that window. A half circle of stained glass. And now that I've noticed this distinctive feature, I recognize the house, too. It's somewhere between my parents' place and Morgan's. It's a house I've passed dozens of times on walks with Bumper, always slowing to admire the pretty glass. Which means—I laugh at the realization: all this time, the house I've been admiring is Jackson's.

The photo blurs before me as I think of his face, just now, telling me my heart is good. His expression was both guarded and vulnerable, like he was risking something by uttering that sentence. I think of my reaction, too—a little dazed by the compliment, when maybe I should have been dazzled.

This is the second time he's visited Just Say Yes in a little over a week, and it's still somewhat strange, seeing him in a setting that feels so personal to me when our relationship has been so professional. That first time he came, informing me of the results of the hair analysis,

I thought he was trying to catch me off guard, coax me into saying something I might hold back at the station.

But what if he had another reason for showing up that day, for wanting to speak to me outside of an interview room?

I swipe out of Instagram and open a text to my dad.

> Hey, I've been missing Bumper the last few days. Okay if I take him for his walk tonight?

After what happened with Blair, Dad told me I was off dog-walking duty for a while. He literally hid Bumper's leash from me and said I needed to spend my time after work relaxing instead.

I'm straightening a rack of dresses when his reply comes in.

> That depends. You feeling okay?

> I'm feeling great.

> Okay. Come on by after work.

I exit the text, smiling, then open my Notes app to start a new entry.

JACKSON DEAN
- Became a homeowner last year
- Participates in a Thanksgiving "Stuffing War" with his sister
- Eyes like gingerbread

I mine my memory for more, absently stroking a blush tulle Marchesa we just got in stock.

- Enjoys cinnamon rolls from Sweet Bean

It isn't much. For all the times he's questioned me these past few weeks, I haven't really bothered to notice his specifics. But there are already two things that connect us—Winnie Dean, and our love of his house—so I bet there are even more.

I put away my phone, satisfied for now. It's been a quiet afternoon at the store, but still a productive one, and tonight, I get to walk Bumper, that sweet, exuberant dog whose heart is the best of everyone's, overflowing with unconditional love.

Maybe, as a treat for both of us, I'll take him down the route he's come to prefer. Maybe we'll walk the shadowy, wooded roads that lead to Morgan's.

And maybe, on the way there, we'll see something worth a closer look.

ACKNOWLEDGMENTS

Thank you to all my readers, past and present. I don't know if I can fully articulate what it means to an author to *have* readers. We type our wildest ideas and hallucinations onto a page, transcribing the words of imaginary people we hear in our heads—and it's an honor to know that someone is on the other side, taking it all in, making those figments of our imagination a little more real. Whether this is the first book you've read of mine, the fifth, or somewhere in between, I'm so grateful to you for devoting time to it, for being the one to hear what I needed to say.

In that vein, thank you to all the people who act as the conduit between authors and readers—the booksellers, librarians, bookstagrammers, BookTokkers, and bloggers who live and breathe books, then help people find their new favorite. Special thanks to BOOK CLUB On the Go, Ink Fish Books, and River Bend Bookshop, who have all been especially supportive of my work.

Thanks, as always, to my spectacular agent, Sharon Pelletier, whose storytelling instincts I trust way more than my own. I often get contacted by querying authors who ask if I enjoy working with Sharon, and I'm grateful that my answer is always an enthusiastic, immediate YES (followed by thirty-seven paragraphs of gushing).

This is the fifth book I've written with Kaitlin Olson as my editor, and I feel extremely lucky that she not only understood my vision for this one from the beginning but also gave me feedback that made my own vision even clearer to me. I'm also very grateful that, in one of our early meetings about the story, she said, "What if you made the ending . . . darker?" (She didn't have to ask me twice!) Thank you, Kaitlin, for helping me make this book—and all the ones prior—exactly what I wanted it to be.

Immense thanks to the rest of the incredibly talented people at Atria, especially Ifeoma Anyoku, Maudee Genao, James Iacobelli, Sara Kitchen, Kelli McAdams, Laurie McGee, and Megan Rudloff. Thanks to the Atria Mystery Bus team, whose stars David Brown and Sierra Swanson always make me smile. (If you're not following @AtriaMysteryBus on TikTok, you must remedy that immediately!)

One of the most important resources I had while writing this book was Amy Silverstein's memoir *Sick Girl*, about the heart transplant she received in her twenties. I was so sad to learn that Silverstein died of cancer while I was writing this book, but I encourage everyone to read her essay for the *New York Times*, "My Transplanted Heart and I Will Die Soon," published less than a month before she passed. The piece not only showcases her resilience, strength, and grief, but also the ways in which the science behind organ transplantation has not progressed nearly as much as it needs to. It was her fervent hope that this would change in the near future, and it's now become mine as well.

Thank you to Laura Heitman for sharing her insights into working at a bridal salon. (Laura is one of my former creative writing students, and it was so fun to have her teaching me this time!)

I often say that my friendships with other authors are the easiest friendships I've ever made. Sure, it might be part trauma bond—publishing is hard!—but I don't know where I'd be in this journey without the support of the people who understand exactly how hard it is. So if you're an author and we're friends (or have even just exchanged a few DMs on social media), please know that I'm so grateful to have you in my life. Special thanks to Andrea Bartz, Layne Fargo, and Halley Sutton, whose text threads keep me sane and inspired. Huge thanks as well to Heather Chavez, Kellye Garrett, Leah Konen, Kimberly McCreight, and Tessa Wegert for their very generous blurbs.

Thank you to my family and (non-author) friends for their continued support; it means so much to me. Thank you to my husband, Marc, who—miracle of miracles—did *not* need to help me with nine hundred plot issues in this book, but I know that if the issues had arisen, he would have let me yammer on about them until we figured out a solution together.

And though I know she'll never read this, thank you to Taylor Swift, whose lyrics have inspired me since I was twenty-six, belting "Dear John" in my car, and whose love songs helped me write this thriller.

ABOUT THE AUTHOR

M egan Collins is the author of five novels, including *The Family Plot* and *The Winter Sister*. She has taught creative writing for many years and is the managing editor of 3*Elements Literary Review*. She lives in Connecticut, where she obsesses over dogs, miniatures, and cake.